When the hairs  he knew that K... the kitchen.

Gideon felt her gaze a... resisting the urge to peer back at her. He dated women all the time, but none of them had caught his attention the way she had.

Deep down he sensed a connection, as if she knew what it was to be hurt deeply and had held herself back from others because of that. Like him. Was that why he got the bright idea to bring dinner to her tonight?

No, it was her sons. They reminded Gideon of himself and his younger brother growing up.

He pivoted toward her, transfixed by the soft blue of her eyes. *Run.* The word set off an alarm bell in his mind. His chest constricted.

In the distance he heard her son Kip speaking to him, but Gideon couldn't tear his eyes from Kathleen, her delicate features forming a beautiful picture that could haunt him if he allowed her to get too close. But he wouldn't do that.

Margaret Daley, an award-winning author of ninety books (five million sold worldwide), has been married for over forty years and is a firm believer in romance and love. When she isn't traveling, she's writing love stories, often with a suspense thread, and corralling her three cats, who think they rule her household. To find out more about Margaret, visit her website at margaretdaley.com.

Irene Brand's first inspirational romance was published in 1984, and she now has more than forty titles, including four nonfiction books, with approximately two million copies in print. Consistent involvement in the activities of her local church has been a source of inspiration for Irene's work. Traveling with her husband, Rod, to all fifty states, and to thirty-two foreign countries has also inspired her writing. Irene is grateful to the many readers who have written to say that her inspiring stories and compelling portrayals of characters with strong faith have made a positive impression on their lives.

His Holiday Family

USA TODAY Bestselling Author

Margaret Daley

&

The Christmas Children

Irene Brand

LOVE INSPIRED
INSPIRATIONAL ROMANCE

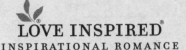

LOVE INSPIRED®
INSPIRATIONAL ROMANCE

Recycling programs for this product may not exist in your area.

ISBN-13: 978-1-335-28492-1

His Holiday Family & The Christmas Children

Copyright © 2020 by Harlequin Books S.A.

His Holiday Family
First published in 2011. This edition published in 2020.
Copyright © 2011 by Margaret Daley

The Christmas Children
First published in 2003. This edition published in 2020.
Copyright © 2003 by Irene Brand

This edition published by arrangement with Harlequin Books S.A.

For questions and comments about the quality of this book, please contact us at CustomerService@Harlequin.com.

Love Inspired
22 Adelaide St. West, 40th Floor
Toronto, Ontario M5H 4E3, Canada
www.Harlequin.com

Printed in U.S.A.

CONTENTS

HIS HOLIDAY FAMILY

Margaret Daley

To Joe, thank you for your support

Therefore my heart is glad, and my glory rejoiceth:
my flesh also shall rest in hope.
—*Psalms* 16:9

Chapter One

Gideon O'Brien hopped down from Engine Two and assessed the chaos in front of him. Strapping on his air pack, he started toward his captain. A hand gripped his arm and stopped his forward progress. He turned toward the blonde woman who held him, her large blue eyes glistening with tears. She looked familiar, but he couldn't place where he knew her from. His neighbor's daughter, perhaps?

"My two sons and my cousin—their babysitter— must still be inside. I don't see them outside with the other tenants." Her voice quivered. She tightened her hand on his arm and scanned the crowd. "I'm Kathleen Hart. My sons are Jared and Kip. I tried Sally's cell but she didn't answer. Please get them out." A tear slipped down her cheek.

"Where are they?" Gideon moved toward his captain, his palm at the small of her back, guiding her in the direction he wanted her to go. Yes, he realized, she was his neighbor Ruth Coleman's daughter.

"Sally's second-floor apartment is on the east side, the fourth one down on your right. Number 212. Hurry." Her round eyes fastened on the fire consuming the three-story apartment building on Magnolia Street.

Gideon paused in front of Captain Fox. "Mrs. Hart says her sons and babysitter are still inside. Pete and I can go in and get them." He looked toward the west end of the large structure where the men of Engine One were fighting the flames eating their way through the top level. "There's still time."

"Okay." His captain surveyed the east end. "But hurry. It won't be long before this whole building goes up."

The scent of smoke hung heavy in the air. The hissing sound of water hitting Magnolia Street Apartments vied with the roar of the blaze. Gideon turned toward the mother of the two boys. "We'll find them." He gave her a smile then searched the firefighters for Pete.

When Gideon found him a few feet away, he covered the distance quickly. "Let's go. There are three people trapped on the second floor. East end."

At the main entrance into the building Gideon fixed his mask in place, glancing back at the blonde woman standing near his captain. He had seen that same look of fear and worry many times over his career as a firefighter. He wouldn't let anything happen to her sons and Sally.

Gideon switched on his voice amplifier and headed into the furnace with Pete following close behind him. Through the thick cloud suspended from the ceiling in the foyer, the stairs to the second floor loomed. Crouching, he scrambled up the steps. The higher he went, the hotter it became.

On the landing, he peered to the right, a wall of steely smoke obscuring his view. To the left, the way he needed to go, the gunmetal gray fog hovered in the hallway, denser at the top.

Gideon dropped to his hands and knees and crawled toward Sally's apartment. Sweat coated his body from the adrenaline pumping through him and the soaring temperature. The building groaned. Visibility only three feet in front of him, he hugged the wall, his heart pounding. He sucked air into his lungs, conscious of the limited amount of oxygen in his tank.

Calm down. Not much time. In and out.

Mindful of every inhalation, he counted the doors they passed in the corridor. One. Two. Three. The next apartment was Sally's. His breathing evened out as he neared his goal.

At number 212's door, Gideon tried the handle. Locked. He rose and swung his ax into the wooden obstruction, the sound of it striking its target reverberating in the smoke-filled air.

When a big enough hole appeared, Pete reached inside and opened the door. A pearly haze, not as heavy as in the corridor, engulfed the room. His partner rushed into the apartment, Gideon right behind him. In the small foyer, he noticed a large television on in the living room but didn't see anyone in there.

"I'll take the left. You the right," Gideon said, making his way down the short hallway to the first bedroom. "Fire department, is anyone here?" His gaze riveted to a double bed. He quickly searched every-where two young boys might hide. Nothing.

For a few seconds a memory intruded into his mind, taking his focus off what needed to be done. He shoved it away, went back in the hall and crossed to the other bedroom. After checking it, he came back out into the corridor and opened the last door to a bathroom. Empty.

He pictured his neighbor's daughter next to his captain, waiting for them to bring her sons out safely. The thought that he might not be able to quickened his breathing for a moment.

When he met up with Pete in the small entryway, his partner said, "All clear in the kitchen as well as the living and dining rooms."

"The same in the bedrooms."

"Gideon, Pete, get out. Mrs. Hart sees her children and their babysitter. They just arrived and are safe," his captain's deep gravelly voice came over the radio.

"We're on our way." Relieved the two boys and Sally were all right, Gideon and Pete made their way back into the main hallway.

The smoke had grown thicker, darker. The crackling and popping sounds of the fire overrode the rumbling noise from the water continually bombarding the structure. A warning went off, signaling Pete only had five minutes of air left in his tank.

Our time is running out.

As those words flashed into Gideon's thoughts, his breathing sped up for a few seconds before he reined it in. He'd been in similar situations. They would make it.

Gideon gestured to his friend to go first. Every second counted. Pete came out of the apartment and got down on all fours, hurriedly heading for the stairs. Gideon crept along a body length behind his partner. As he crawled past the second apartment, his low-pressure air alarm alerted him to the need to move even faster.

But the nearer he came to the stairs, the soupier his surroundings were. He barely made out the back of Pete only a foot in front of him.

Gideon's shoulder brushed against the door frame of the apartment nearest to the steps. Almost there. His inhalations slowed even more to conserve as much oxygen as possible. But heat warmed the inside of his protective suit, and sweat rolled down his face. Its salty drops stung his eyes. He blinked, his vision blurring for a few seconds.

Then suddenly from above, wood and debris came tumbling down. Gideon lost sight of Pete in the dense smoke and dust. The crashing sound of a beam boomed through the air.

Lord, help.

Rolling onto his back, Gideon reached for his radio when another metallic moan cut through the noise of the fire. A piece of timber landed across his chest, knocking his radio from his hand. A sharp pain lanced a path through his upper torso. Then a second slab of lumber fell on top of the first. Gideon stared up as the rest of the ceiling plummeted. Air rushed out of his lungs, and blackness swirled before his eyes.

Holding her two sons' hands, Kathleen Hart watched them carry a firefighter out of the burning building.

Fear bombarded her from all sides. He could die because she'd mistakenly thought her children and Sally were inside. She relived the few seconds when she'd seen Jared and Kip racing toward her with Sally Nance right behind them. The elation they weren't trapped took hold. Then the knowledge she had unnecessarily sent two men into a blaze to find the trio swept away the joy. Now one of them was injured. Because of her.

She turned to Sally. "Please keep the boys with you. I need to see how the firefighter is doing."

"Sure. I'm so sorry you didn't realize I took Jared and Kip to the park. When the weather's good, we've been doing that. With the storm coming, I didn't know when we would get another chance anytime soon. I never in a thousand years thought my apartment building would catch fire and…" Her cousin gulped back the rest of her words and stared at the man on the stretcher being attended to by the paramedics.

"I know, Sally." Kathleen looked down at her sons, whose eyes were round and huge in their pale faces. "We'll talk later." She squeezed their hands gently, drawing their attention. "Stay with Sally. I'm going to check on the firefighter."

Tears shone in Kip's eyes. "Tell him we're sorry."

She stooped and grasped her nine-year-old's upper arms. "Honey, it isn't your fault."

And it isn't my fault, either. It was an unfortunate accident. If only she could believe that.

Even knowing that in her mind didn't make her feel any better as she rose and headed toward the ambulance into which the paramedics were loading the fire-fighter.

One of the paramedics hopped into the back of the emergency vehicle while the other shut the doors and started toward the front of the truck. She knew the paramedic because she worked as a nurse at Hope Memorial Hospital. Kathleen hurried her steps and caught up with the driver before he climbed into the cab.

"How is he, Samuel?"

"O'Brien may have some internal injuries." Samuel gave her a once-over. "Did you just come from the hospital?"

Still dressed in her scrubs, Kathleen nodded. "Will he make it?"

"He should, barring any complications." The paramedic jumped up into the ambulance.

Kathleen backed away from the vehicle and watched it leave the scene. She squeezed her eyes closed, still seeing the flashing lights in her mind. She couldn't shake the tragedy of the situation—one she'd had a part in. Just like another one, not long ago.

She tried to clear her mind of the memory. When would this go away?

Someone tugged on her arm. She looked down at Jared, her seven-year-old son, with worry in his expression. "Sally said he went in searching for us. Is that true?"

"Yes. When I didn't see you outside with the other tenants, I thought you all were still inside."

"Is he going to be okay?" Kip asked as he approached her. Sally followed right behind her son.

"The paramedic thinks so." She hoped Samuel was right.

"Mom, he's got to be." Kip's lower lip quivered. "I begged Sally to take us to the park."

"Honey, you didn't know what might happen." She needed to listen to her own words, but that wasn't as easy as it sounded. "Let's get you two to Nana's, and then I'll go back to the hospital and check on him after the doctor has had time to see him in the E.R." Kathleen shifted toward her twenty-three-year-old cousin. "I'm so sorry about this, Sally. Do you want to go to Mom's?" She threw a glance toward the blaze. "It doesn't look like much will be left. You'll need a place to stay. You're welcome to stay with me and the boys."

"I appreciate the offer, but I can go to my mom's. I need to stay and talk with some of my neighbors. See what happened. Then I'll give Mom a call and have her come pick me up. She should be home. With Hurricane Naomi bearing down on us, I would have stayed at Mom's anyway." Sally looked south toward the water only a few blocks from the apartment building.

Kathleen couldn't think of that. The storm in the Gulf was still several days away from Hope, Mississippi, a quaint town of twenty thousand between Mobile and New Orleans. Her hometown of stately antebellum homes along the water thrived on tourism and the fishing industry. But anything could happen between now and the date the National Weather Service projected Naomi would come ashore in the vicinity of Hope.

"I called your cell earlier when I arrived. All I could do was leave a message."

Sally dug into her jean pocket and withdrew her phone. She winced. "Sorry. I had the sound off." Her cousin peered off to Kathleen's side. "Will Kip and Jared be okay?"

Kathleen followed the direction of Sally's attention. Both of her sons' gazes were glued to the commotion taking place at the Magnolia Street Apartments. Kip chewed his lower lip while her younger son took several feet forward. "I'd better get them away before Jared is in the middle of the chaos. I'll talk to you later. If you need any help, please call." She hugged her cousin, then made her way to her children, who were entranced by the plume of smoke bellowing into the sky being chased by yellow-orange flames.

Her mother would watch them while she went to check on the firefighter. She owed him that much for what he did for her. Kathleen clasped first Jared's hand, then Kip's. "We need to go to Nana's."

"But, Mom, I want to see what happens." He had told her on a number of occasions he wanted to be a firefighter.

"No. They don't need any more people here watching." Kathleen scanned the crowd that had gathered across the street from the apartments. "Besides, if Nana hears about this, she'll get worried."

"Will she even be back from Biloxi yet?" Kip trudged toward her car parked several buildings away.

"I hope so." Because she needed to go to the hospital. The firefighter had to be all right.

* * *

Will he make it?

The question plagued Kathleen the whole way into the E.R. thirty minutes later after she'd left her mother's house. Luckily her mother had returned from her weekly visit to her friend in a nursing home in Biloxi. Activity and tension met Kathleen as she came through the double doors. Ashley, an E.R. nurse who had befriended her when she'd begun working at Hope Memorial six weeks ago, hurried from behind the counter, saw her and came toward her.

"Thank the Lord you are here. We need a hand. One of the nurses got sick and had to go home. Can you help me with a patient? I have two that need attention." Ashley held up several vials of medicines and an IV bag.

"Is one of them the firefighter from the fire on Magnolia Street?" She rushed behind the counter and disposed of her purse in a drawer.

"Yes, he's in room two."

"I'll take him. I just came from the fire. My cousin lives in those apartments. I wanted to check to see how he is."

"I think he'll be all right. I haven't had much time with him yet. Besides him, there was a wreck on Interstate 10. Three injuries. It's been hopping around here. I don't want to even think about how it will be if Naomi hits here."

Neither did Kathleen. As a child, she had gone through two minor hurricanes that had gotten her out of school for a couple of days but, other than that, hadn't changed her life much at all. But Naomi was gathering speed and her winds were increasing.

Ashley thrust an IV bag into her hands. "He needs this."

Her breath caught in her throat, Kathleen took it and started for the second door on the left. "What are his injuries?"

Ashley slanted a look at Kathleen and said, "I think several broken or cracked ribs, possible internal bleeding and smoke inhalation," then entered E.R. unit number four.

When Kathleen went into room two, she stared at the firefighter lying on the bed. His damp black hair was plastered against his head, and there were dark smudges on his tan face. His steely gray eyes locked on her and seized her full attention.

"Pete. What about Pete? Did my partner get out okay?" His raspy voice weakened with each word he uttered.

"Yes, there were no other injuries at the fire." Guilt swamped her at seeing the man she'd sent into the fire hurting, pain reflected in his gaze. The feeling was familiar. Hadn't her husband, Derek, blamed her for causing his stress that led to his heart attack? Shaking away the memory, Kathleen hung an IV drip on the pole and hooked up his line.

"I'll be fine." The firefighter struggled to sit up. His eyes clouded, his face twisting into a frown.

Kathleen rushed forward to restrain the patient's movements. "You need to lie down."

"You're the lady with the boys. Ruth's daughter." He swung one leg to the floor.

"Yes." Kathleen touched his left arm to stop him.

He flinched but proceeded with putting his other leg on the tiles, pushing himself upright. With a moan, he sank to the floor. Kathleen caught him as he went down and lessened his impact with the tiles. Kneeling next to him, she supported his back with her arm.

His head rested against the bottom of the bed. He fixed his weary gaze on her, pain dominating it. "I guess I'm not all right."

"Let's get you back in bed. The doctor will be here soon."

"Yeah, sure." His eyes fluttered and closed.

With her attention fastened on his face, Kathleen settled him on the floor and pressed the emergency call button.

"I thought you left here a couple of hours ago," Mildred Wyman, the floor supervisor, said as Kathleen exited the elevator and walked toward the nurses' station.

"I did, but there was a fire at the Magnolia Street Apartments where my cousin lives." She filled her in on the details. "When I came back to the hospital, Ashley recruited me to help until another nurse was able to come in. She just arrived so I wanted to see if Gideon O'Brien was settled into his room before I go home for sure this time."

"He's in room 345. He was asleep a little while ago."

"I'll peek in. See if he's up. If he needs anything."

Kathleen strolled toward the last room on the west

wing's third floor. The memory of the look on Gideon O'Brien's face wouldn't leave her thoughts. Clearly he'd been in pain but he tried to deny the seriousness of his injuries. If only she had known that Sally had taken the boys to the park, Gideon O'Brien wouldn't be hurt.

She rapped on the door. When she didn't hear anything, she inched it open to see if he was still asleep. The dimly lit room beckoned her. She stepped inside and found him, lying on his bed, his head lolled to the side, his eyes closed.

With the black smudges cleaned from his face, his features fit together into a pleasing picture. High cheekbones, the beginnings of a dark stubble, strong jaw. His features drew her forward until she stood by his side, watching him sleep. She could remember seeing him a couple of times jogging past her mother's house when she had visited. When she'd told her mother who the injured firefighter was, her mom had said Gideon O'Brien had moved in down the street several years before.

"He sure is a handsome lad. Single, too." Her mother's words came back to taunt Kathleen. Before she'd had time to say goodbye to her sons so she could return to the hospital, her mother had ushered her out the door without further questions—which was unusual for her mom. Kathleen knew what was going through her mother's mind. A nice young man would solve all of Kathleen's problems. She would discourage her mother of that thought when she went back to pick up her sons.

Her glance ran down Gideon's length, categorizing his injuries. Two cracked ribs, wrapped but very painful, a broken arm above his left wrist, which would be set tomorrow, and an assortment of bruises. The doctor was still concerned about internal bleeding and wanted to keep a close eye on him overnight.

When her survey returned to his face, it connected with his gaze. Molten silver, framed by long, thick black eyelashes. Captivating. Powerful. Those thoughts sent warmth to her cheeks that she was sure rivaled the fire he'd fought.

Kathleen looked away. "I didn't mean to wake you up."

"You didn't," Gideon said in a scratchy voice. "You were at the fire. In the E.R. Ruth's daughter."

She nodded. "I'm so sorry you and Pete went into the building after my children." She reconnected with him visually. "They were supposed to be there. I had come to pick them up. I didn't know Sally had taken them to the park and was running late getting them back to her apartment."

He shifted, gritting his teeth. "I'm glad they're safe."

"But—"

"So why are you up here?"

She wanted to say so much more to him, but a closed expression descended over his pain-filled features. "I wanted to make sure you were all right before I left."

"Define all right." One corner of his mouth lifted for a second then fell back into a neutral line. He tried to reach for the plastic cup of water on his nightstand and winced.

"Let me get it for you." Kathleen picked up the cup and held it to his lips so he could take a few sips. The scent of smoke clung to his dark hair. "Is your pain manageable?"

"I've had worse."

"You have?" She'd heard from other patients in the past how much broken or cracked ribs could hurt.

"Afraid so." Creases in his forehead deepened. Gideon gulped in a breath of air and started coughing. Agony contorted his features, his eyes shiny. "That hurt."

"Let me see if you can have more pain meds." Anything to help make him feel better. Then maybe she wouldn't feel so guilty.

He coughed again. His pale face urged her to hurry. She left his room and hastened to the nurses' station. "Mildred, can Gideon O'Brien have any more of his pain medication?"

"I'll check and take care of it. I was just coming to get you. Your mother called and said you need to get home right away. Something about Jared falling off the side of the house."

"Is he okay?"

"She didn't say. But she sounded shook up."

Kathleen rushed to the elevator, punching the down button. Seconds ticked by so slowly she started for the stairs when the doors swished open. This day was quickly going from bad to worse.

Two minutes later, after retrieving her purse in the E.R., she hastened out to the parking lot while digging for her cell. She slipped behind the steering wheel of her eight-year-old Dodge and punched in her mom's number.

"How's Jared?" In the background Kathleen heard her son crying, and her grip tightened on the phone.

"I don't know. He's holding his arm. He might have broken it."

"I'll be there soon." She flipped her cell closed and pulled out of the parking space.

Ten minutes later Kathleen turned onto Oceanview Drive. Her seven-year-old son was too adventurous for his own good. She guessed he was going from climbing trees to houses now. Next he'd want to try flying off the roof. The thought sent panic through her as she drove into the driveway and parked.

The front door banged open, and Kip came racing out of the two-story stone house. "Mom, Jared climbed up there." He pointed toward the second floor. "You should have seen him. I can't believe he did it."

"Did you dare him?" Kathleen charged up the steps to the porch. At the door Kip's silence prompted her to glance back at him. "You did."

"Aw, Mom. I didn't think he would really do it."

"We'll talk later." Kathleen entered her childhood home and headed toward the kitchen where the crying was coming from.

Kathleen's mother stood over her son, her face leached of color. "I'm so glad you're here." Relief flooded her features. "If you need me, I'll be—"

"Mom, I'll take care of this. Don't worry." Her mom never did well when someone was hurt or even sick. She usually fell apart. She certainly hadn't gotten her desire to be a nurse from her mother.

Jared sat cross-legged on the tile floor, cradling his

left arm to his chest, tears streaking down his face. His look whisked away any anger she had at him attempting something dangerous.

Kathleen stooped down, putting her hand on his shoulder. "Honey, where does it hurt?"

He sniffled. "Here." He lifted his arm and pointed at his wrist. "Nana thinks I broke it."

When Kathleen gently probed his injury, Jared yelped and tried to pull away.

"Let's take you to the doctor. You'll need an X-ray."

"Am I gonna get a shot?" Jared's brown eyes grew round and large.

"I don't know."

"I am! I don't want to go." Jared scooted back from her. "I can tough it out."

"If it's broken, it needs to be fixed. It'll hurt a lot more than a shot if you don't get it taken care of."

"Don't be a baby," Kip said behind Kathleen.

She threw a warning look over her shoulder. "I'm sure you have homework. Go do it. Have Nana help you if you need it."

Jared stopped moving away from her. He peered down at his wrist, sniffed and then locked gazes with her. "I'm not a baby." He pushed to his feet, tears swimming in his eyes. Blinking, he ran his right hand across his face, scrubbing away the evidence of his crying. "I'm ready," he announced as if he were being led away to some horrible fate.

While Jared trudged toward the front door, Kathleen spied Kip sitting on the stairs. Before her older son could open his mouth, she followed Jared into the foyer. Jared went outside on the porch, sticking his tongue out at his brother as he left.

Kathleen swept around, her hand resting on her waist. "Don't forget you and I need to have a talk. This fighting between you two has got to stop."

"We don't fight."

She arched her eyebrow. "Oh, since when?"

"We're playing."

Gesturing toward the den, she said, "Homework. I want to see it finished by the time I get back to Nana's to pick you up."

Kip leaped to his feet and stomped toward the den, making enough racket to wake up anyone who was within a several house radius.

As Kathleen covered the distance to the den to tell her mother what she was going to do, her mom said, "Glory be. This is great news."

Kathleen stepped through the entrance into the room. "What is?" she asked, swinging her attention to The Weather Channel on TV. She could certainly use some good news.

Her mom muted the announcer. "Hurricane Naomi has changed course. I think we're going to miss most of it. Maybe get a touch of the western tip, but not like they had predicted."

"We don't have to board up our house now?" Kip sat down at the gaming table with his book bag.

"It's not looking like we do." Her mom peered at her. "I know it's not good news for someone else, but maybe it will peter out before it reaches Florida."

Kathleen doubted it from the information she had

heard. "Mom, I'm taking Jared to the minor emergency clinic. I don't know when I'll be back to pick up Kip."

"Fine. Kip and I will put away all the supplies I bought for the hurricane, especially all those boxes of tape I got for the windows, which I really don't need. Don't know why I bought them."

"I'll take a box, Nana," Kip announced while digging into his bag for his homework.

"Sure. Just don't tape up Jared with it." Her mother rose and moved toward Kip. "Kathleen, when you get back we'll order something for dinner. We're celebrating tonight. No Naomi."

Kathleen left her mom's, not feeling the least bit in the mood to celebrate anything—even the fact the town would avoid Naomi. Her cousin's apartment burned today. She could have lost Sally and her sons. A firefighter went into a burning building because of her insistence her family was still inside.

Her life continued to come apart at the seams, starting with the last year of her marriage to Derek. She had wanted coming home to be a new start but hadn't counted on her sons' rebellion against moving to Hope. There was no going back to Denver, however. She couldn't afford to live there, financially or emotionally.

Chapter Two

The crashing sounds of the falling timbers and the crackling of the fire haunted Gideon when he tried to sleep at the hospital. He remembered being put into the ambulance and glancing at the Magnolia Street Apartments as the structure caved in on itself, flames shooting upward as the blaze rampaged through it.

The noises around him amplified in volume. The antiseptic smell of the hospital overwhelmed him. Sweat popped out on his forehead. His breathing became shallow, his throat raw.

Finally, Gideon inhaled a deeper breath and regretted it the second he did. A sharp pain pierced through his chest. He clenched his jaw and rode the wave until it subsided to a throbbing ache. In spite of how he felt, restlessness churned through him. Scanning the hospital room, he resisted the impulse to walk away. The doctor should be here within a few hours to give him the okay to leave. But as he stared at the clock on the wall across from his bed, the second hand seemed to be moving in slow motion.

The sound of the door opening lured his attention away from watching time inch forward. Kathleen Hart—last night he'd finally remembered she'd told him her name at the fire—entered his room. Her long blond hair pulled back in a ponytail emphasized her delicate features—large, blue eyes like the Gulf off the shores of Hope, lips with a rosy tint that wasn't from lipstick, and two dimples in her cheeks as she smiled at him.

Dressed in blue scrubs, she approached his bed carrying a little plastic cup with his meds. "How are you doing today?"

"Well enough to go home." He held out his right palm for his pills.

"Dr. Adams should be here soon. He does rounds after lunch." Dark shadows under her eyes attested to not enough rest.

He recalled her apology and hoped what had happened at the fire hadn't caused her a sleepless night. "Where did you go yesterday? Nurse Ratched brought me my meds. She wouldn't tell me what happened to you."

"I won't tell Mildred you called her that."

He grinned. "She's definitely a no-nonsense nurse. I'm glad you came back today."

"I work on this floor. I had to."

"Ouch. I think my ego was just wounded."

"Only think?" A twinkle danced briefly in her tired eyes.

The shadow in her gaze tugged at him. He wanted

to prolong the light tone of the conversation, but he needed her to understand how he felt. His injuries weren't her fault. "You were upset yesterday. Are you all right today?"

"The more important question is, are you?"

"I will be in time."

"You shouldn't be here right now. If only I had waited a little..." Her voice faded into silence, and she glanced away, swallowing hard.

"I would rather err on the side of caution than have someone trapped in a burning building. What I did yesterday is part of my job. Occasionally we go into a fire looking for a person who isn't there. It happens. You are *not* to blame." He would never forget the firefighters who had rescued him and his younger brother from a fire when he was eight. If they hadn't come into his burning house, he and Zach wouldn't be alive today. "No more guilt over yesterday. I'm glad your sons are safe."

With her gaze still averted, she nodded.

He wasn't totally convinced she wasn't blaming herself anymore, not if the furrowed forehead and the darkening of the blue in her eyes were any indication. "I've been hurt before. I won't let a few cracked ribs and a broken arm get me down."

She swiveled her attention back to him, her expression evening out, but the dark circles under her eyes were still there. "Tell that to my son. He broke a bone in his wrist yesterday after I took him to his grandmother's while I came to the hospital. That's where I had to go. He told me at the doctor's office that he wanted to see the hurricane coming in the Gulf. He thought the view would be better from the roof."

"I heard it turned toward Florida. We might get some high tides and rain, but hopefully that will be all." He shifted in the bed and caused another shaft of pain to constrict his breath, but he tried to keep from flinching. He didn't succeed.

"Are you all right?" The wrinkled forehead returned with a slight tensing.

"Just a twinge. Nothing that won't go away with time. So how did he get to the roof? Ladder?"

"That would have been safer. But he climbed the side of the house on a dare from his older brother. He didn't make it. He fell while trying to hoist himself onto the roof."

Gideon whistled. "You've got a daredevil on your hands. What did your husband say about it?" The second he asked the question he wanted to snatch it back. He didn't see a wedding ring on her left hand, but there was paler skin where one would have been. He couldn't remember Ruth saying anything to him about her son-in-law, but then he and Ruth were only passing acquaintances on Oceanview Drive.

"Derek died last year."

"I'm so sorry. I…" He didn't know what else to say. "Is there anything I can do for you before I leave?"

A professional facade fell into place as she checked his IV drip.

He could respect that she wanted to shut down the subject of her husband. Losing a loved one was difficult. Although he had never been married, he'd lost too many people in his life not to feel a kinship with her.

He grinned, wanting to see the light back in her eyes. "Other than get me out of here, no."

"Sorry, but Dr. Adams might take exception to that. Just as soon as he signs your discharge papers, you can escape."

"A hospital isn't my favorite place." Again he was reminded of his parents' deaths. His father had died in the fire, but his mother with third degree burns had lingered for a day in the hospital. He had only been able to say goodbye to her at the end when she was unconscious. He would never forget that last time he saw her.

"It usually isn't for most people." Her smile reappeared on her face, a sparkle shining in her eyes—making him forget where he was for a moment. "If you need anything, use your call button."

He watched her saunter out of his room. Occasionally he and Ruth would talk when they saw each other on the street, but with his crazy schedule, it wasn't often. She had mentioned she had only one child, and then this August she had talked about her daughter returning home in September to live in Hope. Other than Ruth being excited her two grandsons would be close, she hadn't gone into details about the move.

From his and Kathleen's few exchanges, he had sensed a deep hurt and now that he knew about her husband dying, he figured that must be why. One more reason he didn't get too involved in people's lives. He found after being shuffled between one foster family and another that it was safer to stay emotionally apart from others. Much safer.

After passing out the medication to her patients, Kathleen came back to the nurses' station to write in their charts. Dr. Adams nodded to her as he headed down the hall toward Gideon's room. She smiled, thinking about how the man would finally be able to leave. Even with his injuries, he had exuded restlessness. When he had told her about a hospital not being one of his favorite places, she'd heard pain behind the words though he'd no doubt tried to hide it.

Although he had reassured her she wasn't at fault for his being hurt, she had been married to a man who had blamed her for all his woes. Even with some of his last words to her right before he slipped away after having a massive heart attack at the age of thirty-five, he'd blamed her for the stress he'd lived under. No matter how much she told herself that she hadn't wanted him to take all the money out of their savings for Kip and Jared's college fund to invest in the stock market in risky companies, it didn't ease the guilt. In fact, she hadn't even known about it until after his death. The stocks hadn't done what her husband had dreamed they would. In fact, when he'd had his heart attack, she had discovered Derek had put the family thirty thousand dollars into debt and just that day had gotten notification the bank was foreclosing on their house if the mortgage wasn't paid. She'd tried to do that, but it hadn't been enough.

She shook the past from her mind. Coming to Hope was a fresh start, even if she still had twenty-eight thousand dollars to pay back. When she had lived here, she had flourished in the small-town feel and kindness of others. She desperately needed that now.

An orderly went by her desk and entered Gideon's room. Not long after that she saw Gideon appear in the hallway, dressed to leave, sitting in a wheelchair.

At the nurses' station he had the orderly stop. "Thank everyone for me for their excellent but *brief* care," he told her with a smile.

"I see Nate is helping break you out of here."

"Yep. I was getting ready to walk out of the hospital when he showed up."

"Oh, we cannot have that. Against Hope Memorial's policy," she said in dead seriousness, but the second the words came out she chuckled. "You aren't the first who has threatened that."

He motioned her to bend down closer to him, then he whispered, "Now my only complaint is that I would have liked a prettier escort. Too bad you're busy." Gideon winked and flashed her a grin before the orderly wheeled him toward the elevator.

Kathleen touched her cheek. It felt hot beneath her fingertips. She hadn't blushed in years and this was the second time since meeting Gideon. The injured firefighter was charming, but that was all he was. She didn't have the emotional energy to get involved with anyone, even if she felt guilty for his injuries. Raising her sons and slowly paying off the mountain of bills her husband had left her were enough to deal with.

Her mother kept telling her to turn it over to the Lord. She used to, but in the past two years she hadn't seen any evidence of the Lord in her life. Her prayers for help had gone unanswered. She was still in debt. Her sons desperately needed a man's influence. They hated being in Hope. They fought all the time. Then to top it all off, she felt responsible for Gideon's injuries, no matter what he said.

Which means I'll make sure he's comfortable while he's recuperating at home. That's the least I can do. Then maybe I won't feel so bad when I see him in a cast and wincing from pain.

Kathleen came into the house by the back door, thankful that her car had made it at least to her mom's, although she'd had doubts several blocks away when it died on her yet again. After the third time cranking the engine, it turned over and started.

Her mother told her to use her kitchen to make Gideon something to eat, then she could just walk down a few houses and give it to him. This was something Kathleen could do for him. She'd grown up with neighbors helping neighbors. That was part of Hope's charm. With one arm in the cast it would be hard for

Gideon at first learning to do things one-handed. He didn't need to worry about making something to eat.

Kathleen set the bag of food she'd gotten to make her Mexican chicken dish on the counter. After emptying the sack, she placed the pieces of chicken in water to cook. Then she went in search of her sons to see what kind of homework they had. When her mother didn't go see her friend in Biloxi, she watched Jared and Kip after school until Kathleen got off work and could pick them up. And when her mother couldn't watch her sons, Sally would fill in, no charge. That was a huge help to her because she couldn't afford to pay childcare along with everything else to raise two growing boys.

"Mom, do you know where Jared and Kip are?" Kathleen asked when she entered the den where her mother was watching The Weather Channel.

She peered toward Kathleen. "I didn't hear you come in. Been glued to the T.V. I'm charting the progress of Naomi even if it is going to miss us."

Kathleen wasn't surprised by that fact. Her mom had done that for years. She had a stack of charts of past hurricanes that had come into the Gulf. "I'm going to fix some Mexican chicken for us and take some to Gideon O'Brien down the street like I mentioned to you."

"I'm sure he'll enjoy that. He seems quite lonely to me."

Before her mother had her fixed up on a date with Gideon, Kathleen asked, "Where are the boys? They need to get their homework done. After dinner they are useless. I can't get much out of them then as far as schoolwork."

"They said something about riding those old bikes I had in the garage. I told them they could but not to go farther than this block and not to ride in the streets."

Kathleen glimpsed the time on the clock above the mantel. "It's getting late. I'd better round them up and see where they stand with their homework."

"We'll need to pray for the people in Panama City." Her mother listened to the reporter on the T.V. give the latest coordinates of the hurricane and jotted them down. "I'm sure you'll see the boys if you go outside and look."

That was assuming her sons obeyed their grandmother when she babysat them. Lately there was no guarantee they would. Kathleen made her way toward the front door. Outside on the lawn she looked to the left and saw no one. Then she peered toward the right and thought she saw a bike that was like the one she'd ridden as a child lying on the sidewalk three houses down where Gideon lived.

She remembered Kip's questions the night before about the firefighter who had been hurt in the Magnolia Street Apartments fire. He had wanted to know if he would be all right. Who was he? Could he and Jared make get-well cards for him? She'd kissed her boys good-night and told them she would talk to them today when she got home from work.

She charged down the street. Knowing them, they had taken matters into their own hands without waiting to discuss it with her.

At Gideon's one-story white house with a neat yard,

she skirted around both of her mom's old bikes and headed straight for the front door. After ringing the bell, she waited, trying to temper her anger that Kip and Jared would disturb a man recovering from some painful injuries.

Her older son opened the door. "Hey, Mom. Come in."

"No, I think you all have stayed long enough. You and Jared need to come back to Nana's. You're both supposed to have your homework finished by dinner." *Haven't we done enough to disrupt this man's life?*

"Aw, Mom, Gideon was telling us about some of the rescues he's done."

"Why are you answering his door?" She swung open the screen, the one standing between her and Kip.

"Gideon doesn't move too fast. I told him I'd get it."

Kathleen glanced over her son's shoulder at the slow-moving firefighter making his way toward them with a small white dog with a curly tail. His stiff movements coupled with the sight of his cast only reinforced why the man was in the pain he was.

"Hello, Kathleen. Your sons came over to give me their get-well cards. I asked them to stay if it was okay with you. They assured me it was." Gideon's gaze swept from Kip to Jared, who had joined them in the foyer.

Her younger son poked his head around Gideon. "He has a cast just like me. Isn't that neat? We're twins."

"And that is Butch. He's so sweet," Kip added, pointing to the dog near Gideon.

"It's time for you two to come back to Nana's and get your homework done."

"Mooomm, can't we stay for a while longer?" Kip's mouth formed his classic pout that he had stood in front of the mirror one day to perfect.

"Another time, guys. This is a school night, and you've got work to do." Gideon tousled Jared's, then Kip's hair.

Jared giggled then scooted out the front door.

But Kip remained where he was standing. "Will you tell us some more stories about being a firefighter?"

"Well, sure, anytime it's all right with your mother." Gideon flashed her a grin that melted any irritation she had toward her sons for bothering the man.

"Great. Call if you need us to do anything for you. After school we stay with Nana until Mom comes to pick us up." Kip raced past Kathleen and stamped down the porch steps.

While her sons grabbed their bikes and rode them toward her mother's house, Kathleen faced Gideon. "I know how tired you must be. Your body has gone through a trauma and needs rest, not my sons bothering you. I'm sorry—"

He held up his palm to still her words. "I enjoyed their visit. I was resting on the couch, getting more bored by the second when they came and rescued me from my boredom. I hope you'll let them come again."

She completely surrendered to the kindness in his eyes. Her legs grew weak, and she clutched the door frame to steady herself. "Only as long as they don't pester you." The pale cast to his skin spoke of the strain of standing. "Let me help you back to that couch."

He shook his head. "As much as I'd like a pretty lady to hold me, I can make my own way there."

"Are you sure?"

"Yes. Do you need to watch to make sure I don't falter halfway there?"

She grinned. "I'll take your word for it. Besides, I need to get home and make you a dinner, which I plan to bring you if that's okay with you."

"Normally I would jump at the chance to have someone fix me dinner, but you should see my refrigerator. There is nothing like good ole Southern hospitality. I don't think I'll be able to eat half the dishes stuffed in it. The ladies at my church decided they would stock it for me, so I wouldn't have to worry about what to eat for the next week. Well, more like several."

"Then I'll wait until later when you've run out of their dishes. I know it takes a while for ribs to heal, and they can be painful."

"Like I said, I don't usually turn down a home-cooked meal, so you'll get no argument from me. When it's my time to cook at the fire station, I've actually heard some groans from the other firefighters."

She chuckled. "If you need anything, I only live two blocks away. Down the hill and around the corner."

"On Bayview Avenue?"

"Yeah, the yellow cottage. One of Mom's rentals. Good night." Which was the main reason she could save a little money to pay off her debt. Her mother didn't charge her rent, but Kathleen had insisted on paying all the utilities and other bills connected to the house.

He stood in his doorway with his dog next to him as she descended the porch steps. She felt his gaze on her the whole way down his sidewalk. Heat flared into her cheeks. She couldn't resist glancing over her shoulder, only to find him staring at her, as she thought. He nodded, then swung his door closed.

Kathleen hurried to the foyer to answer the door. When she opened it, her breath caught for a few seconds. Although she'd found herself thinking about Gideon several times since she'd seen him yesterday, she hadn't thought she would see him this soon. "This is a surprise. What brings you by here?"

He lifted two large pizza boxes. "I came bearing dinner. I couldn't stand staying in my home another moment. I immediately thought of you and your sons. You were kind to want to fix me dinner. I thought I would beat you to the punch. I called earlier to see if y'all would be home and Kip said yes. I asked him if you had started dinner. He said you had to run next door and were behind schedule." He handed her the boxes. "He was supposed to tell you I was bringing dinner."

"A minor detail he forgot. I wondered why he kept coming up with things I had to do before starting dinner. You didn't have to bring pizza. I owe you a dinner, not the other way around. Remember?"

"I'm not used to inactivity. It was a spur-of-the-moment decision. I figured the boys would like pizza."

She smiled. "Pizza and just about every other junk food there is." Stepping to the side, Kathleen opened the door wider. "Come on in."

As Gideon entered the house, one corner of his mouth hiked up. "I was hoping you wouldn't send me home with all this pizza."

"You may change your mind after being here a while." She started for the kitchen at the back of the house. "I should warn you. My sons have been fighting most of the day. At the moment they are in time-out. And we've only been home an hour."

"Sounds like a few boys I have in my youth group at church."

"Youth group?"

"I help out when I can with the group for eight-to twelve-year-olds. When I'm not working, we sometimes play a game or two of basketball in the evening at the park near the Hope Community Church. There are several courts there. By the time they go home, they're too exhausted to fight each other. A couple of the dads have joined our little games, too."

"Is that Broussard Park on the Point?"

"Yeah. I like to run there sometimes."

Memories intruded into her mind. Memories of happier times before her father had been killed in an accident at the shipyard. "When I was a child, my family used to go to the Point to watch the sun set and have a picnic dinner."

"Since I came here, I've seen some beautiful sunsets on the Point."

Kathleen went into the kitchen with Gideon following close behind her. After placing the boxes on the table, she peered over her shoulder at him. "Where are you from?"

"New Orleans, originally. I've been here for five years."

"How long have you been a firefighter?"

"Fifteen years."

"Why did you decide to become one?"

He opened his mouth but a few seconds later snapped it closed. A nerve in his jaw twitched. Clasping his hands so tightly his knuckles whitened, he stared straight ahead at a spot over her shoulder. "Someone needs to fight fires."

Behind what he'd said there was a wealth of words left unspoken, but his stiff posture and steely expression told her the subject was off-limits. What was really behind him being a firefighter? On the surface he seemed open and friendly, but deep down she felt his need for privacy as though he were used to being alone and liked it that way. She could respect his need for that.

She'd felt the same way when she'd discovered the extent of Derek's debt and betrayal after he died. Leaving her to deal with the aftermath. Alone. So yes, she was used to dealing with her problems alone.

For a long moment an uncomfortable silence vibrated in the air between them.

Gideon cleared his throat. "I've filled in as a paramedic when they've needed me. I'm surprised I haven't met you before at the hospital."

Covering the distance to the refrigerator, she took

out a carton of milk and a pitcher of iced tea. "That's because I started working at Hope Memorial Hospital a little over six weeks ago. Knowing your aversion to a hospital, I doubt you hung around once you delivered your patients to the E.R."

"Ah, you know me too well. Where did you move from?"

"Denver, Colorado." Kathleen poured milk into two large glasses.

"Can I help you set the table or something?"

"No, I've got this. You brought the dinner. That's enough, and my sons will be ecstatic they aren't having what I planned tonight—tuna casserole."

"I ran into your mother as I was leaving my house. She asked me where I was going when I should be resting. I told her I was feeling better and decided to take dinner to you and the boys. She gave her stamp of approval."

I'm sure she did. Her mother was a romantic at heart and had encouraged Kathleen to start dating almost immediately after returning home. "She goes out every Thursday night with Mildred."

"Not Nurse Ratched?"

"The one and the same."

Gideon rubbed the back of his neck, his forehead creased. "She's a friend of the family?"

"Yes."

"That will teach me to keep my mouth shut."

"She comes across tough and no-nonsense, but she really has a very loving heart. That is, once you get to know her." Kathleen pressed her lips together to keep from smiling at the sheepish look on his face. "I tell you what. You can get the plates down from that cabinet and napkins from that drawer—" she pointed to the locations "—and I'll go get the boys before this pizza gets cold."

As she strolled from the kitchen, the sensation that he was staring at her sent a tingling wave through her. Goose bumps rose on her arms. She quickened her pace down the hallway to Jared and Kip's room. She'd had her younger son go into the bedroom the boys shared while Kip was in hers. Time-out in the same room only escalated their skirmishes, which had been growing worse since they'd moved to Hope.

When she opened the door to the boys' bedroom, Jared sat on his twin bed, chunking paper wads into the trashcan. A whole notebook, almost gone, littered the floor.

"Jared!"

He glanced at her, grinned and said, "Watch me, Mom." He tore the last sheet from the pad and scrunched it up into a ball, then tossed it toward the basket. It bounced off the rim and dropped into the pile of other missed shots. He frowned. "Maybe I should move it closer."

"No, maybe you should clean this mess up and then come to dinner. We're having pizza."

"Not tuna? Yay!" He scooted off the bed, taking half the covers with him. "The only reason I didn't make many baskets was cause I can't use both arms."

"Then I would refrain from climbing houses."

He bent over and picked up the first wad, frowning at his cast on his left arm. "This is gonna take forever."

"You should have thought about that before you decided to make the mess." She turned away before he saw her smile. Natural consequences were great teachers, but her son could have broken something much worse than his wrist.

Across the hall, she found Kip at the door listening to her and Jared. She peeked into her room to make sure he hadn't left a similar mess.

He looked up at her with those big brown eyes and long eyelashes and said sweetly, "I'm sorry I fought with Jared, but he was bugging me. I had to do something to shut him up."

"Getting into a wrestling match isn't an option. Dinner is ready."

"I heard the doorbell. Did Gideon come with pizzas?"

"Yes."

"Sweet." Kip hurried ahead of her toward the kitchen.

"Next time, young man, warn me when someone is coming over, especially with dinner."

Jared came out of his room and followed behind Kathleen. "Why did he bring pizza?"

Kathleen waited for Jared, cradling his cast to his chest. "To see you all."

"Really? Us?"

"I think he enjoyed your visit yesterday. He thought you and Kip might enjoy pizza."

"Kip talked his ear off. I hardly got to say anything.

He was constantly asking him about what a firefighter did."

When she and Jared entered the kitchen, Kip was already seated at his place with three pieces of pizza with all the toppings on it. "I'm starved, Mom."

"We're coming." Her gaze latched on to Gideon standing by the counter. She crossed to the table and took a seat. Gideon moved behind her and helped her scoot her chair forward before he sat. She couldn't remember the last time a man had done that for her.

After Jared plopped down in the last place between Gideon and Kip, Gideon looked at each boy. "I remember Kip mentioning how much he loved pizza yesterday. Earlier that sounded good to me, so I thought I would share some with y'all."

"Pizza is okay." Jared dug into the box nearest him and pulled out four pieces, piling them on his plate.

"Hold it. You never eat that many." Kathleen clasped her hands into fists in her lap. "Take one at a time."

"Kip has three pieces," Jared whined.

"The same goes for him, too." Kathleen pinned her older son with a stare that told him to behave.

"Sorry." Kip began to put his slices back.

"Leave them. You've already put them on your plate, but next time one piece at a time. I expect you two to eat every last bite of what you have on your plate." *Lord, give me patience.* "Remember your manners. We have a guest tonight."

Both of her sons hung their heads but exchanged narrow-eyed glances.

"Jared, it's your turn to say the blessing." Kathleen uncurled her hands.

"Bless this food. Amen." Jared jerked up his head, grabbed his first piece and took a big bite.

When Gideon reached for a slice of Canadian Bacon, her favorite, Jared's gaze fixed on his cast on his left arm that came down to his wrist but allowed him the use of his hand.

"No one has signed your cast," he said with a full mouth of food. Kathleen gave him *the look,* and Jared immediately chewed his pizza and swallowed before adding, "I've got most of my friends to sign mine at school. Annie wanted to, but I wouldn't let her." He held up his arm as though he had a trophy in his grasp.

"Why not?" Gideon poured some iced tea into his glass.

"A girl? No way. I would never hear the end of it." Jared's mouth pinched together, and he tilted his head in a thoughtful look. "Can you work with that cast? I'm having trouble doing things with mine."

A fleeting frown flitted across Gideon's features. "Not where I want to be. I'll be stuck behind a desk at headquarters until this comes off."

"I have to wear mine for six weeks. How about you?"

"Seven or eight weeks."

"Bummer," Kip said, pulling Gideon's attention to him. "That sounds boring."

"Yep. But I'm not much use to the team with only one arm fully functioning. That's why it's important to be as careful as you can, so you don't end up in a situation like this." Gideon tapped his cast. "Not fun."

"Can I sign your cast? I want to be the first." Kip jumped up and headed for the desk to retrieve a red marker.

"Sure. I noticed it was a little bare after seeing yours, Jared."

"Can I sign yours, too? I'll let you do mine."

Kathleen relaxed back against the chair while the boys wrote their names on Gideon's cast. As he searched Jared's cast for a blank space to put his signature, her throat tightened. Lately her two sons hadn't done anything together without launching into a fight. When Kip finally spotted a place for Gideon to scribble his name, Kathleen lowered her head and blinked away the moisture in her eyes. How could she let something as simple as this get to her?

Chapter Three

Later that evening, with darkness beyond the porch light, Kathleen drew in a deep breath of the cool air with a salty tang to it. The Gulf of Mexico was one block away. She could almost hear the waves crashing against the shore. When she got a chance, she loved to run on the beach early in the morning before the town woke up. It had become her haven since she'd come back to Hope.

Still in her scrubs from work, she rubbed her hands up and down her arms. "It's starting to finally feel like fall some. I'd gotten used to having four seasons in Colorado."

Gideon came up behind her and leaned back on the railing. "I'm going to hate seeing October end next week. It's one of my favorite months. In the middle of football season. Not as oppressively hot as in the summer. But I'll take that over cold weather any day. I'm a New Orleans native—hot and muggy is what I'm used to."

"Jared and Kip won't like the fact it rarely snows here. When I was growing up in Hope, it only did once. An inch. Shut down the whole town for a day until it melted."

"Do they know that?"

"I'm not telling them."

The sound of his chuckle filled the space between them, warming Kathleen. His gaze roamed over her features and for a few seconds wiped all thoughts from her mind, except the man who had shared a dinner with them and entertained her sons with stories about his job. Kip had hung on every word Gideon had said. Even Jared had listened until he couldn't sit still any longer. He'd lasted fifteen minutes, five minutes longer than usual.

"Thanks for bringing the pizzas over. You're a big hit with my sons."

"They're good kids."

She opened her mouth to agree with him when she heard a scream then, "Mom!"

She rushed into the house and hurried down the hallway, Gideon right behind her. Past calamities caused by her sons zipped through her thoughts. Jared ran out of his bedroom with Kip on his heels. Her older son tackled his brother to the floor.

"You're dead meat. How many times do I have to tell you not to touch my stuff?" Kip sat on Jared's chest, pinning his brother's arms to the carpet with his knees. He raised his hands and balled them.

"Kip, get off Jared."

Kip flashed her a scowl, his fists still hovering over

Jared's face. "He tore up my notebook. I had my homework in it for school tomorrow."

Kathleen settled her hand on Kip's shoulder. "I'll take it from here."

"But, Mom, I've got to do my homework over. It's all torn up. It was hard. I hate math, and now I've got to figure it all out again."

Gideon stepped into Kip's line of vision. "You know I'm pretty good with math. I'll help you while your mom and Jared have a talk."

Kip's eyes grew round. "You will?"

Gideon nodded.

"I'll get my book. There's paper in the desk in the kitchen." Kip bounced once on his brother's stomach, which produced a grunt from Jared, then stood.

Scrambling to his feet, Jared grimaced, holding his middle. "Mom, did you see him? He hurt me. On purpose."

Kathleen waited to answer him until Kip and Gideon disappeared down the hallway, then she whirled to face Jared. "You used your brother's school notebook to make paper wads?"

He suddenly found a spot on the floor by his feet extremely interesting. Scuffing his tennis shoe against the carpet, he murmured, "He hadn't finished his homework. He only had four problems done. He'd told Nana he had done more than he had after school."

"That's not the point. You have to respect your brother's things."

Jared lifted his head. "I want my own room like I had in Colorado. I hate sharing with him. He's always bothering my stuff. He always has to be first. He always has to have the last word."

"That isn't going to happen anytime soon."

"Why did we move here? I hate this place. I miss my friends." Tears glistening in his eyes, he curled his fingers into tight balls, his face screwed up into a frown.

"I had to sell our house in Colorado. We needed a place to live. I grew up here, and I thought you all would enjoy it like I did."

The frown deepened into a scowl. "You're a girl. All my friends are back home. Not here."

"You've got friends. How about Charlie down the street? How about the kids who signed your cast?"

A teardrop shone on his eyelash then rolled down his cheek. He knuckled it away. "It's not the same." He spun on his heel and raced into his room, throwing himself on his bed and burying his face in his pillow.

After entering, Kathleen sat next to her son and laid her hand on his arm. "Honey, I know this house is small, but it's all I can afford. One day we'll get to move to a bigger place."

Jared popped back up, his eyes flaring wide in hope. "Back home?"

"No. We're staying in Hope. I need my family around me."

"They can come visit. I'll even let Nana have my room when she does and share with Kip."

"Honey, that's not possible."

Jared turned his back on her and hugged his pillow

to his chest. "You don't care about what I want. We were fine where we were."

Coming to Hope hadn't been an easy decision. She'd hated asking for help, but she'd had no choice. She'd needed a support system and a means to save money to pay off the debts. "I'll always care, but we had to move. The cost of living was too high in Colorado."

Still facing away from her, he murmured, "Cost of living?"

"How much it takes to pay for things you need."

"I don't have to have ice cream, and you can forget I want a new bike for Christmas. The one at Nana's is just fine, even if it's a girl's." He twisted toward her. "And I can wear Kip's clothes when he can't anymore. Can we move back?"

"As much as I appreciate your offers, we still can't move back to Denver. This is our home now."

The frown returned, and he faced away from her. "You never listen to me. Only Kip."

"One day you'll understand there are some things that can't be changed no matter how much you want otherwise." Something she had learned painfully the past couple of years. She sat for a few more minutes, but when Jared didn't say anything else, she pushed to her feet. "You need to apologize to your brother. If you bother his things anymore, you'll be grounded next time. Understand?"

"Yeah, you love him more than me."

She leaned over and kissed the side of his head. "I love you both the same. Don't forget to tell your brother you're sorry."

Jared scrubbed her kiss away and put his pillow over his head.

Kathleen walked from the bedroom, releasing a long sigh. *Lord, I need help.*

With his tongue sticking out the side of his mouth, Kip wrote down the answer and waited to see if Gideon said it was right. When he did, Kip beamed. "Thanks, Gideon, I think I get this long division now."

"I'm glad. I used to struggle with math until one year I had this teacher who I connected with. I finally understood what I was supposed to do. After that, math has come easy to me."

"I've only got one more problem. I've never done my homework this fast."

Gideon watched him finish his math sheet. When the hairs on his nape stood up, he knew that Kathleen had come into the kitchen. He felt her gaze on him and straightened his shoulders, resisting the urge to peer back at her. He dated women all the time, but none of them had caught his attention like she had.

Deep down he sensed a connection as if she knew what it was to be hurt deeply and had held herself back from others because of that. Like him. Was that why he'd gotten the bright idea to bring dinner to her tonight?

No, it was her sons. When he'd talked to them there was something that reminded him of his younger brother and him growing up in foster homes— until one day a family had adopted Zach, leaving Gideon alone. It was obvious she needed help with her sons, and for the next seven weeks or so, he would have more time on his hands than usual while he recovered from his injuries and finally could return to full duty.

He pivoted toward her, transfixed by the soft blue of her eyes. *Run.* The one word set off an alarm bell in his mind. His chest constricted.

"Is this right, Gideon?"

In the distance he heard Kip speaking to him, but Gideon couldn't tear his eyes from Kathleen, her delicate features forming a beautiful picture that could haunt him if he allowed her to get too close. But he wouldn't do that.

Run. Now.

He wrenched his gaze away and glanced down at the last problem. "Sure. You did great. I'd better be going. I imagine you need to go to bed early with school tomorrow, and I have a lot to do in the morning. I…" He clamped his jaws closed before he made a fool of himself with his ramblings.

"I'm going to show Gideon out, Kip. You stay in here. Do not go to your bedroom until I get back."

"Can I have some ice cream? I finished my homework, and it's all correct. Gideon said so."

"One small bowl."

As Kip jumped up and went to the refrigerator, Kathleen swung around and exited the kitchen.

"See you soon, sport. I'll see about that tour of the station." Gideon left and found Kathleen in the foyer, waiting for him. "I told Kip I'll arrange a tour of Station Two for him—for all of you. But only if you say it's okay."

"He wants to be a firefighter or a doctor. He hasn't made up his mind."

"I'd say he has a few years to do that. How about Jared?"

She shrugged. "He hasn't said anything. But the way he's going, I could see him being a test pilot or some other kind of job that is daring. Danger means nothing to him while I'm getting gray hairs at the young age of thirty-two."

"How about professional mountain climber?"

"Please don't mention that. Sides of houses are enough for me," she said with a laugh.

He liked seeing her two dimples appear in her cheeks when she laughed. Her eyes lit with a bright gleam that transformed her. "I enjoyed tonight. Of course, I'm not sure what I'm going to do until they allow me to work behind the desk at headquarters."

"Read a good book."

"I'm more an action kind of guy. Reading is too sedate for me. I tried today to circumvent procedures by reporting for desk duty and was told by the chief in no uncertain terms to stay away until I get the go-ahead from the doc. That should be in three days."

"Does that mean your ribs aren't hurting? That's quick."

"I didn't say that." As he stood in the foyer, his cracked ribs were protesting all the activity he'd done that day, but he wasn't going to let that stop him.

She shook her head. "Men. You and Jared are too much alike. I wouldn't be surprised if he tried climbing the house again with his cast on."

He crossed to the door and opened it. "I wouldn't be surprised, either."

"I was hoping you would disagree with me." Kathleen came out onto the porch. "Now every time the phone rings, I'll wonder what else he has gotten himself into."

"My little brother used to be the same way. I had to get him out of a lot of scrapes."

"Does he live here? New Orleans?"

This was the reason he didn't like to talk about himself. So often it led to questions he didn't want to answer. "I haven't seen him since he was four."

The front door swung open and Kip, with his eyes huge, thrust the phone into Kathleen's hands. "It's Nana. She says Hurricane Naomi has made an almost one-hundred-eighty-degree turn and picked up speed—lots of speed—and is heading straight for Hope. It should be here by tomorrow night."

Chapter Four

Kathleen clutched the phone with a trembling hand, hoping somehow Kip hadn't heard her mother right. "Mom, what's going on?"

"Exactly what Kip told you. The hurricane is coming right for us. It has picked up speed. This time I don't think we're going to dodge the bullet."

Kathleen's eyes closed, and she drew in a deep, fortifying breath. "He said tomorrow night—early or late?"

"It will start by early evening, and the eye should be going over us right after midnight if it continues to move at the same speed it is now."

"I guess you don't have to put up those supplies after all. We'll take care of this house and come over to help you after that."

Kathleen hung up and passed the phone to Kip. "You and your brother need to go to bed. First thing tomorrow, we'll have to board and tape up this house then help Nana."

Kip's eyes widened. "How bad will it be?"

Gideon stepped forward. "A lot of wind and rain."

"Like a bad thunderstorm?" Her son gripped the phone tighter.

Gideon settled his hand on Kip's shoulder. "Yeah. You'll be okay."

"Does this mean we don't have school tomorrow?"

"Yes. We'll be busy getting ready as will everyone else." Kathleen opened the screen door.

"Cool. Wait till Jared hears this."

"I don't want any more fighting between you and Jared. We have other things to deal with right now. Okay?"

Kip spun around and charged back into the house, saying, "Yes."

Turning to face Gideon, she let the screen door bang closed. "The last time I was in a hurricane was over twenty years ago. I've forgotten what to do. I remember Mom filling the bathtub and other containers with water. Getting candles, lanterns, batteries for a radio and flashlights…" With memories racing through her mind, it went blank.

"Stock up on food you don't have to refrigerate. We will most likely lose our electricity. Bring indoors everything that can be picked up by high winds. Since this house doesn't have hurricane shutters, tape or board the windows. Then pray. Are you going to stay here?"

"I don't know. I might go to Mom's."

"I think that would be better. If there is a big storm

surge, this house could be flooded. It's nearer the beach than your mom's."

"Then that's where we'll be."

Gideon stared down at his cast. "If it wasn't for this, I'd be at the fire station." Frustration edged his voice.

"I'm on the B team at the hospital. I work post-hurricane. I'll contact work tomorrow morning and see when they want me to come in. There's so much to be done. This house isn't prepared."

He took her hand. "Get a good night's sleep, and I'll come over and help tomorrow morning first thing."

"Only if you'll let me help you."

"I have hurricane shutters, which will cut down on what I have to do. Let's get your house and your mom's prepared first. There shouldn't be too much to do with mine."

"I'll have breakfast ready at 6:30. At least let me feed you before you work."

He squeezed her hand then dropped it and turned toward the steps. "You've got yourself a date. See you at 6:30."

Kathleen stood on her porch and watched him stroll down her sidewalk, hop into his Jeep and leave. As his taillights disappeared down the street, she peered up at the sky. Roiling clouds obscured the moon. It had begun.

The next morning, using the electric screwdriver that Gideon brought, Kathleen secured a large board over the picture window in the living room while Gideon held it in place for her. When she finished with the last screw, she descended the ladder and stepped back. "I hope that will hold."

"You've done what you can." He hoisted the ladder with his good arm and moved toward the detached garage behind the house.

Kathleen followed Gideon toward the backyard where Jared and Kip were hauling the patio items to the garage to store them. She passed several smaller windows she and Gideon had taped in the past hour since they had eaten breakfast.

"You haven't done your share of the work. I've been carrying all the heavy stuff," Kip yelled from the backyard.

Rounding the side of the house, Kathleen found Jared and Kip playing tug-of-war with a seat cushion. She slowed and shook her head. "I guess I should be thankful this hasn't happened before this. Kip still hasn't forgiven Jared for the homework last night."

"I seem to remember Zach and I fighting over nothing at times," Gideon said with a chuckle. "He used to love to bug me."

"I got this first. You take the table." Jared jerked the cushion toward him.

Kip let go of it. "Fine. Take it."

Jared staggered back and fell on his bottom into a puddle of water left by the rain during the night.

Stomping to the table, Kip lifted it and headed for the garage. When he saw Kathleen, his mouth pressed together in a thin line.

"Mom, did you see him?" Jared scampered to his

feet and turned his back to her, showing her his jeans soaking wet with muddy water. "Look at this."

Kathleen inspected the dark clouds surging over them. "Jared, go in and change. Kip, you can help us finish clearing the patio."

"Jared doesn't have to work?" Kip disappeared into the garage.

"I'm counting to ten before I answer that one," Kathleen said to Gideon then trailed her son into the garage. She covered the space between them and blocked his path. "This is not a time for fighting. We have to get this house, Nana's and then Gideon's ready for the hurricane that will be here soon. If you two don't want to be grounded for the rest of your life, you'll work together and be civil with each other."

Tears welled into Kip's eyes. "I'm scared. I've listened to what they've said about hurricanes. I don't want to be here. Why did we move here?"

Kathleen knelt in front of her son and clasped his arms. "Honey, you'll be all right. We are preparing for it. This town has gone through hurricanes before, and it is fine. It has been here for almost two hundred years. It will be here for another two hundred."

"Don't be a scaredy-cat," Jared said from the doorway into the garage.

"Come here, Jared." Kathleen waved her hand toward him. When he approached warily, she took his hand. "We are a family, and we stick together, especially through trying times like this. I told Kip and now I'll tell you, Jared. We can't fight a hurricane and each other. I depend on you two for your help and co-operation."

Jared squared his shoulders and thrust out his chin. "I'll protect you. I'm not scared, Mom."

Kip yanked free from Kathleen and stormed toward the exit. "I'm not, either."

Jared opened his mouth to reply to his brother. Kathleen put two fingers over his lips. "Shh. Not a word. This may seem like an adventure to you, but it's a serious situation that could be dangerous. Like climbing up to the roof. Look what happened when you did that."

"It's starting to rain again." Gideon came into the garage, hauling part of a wooden lounge chair while Kip had the other end. "This is the last of the furniture. Let's get to your mom's and see what needs to be done there."

Kathleen rose. "That's a good idea. I want to get there before Nana decides to climb the ladder and close her hurricane shutters on the second floor."

"I can do that." Eagerness lit Jared's face.

Suddenly, Kathleen pictured her young son with a cast on each arm. "No more climbing for you for a while."

Kip stepped forward, his chest thrust out. "I'll do it."

"No. I'm going to." Kathleen headed into the house to get her purse. "You two go and get into the car."

Gideon followed her inside. "I'll meet you at your mom's."

She snatched her handbag from the kitchen counter and started out to the garage. Gideon touched her arm, the feel of his fingers momentarily grazing her skin, stopping her.

"Everything will be all right. We had a storm the first year I was here. A lot of wind and rain, but the town came through it."

"I hope so. I'm on the team that reports to the hospital right after the storm passes. I hate leaving my boys even then, but at least they'll be with Mom."

"I hate that I can't be out there helping, but my captain told me in no uncertain terms when I called him this morning not to come. Then he went on to give me his brief lecture on being injured. But it's hard standing on the sidelines watching others do what you feel you should."

"If you don't take care of yourself, you'll hurt yourself even more. Cracked ribs and a broken arm take time to heal."

He smiled. "I've never been a good patient."

"I'm used to that."

He strode toward the door. "We'd better go before it really starts raining. The few showers we've had are nothing compared to what will be coming soon."

"I'll follow you to Mom's."

In the car, Kathleen switched on the engine and backed out onto the street as Gideon climbed into his Jeep. Sprinkles fell onto the windshield. Silence ruled in the car. Glares were exchanged between her sons in the backseat. She clasped the steering wheel in such a tight grip, her knuckles whitened. The day had only begun. Before it ended, they would be drenched in water and hammered with wind.

* * *

"Mom, please get down from there. I can do that." Kathleen raced toward her mother, who was on the ladder against the house.

Ruth perched on one of the top rungs, wrestling with the wind to close the shutter. After finally shutting it, she swung around to stare down at her daughter. "What took y'all so long? I've got to go to the filling station and get gas. I only have a fourth of a tank. I should know better with a hurricane out in the Gulf. I always keep it topped off. But the storm fooled me when it turned toward Florida."

Ruth took a step down, lost her footing and began to fall. When she clutched the ladder, it teetered. Gideon hurried past Kathleen and grabbed it with one hand and steadied it against the house. Ruth sagged against the rungs.

Slowly she made her way down to the ground and collapsed back against the ladder, her hands shaking. "My word, I had visions of me landing in the same spot as Jared, but I can tell you I would not be able to bounce to my feet like he did. And a broken arm would be the least of my worries."

"Exactly, Mom. I told you I would do it."

"I'm gladly turning the job over to you—on one condition." Her mother swept around toward Gideon. "You need to hold the ladder for her. The rungs are a little slippery and the wind is picking up. I'll take the boys to the filling station with me."

"I've got a better idea. Take Jared. Kip will stay and

help us." Kathleen picked up the ladder and moved it to the next window.

As the boys slowly walked across the front lawn, their heads down, their arms hanging listlessly at their sides, her mother leaned close to Kathleen and said, "Do you really want to do that? They will fight because one got to go with me."

"Yes. I have a project for Kip."

"Okay, I've warned you. I'll send him over here." She sauntered to the boys, spoke to them and then Jared cheered while Kip trudged toward Kathleen with his shoulders slumped even more.

"I need you to go next door and tell Miss Alice we'll be over to her house to help her just as soon as we get through here. Then stay and make sure everything outside is put in for her." Kathleen ascended the first rung.

"Aw, Mom, do I have to? She's mean. She yelled at Jared and me when we came into her yard to get a soccer ball last week."

Clinging to the ladder, Kathleen shifted around so she could peer down at Kip. "Yes, you have to. We help our neighbors, especially in times of need."

"But, Mom, she isn't our neighbor."

"Go. I've got to get these shutters closed." She waved her hand at Kip in the direction of Miss Alice's house.

When Kip stomped off, splashing water in the soggy grass as he went, Gideon used his lower limbs to anchor the ladder. "You are asking a lot of Kip."

"Tell you a secret. When I was a little girl, she scared me, too. But she is eighty-six and not getting around like she used to. She'll need help through this hurricane."

"I already have it taken care of. Pete is coming over to help me with a couple of the older residents' houses."

"Doesn't he have to work at the fire station?"

"Like the hospital they have two shifts. No one can do a good job if they are dead tired. He's on the second shift after the hurricane passes."

Kathleen proceeded up the ladder and fought to close the shutter, then she descended and started all over with the next one. Three windows later, Kip ran back across the yard.

"Mom. Mom!"

Kathleen jumped down several rungs to the ground and hastened toward her son. "What's wrong?"

"It's Old Lady Beggs. I knocked and knocked, but she didn't come to the door. I peeked through the window. She's sitting in a chair, her eyes closed, her head to the side." Kip stood in the middle of the yard, chewing on his fingernail. "I really banged loud on the door. She didn't move at all. I think she's dead."

"Honey, you stay here. I'll go check." Kathleen started across the lawn.

"I'm coming, too. Kip, when my friend, Pete, comes, tell him where we are."

"Can't I come?"

Both Kathleen and Gideon halted and whirled around. "No."

Kathleen glanced at Gideon and then continued her trek toward Miss Alice's house. On the woman's porch, Gideon pounded on the door while Kathleen checked through the open draperies into the living room. Just as Kip said, she lounged in a chair with her feet propped up and her head lolled to the side, one arm dangling toward the floor.

"Kip might be right. She isn't moving. We need to break in and get her some help."

Gideon came to Kathleen's side. "If she is alive, she isn't gonna like it."

"Do you think she has a spare key somewhere?"

Gideon looked under the welcome mat. When he rose, he shook his head. "This door is pretty sturdy. I don't think I can break it down without an ax, which I left at work. I'll go around and check the windows and back door. Maybe something is unlocked, and I can get in that way."

"Hurry. She might have lost consciousness. I'm calling 911 to be on the safe side."

Gideon started for the back, checking the windows as he went while Kathleen called 911 on her cell. The operator was dispatching an ambulance immediately.

Two minutes later, as Kathleen watched the old lady in the recliner for any signs of life, her white cat came charging into the living room from the kitchen, leaped and landed in the woman's lap. Miss Alice shot straight up at the same time Gideon barged into the room. Miss Alice let out a rip-roaring scream.

Gideon skidded to a stop, his eyes round, his face pale. He said something to Miss Alice, but Kathleen couldn't hear over the yelling. The woman wasn't even looking at Gideon. She stared right at Kathleen, who stood at her window peering inside.

Gideon moved toward her and bent down toward the woman. Miss Alice blinked, clutching her cat to her chest and glaring at Gideon as if he were a total stranger breaking into her house. He backed toward the front door and opened it.

"Kathleen, come in, please." The stress on the word *please* quickened her pace into the house.

As she passed the mirror in the hallway, Kathleen caught sight of herself and paused. From the occasional rain, her wet hair lay plastered against her head and her mascara ran down her face in a couple of places. And Gideon hadn't said a word to her. She scrubbed the black streaks from her cheeks and kept going into the living room.

"What did you say, young man?"

"We thought you were ill. We knocked on the door." His voice rose with each word he said.

Miss Alice shook her head and held up her hand. "Wait a minute." She fiddled with something in her ear then said, "My batteries must be going in my hearing aid. Help me up, young man."

Gideon did as instructed, and Miss Alice shuffled toward the kitchen, yelling, "I'll be right back."

When she left, Kathleen came to Gideon. "Why didn't you tell me I looked like a drenched raccoon?"

He looked away, a sheepish expression taking over his face. "I know better than to tell a woman that. I thought Kip would say something and get me off the hook."

"I scared the poor woman."

"I didn't think anything scared her. I thought she

scared others. At least that's what the boys in my youth group have said when they found out I lived down the street from Alice Beggs." He put his finger into his ear and wiggled it. "I think my hearing is damaged. There is nothing wrong with her lungs."

"I heard that, young man." The woman appeared in the entrance to the dining room. "I should call the police. You broke into my house."

"Oh, no. I've got to call 911 back." Kathleen dug into her pocket for her cell.

Miss Alice's wrinkled forehead wrinkled even more. "You've already called 911 on him?"

Kathleen put the numbers into the phone. "No. For an ambulance. For you."

While she told the 911 operator that Alice Beggs was all right, the older lady shuffled her feet toward her recliner, shaking her head. "I was taking a nap. Can't a woman do that without everyone thinking she's dying? I need more beauty rest than when I was younger." She held out her hand toward Gideon. "Be useful. Help me into this chair, young man."

As Gideon took Miss Alice's arm to assist her into her recliner, Kathleen hung up. "We're sorry to disturb you, but my son thought something might be wrong with you. We knocked a long time on the door, but you didn't move."

"That's because I finally got to sleep after being up most of the night. Why in the world was your son over here trying to wake me up?"

"To see if you needed any help." Kathleen stuffed her cell back into her pocket.

"Yeah, help sleeping. No thanks to y'all."

Kathleen sighed, drawing on her patience she had stored up for dealing with her sons. "I thought we could get your house ready for the hurricane."

"What hurricane? Didn't you hear it's going to hit Florida?"

"No, Miss Alice, it's heading for Hope."

"Where's your mother? She told me yesterday morning we were safe, that it's going the other way."

"It changed its course."

"Why in the world can't it make up its mind? Reminds me of some women I know. No wonder men don't understand us. We don't understand ourselves." Miss Alice leaned back in the chair, fumbling at the side to lift the leg rest.

Gideon stooped and did it for her. "You're perfectly right."

Miss Alice swiveled her attention toward him. "You live down the street, don't you, young man?"

"Two houses away."

"Ah, yes. I've admired you when you've gone jogging."

Gideon's face reddened.

"Miss Alice, your windows need to be covered and—"

The older lady swung her gaze toward the picture window, jerked back and screamed.

Kathleen and Gideon pivoted to see Kip's face pressed against the pane.

Kathleen relaxed and waved him toward the front door. "Sorry, that's my son who was worried something was wrong with you." The one who didn't follow instructions to stay put.

She strode toward the front door to tell him to go back to Nana's, but the second she opened it, Miss Alice shouted, "Have him come in here."

Kip heard the words and shook his head, whispering, "No way, Mom. She's gonna yell at me."

Kathleen took Kip's hand. "I'll be with you."

He took baby steps toward the living room, hanging back from Kathleen. "My friends say she hates kids."

"What did you say, young'n?"

Kip's eyes widened, and he stopped dead in his tracks.

Miss Alice tried to turn her body to glimpse Kip, but she couldn't all the way. "C'mon in. I can't see you from there."

Kip moved forward a few more paces but dropped his head and stared at his feet as he dragged them across the floor.

"So you are Ruth's grandson. I've seen you a couple of times with another little boy. Who is he?"

"That's my other son, Jared."

Miss Alice ignored Kathleen and said to Kip, "What's the matter? Cat got your tongue?"

Kip kept his eyes on the floor.

"Can't you speak for yourself?" Miss Alice's lips thinned and almost disappeared completely. "Where are your manners? I'm here, not on the floor. Look at me when I talk to you."

Slowly Kip lifted his head, but his gaze focused on her chin, the lower part.

"That's better. I'm perfectly fine, but thank you for caring enough to go get help when you thought something was wrong." She flipped her hand toward the door. "Now you can git."

Kip didn't wait for another word. He whirled and ran out the front door and off the porch.

Miss Alice chuckled. "He's braver than most. But that's no surprise since he's Ruth's grandson. Where is your mother?"

"Getting gas because of the hurricane."

Gideon glanced outside, then back at the woman. "Miss Alice, can we board up your windows for you?"

"Don't have any boards. Haven't had a hurricane in years that amounted to much. Not like back in sixty-nine."

"Then we can tape most of them, and I can see if I can get a piece of plywood for your picture window." Gideon turned to Kathleen. "Unless your mom has a tape measure, I'll need to get mine."

Miss Alice twisted her mouth into a thoughtful look. "Who's going to remove all that after the hurricane? I certainly can't."

"I will," Gideon answered before Kathleen could reply. "We'd better leave and get your mom's house done, so we can come over here."

"When is this hurricane coming?" Miss Alice pushed the lever down so her footrest dropped, then she scooted to the chair's edge. "I haven't got all my supplies. I'm not prepared at all."

"Kip knows where the tape measure is. Go have him get it for you," Kathleen said to Gideon, then she put her hand under Miss Alice's arm. "Let's go look at what you have. We'll make a list of what you need, and I'll go get it for you."

"Bless you, child. Hurricane Naomi kept dancing around out in the Gulf, playing with us, that I just forgot about her after a while. Same thing happened a couple of years ago and nothing occurred. Thought that was what would happen this time. Don't keep up with things like I used to."

As Gideon left, Kathleen escorted her mom's neighbor toward the kitchen. The thought of the shutters on the second floor windows in the back of her mother's house still needing to be closed lent a certain urgency to her steps until she realized Miss Alice only moved in slow motion. Contrary to what she'd heard, Hurricane Naomi was finally doing in the Gulf.

Chapter Five

"This will teach me to keep my gas tank filled when there's a hurricane out in the Gulf." Kathleen's mother stood up after scrubbing the bathtub out and making sure the stopper was secured before turning on the water. "There, that is the last one. Both tubs will have water in them."

Kathleen took the cleaning supplies and put them back under the bathroom sink. "I wasn't able to fill Miss Alice's order totally, but I think she'll have enough batteries for her flashlights and radio."

"At least you didn't sit in line at the gas station for three hours only to be told I get five gallons and that is it. Of course, it seemed like half the people in Hope were in that line."

"I didn't have to stand in line because there was little left on the shelves at the store. The other half of the town must have struck the grocery stores."

"Nope. They're on the road evacuating. Are you

sure you don't want to take the boys and go to Aunt Cora's?"

"I can't. I have to go to the hospital right after it passes. You could take the boys."

"No, she only lives about fifty miles north of here. This house sits up on a hill and has never gotten any water. The wind wouldn't be much less than here. But I can go if you want. I'll probably have enough gas to get to my sister's."

"If you don't get caught up in traffic. I can't take the chance of you running out of gas, and I wouldn't trust my car on the road the way it's acting up." All morning Kathleen had wrestled with whether to send her children away with her mother to Aunt Cora's. Jared had flat out told her that he wanted to stay and see the hurricane while Kip told her he wouldn't leave her.

Her mother left the bathroom. "You need to take my car to the hospital when you have to report to work after the hurricane. I'm certainly not going to be going anywhere."

Kathleen headed back to the kitchen where the boys were helping Gideon fill jugs and other containers with water. "Mom, will you ask Miss Alice to come here to stay this evening? I hate her being by herself, but she wouldn't come when Gideon and I tried to get her to."

"I'll try. But she is a stubborn old lady."

Kathleen clamped her teeth down to keep from replying, "Kinda like you." She went into the kitchen to find the water containers all over the counter.

While her mother shrugged into her rain gear and rubber boots, Kip and Jared faced Kathleen with big grins. "We did this," Kip said, gesturing toward the jugs. "Gideon supervised. We did the work. Three gallons of water for each person a day. Isn't that right, Gideon?"

"You've got it. I think y'all are set."

"Did you get yours done when you went home a while ago?"

"Yep. My house is battened down and as secure as it can be. I have my supplies and enough water for a couple of weeks."

Kathleen scanned the kitchen. "The same here."

"Are we staying at Nana's tonight?" Kip started carrying the jugs of water to the pantry on an inside wall.

"We don't want Nana to be alone," Jared added while lugging his share across the room.

"Yeah, we're staying." Kathleen helped her sons store the containers.

"How about Miss Alice?" Kip asked when he came out of the walk-in pantry.

"I'm going right now to see if I can convince her to come over here." Her mother put on her rain hat and tied it down.

"Can I go, too?" Kip crossed the kitchen to his grandmother.

"It's okay with me if your mom says okay."

Kip spun around and asked her, "Can I?"

"Fine. Wear you raincoat and stay with Nana. It's starting to get windy out there."

Jared came out of the food closet. "You're gonna go see Old Lady Beggs? She yells."

"I didn't say anything the first time I heard that

name, but I don't want to hear you two call her that. Either use Miss Alice or Miss Beggs. Understand, Kip?" Kathleen peered at him, then turned to her younger son. "Jared?"

They nodded.

As Kip left with her mother, Jared took another jug to the pantry. "I've got to make sure Bubbles has enough water. Can I go check and fill the bowl up?"

"Sure."

When Jared left, Gideon asked, "Bubbles? I didn't know you had a pet."

"A goldfish. The boys want a dog for Christmas along with a whole list of other things, the top of the list being bikes that are not girl ones like Mom has."

"Christmas? That's two months away."

"Yeah, I know, but they are already thinking about it. Their idea of Christmas is so commercial, and no matter how much I tell them this year that we'll celebrate on a smaller scale, they don't listen."

The door flew open, bringing in rain and wind as Kathleen's mother and Kip entered. "Whew. It's starting to get nasty out there," she said as she untied her rain hat and hung everything on a peg in the mudroom off the kitchen. "We ran back. I've had my exercise for the month today."

"Where's Miss Alice?" Kathleen leaned back against the counter next to Gideon.

"She doesn't like crowds. Told Nana she would be just fine at her house. She planned on turning off her hearing aid and sleeping through the whole thing."

Her mother emerged from the mudroom, fingering

her damp hair. "Actually, I don't blame her. It's getting wet out there, and she moves so slowly."

Gideon released a long breath. "I'd better head home then. Butch doesn't like loud noises."

Kip giggled. "Butch is a funny name for a girly dog."

"Hey, he'll take offense if he hears you say that."

"Yeah, and he might nip my ankle if he did." Kip covered his mouth to keep his laughter inside.

"Why don't you bring Butch and come ride out the hurricane here with us? I personally don't like being alone in a storm." Her mother averted her head, suddenly sliding her gaze away from Gideon.

But Kathleen didn't need to see her expression to know what her mom was up to. Gideon was an available bachelor, and her daughter was available now. Bingo. Why not get them together? As that went through her mind, Kathleen said without really thinking about it, "I agree. You shouldn't be alone. You're injured. I wouldn't want you to do anything to strain your cracked ribs."

"Right, Kathleen has a point."

"Yeah, Gideon, please stay and bring Butch." Kip took his hand and dragged him toward the mudroom where the rain gear was. "I'll come with you and carry your dog."

"I think I'm being bulldozed by all of you."

"If that means we're ganging up on you, yep, we are. I don't want to be the man of the house. I've never been in a hurricane."

Hearing Kip say that twisted Kathleen's heart. Ever

since his dad had died last year, he'd tried to be the man of the house because some of their friends in Denver had said that the job was his now that his father was gone. Although he'd only been eight, he'd taken the role seriously to the point of even bossing Jared around right after Derek's death. That was what had started the fighting between them that had escalated when they'd moved to Hope.

Gideon captured Kathleen's gaze and held it for a long moment. For a brief time a connection between her and Gideon sprang up, taking her by surprise in its strength. They had spent the whole day helping each other and neighbors get ready for the hurricane. Even with his broken arm, he'd managed to participate fully in the preparations and get her sons involved, without any arguing.

"Is it okay if Kip helps me bring Butch?"

Kathleen's throat swelled at the emotions sweeping through her—seeing the eagerness on Kip's face, the compassion on Gideon's as if he knew how much her sons needed a man's influence. "Yes, but hurry."

The clash of thunder boomed as Gideon unlocked his front door. The forty-mile-per-hour wind whipped his poncho about him. Kip huddled close, letting the house block some of it. The second the boy could he charged into the foyer, dripping water all over the tiles.

He glanced down at the puddle forming on the floor. "Sorry."

"If that is all this place gets, I'll be happy. Butch!" Gideon headed toward the back.

His bichon frise yelped, the sound coming from the den. When he entered, he saw the white curly tail sticking out from under the couch. "Butch, come on. We're leaving."

The dog whined, trying to burrow deeper under the sofa.

"What's wrong?" Kip moved toward Butch.

"He's scared. Loud thunderstorms really bother him."

Kip stooped and bent down to look under the couch. "It's okay, Butch. I'm scared, too. We can take care of each other. I won't let anything happen to you."

His coaxing voice held a soothing quality that Gideon's dog responded to. He shifted until his face pressed against Kip's leg. The boy stroked him, continuing to murmur reassurances.

"I'm going to grab a couple of things. I'll be right back." Gideon left the two to bond and went down his hallway to his bedroom.

He retrieved a duffel bag out of the closet and stuck in a high-powered flashlight and then went to the garage for some tools he might need right after the storm. As he gathered his supplies, he thought back to that moment in the kitchen when he and Kathleen had looked at each other. For a moment he saw a future with her. Until he remembered that anyone he had really loved had been taken from him. Usually he could suppress the pain of a loss, but locking gazes with her made him remember the last time he'd seen his baby brother or his parents right before the fire that had taken their lives. His shoulders slumped and his head dropped as the memories washed over him.

"Gideon, Butch is ready to leave," Kip said from the kitchen door to the garage. "I told him I would hold him tight and not let the wind get him."

Gideon sucked in a deep breath, zipped up his duffel bag and rotated toward the boy, forcing a look of reassurance on his face. "First, I need to disconnect some appliances since there's a good chance the electricity will go off."

"That happened in Denver to us during a snowstorm. It got cold in the house. We didn't have electricity for a day." Kip cradled Butch against his chest.

"It might be off longer than that here." Gideon made his way through his house and unplugged various items like his computer and television set. When he was finished, he strode toward the foyer. "Let's get back to your grandma's."

"How long?" Kip stepped out onto the porch, shielding Butch from the wind.

"Could be a week. Could be shorter than that, but it could be longer."

"Longer?" Kip shouted over the howl of the wind and another clap of thunder.

"That's why we have supplies for a couple of weeks. To be prepared." Gideon hurried his pace, crossing Miss Alice's yard and glancing toward her boarded front window. Light leaked out of the slits around the edges of the two-by-fours he found to cover it.

When they reached Ruth's porch, Gideon glanced down at Kip. He chewed his bottom lip and clutched

Butch tight against him. Gideon put his bag down and clasped the boy's shoulder. He lifted his gaze to Gideon's.

"It's always wise to prepare for the worst, but that doesn't mean it will happen. Worrying won't change what is to be. We'll deal with whatever happens. The Lord is with us."

"Mom used to say that. She doesn't anymore."

The front door swung open, and Kathleen stood in the entrance. "I was beginning to worry about you two."

Kip entered, saying, "I had to coax Butch out from under the couch. He's scared." He kept going down the hall to the den.

Gideon moved into the house. "Sorry. I also decided to turn off some of my major appliances in case there were electrical surges."

"Is everything all right? Kip was frowning."

"He's concerned about the electricity going out for a long time."

"Then I'd better not tell him I am, too. I try to reassure him as much as possible, but he worries about everything. It has gotten worse since Derek died. Whereas Jared is fearless, Kip is the opposite."

"I went through that as a boy when my parents died. I cried all the time. I didn't understand why they weren't coming back for Zach and me."

"When anything changes, he freaks out."

"I did, too. That's probably why I didn't do well in a lot of my foster care homes. Things changed all the time. When I couldn't control my life, I acted out. It took me growing up and getting to know the Lord to change that reaction. I'm trying to let Him control my life. But it isn't always easy to do."

"I used to feel that way and look what happened. My husband died and left me with a ton of debt to pay off. To top that, my boys are hurting with everything that has happened. To make ends meet, I had to move here, and they weren't happy about that."

"Because it is a change. Kids depend on stability."

"I wouldn't mind it, either."

He stepped closer in the foyer. "Whether we want it or not, chaos is coming in the form of Hurricane Naomi."

Jared came out of the den. "Kip won't let me hold Butch. I should get a turn, too."

"Ah, I wondered when Kip and Jared's truce would end," she whispered to Gideon then walked toward her son.

He'd wanted to ask questions about her situation, but this wasn't the time. There might never be a good time. It wasn't his business, but he cared about her and beneath her words he heard the pain she carried.

Wind and rain slashed at Kathleen's childhood home as though beating its fists against the exterior and demanding entrance. Sitting in a chair that Gideon had brought into the laundry room—the only interior room in the house—she watched her sons play Go Fish in the glow of the flashlight. Seated in the corner, her mother listened to the radio for any news concerning the hurricane raging outside. The howl of the wind continually pulled Kip's attention away from the game, to the frustration of his little brother.

"Why do we have to stay in here? I can't see what's going on." Jared tossed down his cards after losing again to his brother. "I'm bored."

Kathleen gestured toward two pallets on the floor. "Then try and sleep."

Jared shot her a look as if she'd gone crazy. "What if something happens? I've got to be ready."

Butch yelped at the door right before it opened, and Gideon came into the room. "Everything looks okay right now."

Static suddenly filled the air. "Oh, great, the radio station has been knocked off the air," her mother muttered.

His eyes huge, Kip scooped up Butch. "Did the hurricane get it?"

Her mother turned off the static noise. "No, honey. They either lost their backup power or the storm is interfering with their signal. Nothing to be concerned about."

Gideon picked his way through the pillows and blankets littering the floor to Kathleen and sat next to her. "The electricity is off up and down the street. I don't see any evidence of flooding." He turned his head away from the boys and lowered his voice, "But I think one of us should go out and check every fifteen minutes. The wind has picked up, and I see debris everywhere."

"I'll go next."

"Go where, Mom?" Kip asked, holding the dog close to him, laying his cheek against the animal.

"Just to check the house. We don't have windows in here to look out so it's a good thing to do that every once in a while."

"Why don't we camp out in the den? It's more comfortable." Standing against the washing machine, Kip followed Bubbles swimming around in circles.

"It's safer staying away from windows," Kathleen's mother answered, turning the radio on again and finding more static. Frowning, she switched it off.

The steady sound of the rain and wind hung in the silence that had descended. Even Jared bit his lower lip and hunkered down on the pallet.

"Why don't you listen to your music on your MP3 player?" Kathleen wished she had one to take her mind off the hurricane.

"I forgot mine at home when we packed our bags." Kip flinched when the noise increased in intensity.

"I've got mine." Jared reached for his backpack and dug into it. When he found it, he stuck the earplugs in and lay on the pallet.

The relentless sound pounding at the house continued. Kip chewed on his fingernails, looking at the ceiling. Finally he curled up on his blankets, burying Butch and him beneath the covers.

"I hope he goes to sleep, but I don't think that's going to happen," Kathleen whispered to Gideon.

The blanket flipped back and Kip sat up. "I heard you. I can't sleep. Who can with all this noise?"

"Then why don't you tell me about the snowstorm you had in Denver where you lost your power. How many inches was it?" Gideon leaned forward, clasping his hands, resting his elbows on his thighs.

A crack and boom rent the air. Kip shot to his feet. Butch burrowed deeper into the covers. "What was that?"

"Tell Gideon about the snowstorm. I'll go check." Kathleen schooled her voice and her expression into a calmness she didn't feel. Inside, her heart thundered against her chest, and she squeezed her hands into fists to keep them from trembling. Kip didn't need to see that.

She pushed to her feet and hurried out of the room before her son saw fear on her face. Another sound reverberated through the air. Like a tree crashing into something nearby.

Since most of the windows were shuttered, Kathleen went to the front door and opened it slowly. It was protected from the direction the wind was coming, but she didn't want to take any chances. She knew the folly of going out in the storm, but she needed to discover the source of that noise. The yard had tall pines and live oak in it. She moved a couple of feet out onto the porch with Gideon's powerful flashlight.

When she peered out at the rain and wind lashing the ground at a forty-five-degree angle, she couldn't see anything. Through the early morning light she accounted for all the trees in front. As she started to back away and close the door, she noticed out of the corner of her eye the base of an uprooted pine in Miss Alice's yard.

Quickly going into the house, Kathleen slammed the

door closed and rushed into the garage where there was a taped window that faced Miss Alice's place. Through the strips she spied the pine. Its massive trunk halved the one-story house right where Miss Alice's bedroom was. Rain and wind whipped through the hole in the structure. Kathleen remembered the older woman had planned to sleep while Hurricane Naomi raged outside.

Chapter Six

That Miss Alice was probably trapped beneath the pine tree gripped Kathleen with immobility for a few seconds as the howling wind vied with the drenching downpour. Then another crack followed by a boom propelled her into action. She whirled around and raced toward the door into the house. When she burst into the laundry room, Jared lay curled on his pallet, asleep finally, while Kip, buried by mounds of covers, stayed hidden with Butch.

Her mother glanced up. "What's wrong?"

In midstretch, Gideon riveted his attention to her.

"Miss Alice's house was struck by a tree right through her bedroom where she was going to be. We've got to help her."

Gideon bolted to his feet. "I'll go."

"No, not alone." Kathleen blocked his exit. "Mom, remain here with the boys. If you can get through to 911, let them know about Miss Alice."

"Hon, I doubt I'll be able to, but I'll try. What if Jared or Kip wakes up?"

"Tell them we went to help Miss Alice, and we'll be right back." Kathleen spun on her heel and moved into the hallway, waiting until Gideon left and closed the door.

"I heard another tree either go down or split, but I didn't see where."

"You should stay here." Gideon began donning his rain gear.

When Kathleen finished snapping her waterproof jacket, she grabbed her heavy-duty flashlight and started for the back door. "I'm a nurse. If something is wrong with Miss Alice, I might be able to help."

Right behind her, he stopped her progress. "I'm a paramedic. Let me handle this. You take care of your family."

She tapped his cast underneath the rain slicker. "With only one arm?"

He scowled. "Let's go. Take hold of me and stay close."

As she stepped out into the wind, its force nearly snatched her flashlight from her. She tightened her grip and lowered her head. She dragged one foot forward, then another, fighting the crosswinds and the driving rain. The beating of her heart battered at her chest as the hurricane battered Hope.

Gideon paused near the downed tree, inspecting what he could, but the downpour and high winds made it hard to see anything. Hugging the side of Alice's house, Kathleen used it to shelter herself from the fierce storm and continued toward the back door. She reached it and tried the handle. Locked. She peered back toward Gideon approaching her.

"It's locked. How do we get in?" Kathleen asked.

"I'll try to climb in through the hole the tree has created. There's a gap. I might fit," he yelled over the din of the hurricane.

"I might be able to better than you. Let me try first."

"But—"

"I have two arms I can use to climb." She started back the way she'd come.

Gideon dogged her steps, and when she arrived at the place where he thought he could get into the house, Kathleen examined it and wondered how she would get through the slit. She grabbed hold of the trunk, the rain pummeling her. Gideon positioned himself next to the tree, and she used him to hike herself up and into the small opening.

The wet bark scraped against her as she wiggled through the hole. Her raincoat snagged on a broken branch, stopping her progress. She yanked on her slicker and freed it, then slithered through the rest of the opening.

With her flashlight she inspected the area where the tree came down. All she could see was the edge of the bed. The pine obscured the rest of it. She stepped closer and peered through the limbs to see if she saw Miss Alice. The storm still hammered at her.

She knelt next to the bed and probed the green foliage for any sign of Miss Alice. She couldn't see anything. "Miss Alice!" she yelled several times over the

noise of the storm. Even though her neighbor had intended to turn off her hearing aid, she had to try in
case Miss Alice hadn't.

Standing, she hurried into the hallway and closed
the bedroom door to keep some of the wind and rain
out although part of the corridor's ceiling had caved
in as well. She headed toward the kitchen to open the
door for Gideon.

After letting him into the house, she pointed toward the dining room and living room. "Let's check
the house. I didn't see her in her bedroom. Maybe she
used her other one. Or maybe she's on the other side
of her bed where I can't get." As she voiced that last
fear, she sent a silent prayer to the Lord that Miss Alice
would be safe somewhere else in her house.

"We'll find her."

Kathleen swept her flashlight in a wide arc on half
the dining room while Gideon took the other part, making her way toward the living room. *Please let Miss
Alice be safe in her recliner as before.*

But when Kathleen entered the room ahead of
Gideon and shone her light on the chair, its emptiness
mocked her. "Where's Miss Alice's cat? I haven't seen
or heard it."

"With her probably. Or hiding."

A slamming sound caused Kathleen to jump, nearly
falling back into Gideon. He steadied her with one
hand, then skirted her and strode toward the noise. In
the hallway he slowed his quick pace. Kathleen spied
the bedroom door she'd shut banging against the wall
as the wind whipped through.

"Let's finish checking the rest of the house then re-check her bedroom." Gideon covered the distance to Miss Alice's other bedroom.

Kathleen took the closed door across the hall. When she entered the bathroom, she came to a halt, her light illuminating a sleeping Miss Alice on a small, blow-up mattress with her cat curled next to her.

"Gideon, she's in here." Kathleen knelt next to Miss Alice and shook her shoulder.

The woman's eyes popped open. For a few seconds confusion marked her expression until recognition dawned in her gaze. "Why are you here? I'm perfectly fine. I told you I was going to bed and sleep through this."

"Miss Alice, a pine tree fell on your house. On your bedroom. I was afraid you went to sleep in your bed."

The older woman's eyes grew round. "My bedroom? Something told me to set up in here. This is the only room without windows." She struggled to sit up.

Kathleen helped her. "Please come over to Mom's house. We'll help you. You've got a couple of other trees close to your house."

"I'll be all—"

Gideon moved into the bathroom. "Miss Alice, do you want us to worry about you? Because we will if you don't come with us. There is no way we can leave you here with your house damaged like it is."

"A tree could fall on Ruth's house."

Gideon plowed his hand through his wet hair. "Yep, you're certainly right, but right now one hasn't. At least wind and rain aren't blowing through her place."

"What about my things?"

"You're more important than any of your possessions. I'll help you carry what you think is important."

"I've got to take Cottonballs. I can't leave him here." Miss Alice scooped up her white cat and held it against her chest. "Help me up. My knees don't work like they used to."

Gideon took Miss Alice's left arm while Kathleen clasped her right one, and they hoisted her to her feet.

"I have to have my pocketbook. I don't go anywhere without it."

"Where is it?" Kathleen scooted the air mattress back so Miss Alice could walk unhindered.

"In the bathtub along with some of my most prized possessions. I need them, too."

"I'll get them while Gideon helps you."

"Miss Alice, you'll need to stay close to me. The wind is fierce."

"Don't you worry about me, young man. I've been through some bad storms before. You don't live to be eighty-six and not. I could tell you some stories…" As she and Gideon made their way toward the kitchen, the roar of the wind streaming from the bedroom drowned out her words.

Kathleen turned toward the bathtub and saw Miss Alice's purse along with a sack of other items. Taking the paper bag, she panned the room for something to put her possessions into that wouldn't fall apart the minute she stepped outside. Finally, she dumped the contents of the trash can out on the floor and stuffed the sack down into it, then hurried into the hall.

Her slicker flapped in the wind coming from the bedroom. She didn't want to think of the damage being done to the inside of the house. In the kitchen, before she followed Gideon and Miss Alice and her cat out into the tempest, she drew in a fortifying breath.

Lord, please help us get back to Mom's safely.

A couple of hours later, Gideon opened the front door and stood in the entrance to Ruth's house, surveying the street. The rain still fell, backing up at the drains and flooding the road. He ran his fingers through his now-dry hair then kneaded the tight cords of his neck. Tension gripped him.

Limbs, leaves and debris cluttered the rain-soaked ground. Downed trees crisscrossed his neighbors' yards. A small magnolia in front of Ruth's lay uprooted and blocking the sidewalk. Months of work stretched before the town. It took a day to destroy, but it would take a long time to repair.

"How bad is it?" Kathleen came to his side to peer outside.

"We probably fared better than some areas nearer the water. The storm surge was supposed to be bad. I think most of those people evacuated. At least I hope they did."

She clicked off her flashlight. Although it was daylight, a steady rain grayed the sky, and the shuttered windows darkened the interior of the house. "I'm afraid of what I'll find at the cottage. It sits at a lower elevation near the beach."

"When do you have to report to work?"

"I should go in as soon as possible. The people who've been at the hospital have been there for over twenty-four hours."

"I want to drive you. You said your car has been giving you problems. I don't want you to get stranded."

"Thankfully, the hospital isn't but a few miles from here. If I have to, I can walk."

He turned toward her, grasping her arm. "No, I will take you. It's going to be dangerous with flooding and downed power lines."

"I hate leaving Mom and the boys, but they need me at the hospital."

"Don't worry about them. I can stay here and help."

"Don't let Miss Alice go home. It isn't safe."

He grinned. "I'll do my best, but she's stubborn. I thought for a moment last night I was going to have to throw her over my shoulder and carry her out of her house."

"That would have been a sight, especially with your cracked ribs and broken arm."

"Yeah, I was doing some heavy-duty praying she'd agree without a fight."

The look in Kathleen's eyes softened. She took hold of his hand. "Thank you for being here. I think your presence helped the boys, especially Kip."

"It's much better to ride out a hurricane with someone than by yourself." Most of his life he had been by himself, but when he said that to Kathleen, he realized he meant every word. He'd felt needed and liked that feeling.

"I'd better get ready," Kathleen said with a deep sigh.

"I'll get my Jeep and be back to take you."

She turned back into the house and crossed to the hallway, using her flashlight to guide her. Gideon shut the front door and went to the kitchen to get into his rain gear, then he headed out the back and cut across Ruth's yard toward Miss Alice's, circling around toward the front. As he strode past her place, he took note of the extensive damage. Another tree had fallen on her porch and crashed through its roof, barely missing the main house.

When he arrived at his home, one of his shutters was ripped off its hinges and the window was broken, allowing rain into his place. He went inside and hurried to the front spare bedroom. Now that the wind wasn't driving the rain at an angle, water was no longer pooling on his hardwood floor. He would take Kathleen then come back to patch the hole the best he could. Maybe he could get Kathleen's sons to help him now that the rain had lessened and the wind had calmed. It would be good to keep them busy, especially Jared.

Ten minutes later he pulled up in front of Ruth's. Kathleen came out before he could get out of his Jeep. She hurried toward his car and climbed into the passenger's side.

"Jared wanted to come with us. I told him he can't leave the house until it's safe."

"I thought I would see if Kip and Jared would help me repair one of my windows. Other than some rain damage in that bedroom, I think my house weathered the storm okay. I noticed some shingles off the roof and some branches down but nothing like Miss Alice's place."

"I went upstairs and the ceiling in my old bedroom is leaking so I'm sure Mom's roof has some problems, too."

"There's a lot of work to do, but first I need to get you to the hospital."

He came to a stop at the end of the block where a downed tree impeded his progress. Climbing from the Jeep, he started for the medium-size pine to move it. He grasped it and started dragging it, a grimace of pain on his face. Kathleen joined him and took hold of it as he did. Together they managed to drag it off the road enough to allow cars around it.

Back in the Jeep a few minutes later Gideon threw the car into Drive and pulled forward. "That probably won't be the only time we'll be doing that." He steered clear of a power line down on one side of the street and continued toward the hospital.

By the time he reached the front doors of Hope Memorial, his hand ached from gripping the steering wheel so tightly and the tension in his neck had intensified. What little he'd seen of the town left an impression of chaos, as though he'd driven through a war-torn area.

When he parked, he angled toward Kathleen. "When do you want me to pick you up?"

"My shift will end tomorrow morning at this time. We'll rotate teams until things calm down, but from the looks of the town that may be a while."

"This is the worst possible time to be on medical leave."

"But you are for a good reason." She touched his cast.

He captured her hand and laced his fingers through hers. "I know, but it doesn't make it any easier to accept it. Thanks for trying to make me feel better. The department can't curtail my activities around the neighborhood, though. I can focus my energy helping people on my street. There will be a lot to do there."

Smiling, Kathleen shook her head. "Why does that not surprise me? Just remember it has been less than a week since you were injured. Don't overdo it and make your situation worse. Promise me you'll take breaks, at least."

The concern in her expression warmed him. She had a kind heart. From what he'd seen, that made her a good nurse. But she was able to do her job while he wasn't. He had never been an inactive person, and it would be hard to start now, especially with all that had to be done.

He cocked his mouth into a grin. "I promise. I want to get better so I can go back to work."

She leaned across the seat and gave him a quick kiss on the cheek then opened the door and slipped out of his Jeep, leaving him to wonder about that brief touch of her lips on his cheek. He closed his eyes for a few seconds and could imagine the kiss all over again. He could smell her lingering scent of vanilla. The sensations she'd produced in him had nothing to do with friendship. Whoa! This was not good. He had no business being anything other than a friend to Kathleen. Neither of them was looking for anything more.

"Mr. Miller in room 320 is finally settled down. Per the doctor's orders, I increased his pain meds." Kathleen took the chart of the older man who had broken a hip when he fell off a ladder. She made some notes, then placed it back behind the counter at the nurses' station.

"We've been so busy I never got to ask you how Ruth fared in the hurricane." Mildred eased into a chair and massaged her temples. "I don't think I've slept in forty-eight hours."

"Who can sleep through a hurricane?" Kathleen snapped her fingers. "Oh, I forgot. Miss Alice slept through a good part of it until Gideon and I came to rescue her. Then she was up with us in the laundry room, refereeing between her cat and Gideon's dog. Not a pretty sight. The cat kept hissing the whole time. A couple of times his banshee cry rivaled the noise of the storm."

"Ah, poor thing. Alice Beggs can be a handful."

"Mom!"

Kathleen peered toward the stairs and spied Jared and Kip racing toward her. She held up her hand to slow them down, but Jared crashed into a doctor coming out of a patient's room, knocking the distinguished-looking man to the floor while Kip skidded to a halt a foot from him. Not far behind the boys, Gideon came down the hall, a frown on his face.

"Sorry, Kathleen. They got ahead of me racing up the stairs."

The six-foot-five doctor picked himself up from the floor and glared down at her sons. "No running in the hospital. We have injured people here, and I don't want to be one of them."

Jared leaned back and looked up at the man. "Sorry."

"What are you doing here?" Dr. Allen set his hands on his hips. "This isn't a playground."

"Mom works here." Jared pointed toward her, then turned his big eyes on the man, pure innocence in his expression. "I'm really sorry, sir. I won't run again."

And her son believed that until the next time. Kathleen quickly covered the space between Jared and Dr. Allen.

Dr. Allen straightened his white coat, saying, "I'm glad to hear that," then nodded toward her and made his way to another patient's room.

Jared grinned from ear to ear, turning on that little-boy look intended to melt her heart. "I'm sorry, Mom. I was just glad to see you."

"They worked so hard yesterday helping the neighbors and your mom clean up that I couldn't say no to coming with me to pick you up."

Jared spotted the head nurse behind the counter, waved and said in a loud voice that could carry beyond down the hall, "Hi, Miss Mildred. Do you need any help? I've been helping anyone that does."

Kip punched him in the arm. "Shh. This is a hospital. People are sleeping."

"But it's ten in the morning."

"Boys, why don't you go downstairs with Gideon? I'll be right there."

"We're parked in the left lot when you come out the front entrance. The other one is still blocked with a downed oak." Gideon grabbed Jared's hand before he shot for the stairs.

Mildred came up behind Kathleen. "Go home and sleep. Be with your sons. I'll see you in two days."

"Call me on my cell if someone can't come in. I don't live too far away, and we are in okay shape." With cell reception working some of the time, she'd talked to her mother yesterday evening, and she reconfirmed what Kathleen had thought. Her childhood home didn't have too much damage, especially compared to Miss Alice's house and others she saw on the way to the hospital.

"Knowing Ruth, she has the neighborhood organized with the cleanup."

Kathleen walked into the room behind the counter and pulled her purse out of her locker. "You know my mother well," she said with a laugh. "The trick will be getting some rest before I'm put on a work crew. How about you? When are you going home?"

"I'm camping out here for a few more days. I don't have family and unfortunately my duplex near the beach didn't make it. Thankfully I was here, but one of my neighbors let me know when he went back after evacuating."

"Then you need to come to Mom's. She has the room."

"Aren't you and your sons staying with her? And how about Alice?"

"I hadn't planned on it, but with all that has happened here I haven't had time to check about Mom's rental I was living in. It wasn't as close as you were to the beach so it might be all right. Still, you know Mom will insist. You are like family."

Mildred smiled, a tired gesture because she'd been working for two straight days. "I'll think about it. Now you'd better go before your boys overpower that nice young man and come looking for you."

Kathleen laughed at the image that came to mind. "Don't forget there's a place for you if it doesn't work out at your sister's. The hospital isn't where you should stay. You'll work all the time."

"We're mighty busy, but I could use a break."

Kathleen hugged Mildred then walked toward the stairs. Five minutes later she climbed into the front passenger seat of Gideon's Jeep while Jared and Kip were sitting still and quiet.

"Okay, what have you done with my sons?" She slid a look toward the backseat.

"We're being good." Jared folded his hands in his lap.

"Yeah, Mom. We want to go to our house, and if we don't act good, Gideon will take us back to Nana's."

"Oh, I see." She straightened forward, slanting a glance toward Gideon. "We're going by the cottage?"

"Your mom wanted me to check on it. We've heard that area was flooded."

"Why didn't someone tell me?" She'd thought about it while working then another emergency had come in and she hadn't had time. That had been her past twenty-four hours—one crisis after another.

"Because your mom didn't want you to worry. We had so much to do in the neighborhood yesterday just to make it safe. We didn't have time for anything else. A couple of people have generators. One is keeping food cold. Another is where people can do their laundry. I brought mine down to your mom's since y'all and Miss Alice are staying there. Between those two generators they're cooking a hot meal for everyone on the street. Your mom has set up headquarters for the hurricane cleanup."

"Headquarters?"

"She has organized all of us. She's very good at getting things done."

"Miss Alice didn't demand to go home?"

"At first, until she saw her house. She may be stubborn, but she's not a fool. She's actually settled in at your mom's quite well. Now, her cat is another thing."

"Is Butch still there?"

He turned onto the street where the rental cottage was. "I fixed my window so there won't be anymore rain damage, and Butch is happily back at his house."

Kathleen scanned the houses where she lived, sucking in a deep breath and holding it. The sight of the destruction churned her stomach. She could see where the water had come up to houses—some over their first story. The smell of rotting vegetation and rancid water saturated the air, causing her stomach to roil even more.

Gideon pulled into the driveway and switched off his engine. The silence from the backseat spoke of the horrific sight where the cottage used to be. All that was left was the foundation with pieces of what could be their place scattered around it, but Kathleen couldn't tell for sure. The neighboring homes were gone too, as if a surge of water had focused its power on this area that dipped down. It probably had formed a river in the middle of the hurricane.

"Mom, where are our things?" Kip finally asked in a choked voice.

"I don't know, honey. Maybe we'll be able to find some out there." She waved her hand toward the litter mixed in with the dead foliage and tree limbs. She thought she saw Kip's skateboard sticking out from under a pile of debris, but wasn't sure.

She heard the back door open and angled around. "Jared, I don't want you getting out."

Tears shone in his eyes. "Why not? We've got to look for our stuff."

"Tell you what. I'll check the area out and make sure it's safe and then you all can come over and go through everything. How about tomorrow?" Gideon started his Jeep.

Jared slammed the door closed. "What if it rains today?"

Kathleen bit her lower lip, her own tears making her vision blurry. "Hon, I don't think that will make a difference. If it's out there, it has survived a hurricane. A little rain won't hurt it. Everything we had can be replaced." Except the pictures and a few treasures, but she didn't want to say anything about them right now. It was hard enough seeing the destruction. "Let's go to Mom's."

Gideon sent her a reassuring smile. "I'll take care of it later today."

"I appreciate that." The sight of what was left of her cottage drained what little energy she had. The past two days had finally crashed down on her. All she wanted to do was sleep.

Later that afternoon as she awakened from a long nap, the scent of coffee brewing drifted to Kathleen. The aroma lured her to full alertness. She glanced at the battery-operated clock on the nightstand and bolted up in bed. Four o'clock. She hadn't wanted to sleep almost the entire day. Now she wouldn't get to sleep later tonight. That thought broke the dam on her emotions she'd kept reined in ever since she'd seen the destroyed cottage.

Her tears finally streamed down her face, flowing freely. Could things get any worse? Hope was devastated. The house she'd been living in was gone. She was drowning in debt her husband had accrued. Her sons were hurting emotionally. The tears turned to sobs that shook her. She drew her legs up against her chest and clasped them. For so long she'd been desperate to hold it together. Now she couldn't.

A soft knock at the bedroom door startled her. She tried to scrub away the evidence of her sorrow as she asked, "Who is it?" If it had been her sons, they would have burst into the room.

"Gideon."

She glanced down. Having no energy to change when she got home at ten-thirty this morning, she still wore her blue scrubs. As she swung her legs over the side of the bed, she continued to swipe at her tears.

"Are you all right?"

She stood—too fast. The room swirled before her eyes, still swimming with tears. "Yes. Be right there."

Steadying herself, she started for the door but caught sight of herself in the mirror. A gasp escaped her lips as she stared at the hollow look in her gaze staring back at her. Other than holing herself up in the bedroom, there'd be no way he wouldn't know she'd been crying. Inhaling several times, she opened the door.

He peered at her with an intensity that robbed her of the decent breath she'd just taken in. "Can I come in? I went by your house again while you were sleeping."

She stepped to the side and allowed him into her childhood bedroom, then shut the door. She didn't want her sons to overhear anything concerning the house. They already had enough to deal with.

"I'm glad I did. I found a nest of snakes under a pile of limbs and lots of boards with nails sticking up, but I think I've made the area safe enough for you and your sons. There are a lot of items among the debris that might be yours. It's hard for me to tell."

Kathleen sank down on her bed. "I don't want Jared or Kip going back there right now. I'll go over tomorrow and look around. They've lost so much. I don't want them to see their possessions destroyed. If I find any of their stuff, I'll bring it back."

"You know they won't like that. They've been very

quiet today, but when they talk, they discuss what they're going to do when they go back home."

"Home?" The word came out on a shaky breath. Tears clogged her throat. She didn't want to cry in front of Gideon. She'd shed enough tears over the past year since her husband's death but always in private. "I don't know what that is anymore. When I came back to Hope, I felt this would be it. I wanted to make a home for my sons. I had hoped I could save enough money to buy the rental from Mom eventually. It was starting to feel like a home to me. Mom wanted to give me the cottage, but I wanted to make this work on my terms. This hurricane changed everything."

The overwhelming sense of loss suddenly hit her. She could no longer contain the sorrow. It swelled up and spilled down her cheeks.

Gideon put his arm around her and tugged her close to him. "You aren't alone."

Through the sobs, she mumbled, "I know the whole town feels that way right now." She swallowed hard, trying to tamp down her tears. What good did they do?

"No, I mean the Lord is with you through this. He is here to give us what we need."

"I need a home for Jared and Kip even if it is a two-bedroom house and they have to share a room. It was our home. We had one in Denver until it was repossessed and we had to move."

He tilted up her chin so their gazes connected. "Your home isn't a physical place. It's people. I know. I've been searching for one most of my life."

For a few seconds she thought she saw bleakness in

his expression, but it vanished so quickly she wasn't sure. But he was hurting, too, and it had nothing to do with Hurricane Naomi. "What happened?"

"I lost my parents to a fire when I was eight. My brother and I were put in foster care and finally he was adopted. I wasn't. I had a lot of anger. Not your easiest child to handle. Zach's family moved away and over the years I've lost touch with him. He was five years younger than me and I couldn't keep us together. I blew it."

"Have you tried to find him?"

"Yes. I connected with him finally online about six months ago. He's serving in the marines and is overseas right now. I don't think he really remembers me. He was only four when he was adopted."

"I'm sorry. Don't give up on him."

"I'm not, but I'm not getting my hopes up that I'll suddenly have my brother back."

She came from a large extended family, many with roots around Hope. She couldn't imagine her life without them. Sniffing, she took his hand. "I know that my boys fight a lot, but they really love each other. If anyone threatened Jared, Kip would be there defending his brother and the reverse would be true. I've seen it happen right after they were yelling at each other."

"My family now is Station Two. The guys would do anything for each other. If Zach and I ever get together, fine, but I'm not counting on it."

"The people at the hospital are becoming an extended family to me. The way I've seen them coming together during this crisis awes me. Mildred—Nurse Ratched to you—is staying at the hospital. Mostly I think because she wants to let others stay home to help with their families. She doesn't have one. I hear she's always filling in during the major holidays so people can be with family."

He winced. "Okay, let's agree to forget my name for Mildred."

"I don't know. I may not let you live that one down."

"What can I do to change your mind?"

"Hmm. I'll have to think about that."

"When things calm down, I'll give Kip a grand tour of Station Two."

"You were already going to do that."

"A ride in a fire truck."

Kathleen tapped her chin with her forefinger. "Tempting. I'll keep that in mind."

Gideon rose and tugged her up, her body close to his. His masculine scent surrounded her, and the gleam in his eyes warmed her as the feel of his hand on her arm sent shivers down her spine. "I'm just gonna have to persuade you I'm one of the good guys."

He dipped his head toward her. Every nerve became alert, anticipating the meeting of their lips. Wanting it. She leaned toward him.

A knock sounded on the partially open door and her mother stuck her head through the opening. "I can't find Jared and Kip. They told me they were going upstairs to play in their room for a while. I went there to get them to do something for me and they aren't there. I've looked everywhere in the house and even in the yard. They're gone."

Chapter Seven

Kathleen quickly stepped away from Gideon. "Do you think they went to help someone in the neighborhood?"

"They've been helping the Johnsons but they've been good about letting me know and getting my okay." Ruth pushed the door open wide.

"Would they have gone back to the cottage?" Gideon headed for the hallway. "I can go look for them."

"They know never to leave the block without talking to me first or Mom and that is without a hurricane." Kathleen followed Gideon into the corridor.

"Gideon might be right about the cottage. I heard them whispering before they decided to go play in their room. That in itself should have been a red flag, but I've been cooking all afternoon so people on the block can have one hot meal a day. For a while they were helping me."

"Since this house is in the middle of the block, I'll go one way toward the cottage and you go the other,"

Gideon told Kathleen, then strode toward the front door. "We'll find them."

"Mom, you go on and finish cooking. Don't worry." Kathleen joined Gideon on the porch, the creases on her forehead deepening. "Now if only I could follow my own advice."

"Maybe they thought they could join me while I was over there. One of the neighbors helped and then I went to the fire station to see if there was anything I could do there. The boys wouldn't have known that."

"I'll go this way." Kathleen pointed east.

Gideon made his way to the end of the block and turned the corner, glancing back at Kathleen who'd been stopped by a neighbor. When he started down the street where the cottage was, he spied Kip out in front. He quickened his pace.

Kip looked up from digging through a pile of trash, grinned and waved at him. Hopping up, he yelled to Jared then ran down the middle of the road toward him. The boy's foot caught on a limb on the ground and he went flying forward, hitting the asphalt with a jolt.

Gideon rushed to the child, who had tears rapidly filling his eyes. Kip rolled over and held up his hands. They were bleeding. Gideon knelt next to him, noticing his jeans were torn at one knee. "Are you okay?" Taking Kip's hands, he examined the palms.

"It hurts."

"I know. It needs to be cleansed. Let me help you up."

The boy pushed up to a sitting position but didn't move any more than that. Suddenly he burst out crying and hugged his arms to his chest, rocking back and forth. For a moment Gideon didn't know what to do.

"Besides your hands, where else does it hurt?"

"Everything is gone. I can't find anything of mine."

Gideon settled his hand on Kip's shoulder. "You might not be able to. I know how hard that can be."

Kip looked up at him, his eyes shiny, tears coursing down his face. "But your house is all right."

"When I was about your age, my home burned down. Everything was destroyed. All I had was the clothes I had on when I escaped from the house."

Kip's gaze widened. "It did? What did you do?"

"Exactly what you did. I got upset. Then I grew very angry at the world. In the long run, that didn't help me at all. I pushed everyone away, even people who were trying to help me. I became so difficult that I ended up being moved from foster home to foster home. I never stayed in one place long. I was the one hurt by that."

"Like Mom moving here?"

"Not exactly. You still have your brother and mother. She will provide a home for you even if that means living with your grandmother. Y'all will be together."

Kip dropped his head and knuckled his eyes.

"I'm not gonna kid you. The next months will be hard. Everyone in Hope will have to pull together to put the town back even better than it was. You and your brother will have to do your part. The more united we are, the faster Hope will recover."

The child lifted his face, squaring his shoulders. "I can do my part."

"C'mon. Let's go get Jared. Your mom is worried

about you two. She should be here shortly." Gideon rose and offered Kip his hand.

As the boy struggled to his feet, grimacing as he put weight on his leg with the torn jeans, Gideon saw Kathleen hurrying down the street toward them. A frown carved deep lines into her face.

"Kip, what happened?"

"I tripped, but I'm okay," he said in his tough-boy voice Gideon remembered using even while inside he'd been hurting.

"I found your skateboard," Jared shouted, holding it up.

"My skateboard!" Kip limped toward his little brother and took it from him. He turned and grinned at Gideon and his mother. "I didn't lose everything."

"How am I supposed to get angry at them when I see that?" Kathleen whispered, shifting toward him.

"Kip and I talked. They're scared. Everything familiar to them has been changing lately. They came over here to find anything of theirs they could cling to. I remember when I escaped the fire at my home, I grabbed my baseball card collection my dad and I started. It was my most prized possession."

"Do you still have it?"

Memories washed through him, sharpening the pain of loss. "At one of my foster homes someone stole it from me. I thought I knew who had it and started a fight with him. He didn't have it, but it got me thrown out of the house. It had been the last straw with the couple I lived with."

Kathleen covered her mouth and shook her head. "You never found it?"

"No. But no one can take away the memories I have of my dad and me going to the store, deciding who to buy, putting it in a scrapbook."

Kathleen cleared her throat and turned back toward her children. "Do you mind if we take a little while to look around for the boys? Maybe there is something besides the skateboard."

"I was going to suggest that. At least until we find something of Jared's."

She threw him a grin as she moved toward her sons. "Or it gets dark."

"Good idea. Besides, your mother was determined to fix a big batch of spaghetti for everyone."

Kip heard Gideon. "Spaghetti! This day is getting better and better."

Kathleen stopped next to Jared. "Let's see what we can find of yours."

"Mom, I've looked everywhere. I don't think there is anything. At least I've got Bubbles at Nana's."

Gideon stood back for a few seconds while Kathleen and Jared went to a pile of items he'd stacked up earlier after clearing some debris and limbs away. These past few days had made him think about having a family. Years ago he'd given up on that idea. He'd been determined to go it alone in the world. But being with Kathleen and her sons revived that dream he'd had as a little boy. He'd been by himself for so long he didn't know if it were possible.

* * *

Half the neighborhood sat in her mother's living and dining rooms. Kathleen handed the last person to arrive a plate with spaghetti. Someone else had brought a premixed salad and another person had two loaves of French bread. As she scanned the faces of the people on the street, tired expressions met her perusal but each person gave her a smile.

When everyone was served and had a seat, her mother stood in the wide entrance between the two rooms and said, "I'd like to offer a blessing." After several people bowed their heads, she closed her eyes and continued, "Lord, I know You are here with us even if at times it doesn't seem like it. We need You. We need Your help rebuilding Hope. Bless this food we are sharing and the people who are gathered here. Amen."

A few around Kathleen murmured amen, but there were some people who grumbled. At the moment she didn't know what to feel. She fought the urge to shut down physically and mentally, but spiritually she was teetering on a ledge—ready to fall any second.

Gideon leaned toward her. "You okay?"

"Yeah, I'm still trying to sort out all my feelings. I feel like I'm at a boxing match and I'm down for the count. And it looks like most of the people are experiencing that, too."

"There's a lot to do in the coming months."

"Jared informed me earlier today that Christmas isn't too far away."

"The first of November is in a few days. I can't believe it."

"I think Jared wants to start a new rock collection. He was disappointed that he couldn't find it at the house."

"There's still more to go through. It might turn up."

"I'm not telling him that, or he'll get his hopes up. I don't want him to be any more disappointed than he was when we left the cottage this afternoon."

"What was it kept in? That way I'll know what to look for."

"It was in a wooden chest. He'd carved his name into it and about scared me to death. He'd gotten a hold of his dad's pocketknife. I wondered why he was so quiet. When I found him in his room, he had all but the *d* carved in the box. Kip had helped him. The rocks are some we found on our hikes in Colorado." *When we were a family before the trouble started.* "He had a rock tumbler that polished them and made them shiny."

"And that's gone, too. That doesn't mean we can't collect rocks around here."

"He already has. He found one on the ground by the cottage and put it in his pocket."

"Kids have a way of bouncing back."

Kathleen chuckled. "Probably before us adults." Her gaze found Miss Alice sitting in a chair with a stool because her mother didn't have a recliner like Miss Alice was used to. "I hear she threatened to go home when she discovered there was no recliner here."

Gideon followed the direction of her look. "I fixed that stool for her. She calmed down after that."

"I imagine being here with Kip and Jared is a bit much for her. She never married and had children. I don't think she's been around very many."

Kip approached Miss Alice and said something to her. Handing Kip her plate, the older lady smiled, a dimple actually appearing in her wrinkled face. He darted away and threaded his way through the crowd as the neighbors finished and began standing.

"Mom told me that he's been trying to help her, whereas Jared is staying as far away from her as he can living in the same house."

Tom Baker, who lived across the street, stopped in front of Gideon. "Some of us are going to help remove the tree and cover the hole in Miss Alice's house tomorrow. The weatherman is saying there could be rain in a few days."

"Great. I want to help. What time?"

"We're thinking eight. It's gonna take a good part of the day. Her house is the worst one hit on the block."

"I'll be there."

Tom nodded at Gideon. "I figured you would say that. Do you have a chainsaw?"

"Yes."

"We'll need it."

"Is there anything I can do?" Kathleen asked.

Tom peered at her. "We could use some people to help haul the branches away."

"I can do that. Does Miss Alice know?"

The man stared down at the floor for a moment, dragging his hand through his hair. "I figured you could tell her. You two have a way with her."

Kathleen pressed her lips together to keep from laughing. Miss Alice's reputation was far worse than the woman really was. "I will."

"Good. We aim to help everyone on this street, even Miss Alice."

When he left, Gideon shifted toward her. "What about your house?"

"It's gone. There isn't much we can do now but look for some of our possessions. If we have time, we'll do it tomorrow afternoon."

"We? You mean Jared and Kip?"

"Yes, today I realized they need to do that. They need some closure. We'll be staying at Mom's for a while. I think it will help them to understand the why of the tragedy by helping others and cleaning up the mess at the cottage."

"Besides, it will keep them out of trouble if they're working."

"Well, that, too. At least until school resumes."

"At the fire station I heard that might not be for a couple of weeks. Some of the schools sustained serious damage. The one on the Point flooded. They're going to have to find another place for the children to go to school—at least for most of the rest of the school year."

"Mom!"

A silence fell over the room at the sound of Jared's yell.

"Mom! Cottonballs is gonna eat Bubbles."

All gazes turned to her. She rose. Miss Alice struggled to sit forward in her chair.

"I'll take care of this, Miss Alice." Kathleen hurried from the room and up the stairs with Gideon following.

Upstairs in the room Kip and Jared shared at her Mom's, she found Jared holding a dripping wet white cat. Kathleen immediately looked at the goldfish, which was swimming around the bowl as though nothing had happened.

"He's a menace. We need to lock him up until he leaves." Jared's forehead was scrunched, his eyebrows slashing down. He held at arm's length a wiggling Cottonballs with his claws out, waiting to sink into something soft like flesh.

Gideon crossed the room and gingerly took the cat from Jared. The beast kept squirming, determined to get back to his food in the bowl. "I'll take him to Miss Alice."

After Gideon left, she shut the door and turned toward her son. "Let's keep this closed while Cottonballs is staying here."

"Why is he, Mom? Miss Alice is always frowning at me. She doesn't like me."

"Have you tried to talk to her?"

"Well, no. What do I say to her? She isn't like Nana. I've heard her yell at kids in her yard."

"I don't think she is used to kids."

"What do you mean?"

Kathleen sat on the twin bed nearest her. "She isn't around children much."

Jared gave her a confused look.

"Sometimes kids require a certain kind of patience not everyone has."

"I was thinking the same thing about Miss Alice."

"Hon, it won't be too long. Once her house is livable she'll want to leave. Put yourself in her shoes. She has always lived alone. Now all of a sudden she is living with two children and two adults. She knows Nana, but she really doesn't know us well. We're all family. She isn't part of our family and may be lonely. Maybe she feels left out a little. And she can't do much to help everyone with cleanup."

"Why not? She could help Nana fix the meals."

"You're right. I don't think anyone has asked her. But remember, Jared, she's a guest in our home."

"This isn't our home. It's Nana's. We don't—" His voice caught. "We don't have a home."

"Yes, we do. Home is where we are together even if it is at Nana's. We might not have a house or apartment for a while, but we have a home."

He cocked his head to the side. "Why can't we?"

"Because we were not the only ones who lost their house. There will be a shortage of places to live until people can rebuild. That will take time."

"Like Miss Alice's house?"

"Yeah. Her place will need extensive work to be livable again."

"While Nana's and Gideon's don't?"

"You're right. We only sustained minor damage compared to others." Kathleen shoved to her feet. "Now I need to go help Nana clean up. Are you coming downstairs?"

"No, I need to make sure Bubbles is all right."

Kathleen hugged Jared. "I love you. Everything will be all right in time."

As she left her sons' room and descended the steps to the ground floor, she wondered if everything really would be all right in time. She hoped—prayed—

it would be, but she felt buried under a pile of rubble the storm created.

Seeing the house cleared of neighbors now that darkness was settling outside, Kathleen checked in the den where the sleeper sofa was set up for Miss Alice to see if she needed anything. The woman wasn't in the room. Voices coming from the kitchen drew her toward it. When she entered, she found Miss Alice drying the dishes while her mom washed and Gideon put them away in the cabinets.

"This is an efficient team. I guess you all don't need me."

Gideon slanted a look over his shoulder then continued to stack the glasses into the cupboard. "Yeah, we'll have this cleaned up in no time. Miss Alice was telling us about her first job when she was a young girl. She was a dishwasher in a fancy restaurant in New Orleans. I've eaten in the place a couple of times."

"You lived in New Orleans, Miss Alice? I thought you'd lived here all your life."

"Child, I lived all over the world until I was thirty and retired to Hope."

"Retired? At thirty?" Kathleen bridged the distance between them and made herself busy putting away the rest of the food.

"That's what I call it when I stopped traveling and put down roots in one place. I chose Hope for that."

"Why?" Gideon took the dried plate from Miss Alice.

"It was smaller fifty years ago, quaint and hospitable. I didn't want a big city where I didn't know many people. You might not believe this, but at one time I was a mover and shaker here in Hope. I've been through my share of hurricanes. I even organized groups to deal with the aftereffects here in town."

Kathleen shut the pantry door. "What did you do?"

"If people group together, the cleanup can go faster. A lot like what you've gotten this neighborhood to do, Ruth."

Her mother grinned at Miss Alice. "At your suggestion."

"Like what we're doing right now, cleaning up after dinner. Teamwork." Miss Alice's eyes twinkled as they fell on Gideon. "Like you do as a firefighter."

"It's hard fighting a fire without teamwork." Gideon put away the last dish.

What happened to Miss Alice while she was upstairs? Kathleen wondered. For the past couple of days, the old woman had been depressed and quiet but for now. Kathleen stared at her, trying to figure out the change.

Miss Alice caught her attention and winked. "It was Kip who reminded me I still have a lot to give. That I could still be part of the team."

Kathleen's mouth fell open, feeling as though the woman had read her mind.

"When Gideon brought Cottonballs downstairs a while ago, Kip hurried and took my cat, telling me he would take care of him. He knew I must be tired so I should rest. I suddenly realized that had been the way I had been acting for the past two days. No more. I may be eighty-six years young, but I'm not gone yet.

So tomorrow I'll be at my house helping with whatever I can."

"You know what the neighbors are going to do?"

Miss Alice grinned. "Gideon broke the news to me. I may be set in my ways, but not that set, I can't appreciate the help." She folded the dish towel and shuffled toward the door that led into the hallway. "With that in mind, I need to get my sleep so I'll be ready. Good night. Ruth, the dinner was delicious."

When Miss Alice left, Kathleen swung her gaze between Gideon and her mother. "Is that the same lady who we kept over here during the storm and sat in a chair, not speaking or doing a thing for hours?"

"I've heard stories about Miss Alice in her younger days. She's right. She was a regular dynamo. Then about fifteen years ago she stopped going to church, being involved with others, and holed herself up in her house. I was never sure why." Kathleen's mother started for the same exit. "I think I'll follow her. Good night."

Kathleen released a slow breath. "It's only eight but I feel like I've been up for the whole day instead of four hours."

"A lot has happened in that time."

"I'm tired but not sleepy."

"Me, too."

"Where did Kip go?"

"To feed Cottonballs and settle him in the laundry room. I guess I probably should also leave. I have some work I want to do at home."

"In the dark? We have your generator."

"I have lanterns like you do."

"Stay." The word came out before Kathleen could censure it, but she didn't want to be alone at the moment.

"I should— Okay, for a little bit."

Out of the corner of her eye, Kathleen saw a flash dart by the doorway. "Why don't we go out on the porch so little boys with big ears don't eavesdrop?"

Gideon glanced toward the entrance and laid his forefinger over his mouth. "Surely you don't mean Jared or Kip?" he asked as he crept out of the kitchen through the dining room.

"Well, they have been known to listen when they shouldn't. You can never tell if…"

A roar erupted in the hallway followed by a yelp from Kip. Two seconds later her older son and Gideon came into the room.

"Look who I found standing by the door. Listening."

"Imagine that. My son with the big ears."

Kip frowned. "I don't have big ears. Jared does, but I don't."

"No, I don't," Jared squeaked from the dining room.

Kathleen made her way to where the sound came from and peeked around the door. "Come out. What were you doing behind there?"

Jared trudged into the kitchen, his eyes downcast. "If Kip can listen, so can I."

"Both of you need to get ready for bed. Now."

"But, Mom, it's only eight-twenty, and we don't even have school tomorrow." Kip's mouth twisted into a frown that he shot at his brother. "See what you made Mom do."

"I did not."

"Jared. Kip. Enough. We have a lot to do tomorrow, and we need to get up early. I don't want two cranky kids. That's why you're going to bed a little early. I understand from Nana you both were up late last night. You've got some sleep to make up."

"I don't need a lot of sleep. Besides, I shouldn't have to go to bed at the same time as Jared. I'm older. Age should have some privileges."

"I agree. And I'm older than both of you. So I get the privilege of you two listening to me then doing exactly what I say."

"But that's not what I meant."

"Go." Kathleen fluttered her hand toward the hallway.

"See you two tomorrow bright and early. I'm going to need two helpers. I can't do all I would like to do because of my cast." Gideon struggled to maintain a serious expression, but the second they disappeared into the hall, he chuckled.

"I heard that," Kip said right before he stomped up the stairs.

Gideon laughed even more. "Finally alone at last," he said to Kathleen.

"You think this will last? You don't know my boys. They'll come up with one excuse after another to come down here just so they can stay up."

He grabbed her hand and tugged her toward the

foyer. "Then let's escape onto the porch like you suggested."

"Great minds think alike."

As Kathleen shut the front door, she glimpsed Kip at the top of the stairs staring down at them. When he saw her, he turned around and went into his room.

The cool night air washed over Kathleen. She sat next to Gideon on the top step and surveyed the neighborhood. Dim lights, from candles and lanterns, shone from some of the houses, the only illumination on the street. The darkness hid the piles of debris and torn up landscape. Across from them, Tom Baker had a tarp over part of his roof covering a hole where some of the shingles had blown away. The place next to him had its carport ripped away from the house, pieces of it lying scattered all over the yards along the street.

The scent of salt water drifted to her, reminding her of how far the Gulf came ashore and covered the area near the beaches and swamped the whole peninsula known as the Point in Hope. The sea retreated but had left its mark on the town, the stench of dead fish and rotting vegetation.

Gideon laid his flashlight down beside him. "When I went to the station, I felt so useless. An alarm went off while I was there, and I had to stand by and watch the others leave to fight the fire."

"I'm so sorry. I'm the reason you're in that situation."

"Hold it. That isn't the reason I told you that. You're not to blame for my injury. I thought we were past that. What do I have to do to make you understand that?"

Her husband had always made her feel she was the cause of things that had gone wrong in their marriage. As though she had been the one to get them into debt. She'd begun to wonder if she was the reason. Had Derek thought she'd wanted a new car or a swimming pool? She hadn't, but he'd acted as if she had.

"Old habits die hard." Placing her elbows on the tops of her thighs, she leaned forward and clasped her hands.

"What do you mean?"

"According to my husband, I was the reason everything went wrong." She turned toward him and realized how close he was to her on the step. Their arms brushed against each other. His coffee-laced breath mingled with the night scents. Her heartbeat reacted to his nearness by speeding up. "Don't get me wrong. I know marriage is a two-way street. We rushed into it. I think I was in love with the idea of marriage. I won't make that mistake again."

"What mistake?"

"Marrying. The year before Derek died I felt like I had to guard everything I said. I even went to the doctor because I was so anxious. I would cry at the drop of a hat. I was always so tired, and it wasn't from work like it is now. My husband didn't want me to work after Kip was born. I agreed with him." *To keep the peace.*

Gideon covered her hands with his. "You'll feel different with time. It hasn't been that long since he passed away."

She nodded. "Fifteen months. But I don't think time will make a difference."

"You're a great mother, patient with your sons even when they test you. You might want to marry again, have another child. Your mom told me you once said you wanted six kids."

"I was fourteen. When did she tell you that?" She was going to have to keep an eye on her mother. Next she would be bringing out her baby pictures to show Gideon. She knew what her mom was up to, and she needed to put a stop to it.

"When she was quizzing me about when I was going to start a family. I don't think your mother knows the meaning of the word subtle."

"I'm finding that out lately. Don't mind her. She thinks the answer to my problems is a man. She doesn't understand a man got me into the mess I'm in." The second she said that her cheeks flamed, heat radiating down her neck. "I mean…"

His hold on her cupped hands tightened as he shifted toward her. "Shh. I understand perfectly."

In the soft glow she could barely make out his face. But she couldn't read the expression on it. Which meant he couldn't read hers. Relief trembled through her because embarrassment still heated her cheeks. The cool breeze flowed over her, but it did little to ease the warmth suffusing her.

"This past week you and your family have kept me sane. You have given me a purpose at a time when I haven't been feeling so useful. You have to understand I'm a man of action. That came to a grinding halt with the accident."

She opened her mouth to tell him she was sorry again, but he covered her lips with his fingers.

"Not a word about you causing it or I will leave."

"Do you always threaten friends?" She tried to school her voice into a serious tone, but laughter leaked through.

"I'm not answering that on the grounds that it might incriminate me." He cradled her face in his large palm. "When do you go back to the hospital?"

"The day after tomorrow. I think we'll be back on our regular schedule soon unless something further happens. How about you? When do you report to headquarters for desk duty?"

He groaned. "Don't remind me. In two days, but I guess it's better than doing nothing."

The feel of his skin against hers momentarily robbed her of speech. She frantically tried to put together a coherent sentence, but every inch of her was aware of the man sitting next to her, so close his breath fanned her chin. "You call what you've been doing nothing, and you've been doing it with only one arm. I certainly have appreciated all your hard work around here and at the cottage."

"I'm glad." He bent a few more inches toward her, their mouths only a breath away.

Her pulse accelerated. Her throat went dry. Her stomach tightened.

His hand ran down her jawline until he took hold of her chin and tilted it up toward him. Her lips parted as she inhaled deeply.

Chapter Eight

All evening Gideon had wanted to kiss Kathleen, so when his lips touched hers, it felt right. Better than right. He wound his arm around her and drew her to him. His mouth settled on hers as he deepened the kiss, pouring into it all the feelings he'd experienced whenever he was near her. Earlier, he'd watched her mouth move as she talked, smiled or frowned. He'd wondered what it would feel like when his moved over hers. Now he knew.

But in the back of his mind he heard Kathleen's words again. She didn't want to become involved with any man. She'd been burned by her deceased husband. She had been warning him. And he needed to listen.

When she slid her arms around his neck, he pulled back, his ragged breath sounding in the sudden quiet of night. "I'd better be going."

Pushing to his feet, he hovered over her. She peered up at him, but he didn't want to see her expression. He wanted to think she enjoyed the kiss, at least some. But he also needed to remember she didn't want to get involved with a man. He had lost too many special people in his life. There was no way he would go through that kind of pain again. So he had to back off before he fell in love and ended up hurt.

"Good night. I'll see you tomorrow." He descended the remaining two steps, wanting to stay and pursue the feelings rampaging through him, but needing to go because of those feelings. He pivoted and started down the sidewalk.

"Gideon."

He stopped and turned but he didn't say anything. No words would describe the conflict raging in him.

"I— Thank you for your help today."

"Anytime." This time he rotated around and hurried away.

Kathleen watched Gideon almost flee from her. What just happened?

She ran her fingers across her lips. *I was kissed by a dynamite, caring man. I was...*

She didn't know what to think. Instead, she sat there letting her feelings dominate her—no, overwhelm her. From her hammering heartbeat to the tingling awareness of everything about Gideon.

What made him stop and pull away?

Did I do something wrong?

Derek's rejections the last year and a half of their marriage mocked her. Would she ever be free of those memories?

She stood, pulling in deep breaths over and over to

calm her. She hadn't come to Hope to find a man. She didn't believe, like her mother, that a man was the solution to her problems. A man had put her into debt, attacked her self-confidence. No, she would be fine by herself. She would put her family back together.

But still she had wanted that kiss to continue. She'd wanted to bask in the feeling of femininity it had brought out in her for a while longer.

The next evening after spending the day at Miss Alice's and then at the cottage picking through the rubble, Kathleen helped her mother put together soup and sandwiches. The back door opened and in came Jared.

"Did you two invite Gideon to dinner?" her mother asked as she put the soup onto the stove to heat.

"Yep. He's going home to wash up and feed Butch. Kip went with him."

"He did?" Kathleen needed to say something to Kip about bugging Gideon too much.

"He wanted to help with Butch." Jared's gaze lit upon Miss Alice sitting at the kitchen table.

"Whatcha doing, Miss Alice?" Jared plopped himself down across from the older woman, put his elbow on the tabletop and settled his chin in his palm.

"I had to do something. Your mom and grandma didn't want me to help with dinner so I'm playing solitaire."

"Can I watch?"

"Sure, if that floats your boat."

"Floats my boat? I don't have one."

Miss Alice laughed. "If that makes you happy."

"Nana plays solitaire sometimes, but it doesn't look like that."

"There are hundreds of different kinds of solitaire."

"Why don't they have different names?"

"Solitaire really means any card game you can play by yourself."

"Oh."

"Why didn't you go with your brother?"

"I don't know." Jared shrugged. "I guess 'cause I'm tired after working all day."

"You did good."

Jared beamed. "I did?"

"Both you and Kip really helped Gideon. I heard him say so. I just wish I could have done more."

"But you're an old lady."

"Jared!" Kathleen closed her eyes and waited for Miss Alice's reaction.

"And proud of it. I've seen and done many things." A chuckle accompanied her declaration.

"Like what?" Jared moved around to the seat next to Miss Alice to watch her play the card game.

"I've ridden a camel in the desert and an elephant in India. I've dived with sharks, and I've climbed some of the tallest mountains in the world."

His eyes grew round. "Weren't you scared the sharks would eat you?"

"Tell you a secret." Miss Alice leaned close and whispered something in Jared's ear.

Kathleen didn't think her son's eyes could get any bigger. "The first time! How many times did you swim with them?"

"Half a dozen times. I'll show you some of my pictures when I can get back into my house."

"I'd like that."

"Now let me show you how to play this version of solitaire." Miss Alice shuffled the deck and laid the cards down in a pyramid, telling Jared what she was doing as she did it.

When Kathleen heard a knock on the front door, she merely continued making the sandwiches. Her mother looked over at her and said, "That must be Gideon. Would you answer the door?"

Kathleen thought about refusing her mother's request, but that would start a whole series of questions she didn't want to answer. Besides, she and Gideon could be casual friends.

She finished cutting the last turkey and Swiss cheese sandwich in half, then hurried into the foyer. Gideon stood on the porch. A picture of him kissing her the night before flashed into her thoughts—along with an image of him ending it suddenly and leaving right after that. All day she had avoided being near him and now she was face-to-face with him, only two feet from him. Way too close for her peace of mind.

He had kissed her and found her lacking. The insecurity she experienced reminded her of Derek that last year of their marriage. He had hardly ever touched her.

"Where's Kip?" Her voice cool, she stepped to the side to let him into the house.

"Butch needed walking, and he wanted to do it. I said okay. I hope that's all right with you."

"That's fine."

She swept around to go back into the kitchen, but Gideon grasped her hand and stopped her. "Is something wrong?"

Yes. His warm touch only reinforced his rejection. "No, everything is fine."

"I'll go get Kip. I shouldn't have let him do it." He released her hand and started to open the door.

"Leave Kip. I said it was fine. I know how much my children love animals."

"Then this must be about last night. You've hardly said two words to me today. I know I shouldn't have kissed you. I was presuming something between us that's not there."

Being punched in the stomach would be better than what she was feeling right now. She backed away. She gritted her teeth and tried to think of something elegant to say. Nothing came to mind except all the hurt his words produced.

"I'm not explaining myself well. I mean—"

"Please, you've made yourself quite clear. Now, if you'll excuse me, I need to help Mom get dinner on the table."

This time he didn't stop her from leaving. Thankful he hadn't, she fought the tears jamming her throat. All she wanted to do was get through this evening without saying or doing something she would regret.

In the kitchen, her mother studied her for a few seconds then went back to setting out the paper goods they were using so they didn't have as much to wash. "Dinner is ready." She looked behind Kathleen. "Where's Kip?"

In the doorway Gideon replied, "I'll go see what's

keeping him." Then he disappeared down the hallway before anyone could say anything.

The sound of the front door opening and closing filled the quiet.

Miss Alice swung her attention from Kathleen to her mom, then rose and asked Jared, "Will you help this old lady to the restroom to wash her hands?"

Jared jumped up and held Miss Alice's arm.

"We'll be gone for a few minutes," she announced as she and Jared left the kitchen.

Her mom leaned back against the counter. "Okay. What's going on? I noticed all day you didn't say anything to Gideon. Are you two having a fight?"

"That would imply there was something between us."

One of her mother's eyebrows rose. "And there isn't?"

"No, we're barely friends."

"Oh, I see. So you two did have a fight."

"No, we didn't and I don't care to talk about this anymore. I'm starved. I worked up quite an appetite today."

"Ignoring your feelings will not make them go away. Since you and Gideon were getting along so well yesterday, I guess something happened after I went to bed last night. Today you wouldn't even think y'all knew each other. What happened?"

The tears fought to be released. Kathleen swallowed again and again. "On second thought, I'm not very hungry. I have to be at work at seven tomorrow. I'm turning in early tonight." Biting her lower lip to keep from crying, she headed for the hallway.

"But, honey, it's only six."

She ignored her mother's words and rushed up the stairs before Gideon returned with Kip. She didn't want to run into him. She didn't understand what she was going through, but she was determined to get a handle on it before she saw him again.

In the safety of her bedroom, she closed the world out and sank onto her bed. What happened last night was a good thing. It reconfirmed that she didn't need to get involved with anyone. Maybe after her children were grown up, when what occurred between her and a man would only affect her. Her sons didn't need to be subjected to a volatile situation as they were the past few years no matter how much she tried to protect them. Jared and Kip needed stability. That needed to be her focus.

A rap at her door startled her. "Who is it?"

"Gideon. May I talk to you?"

No, she wanted to shout, but instead she closed her eyes, fortified herself with a lungful of air and rose. Her pace slowed as she neared the door, and when she opened it, she still wasn't prepared to see him. Nor the angry expression on his face.

"Can I come in?" Steel accompanied each word.

She backed away and let him into her bedroom.

She opened her mouth to speak, but he cut her off. "I asked you if there was anything wrong and you kept telling me everything was fine. Friends don't do that to each other."

"Friends. Is that what we are?"

"Yes." He paused and averted his gaze for a moment. "At least that was what I thought."

"And so friends kiss each other like we did last night?"

"I knew it. I knew I shouldn't have kissed you. I've ruined everything, and I didn't want to do that."

"Wow. That certainly makes me feel better. You regret kissing me."

"I never said that. I shouldn't have kissed you because it led to complications, and I don't want to lose your friendship."

"That's nice to know."

"Sarcasm doesn't become you."

She closed the space between them, her own anger surging to the surface. "Tell me why you kissed me last night. What were you trying to prove?"

"All day I'd been thinking about kissing you, and I thought if I did, that would be it."

She sucked in a ragged breath. "I guess I should appreciate your honesty." But her self-confidence had taken a beating the past couple of years. She hadn't realized how much until he'd pulled away and left so quickly the night before.

"You want honesty?" He got in her face.

She stood her ground. "Yes."

"After you said that you weren't interested in getting involved with anyone, I had decided that was fine. I could respect your wishes. Then before I realized it I was kissing you, telling myself that at least I could satisfy my curiosity then let it go."

"I'm so glad I could accommodate you. Now you won't lose any sleep over that."

A humorless laugh escaped his lips. "I wish that were the case."

"What do you mean? You pulled away and left in such a hurry I wasn't even sure what had happened. I figured you regretted—" She stopped, realizing what she was revealing.

"If you were going to say I regretted kissing you, you're right."

Her anger dissolved into hurt with his declaration.

"And you are wrong."

"What do you mean?"

"I mean that kiss was amazing, but after what you said I shouldn't have done it. I should have respected your wishes and not complicated our relationship. I'm sorry I didn't communicate that well to you last night or earlier this evening."

"The kiss was amazing?"

He looked at her for a long moment then grinned. "Most definitely. Everything I anticipated and more."

The words washed away the hurt and lifted her spirits. "I thought—"

He held up his hand. "No more speculation. If something is wrong, we need to talk it out. That is what friends do. You and your family have made my medical leave bearable, and I appreciate that more than you can know."

"I guess this isn't the time to point out I was the reason for the medical leave."

A stern look descended. "This is the last time I am

going to speak of this." He rapped his knuckles against his hard cast. "I forgive you. Totally. One hundred percent."

Kathleen chuckled. "Okay. I believe you. I promise."

"It's about time. Because I didn't know what else I could do or say to convince you. I guess I could have had my friend write it in the sky for the whole town to see."

"Don't you dare." Laughter overtook her as she pictured the words. *Kathleen, you are forgiven. Gideon.* "That would set the tongues wagging in Hope. I probably wouldn't be able to show my face. Of course, it would take everyone's mind off the hurricane."

"Well, then I'll do that."

She punched him playfully in the arm. "You'd better not."

"I won't. I don't want to get on your bad side again."

A shriek and barking reverberated through the house. Kathleen started for the door. "Kip brought Butch back here?"

"Well, not exactly."

"I'm not sure I want to hear what you mean by that."

"That will depend."

Kathleen opened the door and stepped out into the hallway at the same time a small brown wiry-haired dog ran down it with Cottonballs on its tail. Kip raced after the pair toward the living room.

"*That* is what it depends on?" Kathleen gestured toward the dirty dog.

"Yep. How do you feel about adopting a homeless dog?"

Kip skidded to a stop at the end of the corridor and

swept around toward her. "I found him hiding under a bush. He was scared, shaking and whining. He's lost. I had to bring him home." Then before she could reply, he hurried down the stairs after the fighting animals, drawn no doubt by the racket the mutt and Cottonballs were causing in the living room.

"I'm not sure this is the best time. I never got to have a dog when I was younger. Mom didn't want any pets." Kathleen entered the living room to the picture of Kip kneeling by the couch and trying to coax the dog out from under it while Cottonballs stood next to him, tail puffed out, teeth bared and giving off a banshee cry that made *her* hair stand up.

Miss Alice, Jared and her mom came into the room from the kitchen.

Kip lifted his head, looked at Kathleen and said, "Mom, he is so scared. Do something," then went back to trying to soothe the animal.

"Jared, can you get Cottonballs and take him to the laundry room for me?" Miss Alice moved slowly toward the sofa while Jared darted around her and scooped up the cat that continued to hiss and scream as he took him away. Miss Alice trailed after Jared.

Her mom stepped over to the sofa. "What's going on here? What is under there? Another cat?"

Gideon inched closer to Kathleen and whispered, "Kip brought the dog in through the front door and was taking him upstairs when Cottonballs sensed his territory had been invaded and went on the defensive. I didn't have a chance to say anything to your mom."

Kathleen stooped next to Kip and leaned down until

she saw the mutt cowering in the back. On closer inspection the dog appeared underfed. His ribs showed, and that sight squeezed her heart. "Maybe if we moved the couch, he'll come to you, Kip."

"What's going on?" Ruth asked again. "What's under there?"

Kip peered up at his grandmother. "I found a dog that needs a home. Can I keep him? Please."

"I don't know if that is such a good idea. I'm not a pet person."

"But, Nana, he's homeless. We can't turn him away. We've got Cottonballs here. He's a pet, and Gideon had Butch here during the hurricane. Pretty please."

"But that's the reason why. We do have Cottonballs here. One pet is enough. Look what nearly happened with Bubbles."

"No one will know he's here. I'll keep him in my room. Feed him. Bathe him. Walk him. Besides, Miss Alice will be leaving soon when her house is fixed up."

Her mother sent Kathleen a beseeching look.

"Honey, let's get him out from under the couch first. Gideon, will you help me move it?"

"Sure. Kip, be ready to snatch him if he makes a run for it."

Kathleen stood on one end of the sofa while Gideon took the other. "One, two, three. Lift."

Positioned to grab the mutt when the couch was moved, Kip lunged forward and scooped up the medium-size dog, skinny with his ribs showing. "See. He's been homeless for a while and he has no collar."

"It's dirty." Her mother wrinkled her nose and

backed away. "He needs to be outside. We don't have enough water yet to bathe him."

"I can't keep him?"

"Certainly not in this house until he is clean. No telling what he's brought in here. Fleas. Ticks." Her mother folded her arms over her chest.

"I don't have to drink any water. He can have my share."

Kathleen's gaze fastened onto the dog's sad face as he laid his head on Kip's shoulder. The animal's brown eyes latched on to hers. "Mom, why don't we keep him in the garage for right now? At least for the time being while we decide what to do with him."

"Please, Nana. I promise he won't be a problem."

"Fine, for now. But you have to do everything for it. And you have to keep it away from Cottonballs. I thought an animal was dying in here."

"Thanks. I will. You'll see."

Gideon scratched the animal behind his ears. "C'mon. I'll help you set up a bed for him. We'll make him feel right at home in the garage."

Kip rushed past his grandmother as though he was afraid she would change her mind.

Which given a chance, she might. Kathleen closed the gap between her and her mother. "Thanks. This means a lot to Kip."

"It stays only as long as it isn't any problem. We don't know what kind of diseases it carries. It's so mangy looking."

"I think some food will help with that, and I'll have a vet look him over. The dog must have been on his own for some time. Probably before the hurricane. He looks like he hasn't eaten much lately."

"So what do we feed him? I don't have any dog food here."

"I'll talk with Gideon. Don't worry." She hugged her mother then headed toward the garage.

Kip found an old comforter in the Goodwill bag her mother kept and put it down near the door into the house. When he set the dog on it, he stroked the dirty fur on the animal's back and murmured, "You're all right now. I'm gonna take care of you."

"How about food?" Kathleen asked as the dog curled into a ball, laying his head on Kip's leg.

"I can get some of Butch's dog food. I stocked up when the hurricane was coming. He'll need a bowl of water, too."

Kip grinned up at Gideon. "Thanks. He needs a lot of it."

"I'll find a bowl and fill it with water." Kathleen snagged Gideon's attention. "May I have a word with you?"

He nodded and backed toward the door into the house.

"Mom, tell Nana it's my share of the water."

"We'll find a way for everyone to have water, even your dog. I think the water will be restored soon anyway, so we'll be fine."

"See, I told you everything would be okay." Kip put his arm around the mutt and rubbed his face against the matted, dirty fur.

Kathleen hurried inside before she threw herself

between the dog and her son. *Boys like to get dirty. Boys like to get dirty.*

In the kitchen she shifted toward Gideon. "Which vet do you take Butch to? I hope he can see Kip's dog tomorrow."

"Dr. Anderson. Let me see if his clinic is set up to receive patients. The area of town it's in didn't get hit as hard as some. When are you off work tomorrow?"

"I should be home by four."

"We can do that, then stop by the beach afterwards."

"Why?"

"It's not the most ideal bathtub to bathe an animal in, but it's better than nothing."

"Good thinking."

"I'll have everything set up tomorrow for the dog. You can go to work and not worry about it."

As he left the kitchen, Kathleen began searching for a bowl for the water. When pulling down a plastic dish to use, she stopped in midmotion. In a short time she was beginning to depend on Gideon, to turn to him for help with certain problems. She had to put a halt to that or she would fall right back into the role she had in her marriage where she'd let Derek run everything. She really had only herself to blame for the situation she'd found herself in. She'd never insisted to be informed about their finances. Their marriage had never been a partnership, and she just now realized she was partially the reason it hadn't been.

Chapter Nine

Kathleen surveyed the live oak that remained standing guard near the old white lighthouse on the Point. From what she understood, the historical tree, more than two hundred fifty years old, would live in spite of the fact the hurricane had stripped off all its leaves. Seeing it gave her hope that the town would revive and be better than ever. The Peace Oak, as it had been known through history, had been where a treaty had been signed between the French and the Indians in the area.

Gideon came up behind her and stopped next to her, staring at the lighthouse. "It makes me feel good to see these two landmarks here after the surge of water covered most of the Point."

The past two weeks she and Gideon had seen each other in passing and a couple of times had stopped to talk but that had been all. With the power and water back on, most of the neighbors had retreated to their own houses to repair what they could. She missed the camaraderie of working on a team. "The lighthouse definitely needs a fresh coat of white." Four feet up the structure all the paint was gone and above that band the rest was dull from years of wind and weather.

"That's one of the projects we are tackling today. If we can get the park back into some kind of order, then we'll be able to decorate it for Christmas."

"So they'll still turn the holiday lights on Thanksgiving evening?"

"Yep, twelve days away. That's why we're here. The powers-that-be want the holidays to be like every other year."

"Actually, that's a smart move." Kathleen pointed toward the Peace Oak. "Now if we could glue the leaves back on it, it would be like every other year."

"Gotta find those leaves first."

"They're probably somewhere around Jackson." She turned away from the tree and lighthouse and scanned the beehive of activity all around Broussard Park that was one of the favorite spots for the townspeople. "So what are you doing here today?"

"Helping rebuild the playground. Zane Davidson is donating the new equipment along with some help setting it up." He nodded toward a large truck pulling into the parking lot. "In fact, he's here with it now. What are you doing?"

"Helping to lay gravel for the playground."

"Ah, so we'll be working together. Since Miss Alice's house, I've missed that."

For the past two weeks she had been pulling double duty at the hospital, coming home and helping her mother repair what they could or going to the cottage to dig through the debris for anything of hers or her sons'. "I'm almost through with the cleanup at the cottage. The city should be around at the end of the week to pick up the trash."

"Where are Jared and Kip?"

"Coming later with Mom and Miss Alice. They're contributing lunch for the volunteers."

"Good. I've arranged for your sons to tour Station Two next Saturday. I want to tell them today, but I want your okay first."

"They'll enjoy it."

"How's Rocky doing?"

"The second Kip was able to give him a bath he started bugging Mom about letting him come in and stay in his room. I think he's been counting down the days until Miss Alice goes back to her house. Davidson's Construction Company will be starting on her home Monday. Do you know Zane is only charging her whatever the insurance company gives her to repair her home? She won't even have to pay the thousand dollar deductible. When Zane told her that, I thought for a moment Miss Alice was going to do a jig."

"Now that I would have liked to see."

"I went to school with Zane, and if you had told me he would be doing so much for Hope, I would have scoffed at that."

Gideon's forehead crunched. "Why? Since he returned to Hope, he's been doing a lot for the town."

"When he was in high school, he had quite the reputation of being the bad boy. He rode a motorcycle way too fast and drank. But when I saw him at Miss Alice's house yesterday, I hardly recognized him."

Gideon waved at a tall, black-haired man talking to the driver of the truck.

"You know him?"

"Yeah, this past year he's been coming to this park to play basketball with my youth group."

"What's going to happen to Hope Community Church?" She glanced toward the church across the street from the park. All that remained of the front building was the bell tower. The older original church that had stood behind the newer part was still intact, not having received any water damage because it sat on a rise that had protected it from the flooding.

"We have plans to restore the worship area in the original church. The pastor hopes to have it complete by Christmas Eve services, even if the rest of the church restoration hasn't been done. It amazes me how the building built a hundred and fifty years ago withstood the hurricane but not the one built seventy years ago."

"Have you ever wondered why certain things happen while others don't? Like the church or the tree falling on Miss Alice's house. It could have fallen on Mom's."

"That's why I've always felt being prepared for everything is better."

"But you can't always think of everything. Events occur out of the blue that throw your life into a tailspin."

"Is that what happened when your husband died? He had to be young."

She nodded. "Thirty-five. That's young for a heart attack, but he had been under a great deal of stress. He'd tried to hide the trouble he was in, and it had taken its toll on his body."

"What kind of trouble?"

"Financial. He got himself into debt. He took a second mortgage out on the house. When he died, I couldn't make the payments. The bank foreclosed on us. I tried to stay in Denver for the boys. So much had changed in their lives, I didn't want to move away from what they were familiar with. I sank deeper into debt. Finally, I came home."

"And now with the hurricane, you've lost what you had when you came back to Hope?"

"Yes. Some pieces of furniture and boxes of possessions were still at Mom's, but most of what we owned was in the cottage. I hadn't gotten renter's insurance yet. All we have from the cottage fits in two boxes."

He moved close and took her hands. "But you and your sons are alive."

"Yes, and my car was at Mom's so it wasn't a total loss."

"Many people are in the same predicament. We just have to pull together. One prayer is good, but when it can be many, that's even better."

As before, Gideon's nearness sent her pulse racing. Her senses became attuned to him, everything else fading into the background. As far as she was concerned, they were alone in the park. The breeze from the Gulf carried the scent of the sea. The warmth of the sun canceled out the slight chill in the wind. It was a perfect day, a day to enjoy a picnic, like when she was a child.

"Mom!" Jared ran across the parking lot toward her.

Life intruded. Kathleen tugged her hand from Gideon's and stepped back, turning toward Jared and smiling. This wasn't a day to enjoy a picnic. It was a day of work, a day to remember what happened in Denver with her husband. A day to remind herself not to rush into anything, to be cautious.

"I helped Miss Alice and Nana with the sandwiches. Kip didn't. He was playing with Rocky." Jared skidded to a stop in front of her. "Nana told me to tell you her and Miss Alice are setting up over by the bell tower." Facing Gideon, he stood at attention. "What can I do? I'm here to help. Nana said we have to if we want a playground."

Gideon clasped his hand on Jared's shoulder. "Let's go see what we can do."

She watched her son walking off with Gideon, both with casts on their left arms. The sight thickened her throat. Often when she was working and Gideon was off, her sons spent time with him, helping around his house or a neighbor's. Butch and Rocky had become "best buddies" according to Kip.

Jared stopped and whirled around. "Aren't ya coming?"

"Yes," she answered, noticing Kip helping her mother carry the food to the church.

If she could ignore the damage all around her, she could for a moment see a glimmer of hope. Jared and

Kip had settled in at her mother's. She had a good job, which would help her get back on her feet. She was surrounded by family and friends who cared. But she knew this moment would never last. Worry nibbled at her composure. She kept waiting for the other shoe to fall.

Zane approached Gideon. "You're determined to ignore that cast on your arm, aren't you?"

He laughed. "I keep trying to get my captain to ignore it."

"Obviously desk duty isn't setting well with you."

"Would it with you? You own a large construction company, and yet I see you often working at one of your sites. How come?"

"I enjoy it. Hard work makes me feel alive."

Gideon stared at his friend he'd met while trying to put out a grass fire threatening the pine forest along Interstate 10, all because someone had thrown out a lit cigarette. "It's scary how alike you and I are."

"That's why I want to know what is going on between you and Kathleen. I knew her in high school. She was a freshman when I was a senior. Nice girl."

"She's a nice woman."

Zane cocked an eyebrow. "Don't tell me you're abandoning me. I thought we would go into old age as confirmed bachelors."

"How did you get *nice woman* to mean marriage? I think all this hard work is going to your head."

"In all the years I've known you, I haven't heard of

you dating a woman longer than a couple of weeks. Long-term isn't in your vocabulary."

"And it is in yours?"

"No," Zane said with a chuckle.

"For your information, three years knowing me isn't that long. I've dated women longer than two weeks."

"Who?"

Gideon stuck up his forefinger. "One is Missy Collins, two is…" He could hardly even count Missy because they were more friends than anything else.

"Two?"

"Okay, I haven't found the right one yet." And most likely wouldn't since he wasn't looking for any long-term commitment.

"So this makes Kathleen special."

"Of course she's special, but we haven't even gone out on one date."

"From what I've heard from Pete, you're always over at her mother's. He said something about arranging a tour of the station for her sons. I just saw you a while ago having an intense conversation with her. It looks serious to me."

Gideon released a frustrated breath. "You're not going to rile me. Since when have you listened to gossip?"

"Pete seemed to think it might be something."

"Since when have you listened to Pete?"

"Since high school. Why haven't you gone out on a date?"

"Hurricane Naomi. Did you forget about that?"

"Not all dates are at a restaurant, the movies or something like that."

"Now you're giving me dating advice?"

Zane clapped him on the back. "Someone's gotta help you. That's what a friend is for—giving you unsolicited advice. I'm quite good at it."

Gideon gestured toward a worker. "I think one of your men needs your unsolicited advice."

"I think I've treaded on a touchy subject."

"Bye, Zane."

His friend's laughter as he strode toward his worker grated on Gideon's nerves. Why would he risk getting hurt after Kathleen made it clear she wasn't interested? But Zane was right. They didn't have to go to a restaurant for a date, and friends could go out together. Kathleen deserved something special. She'd been working nonstop since the hurricane. Maybe he could do something about that—as a friend.

"Hey, Gideon, we're taking a break. Wanna shoot some hoops?" Kip approached him with a basketball under his arm. "I got this from the church. Nana said it would be all right to take it so long as I put it back."

"Sure. Let's see if we can get some other boys and maybe a couple of dads."

Kip turned in a slow circle, going from one father and son to another. A frown creased his forehead.

It didn't take much for Gideon to figure that Kip was missing his dad. He could remember the first few times after his dad had died and he'd seen a father and son together how much it had hurt him to realize he would never have that. He'd gotten really good at avoiding situations where that might take place. The hurt had faded but never totally went away.

"Trust me," Gideon said the next Friday and turned Kathleen away from him. "Close your eyes. I'm putting a blindfold on you."

"Blindfold? Why?"

"It's a surprise and I don't trust you will keep your eyes closed."

"Do you hear yourself? You ask me to trust you and yet—" The feel of the cloth over her eyes interrupted her train of thought. Actually it was more the close proximity of Gideon and the lime-scented aftershave she smelled that affected her thinking.

He leaned near her ear and whispered, "And yet I don't trust you to keep your eyes closed? Sometimes life doesn't make sense."

"More like you don't make sense," she said in response to him but was amazed she managed to utter those words when she still felt the tickle of his breath on her neck. She pictured him nibbling on her lobe and nearly melted into her mother's front lawn.

He chuckled. "I've been told that before. Now quit complaining and relax. You've been working too much lately."

"And you haven't?" He took her hand and led her to his Jeep.

"I have called in a few favors to pull this together so I want you to sufficiently appreciate my efforts."

"But there is so much to do."

"I agree and it will be there tomorrow. Have you

taken any time for yourself in the past three weeks since the hurricane?"

"Are you kidding? With the cleanup and the demands at the hospital? Just yesterday a man came in who was trying to repair his own roof and fell off. He broke several ribs, and one punctured his lung." She relaxed back against the seat while he pulled out of the driveway.

"When the power came back on, we had several electrical-caused fires. It's bound to happen with all the damage."

"We take for granted electricity until we lose it. So much of what we use is run by electricity and without it, we become lost."

"One good thing was the hurricane was late in the season and the temperature wasn't as unbearable as it can get in the summer."

"Or cold like in Denver, even in November."

Gideon slowed down then made a right turn. Kathleen tried to figure out by the direction he drove where he was taking her, but she wasn't as familiar with Hope as she had been growing up and with the hurricane, detours were necessary in some places. Sections of the road along the coast were still closed off because of extensive damage to the pavement.

When he stopped, he opened the door and said, "Stay right there. Don't take off the blindfold. I'm coming around to lead you to my surprise."

She was tempted to peek but then decided to give in to what Gideon was doing. He'd gone to some trouble to do this, and she didn't want to disappoint him. He'd done a lot for her family. Jared and Kip were constantly making excuses to go down and see Gideon. She'd even found herself trying to come up with one, especially since the day at Broussard Park. Seeing Gideon playing basketball with her sons made her realize how much anger she still had toward Derek. It should have been him, but he'd chosen a destructive path. He'd wanted possessions over his family.

When Gideon opened her door, he clasped her arm and assisted her out of the Jeep. A light breeze blew, carrying the scent of the sea. Only three weeks ago that same water had raged against Hope. The shrieks of the gulls echoed through the air, and the noise of waves washing onto shore soothed her even more. She loved that sound.

As he led her toward his surprise, she asked, "Can I take off the blindfold now? I know we're on a pier."

"But where is the pier?"

"On the Gulf. Not too far from Mom's. It didn't take us long to get here."

"Hope isn't a huge town and traffic was light." Finally, he came to a halt and reached behind her to untie her blindfold.

When the cloth fell away, she faced a twenty-foot sloop, bobbing on the water. "Is this yours?"

He shook his head. "It's Zane's. I learned how to sail when I came here. Zane lets me borrow it when I want to go out on the sea and be truly alone."

"How did it survive the hurricane?"

"Zane took it out of the water."

"Do you sail alone often?"

"I get the hankering about once a month." He hopped down onto the sloop and held his hand out to help her. "My trip is well overdue."

"But if I go, you won't be alone." Stepping down onto the craft, she came up against him as the boat rocked.

He steadied her. "I know, but I thought you could use this time away. I love getting out on the sea, listening to the waves lap against the hull, feeling the sun on my face and the salty breeze powering the sloop to parts unknown. No agenda. Just sailing."

"You've sold me on it. Let's go." She settled herself on the sailboat. "But I've got to warn you, although I grew up on the Gulf, I never learned to sail. I went sailing with friends, but never took lessons. Always too busy doing other things."

"No worries. I've done this many times. This is my gift to you. Enjoy the sun and sea, and don't think about what has to be done when we get back. Okay?"

She smiled as he untied the sloop from the dock. "I like that."

He steered the sloop away from the pier and headed out into the Gulf. "Are you still trusting me?"

"Yeah," she replied slowly, wondering what he was up to.

"I have a destination in mind."

"And you're going to tell me?"

"Nope. You'll figure it out soon enough." He adjusted the mainsail. "I'm curious. What kept you so busy while you were growing up here that you couldn't learn to sail?"

"Two things—dance and cheerleading."

"Neither of which I would have guessed."

"What do you think I did in high school?"

"National Honor Society, Science Club."

"Why?"

"Your mom told me you were valedictorian."

"What else has my mother told you?" She was going to have a word with her mom when she got back home. Every opportunity she got she invited Gideon to come eat with them. On several occasions Kathleen had caught her mother and Gideon laughing over something, but the second she came into the room they would go quiet.

"Just that."

"I did those, too, but my passion was dance."

"Which kind?"

"Ballet."

"Like Swan Lake and the Nutcracker?"

She nodded. "Have you been to a ballet?"

"No, there isn't much opportunity around here."

"True. What did you do in high school?"

"I tried to stay out of trouble."

"No wonder you and Zane are friends. That about describes him."

"I was an angry teen until my last foster parents dragged me to church. At first I sat in the pew determined not to hear anything the pastor was saying." He hitched up one corner of his mouth. "That didn't last long. Once I began listening I realized all that anger at the world was only hurting me. Yeah, I got a raw deal with the death of my parents, but that didn't have to define who I was. So the spring of my junior year, I went out for football."

"You were a jock. That doesn't surprise me."

"Football taught me the importance of being on a team. From there when I graduated from high school, I decided to do something to help others not go through what I did as a child."

"So you became a firefighter."

"It was a kind of therapy for me. I faced what I had feared for years and came out on top."

Had he really? By his own words he kept people at a distance—just like her—afraid to risk getting hurt again.

"What made you become a nurse?"

"Actually, I wanted to be a doctor, but I met Derek and not long after we got married, I became pregnant. My plans changed."

"Why?"

"It didn't seem to fit our future. I loved being a mother and wanted more children. The cost was too much to do it all so I remained a nurse and gave up my dream of being a doctor. I didn't work much though after Jared came along. Derek wanted me to stay home. He never liked the idea of me working." And she had agreed because she had enjoyed being a full-time mommy, but once her sons started school she'd wanted to go back to work. She and Derek had fought a lot over that. In the end it was easier to volunteer her time than disrupt her family.

"It's not too late."

"Yes, it is. I have a debt to pay off. There's no way I could afford med school."

"Where there is a dream, there is a way."

"Sometimes dreams have to change. Reality has a way of doing that." She shielded her eyes to look out over the glistening water, so tranquil now.

"True. I know that better than some. The day my parents were killed changed my dreams and my reality."

"What was your dream?"

"At eight I wanted to be a firefighter or police officer."

"Then you're living your dream."

"Not exactly. I wanted to grow up to be just like my dad. He was a great father. He wasn't a firefighter, but he was a police officer. My dad would have been so disappointed in me as a teen. I rebelled every chance I got."

With the sails completely up and catching the wind, the boat glided over the smooth water. The shoreline faded the farther out they went. Kathleen relished the beautiful day—the peace, the sense that all was right with the world, that a hurricane hadn't plowed through her hometown.

But on the sloop emotions churned. The past lay exposed between Kathleen and Gideon. She decided to share more of hers. "The disappointment I faced was from my husband. I could never do anything right. I'd made a commitment to him and was determined to make our marriage work, but it was getting so hard. My self-confidence felt attacked from all sides. I questioned everything I did. Then he died and I learned the extent of his betrayal. He kept so many secrets, but right after his funeral they began to come out. By the time the will was read, I realized there was no money, and I most likely would lose the house that meant so much to Derek."

"I'm sorry, Kathleen. That couldn't have been easy."

"The day the bank foreclosed was one of the lowest in my life. I felt a complete failure. My sons were so upset. Their father's death totally changed their lives, and they were groping for stability. That's why I finally decided to come home. That's what Hope has always meant to me." She gestured toward the distant strip of shoreline. "We're here for seven weeks and a hurricane strikes, totally disrupting Hope. Even moving here hasn't been the stability that Jared and Kip need."

"Maybe you're looking for the wrong kind of stability."

Squinting, she stared at Gideon. "What do you mean?"

"Objects and places don't really offer true stability. They are temporary as we in Hope have found out lately. It's something that happens inside you, a sense of yourself, a peace with yourself." He laughed, little humor in the sound. "Of course, it took Pastor Michael to show me that true stability comes from faith."

Instead of turning away from her faith because of her struggles, should she have turned toward the Lord? Was Gideon right? She did know firsthand how possessions were fleeting. First in Denver and now in Hope, much of what she owned had been taken from her and her sons.

"We're almost to our destination."

Kathleen shifted forward and gazed across the calm sea to an island. She hadn't been paying attention to where they were going, only where they had come from. Much like her life of late. "Which island is this?"

"Dog Island. Zane is one of the owners, and he asked me to check out what the hurricane has done to the place. I told him I would be glad to. He has been turning this island into a refuge for certain species of animals like the different types of eagles. There's a cabin in the heart of the island. He didn't know if it made it or not. He hasn't had time to come out here."

"It sounds like I'm not the only one working too much."

"There is so much to be done rebuilding Hope, and that is what his company does the best. I'm glad he took on Miss Alice's house for cost of supplies. I've heard he's been doing that a lot." Gideon guided the sailboat toward the center of the island to what remained of a pier, a couple of pilings sticking up out of the water.

"The dock is gone."

"Yeah, I was afraid it would be. We can bring this sloop in close. You might roll up your pants and take off your shoes. We'll wade into shore. It shouldn't be too deep."

"Speak for yourself. You're over six feet. I'm only five-two."

"Don't worry. I'll take care of you."

A few minutes later, after Gideon had tied the boat up to the piling nearest shore and thrown an anchor overboard to keep the craft in place, he hopped into the water, holding their shoes and a towel in a bag. "Here, take this." He gave her their belongings. "I'm carrying you to the beach."

She glanced at the water lapping against the bottom of his jean shorts and thought of that foot difference in their heights. "Won't it be hard with your cast?"

"I'll manage." His grin rivaled the sun.

She eased into his arms, conscious of his cast on the left one. He nestled her against him, with the bag clutched to her chest, then waded toward shore but didn't stop until he was up the rise of the beach where the sand was firmer. Then he set her down near a log from an uprooted tree, probably during the hurricane.

"We should wear our shoes. No telling what is hidden in the sand or ground on the island." He sat on the log, leaving her enough room to do the same.

She did, then took her footwear from the bag and passed it to Gideon who used the towel to dry off his wet feet before putting on his deck shoes. After tying her tennis shoes, she glanced up at the area around her. It looked a lot like the beach area in Hope. "I'm not sure this place fared very well."

"At least the island looks like it's intact. Remember the hurricane that split Ship Island into two parts?"

She nodded. "But Fort Massachusetts remained."

"Ready? We'll walk to the cabin before I show you the other side. The waves are a lot bigger on that side. The boys would enjoy swimming here in the summer."

"So you've come out here before. How many times?"

"A few times a year. Sometimes by myself, sometimes there is a group of us to make improvements."

He rose, took her hand and tugged her to her feet. "We can't stay too long. I'm just checking to see what will need to be done later."

"I didn't know you and Zane were such good friends."

"We both want to preserve the Barrier Islands and the habitat on them. Most are a part of the park system. This is one that isn't. He didn't want to see it fall into the wrong hands so he got a group together to buy it."

"Zane certainly has changed. Back in high school my best friend's cousin had a crush on him and he hurt her. They dated for a while then he just stopped all of a sudden. He left that summer after she graduated from high school. She didn't know where he went or why. I can still remember listening to her cry in her bedroom."

"People change from when they were teenagers. I certainly have. If I had kept up doing the things I was doing, I would probably be dead by now. I took chances I should never have taken."

She'd changed, too, from having a direction to not having one. From having a dream to living one day at a time with no purpose but to keep her family together, even if it meant losing herself in the process.

"Let's go. Evening will be here soon enough. This will be a whirlwind tour, but I promise I'll bring you and your sons back here to explore the island leisurely, maybe ride the waves."

"Please don't say that to Jared. He'll want to do more than that."

"He's been really good lately. No risks."

"Wait until his cast comes off. I think he has been biding his time."

Gideon waded through the debris and downed tree limbs scattered about the island. "I know that feeling."

"How many more weeks?"

"I go back in four weeks. I've starting doing what Jared does—marking off the days on the calendar."

"But before that there's Thanksgiving and my mother's ambitious plans to celebrate it."

He paused in the path and cupped her face. "She has risen to the occasion as well as you. I'm continually amazed at her ability to organize it. It will be the best Thanksgiving ever."

"Leave it to my mother to find the way to show our thanks and involve hundreds of people."

His warm palm against her cheek rooted her in place. In spite of how the kiss ended the last time, she wanted him to kiss her again, but she would never make the first move. And she didn't have to. Gideon dipped his head toward hers. She dissolved against him, her fingers entwined behind his neck as his mouth settled over hers. For a moment she felt that peace he'd talked about earlier.

Chapter Ten

Next to the lone bell tower at Hope Community Church, Kathleen's mother stretched her arms out wide. "Thank the Lord for this gorgeous day. We have been blessed. This will be the best Thanksgiving ever."

How could her mother say that? There were so many people in need. Kathleen's gaze shifted to the tall pile of boards and debris off to the side of the destroyed newer church. The town had finished the initial trash pickup from the storm and was just starting its second round. It would take more than a few rounds to clean up Hope.

"Why did you want to serve the people here?" Kathleen asked her mother as Gideon pulled up with Jared, Kip and Miss Alice, who had wanted to ride with him.

Sweeping her arm out, she rotated in a full circle. "Look what we have accomplished so far. Broussard Park is ready for our kickoff of the holiday season tonight. Even the church is coming along. It should be ready for Christmas Eve service in the original church.

The Point was one of the hardest hit and after a month, it's beginning to show signs of restoration. That's due to the townspeople."

"You should run for mayor, Mom."

Kip, carrying two sacks of groceries, came to a stop between her and his grandmother. "Mayor? You're running for mayor, Nana? Neat."

"No, please don't say that to anyone. What would I do as mayor?"

"Motivate the town. You're a great organizer. Our current mayor has decided not to run again. In fact, I hear he's thinking of moving away from Hope." Kathleen caught Gideon's gaze as it skimmed down her length, leaving a warm trail where it touched. "What do you think, Gideon. Should my mother run for mayor in the spring?"

"I'd vote for you." He set his paper bags down next to Kip's.

"Me, too." Miss Alice joined them with Jared.

"How did we get from feeding the people who lost their homes to me running for mayor?"

Kathleen shrugged. "But it is still something you should seriously consider."

"Let's get through today first. I think we should set up the tables in the park instead of the church's meeting hall. It's just too pretty to be inside and the park looks great after last week's cleanup. The kids can enjoy the new play equipment."

"Yes, I think we should try it out. Come on, Jared." Kip didn't wait for his little brother. He raced across the park to the new playground.

"Miss Alice, do you need me to bring the rest of your pies?" Jared asked while his gaze strayed to his older brother.

"No, I can manage. You go check out the equipment. We wouldn't want anyone to get hurt if there was a problem."

"Yeah, you're right." Jared gave Miss Alice the two pies he held, then sprinted toward the playground.

Miss Alice laughed. "I didn't have the heart to tell him no. Wait till you see the pie Jared helped me make."

"Should we serve it?" Kathleen remembered her son coming back from Miss Alice's with flour all over him yesterday evening. That had been the first day she'd been back in her mostly repaired house. Zane and Gideon had made it a priority.

"Most definitely. He baked an apple pie and did a great job." Miss Alice winked. "With some assistance from me."

More cars arrived with helpers that her mother had solicited to set up the big Thanksgiving feast she'd planned. Zane stopped to talk with her sons while Pete, his wife and two children joined them with their contribution to the meal—deep fryers for the turkeys. Pete and Gideon went to work setting them up and preparing the birds for the oil. The last of the volunteers— Mildred, a couple of firefighters, her cousin Sally and some of her mother's friends from the ladies group at church appeared with their food and willing hands.

Kathleen's mother asked Gideon to whistle. He put two fingers into his mouth and let out a shrill sound. Everyone turned toward him.

Ruth ascended the steps of the church halfway then turned toward the crowd. "We have three hours to get everything set up. Let's make it special for the folks who have lost most of their possessions."

Kathleen sensed someone approach her from behind and slanted a look at Gideon. The kiss they'd shared last week on Dog Island had haunted her since it occurred. She couldn't seem to get it out of her mind. "Thank you for taking Jared and Kip to the fire station. I wanted to come, but one of the nurses had an emergency and I agreed to fill in for her."

"Did they tell you about the tour?"

"Oh, yes, I heard about it all evening when I got home. Kip's favorite part was the slide. But then I don't know if he enjoyed doing it the most because he truly liked it or because Jared couldn't go down the slide with his cast. Kip made a point of telling me over and over about pretending he was called out to a fire and having to slide down the pole."

"That's okay. I let Jared sound the siren."

"I know. I got dueling stories after that. I went to bed with a headache and those stories running through my mind." But not as much as the kiss she'd received a couple of days before that from Gideon.

"I'm sorry." He circled around in front of her and cut the distance between them. "I didn't mean for you to lose sleep over it."

"I didn't exactly lose sleep over it as much as I had a weird dream with Kip sliding down the pole over and over while Jared sounded the siren continuously. Kip said something about going back again. Are you sure?"

"We have an open house every Christmas. A lot of the kids come and get to play firefighter for a little bit. One year we had to leave because of a fire, and instead of being a disappointment to the children, they were excited to see us in action."

"Kids have a way of turning something around and looking at it from a different view."

"Are you all coming tonight to the Lights On Celebration?"

Kathleen nodded. "We may just stay here until it gets dark. With the church open, we have all the comforts of home. Zane has been busy."

"Yeah, he's finished the structural restoration of the original church. Now all that is left is the interior makeover."

"Not a small task."

"After church in the meeting room on Sunday, some of us are staying to work on the chapel and classrooms. If you don't have to be at the hospital, why don't you stay and help?"

"Unless an emergency occurs, I should be off."

"Great."

"Hey, you two. We could use some help over here. You can chat later."

Kathleen glanced toward her mother. "The general has spoken. Maybe we should say the mayoral candidate has spoken."

"Do you think she'll run?" Gideon started toward the stacks of tables that Zane had delivered for the people to sit at.

"I hope so. Mom needs a purpose. She was getting

too caught up in her soap operas and The Weather Channel. There isn't anyone who knows Hope better than her."

"Everyone needs a purpose."

"Since coming to Hope, I've looked forward to getting up in the morning. The last few years of my marriage, I felt at such a loss, aimlessly going through life."

Gideon hefted one end of a folding table while Kathleen took the other end. "I've been to that place and don't care to go back there."

Kathleen set her part down and flipped the legs out then looked toward Gideon. He stood perfectly still, staring toward the water, his eyebrows slashing downward.

"Gideon?"

When he didn't respond, she said in a louder voice, "Gideon, what's wrong?"

He jerked around, said, "It's Kip. He was by the water and now he isn't. Something's wrong. It doesn't look right," and then began running toward the edge of the Point overlooking the Gulf.

Kathleen heard Gideon and the concern in his voice but for a few seconds the meaning didn't register in her brain. When Gideon was a hundred yards across the park, she raced after him, all the while her heartbeat thundering against her skull.

Gideon reached the edge of the ten-foot cliff, whirled toward her and called out, "Get help. The ground has given way and he's buried under the dirt. There's his ball cap."

Bracing himself with his good arm, he went down

the incline. Kathleen hesitated for a breath, wanting to continue toward Kip but instead she hastened back toward the crowd, homing in on Zane and Pete.

"Gideon needs your help. The ground over there—" she wildly waved her hand toward the cliff "—gave way and Kip is buried in the dirt."

Zane was already moving toward his truck before Kathleen had arrived. "I've got some shovels."

Pete and a couple of other firefighters headed across the park toward the water. Kathleen followed. When she reached the men, Pete and their captain clambered down the incline to help Gideon. She started after the pair.

The firefighter left on top stopped her. "Let them take care of it, ma'am. It's a closed-in space and the tide is starting to come in. They need to get him out before that. I've called 911. We'll get him out before they arrive."

She tried pulling away, everything in her screaming for her to be down in the hole created by the ground giving way, but the man clasped her to him. Zane, along with a crowd of people, arrived. He ducked around the firefighter and Kathleen and started down into the hole.

"I need to be there," Kathleen said, watching Zane disappear with the shovels. "Kip needs me."

"They need to get him out first."

The firefighter's calm voice didn't appease the terror building up in Kathleen. The man handed her off to her mother and Sally then corralled everyone back from the edge.

"Get back. The ground has been undermined, probably by the hurricane."

"Mom. Mom. What's wrong with Kip?" Jared clasped her around the waist, fear on his face that matched what she was feeling.

She had to hold it together for both her sons. They would get Kip out, and he would need her then. *Please, Lord, save him.*

Gideon tore at the dirt with both his hands as Pete and his captain joined him. "He's under here and the water's coming in." His tennis shoes sank into the mud at the bottom of the cliff.

As the water rose, the dirt turned to mud, making their digging more difficult. Zane slid down the incline with two shovels and a spade.

Gideon grabbed the smaller tool. "We'd better not use the shovels. We could hit Kip."

"I'll work from the edge inward, carefully." Zane propped one shovel against the bank of dirt behind him while grasping the other one to use.

"I found something!" Pete shouted and scooped up another handful of mud. "A leg."

Gideon and the others concentrated in that area. Kneeling in the water coming in, Gideon estimated where the boy's torso and head would be. Soon he felt Kip's shoulder and increased his speed, working to uncover the child's face while his captain removed the pressure from Kip's chest.

Gideon removed the last layer of muck from around the boy's mouth and nose, then his eyes. Finding his thready pulse at the side of Kip's neck, Gideon released his bottled-up breath. "He's alive." As more of the child was unearthed, Gideon looked up. "Call 911."

"Taken care of!" someone shouted from above.

Wound tight, Kathleen paced in the hallway outside the waiting room. She couldn't sit still while waiting for Kip to come out of surgery. "A collapsed lung, internal injuries. He was standing on the cliff looking out into the water and the next moment he is being swallowed by the ground. Why didn't anyone check the stability of the cliff after the hurricane? Children play in that park. The town is having the Lights On Celebration tonight."

"Not anymore. The mayor has called off the celebration until the park can be checked." Gideon leaned against the wall.

"If you hadn't seen him going over there, he might have disappeared. He could have died before we found him. He could..." She couldn't get the rest of the sentence pass the lump in her throat. She swallowed several times, but it was still too painful to speak.

Gideon pushed himself away from the wall and stepped forward. Drawing her into his embrace, he whispered against the top of her head, "He's all right. They will patch him up and in no time he will be back playing with his friends and Rocky."

"I know the things that can go wrong. What if—"

He pressed his forefinger over her lips. "Have faith he will be all right. Believe it, Kathleen."

"I wish I could. When are things going to stop going wrong?"

He backed up slightly and looked down at her. "Want the truth?"

She nodded. Her throat burned, her stomach roiled.

"Things will never stop going wrong. That's part of life. Problems and complications happen."

"To me," she said. "But why Kip? He's a little boy."

Her mother appeared in the waiting room doorway. "Jared is awake and needs you."

She'd left her younger son on the couch when he'd nodded off a while ago. Before that, he'd been so quiet she'd known he was trying to process what had happened to his big brother. He had rebuked her attempts to talk with him. Now Kathleen hurried to the couch where Jared sat, his shoulders slumped, his hands twisting together. When he lifted his head, a bleakness seized her heart and squeezed.

"Hon, Kip is going to be all right." She had to have faith, as Gideon had said. The alternative was not acceptable.

"He was mad at me for hogging the tire swing. He stomped off. That's why he was at the cliff. He wouldn't have been there—" Her son burst into tears and flung himself into her arms. "I'm sorry. I'm sorry."

"Jared, you did not cause what happened to your brother. It was an accident."

"But it's got to be bad. They're operating on him."

"To fix him up." She placed her finger under his chin and raised it toward her. "He'll be fine. Good as new. You two will be back to arguing in no time."

"Nope. I'll never argue with him again." Tears continued to leak out of Jared's eyes. "Dad had an operation and died a few days later." He clasped himself against her. "What if the same thing happens to Kip?"

His question stole her breath. She gasped for air and tightened her arms around her son. Kathleen closed her eyes, and when she opened them a few seconds later, Gideon stood in front of her, the concern etched into his expression threatening her composure. Jared needed her to be strong, and she didn't feel very strong at the moment.

Gideon knelt and laid his hand on Jared's back. "We can pray for Kip."

Jared's sobs quieted. He pulled back and peered at Gideon. "You think it will help?"

"Yes. God can always help."

Jared shifted toward her. "Mom, can we?"

"Of course, honey. Gideon has an excellent idea."

Gideon reached out and took both Kathleen and Jared's hands, then bowed his head. "Father, we place Kip's care and recovery in Your capable hands. Be with him during this time and surround him with a protective shield. In the name of Jesus Christ. Amen."

The surgeon appeared in the doorway, spied her and crossed the room. "Mrs. Hart, Kip is in recovery. The surgery went well. We were able to stop the internal bleeding, remove his spleen and repair the lung that was punctured."

"Can I see him?" Kathleen rose.

"Yes, you can stay with him in recovery, then we'll move him to his own room."

"Can I see him, too?" Jared hopped up.

"Just your mom right now, but it won't be long before you'll be able to see him," the doctor replied.

Gideon interjected, "While your mom is with Kip, why don't you, me and your grandmother go get something to eat? We didn't get a chance to eat our Thanksgiving feast so let's check out what they have in the hospital cafeteria."

As Kathleen walked toward the exit right behind the doctor, Jared called out, "Promise me you'll come get me the second I can see Kip."

She turned and smiled. "You will be the first one."

"Kathleen, I'll let everyone know about Kip."

"Thanks, Mom."

When she found her son in the recovery room, his eyes closed, his breathing even, she collapsed in a chair near the bed and finally cried. *Thank you, Lord.*

"When can I go home? Rocky has to be missing me." Kip lay in the hospital bed with his IV still in him, his face pale, his eyes dull.

But for a few seconds Kathleen glimpsed a sparkle in his gaze. After five days, Kathleen saw an end to his hospital stay. His chest tube had been removed after the lung re-expanded. He wasn't on as much pain medication from the abdominal surgery and he was complaining. Always a good sign with Kip. "Tomorrow. This will be your last night in here." And mine. She could certainly understand Kip's impatience to be out of the hospital. She'd spent most of her time here with him except when her mother or Gideon relieved her to go home to see Jared and shower.

The door opened, and Jared charged into Kip's room. "I've got more get well cards from your class. After school Amanda gave this one to me and made me promise you'd read it first." He plopped the stack on Kip's bed. "I think she likes you."

"We're friends. That's all."

"What about Ginny? She follows you around on the playground." Jared positioned himself next to Kip as close as he could get.

"Who brought you?" Kathleen asked before her sons got into a fight over girls.

"Gideon."

"Where is he?" She smoothed her hair, hooking it behind her ears.

"I got on the elevator before him and the door closed. He'll be here. He's way too slow."

At that moment Gideon entered the room, carrying a duffel bag that was partially unzipped. A yelp sounded from it.

"What do you have?" As tired as she was, it was so good to see him.

"A surprise." Gideon placed the bag on the empty chair near the bed and lifted Rocky out.

The grin that spread across Kip's face endeared her even more to Gideon. But still… "Dogs aren't supposed to be in here."

"Shh. Don't tell anyone." Gideon passed the wiggling pet to Kip but kept one hand on the animal. "We can't stay long, but he has been missing you."

Kip buried his face in Rocky's fur. "I've missed him, too."

Jared puffed out his chest. "I didn't say a word about the dog to them."

Gideon ruffled the child's hair. "I appreciate that." He stepped back, allowing Jared to pet Rocky, too.

The dullness in Kip's eyes was replaced with a twinkle. Two patches of red colored his cheeks. The sight of Rocky had done more to lift his spirits than anything else.

"Thanks for doing this, although I should report you to hospital security," Kathleen said.

"I talked with Kip's doctor to make sure it was all right. I'd never do anything to hurt him."

She looked into his gaze. "I know. That's one of the things I like about you." Although Derek had never harmed his sons, those last few years he had been emotionally distant. He stopped doing things with Jared and Kip, and they hadn't understood why. She hadn't either—until she'd discovered her husband's money troubles.

"I gave him a bath so he would be as clean as possible. I figured with Kip coming home tomorrow, Rocky would be all over him then. I didn't think one day would make much difference."

"One day has made a difference. He has been moping around here all day. Even complained there was nothing on TV to watch." She nodded toward the bed where the two brothers were talking civilly and loving on Rocky. Both the boys grinned from ear to ear. "That's a big difference."

"Miss Alice and your mom are planning a small homecoming celebration tomorrow. People have been asking about Kip in the neighborhood. The mayor told Ruth this morning he's waiting to have the Lights On Celebration so Kip can throw the switch on the lights."

"Usually it's a town dignitary. I'll talk with the doctor and find out how restricted Kip's activity will be over the next couple of weeks. So they have reopened the park?"

"Yes and different groups are decorating the whole area. Before it's over with, it's going to look like a Winter Wonderland without the snow. The fire department is taking care of the lighthouse, and we're not sparing anything. It's going to be the best Christmas lighthouse this town has ever seen."

"That's nice," she said while watching Jared open the cards for Kip to read since her older son was hugging Rocky against his side.

"Nice? It's going to be spectacular. I'm in charge— a desk duty I don't mind."

Kathleen chuckled. "Jared gets his cast off at the end of next week. What about you?"

"The fifteenth of December and I'm counting down the days."

"That evening let me make you that dinner I owe you from way back before the hurricane."

"Sure, I can come to your mom's."

"No, I'm coming to your house. The dinner isn't a family affair."

"Oh, then you've got yourself a date."

"Yes, a date." Ever since that kiss on Dog Island,

they had been dancing around each other—friends and yet more.

"That's the best news I've heard all day." Gideon winked then made his way to the bed. "I hate to break up this reunion, but I promised the doc I wouldn't tire you out. Rocky will be waiting for you at your house tomorrow. Jared, can you get Rocky?"

As her son scooped up the dog, Gideon opened the duffel bag. When the animal was inside, he zipped it partway. "I don't want others to get the idea that they can break hospital rules so mum's the word."

Jared paused at the side of his brother's bed, then suddenly he bent down and gave Kip a hug. "See you tomorrow. I've been taking good care of Rocky for you."

"Is something wrong with Jared?" Kip asked, staring at the door as it closed behind his brother leaving.

"I think he blames himself for what happened to you."

"Why?"

"He said something about a fight you two had over the swing."

"Oh, that. That had nothing to do with the cliff giving way."

"You left the playground and went over to the edge. He thought it was because you were mad at him."

"Not really. I was tired of playing. I like watching the water. One day I'm gonna get myself a boat. I saw one I liked and went over to look at it as it passed by."

"You might say something to Jared about that."

"Why? I think I'll let him suffer a little more. It's kinda nice not arguing all the time."

Kathleen stuck her finger in her ear and wiggled it. "Say that again. I don't think I heard you correctly."

"Oh, Mom. I'm growing up. Fighting is for babies."

"I see. I'll remind you of that when you fight with Jared again." Because as the sun rose each day, she was sure they would fight again.

The next afternoon, before taking Kip home from the hospital, Kathleen had gone down to the office on the first floor to make arrangements about the bill. With the length of stay and the surgery, even with the insurance she had, her part would be thousands of dollars she didn't have. She still hadn't paid for Jared's broken arm. The woman she'd met with had given her a rough figure—worse than she had thought—but had said not to worry about it just yet until the insurance company settled their part of the bill.

Pulling into her mom's driveway, she switched off the engine and tried to paste a cheerful expression on her face as she turned toward the backseat where Kip was. "Ready? I understand Miss Alice baked you a welcome-home cake. Your favorite—chocolate fudge."

"Really. How did she know? Nana?"

"Yep. There are a few people here to see you, but the second you're tired let me know. I'll clear them out. I don't want you overdoing it."

"Mooom, quit babying me. I'm almost ten."

She climbed from her car and opened the back door. "I've got news for you. I'll always be concerned about you even when you are a grown-up and living on your own."

Jared slammed open the front door and ran down the steps, barely managing to stop before barreling Kip over. "You're home. I'm starved, and Nana said I can't have any cake until you're here."

Kip rolled his eyes. "You'll survive."

"C'mon. You get the first slice. Miss Alice said so." Jared pulled on Kip's arm.

"Jared Taylor Hart, let go of your brother's arm. He will be inside in a second. How about you come over here and help me take our stuff inside." Kathleen swung the small suitcase out of the back and handed it to Jared, then faced the house. "When did you all put up the Christmas decorations?"

"Yesterday afternoon. Gideon helped me and Nana. We've got the tree up but no decorations on it yet. We were waiting for you to come home. Maybe we can do that later today."

"Slow down, Jared." Kathleen grabbed the sack of items she'd been given at the hospital for Kip. "I doubt we will tonight. Maybe tomorrow."

"Do you know Miss Alice doesn't put up any decorations? She told me it was too much effort for just her." Jared walked ahead of her and Kip toward the porch, jabbering and not caring they weren't keeping up.

At the front door, he finally stopped and waited for them. "So what do you think?"

Kip scrunched his forehead. "What about?"

"Decorating Miss Alice's house for her. Our gift to her. Wanna help me?"

"Before you go planning your brother's life, I think you need to realize he will be restricted for the next several weeks while he continues to heal. He won't be able to do a lot of what he used to. Recovery from surgery takes time."

"Sure, Mom." Jared opened the screen door then the main one. "But he can help me with Miss Alice. That shouldn't be a lot of work."

When Kathleen, Kip and Jared entered the living room, she came to a halt, taking in the sea of people crowded into the small area. This was not her definition of a small celebration.

Gideon moved to her side. "Glad you're here. I didn't know what we were going to do with Jared."

"We need to use the same dictionary. In mine, this wouldn't be defined as small."

"Well, it started out that way, just a few friends and family. Then the firefighters who helped rescue Kip wanted to come. After that, one neighbor after another asked if they could drop by and see how he was doing. They all dropped by at the same time."

Stunned, Kip scanned the people in front of him, his gaze pausing on several of his classmates, especially a pretty young girl with long brown hair and blue eyes. Amanda? Ginny? Kathleen peered at her son. His cheeks reddened, and he looked down at the floor by his feet.

She turned and whispered into Gideon's ear. "It looks like my son doesn't care who is here so long as that pretty brunette is."

"Ah, Amanda, the one who decorated his card with glitter and hearts."

"I thought that might be her."

Her mother climbed up on the coffee table, nodding to Gideon. He gave a loud whistle and the room quieted, except for a few whispers and giggles. "Mayor Thomas has a few words to say before we cut the cakes."

Kathleen leaned toward Gideon again, taking in a whiff of his lime aftershave lotion. She immediately thought of her favorite pie—key lime. "I thought there was only one."

"When your mother saw all the people showing up, she had me go buy a couple more, along with some drinks and ice cream."

"You'd think this was a birthday party."

"The ice cream was Jared's idea. He went with me. Guess what kind I have."

"Vanilla."

"Yep. I tried to talk him into chocolate, but he told me he didn't like chocolate. What kid doesn't?"

"My son. He's never been a big fan of it. But give him a bowl of ice cream, so long as it isn't chocolate, and it will be gone in no time. Takes after his mother."

"What flavor do you like?"

"Cookie dough. I never got many cookies baked because I ate half of the dough. Got sick a couple of times when I ate too much. My mother didn't take pity on me. How about you?"

"Chocolate. I do like chocolate in any form."

One side of his mouth quirked into a grin that

flipped her stomach. He was totally focused on her, and her knees went weak. She gripped his arm to steady herself. "Sorry. I haven't slept much the past week. You know it isn't easy sleeping in a hospital unless they knock you out. Too much noise and people."

"Yeah, you would have thought you had that figured out since you work in one."

"Didn't think about it until I had to stay five nights. When my husband was in the hospital, he didn't want me to, and I needed to be home with the kids."

The mayor made his way to the sturdy coffee table and joined her mother. "This is a great time for me to ask Ruth if she will run for my office. Don't y'all think she should?"

Her mother blushed beet red. "When you said you had a few words to share with the crowd, I didn't think it was about me running."

"I've been hearing rumors and I thought it was time I tried to talk you into running for mayor."

Everyone cheered, Kip and Jared the loudest with Gideon whistling.

"See. They all want you to be our next mayor."

"I have no experience."

"Have you lived in Hope all your life?" the mayor asked her mother.

She nodded.

"You know everything about Hope and probably just about everyone in town. C'mon, let's hear it for Ruth as our next mayor."

Ruth raised her hands to calm the roar of approval. "Why don't you run again?"

"Because I've been mayor for eight years, and it's my time to step down. I'm retiring."

"I've already retired from one job. I don't need a second one."

"You might not, but the town needs someone who cares. That's you, Ruth. Look at the Thanksgiving feast you organized."

"We had to postpone it because of the accident."

"Just the celebration part. The food was distributed to the people who needed it." Mayor Robert Thomas took her mother's hand. "We've been friends for a long time. Since elementary school. You're what this town needs now. Promise me you'll think about it."

"I—I—" Her mother stared down at their clasped hands. "I don't know what to say."

"All I'm asking is you think about it." The mayor's face lit up like a Christmas tree.

"He knows he's got my mom," Kathleen whispered to Gideon in the silence that enveloped the room. She lowered her voice even more and bent close to Gideon, saying, "I heard that once they were an item before my dad came on the scene. You would think he had proposed to Mom in front of the neighborhood the way she is acting."

Gideon laughed, breaking the quiet. Suddenly, the room was filled with chatter and cheers.

Her mother extracted her hand from the mayor's and stepped down from the table.

Robert Thomas raised his arms and signaled for silence. "My other reason for being here is to welcome Kip Hart home from the hospital. His accident only reinforces how cautious we need to be. We're still discovering all the effects of the hurricane on Hope. We don't want any more children hurt."

Jared took Kip's arm and tugged him through the crowd toward the dining room. "I don't know about you guys, but I'm starved. Time for cake and ice cream."

A sprinkle of laughter rippled through the group, neighbors parting to allow Jared and Kip through.

"They know it's dangerous to get in the way of a child and cake and ice cream." Practically plastered against Gideon, Kathleen moved away from him. She released a long, slow breath. "I'd better go rescue Miss Alice and Mom."

"Those ladies don't need rescuing." He grasped her hand and drew her toward the front door. "You need to rest."

Before she could say anything, Gideon had her on the porch and sitting in a white wicker chair. "What just happened?"

"I'm rescuing *you*. You're tired. The past week has worn you down."

She cupped her face. "I look that bad?"

"No, but I can tell something is wrong. Did the doctor say something today?"

She shook her head, wishing that she didn't always have a hard time hiding her feelings. "Kip will be fine in time. By Christmas he'll probably be chasing Jared around the house."

"Then what is it?"

"Quit being so perceptive."

"I haven't been accused of that before."

"It's really nothing. There is just so much to do. I can't believe Christmas is weeks away. I started thinking of all I need to do, and I got tired."

He scrutinized her for a long moment, his eyes boring into her as if he were trying to read her thoughts.

She stiffened, determined not to squirm under his probing.

"As you know, I have a fairly normal schedule until after I see the doctor on December 15th, so what can I do to help you?"

"You've already done enough."

"That's not the point. The point is you need help. How can I help you?"

Don't press me about what's wrong. She couldn't tell him she was even more in debt than before in spite of having health insurance. Twenty percent of thousands was still a lot of money—money she didn't have. She would have to figure out something when she wasn't so exhausted.

She had to say something to Gideon. The expectant look on his face told her he wouldn't let it go until she did. "You could come tonight and help us decorate the tree. I don't think Jared will rest until the tree is fully up. We usually do it Thanksgiving weekend. One of our long-standing traditions."

"That's all?"

"Well, it's a start. If I can think of anything else, I'll be sure to say something. Truthfully, you being here is nice."

"Nice?" His smile grew. "I guess that is better than okay."

His infectious grin spread through her. "That's all you're gonna get. We'd better get back inside. I want some of that ice cream. I know where my mom's stash of caramel sauce is. That goes great with vanilla ice cream." As she pushed to her feet, she prayed that Gideon dropped the subject of what was wrong. Her problems were hers—not his.

Chapter Eleven

"Mom, where's the hot chocolate?" Kip sat on the couch putting hooks on the ornaments.

"Hot chocolate? You want that? It's fifty-eight degrees outside." Kathleen took another Christmas ball from her son and found a space on the eight-foot artificial tree.

"Yeah, it's a tradition. We've done it *forever*."

"That was in Denver where it's cold."

"Please."

"I don't have the ingredients for hot chocolate." Her mother handed a homemade decoration, one Kathleen had made in grade school, to Jared to place near the top of the tree.

He climbed the stepladder and reached up to hang the ornament on the fake pine. "You can go get some. I'm with Kip. We can't decorate the tree without hot chocolate."

Kathleen peered at the nearly finished work of chaos standing in front of the picture window in the living room.

"I'll go get it. What do you need?" Gideon asked.

"Tell you what. We'll take a break. You need to rest, Kip. Gideon and I will go to the store and get the ingredients. Then after we've had our hot chocolate, we'll finish the tree."

"I'm on a roll. I don't need to rest." Jared hooked another ball on the same limb as two others. The artificial limb drooped.

Ruth sat in a chair near the tree. "Tell you what, Jared. Why don't you go see if Miss Alice would like to share some hot chocolate and leftover cake with us?"

Kip laid his head on a sofa pillow and closed his eyes. "Hurry back."

Jared went out the front door with Gideon and Kathleen and raced across the lawn to Miss Alice's.

"Let's take my car. It's right here." Kathleen dug into her purse and retrieved her keys, then tossed them to Gideon. "I'll even let you drive."

When he tried to start the vehicle, a loud cranking sound echoed through the interior, grating on her already frazzled nerves. She held her breath when he attempted it a second time. Dead. Now what?

"I don't think it's going to turn over this time." Still, Gideon turned the key in the ignition again.

She heard nothing but the choking noise of a dying car. She didn't have any extra money—not for Christmas, not for the hospital and certainly not for car repairs.

"Let me get my Jeep and use that. Pete knows about cars, and I'll have him come over and take a look. It could be something simple he can fix." He opened the door. With the interior light shining in the darkness, he angled toward her. "Don't worry about it tonight. We'll make hot chocolate and sit around and pretend we are in front of a fire."

Tears tightened her throat. *Don't cry. Don't ruin this evening.* It wouldn't change the fact that the car would need an infusion of cash to get running.

Gideon sat there, his gaze fixed on her. "Are you okay?"

Her emotions screamed for release. She wanted to rile, to yell, to cry. "Fine," she said. Averting her face, she fumbled with the handle to open her door.

His hand on her shoulder compelled her to shift toward him. "I thought so earlier. Something is wrong. Sometimes talking about it helps."

"No, it won't. I'm tired. That's all. Don't make it out to be something it isn't. Lately a few things have gone wrong. Haven't you had one thing too many happen to you and you just want to give up?"

"Sure, but Kip is on the mend and the town will recover."

Tears crowded her eyes. Why couldn't her body do what she wanted? Frustrated, she balled her hands, fingernails digging into her palms. "I'll be much better tomorrow after a good night sleeping in my own bed. Hospital cots aren't the best place to sleep." She hurriedly thrust open the passenger door and exited before he asked any more probing questions. The money was her problem, and she'd never been comfortable sharing her problems with others. She'd learned in her marriage to keep them to herself.

* * *

Standing back in the dining room doorway, Gideon finished the last sip of his delicious second cup of hot chocolate, watching the last of the decorations being put on the tree by Kip, Kathleen, Jared and Ruth.

"I declare that is the most unusual Christmas tree I've seen in a long time. There is a pine tree under all those ornaments, isn't there?" Miss Alice staked her claim on the chair with the stool in the living room.

"Somewhere under there," Ruth said with a laugh, moving back to get a good look at the overall picture. "We do have a lot of decorations, an accumulation of many years of collecting Christmas memories."

"Jared, you might go a little to the left then reach up a few inches. There's one blank space left without anything on it." Miss Alice pointed toward an area on the tree.

"Oh, yeah, I see. Thanks." On the stepladder, Jared glanced over his shoulder at Miss Alice at the same time he leaned to the side.

The child wobbled. Jared flapped his arms to get his balance. The sequined ball went flying across the room as he finally grabbed hold of the nearest object—the Christmas pine—to steady himself on the ladder. But instead, he kept plunging downward to the floor with the tree tumbling with him.

Gideon shot forward but all he caught was air. He looked down. Jared lay in the middle of a mountain of ornaments, some broken, with some green pine poking out. The look of confusion on the child's face evolved into horror as he took in what happened. His eyes became round like perfectly drawn circles.

There was nothing but complete silence for a few seconds until Jared struggled to get up and crushed several more decorations under him. Gideon offered the child his hand, which he took. Gideon lifted him free of the mess and set him a couple of feet away.

Jared opened his mouth to speak. Nothing came out. He snapped it closed.

Finally, Ruth began laughing. "Well, that is one way to weed out some of the ornaments."

Kip chuckled, followed by Miss Alice.

Gideon's attention riveted to Kathleen, who stood frozen, shock on her face.

"Are you all right, Jared?" she finally asked, a taut thread woven through her words.

The child nodded.

Kathleen's stunned expression melted into relief, and she sagged back against the windowsill.

"I think we can salvage this." Gideon stooped and grasped the trunk then hoisted the tree to an upright position.

Some of the loose ornaments fell to the floor, a couple shattered among the shards of other broken ones. Gideon made sure the pine was stable, and then he backed away. "In answer to your earlier question, Miss Alice, there is a tree underneath there."

Kathleen shoved herself from the window ledge. "More hot chocolate anyone?"

Everyone quickly said yes.

"I'll help you get it." Gideon quickly trailed Kathleen into the kitchen while the others discussed how to clean up the mess.

Kathleen covered the distance to the stove where a pan of hot chocolate was still on a burner. "Poor Jared. He's going to be so upset with himself." She slanted a look at Gideon. "Mom really did have too many ornaments, but she never would get rid of any of them. She has been collecting them from before I was born. She always insisted the boys make her something for the tree as her present every year."

A memory invaded his thoughts. The boxes of Christmas decorations stored in his childhood home in the attic. All burned up—gone forever. After that he hadn't collected many—only a handful given to him by friends over the years. The small two-foot tree he put up at Christmas had a lot of bare places on it.

As Kathleen poured the drink into the mugs, he came to her side, inches from her. The sound of laughter drifted from the living room. He smiled. "This could have been a disaster."

"Next year all those bare places on the tree now will be filled with new decorations. It was an accident. The topping on a difficult day. I figure I need to cut my losses and go to bed."

"That might not be a bad idea. I'll help your mother clean up the mess. Go on. You're right. This past week has been hard on you."

"But what about the ornaments that have to be put back on the tree?"

"We'll take care of it." He captured her hands and turned her toward him. "Go. Rest. You deserve it."

"But this is my…"

"What?"

"My family. I can't ask you to fill in for me."

"You aren't asking me. I'm volunteering. No, I'm insisting." He cupped her chin and lifted her head so he could look into her eyes. He grazed his forefinger across the top of her cheek. "I see it there. You're exhausted."

"I can't let you do my job. This is my family."

"Why not let me? I'll borrow yours for the rest of the evening. Tomorrow you'll be better rested."

"You know when I agreed to decorating the tree tonight, I'd forgotten how much work it could be, especially a second time."

"I saw that when all you did was sink down on the windowsill and stare at your son when he fell."

"Yeah, I didn't have the energy to react. He has his share of accidents, but this was a doozy. I'm glad Mom took it so well."

"Ruth goes with the flow."

"That's something I'm still learning from her," she said in a voice that reflected the world crashing down on her.

He brushed his lips across hers, then urged her toward the door into the hallway. "C'mon. Off to bed with you." He watched her walk toward the stairs, her shoulders slumped, her step slow.

She bent over the banister to look at him. "Thank you."

"You're welcome."

As she disappeared from his view, he remembered

bits and pieces of their interaction throughout the day. Something was wrong. Kip's accident had been traumatic, but there was something else going on with Kathleen. He'd given her several opportunities to confide in him, but she hadn't. Frustration churned his gut. He was falling for her, and she was putting up barriers between them. He needed to shore up his own walls, protect himself, but he was afraid he was too late.

"Kip wanted to know where the hot chocolate—" With glitter sparkling in the light on his jeans and shirt, Jared paused in the entrance from the dining room and panned the kitchen. "Where's Mom?"

"It was past her bedtime."

"She doesn't have one."

Gideon crossed to the tray with the full mugs and picked it up. "She was tired, and I told her I would make sure everything was cleaned up from your little disaster."

Jared yawned. "You know, I'm tired, too. I think I'll go to bed—after my hot chocolate."

"Sorry, I'm not buying it." Another yawn made Gideon chuckle. "Still not. You're stuck on cleanup duty."

A grin spread over his face. "Oh, well, at least I get to stay up past my bedtime."

"When is it?"

Jared leaned to the side and peered at the clock on the wall behind Gideon. "In ten minutes."

"Guess you're gonna miss it."

"Yes." Jared pumped his arm in the air.

Gideon carried the tray into the living room and

passed the mugs around to everyone, except the one who requested the hot chocolate. Kip lay on the couch asleep.

"Should I wake him?" Gideon set the tray with the last mug on the coffee table in front of the couch.

"Young man, don't you know you never wake a sleeping child? Wait, maybe that's a sleeping baby." Miss Alice sipped her drink.

"Where's Kathleen?" Ruth put the lid on an empty ornament box then sat with her hot chocolate cupped between her hands.

"She went to bed." Gideon looked back at Kip. "I can take him up to his room."

"That would be great if you think you can with your cast." Ruth took a swallow from her cup.

"Sure." He thought about the time he'd carried Kathleen to the beach on Dog Island. He'd enjoyed the feel of her in his arms.

Squatting by the couch, Gideon carefully scooped up Kip and rose. The boy snuggled against Gideon and draped one arm over his shoulder. His eyes closed, Kip murmured something Gideon couldn't understand and settled against him.

A few minutes later, he laid the boy on his bed and covered him with a blanket. He stared down at the child and wondered what it would feel like being a father. When Kip had fallen last week, his heart had plummeted and a gripping fear had taken over as he'd never experienced. He'd rescued children before, but that had been different.

When he returned to the living room, Miss Alice sat forward, then stood. "I'd better be going."

"Let me walk you home." Gideon started for the foyer and opened the front door.

"Good night, y'all. Thanks for sharing this with me. It's been years since I've participated in decorating a tree." Miss Alice shuffled toward Gideon, a softness in her expression that a month ago hadn't been there.

He offered her his arm, and they descended the porch steps.

"Those boys are good kids, but they need a father." Miss Alice's declaration broke the silence between them halfway up her sidewalk to her house. "If you're not interested, maybe one of your friends. That Zane fellow is nice. I like him. He did a good job fixing my house."

"I don't think Zane is looking for a wife."

"Are you?"

He nearly faltered on the stairs leading to the porch, quickly grabbing hold of the railing. "I hadn't really thought about it."

"You'd better stake your claim fast. She needs a good man to take care of her."

"Why do you say that?" Gideon stopped at the front door, shifting from foot to foot.

"She's sad. I see it in her eyes. From what Ruth has told me and what I see, I don't think her path has been easy."

"What has Ruth told you?"

Alice dug into the pocket of her sweater and pulled out her key, then inserted it into the lock. "That, young man, is something you will have to ask Ruth or Kathleen. I don't gossip. Well, occasionally I have but not in this case."

"Good night, Miss Alice." He turned to leave.

He descended the steps when Miss Alice said, "Don't end up like me—alone all your life. It isn't all it's cut up to be."

He glanced back at the woman, but she went into her house and shut her door. As he walked back to Ruth's, darkness surrounded him with a hint of a chill in the air. Could he risk his heart with Kathleen? Miss Alice's words about being alone pricked his heart, threatening his belief that he was better off not caring too much for others and going through life more an observer than a participant. This past month he hadn't been. Was it because of the hurricane or Kathleen that he'd gotten more involved than he usually did?

When he reentered Ruth's house, he found Jared and her in the living room with broom and dustpan, cleaning up the pieces of broken decorations. "I thought if I stayed gone long enough you two would have this all taken care of."

Jared giggled. "I should have asked to take Miss Alice home." He moved the dustpan away, tilting it forward enough that its contents spilled all over the floor again.

"Jared, pay attention." Ruth's loud sigh conveyed her annoyance.

Gideon bridged the distance between them and took the broom from Ruth. "I'll help Jared in here."

She gave him a grateful look. "Then I'll take care

of cleaning up the dishes we used." After gathering the tray and mugs, she strolled toward the kitchen.

"I didn't mean to dump the pieces." Jared's mouth drooped in a pout. "I don't mean to cause trouble."

"I know. Sometimes it just happens. Here, hold the pan while I sweep it up again." As he worked, he saw Jared's sagging shoulders and tight mouth. "What happened tonight reminded me of a time when I was eight and couldn't wait until Christmas Day to open all the presents under the tree. My parents were getting ready in their bedroom to go out. I decided to sneak a peek when they weren't in the room. I wheedled my way under the tree, wanting to get my hands on the big box in the back. I wiggled the wrong way and the tree came down on top of me."

"You did? What did your parents do?"

The memory was seared into his mind as though it had happened yesterday. "They heard the noise and came running. When they found me, they must have laughed for five minutes before they got the tree off me. I didn't understand why they weren't mad at me. It had taken us hours to decorate the tree, and I had destroyed it in seconds."

"They didn't do anything to you?"

"Oh, they did. I had to clean it up all by myself and put everything back on the tree without their help. They decided not to go out that evening and instead sat there on the couch watching me, talking to each other and ignoring my whining." He wouldn't trade that memory for anything. It made his parents seem so real to him for a few minutes.

"Where are your parents?"

"They died years ago."

"My dad did. I miss him every day."

"I miss my parents every day."

"Everything is so different now."

"How so?"

"Mom has to work a lot. She's always worrying. Nana told me worrying only makes the problem worse."

Grinning, Gideon finished sweeping the last pieces into the pan. "She's right. But it doesn't stop me from worrying."

"Why doesn't it?" Jared kept his gaze fastened onto the pan as he lifted it and walked slowly to the trash can, then dumped the contents into it.

"I've never really found that worrying about a problem solves it. It just makes me stressed over it, but for so long it has been a habit of mine I'm trying to change."

Jared cocked his head to the side. "Yeah, you're right. I worried about Kip when he was in the hospital. But that didn't really make him get better. I think my prayers helped. Nana and me prayed every night he was there."

"That's great. You're a good brother."

Jared puffed out his chest. "Yeah, I am."

Ruth reappeared in the living room. "This looks nice. You wouldn't know you toppled the tree."

"Except there aren't as many ornaments on it. Maybe Kip and me can make some to put on it this weekend."

"I'd like that." Ruth hugged her grandson.

"How about you, Gideon? Will you help us on Saturday?"

"Sure. I can't think of a nicer way to spend the day." As he said those words, he realized he had meant every one of them. When he had kidded Kathleen about borrowing her family for the night, he hadn't realized how it would affect him. He wanted a family for himself.

Kathleen sat at the kitchen table gluing sequins on a plain gold ornament while Jared and Kip glued paper rings together to make a garland for Miss Alice.

"Did ya get it?" Jared asked the second Gideon came into the room on Saturday.

"No *how are you?*" Gideon bent down and rubbed Rocky behind his ears.

"Hi. They've been wondering what was taking you so long. They wanted me to take them to the store to find you," Kathleen said with a chuckle. "I had to remind them my car is being fixed and they would have to walk. They decided to wait a little longer."

"Miss Alice is gonna be so surprised." Kip used the scissors to cut some more red and green strips of construction paper.

"How big is the tree?" Jared dabbed some glue on the end of the ring to hold it together.

"I got a live tree in a pot. It's about three feet high. Then if she wants me to, I'll plant the pine after Christmas."

"To replace the tree she lost. I like that." Kip paused and leaned down to pay attention to Rocky sitting by his chair.

"Where's Ruth? I thought she would be in the middle of this."

"She's getting ready to leave. We decided Nana should take Miss Alice out shopping while we decorate her house. That was my idea." Jared patted his chest.

Gideon took the chair next to Kathleen across from the boys. "How are we going to get into Miss Alice's house?"

"She gave Mom a spare key when she moved back into her house. I guess with everything that has happened, she has decided that might be for the best rather than us breaking down her door if we think she's in trouble." She'd missed Gideon the past few days, working at the hospital as much as possible to make up for taking off while Kip was there.

"How long do you think we'll have?" Gideon scooted his chair closer to the table, his arm brushing against Kathleen.

"An hour, probably, so we need to be finished with these decorations when Mom leaves."

"We're almost done. Look at this." Jared, with Kip's help, held up the long paper garland for Miss Alice's tree.

"That ought to go around all of it." She slanted a glance toward Gideon who made a design with glue then sprinkled red glitter on the plain gold ornament. "What time are we going to the Lights On Celebration at the Point?"

"Six. With Kip throwing the switch we want a good place to see it. Wait until you see what the fire department did with the lighthouse. We went all out this year. Y'all might want to bring your sunglasses."

"At night?" Jared wrinkled his nose.

"You'll see what I mean in a few hours."

"The hospital did the Christmas tree." Kathleen began gathering the decorations in a box to take to Miss Alice. "I helped some yesterday afternoon after work."

"I wanted to come, but Mom wouldn't let me. She said I needed to rest. That's all I've been doing. I'm getting bored with watching TV and sleeping." Kip put the last ring on the garland.

"I don't want you to overdo it."

Purse in hand, Ruth stopped in the entrance into the kitchen. "I'm going to get Miss Alice. Give me ten minutes then go on over. We won't be gone more than an hour. She wants to rest before tonight's celebration."

After her mother left, Kathleen placed the paper garland on top of the ornaments. "Let's clean this up. We won't have a lot of time when we come back here before dinner."

"Mom, I think someone needs to keep a lookout for Nana and Miss Alice leaving. I'll do it." Jared hopped up from his chair and raced toward the living room.

Kathleen opened her mouth to tell him it wasn't necessary, but he'd fled so fast she'd barely formed the first word in her mind. "I've got to harness some of his energy. I could use it."

"I'd better help him." Kip followed his little brother from the room although at a much slower pace.

"We're alone at last." Gideon waggled his eyebrows. "I thought they would never leave."

Kathleen laughed. "And what did you have in mind?"

He bent toward her and kissed her quick on the mouth. "That. I'd been thinking about it since I first came in here." He started to pull away.

Kathleen stopped him with a hand on his arm. "Hmm. I don't call that a kiss. Maybe a peck, but certainly not a kiss."

He locked his gaze on her lips. "You're mighty picky today. What is a kiss in your book?"

She smiled, one that came from the depths of her heart, and wound her arms around his neck, tugging him toward her. Her mouth connected with his, and she poured everything into it until she forgot to breathe and finally had to step back to take a deep gulp of air.

"Ah, I see what you mean. We might need to practice some more later." He moved back quickly as the sound of footsteps neared the kitchen. "When we're alone again," he added in a whisper as Jared and Kip burst into the room.

"They're gone," both boys said at the same time.

"Let me get the key. Jared and Kip, carry one of the boxes of decorations. I'll bring the large Christmas card you two made for her." Kathleen crossed to the desk and pulled out the drawer where Miss Alice's house key was.

Jared examined the kitchen table. "You two didn't do a good job of cleaning up. The glitter is everywhere, paper on the floor. What were you all doing?"

Kathleen wasted no time coming up with an excuse. "I decided to leave some for you and Kip while we wait for the pizzas to be delivered."

Kip punched Jared in the arm. "Why did you go and say that? When are you gonna ever learn to keep your mouth shut?"

"I was just wondering." Jared stuck his tongue out and hastened from the room with his box.

When Kip went after his little brother, Gideon blew out a breath of air. "Quick thinking."

"If we aren't one step ahead of our kids, we get trampled. Not fun in the least."

Gideon grabbed the pot with the small pine. "Sounds like you've been trampled a few times."

"I wish it were only a few. I lost count way back."

An hour later the four of them finished with Miss Alice's living room, confining their holiday decorating to that one room she spent most of her time in. On the front door the boys hung their three-foot-by-two-foot card with the outside displaying a huge fir dripping with ornaments and lights and packages beneath it.

With Kip on one side and Jared on the other, Kathleen stood in the middle of the living room. Voices from the front porch announced her mother and Miss Alice's approach.

"We should hide like a surprise birthday party." Jared scanned the area. "I can, behind that chair."

He started for his hiding place, but Kathleen grasped his shirttail and halted his movement. "I think she'll know something is up with that huge card on her door. Besides, we don't want to give her a heart attack."

Cottonballs whined and weaved in and out of their legs as the knob on the front door turned.

"Let me put this sack down and get my reading glasses on. Who would leave me such a big card?" Miss Alice moved into the foyer and caught sight of them in the entrance to the living room. She gasped, dropping her sack and splaying her hand over her heart. "Oh, my, what are y'all doing here? Y'all scared the—" Then she took several more steps until she saw all the decorations. Her mouth fell open.

While Miss Alice remained rooted to the floor, Jared came up to her and pulled on her arm. "Something's leaking all over the tiles."

Miss Alice blinked and swept around, her hand covering her mouth. "My eggs. They're broken."

Kathleen skirted around the woman and stooped to clean up the mess. "I'm sorry. I'll replace them. We wanted to show you how much we care about you and give you a little bit of Christmas." Gathering up the egg carton, she placed it into the torn sack while taking out the other grocery items. Thankfully, none of them were broken.

A suspiciously shiny sheen to her eyes, Miss Alice surveyed the living room, saying, "Don't worry about the eggs. I can't believe y'all did this for me. No one has done…" Her voice cracked, and she lowered her head, pulling a tissue from her coat pocket and dabbing at her face.

"It was my idea," Jared piped in.

Kip stepped forward. "No, it wasn't. I thought of it

and talked to you about it. I came up with the big card on the door."

"No, you didn't." Jared sent his brother a glare.

"Boys, that's enough. Let's say this was a cooperative idea between Jared and Kip." Kathleen walked toward the kitchen. "I'm throwing these away. I don't want to come back in here and see you two fighting."

She strode to the trash can and dumped in the sack and carton of eggs, straining to hear what was going on in the living room. All she heard were murmurs. She rushed back to find Miss Alice seated in her recliner, tears streaking down her face.

"I'd forgotten what Christmas was about until this year. You couldn't have given this old lady a better gift."

"We made everything in here." Kip beamed.

"Well, except the tree. But everything else." Jared stood next to his brother, his grin as big as Kip's.

"I'll never forget this. And you two can play soccer in my front yard anytime you want." Miss Alice swiped the tissue across each eye, then stuffed it back into her pocket.

While Kip brought Miss Alice the Christmas card from the front door so she could read the inside, Kathleen watched their neighbor interact with her two sons. A warmth flowed through her. Her sons still bickered, but for this project they had worked side by side with little fighting. In the past week they hadn't said once they wished they were in Denver. Hope was becoming their home. At least one thing was working out as she'd prayed. If only the rest of it would.

* * *

At the front of the crowd at Broussard Park in a semicircle around the lighthouse, Kathleen huddled in her light jacket, not having expected the wind to be as cold as it was, blowing off the water. She hugged herself and tried to focus on what Mayor Thomas was saying.

Next to her, Gideon drew her close to him, wrapping his arms around her. His warmth spread through her, alleviating the chill some. She cherished the feel of his embrace, the sense of being protected from the elements. "The temperature is dropping. A front must be moving through. It's always a little cooler here, which is great in the summer."

She turned her head and whispered, "Some people came better prepared than I did. I'm looking forward to a cup of hot chocolate."

Gideon's face, only inches from hers, threw her heartbeat into a fast tempo. The cold fled completely as the mayor finished his little speech about the future of Hope.

"It's time to turn on the lights. A beacon of hope in the dark. Ships passing by will be able to see our little light display. Hope may have been hit six weeks ago, but we aren't down. There will be a new Hope rising even better than before. Kip Hart will flip the switch this year on our Lights On Celebration. Kip, are you ready?"

Nodding, her son positioned himself next to a big red button.

"Okay. Ten. Nine," the mayor said with everyone

as usual joining in the countdown. "Eight. Seven. Six. Five. Four. Three. Two. One."

Kip pressed the button and bright lights flooded the park—thousands and thousands of them, glittering and dazzling.

But Kathleen's gaze fastened onto the lighthouse the fire department had decorated. Red, white and blue lights covered the whole surface of the white structure as though the building was wrapped in an American flag. "Stunning."

"I'm glad you like it. It was my idea. A tribute to our soldiers and citizens who continually fight to make this country better. All I have to do is look around at the people in this crowd."

The warmth of his breath tickled her neck. She shivered.

"Still cold?"

The crowd began to clap at the display not only on the lighthouse, but on the ten-foot Christmas tree standing tall at the edge of the cliff as if it defied the sea to take it down as it had so many others in the hurricane. The park's pines, live oaks, stripped of their Spanish moss, and magnolia trees left from the storm were lit up in white like stars glinting in the night sky.

Kip made his way through the people surrounding the mayor. "Mom, what did ya think?"

"You did great."

"The mayor told me they found a few more areas along the cliff that had to be shored up. That I prevented others from being hurt. I helped save some people."

She was glad some good had come out of the tragedy, but it didn't make it any less painful.

"I'm hungry. Can I go get some dessert and hot chocolate?" Jared wedged himself in front of Kathleen.

"I was thinking that very thing." The church would block a lot of the chilly wind. A much better place to enjoy the treats her mother's ladies' group had fixed. "If we hurry, we can be first in line."

Jared shot forward, nearly knocking into a young woman in his haste. Kip trailed his brother at a more sedate pace, still not up to his usual active level.

"I probably shouldn't have said that. But then with everyone who turned out for the celebration, it would be nice to be at the front of the line."

Gideon glanced around. "I think others have the same idea."

"At least we'll be out of the wind."

Gideon waved at Pete and his wife. "We could break in line."

"You're such a rebel."

"Your mom said something about making divinity."

"She makes the best in town. Probably the state. I don't know how I'm going to carry on her tradition. Mine isn't nearly as good."

"Y'all have a lot of traditions at Christmas."

"Yeah, passed down from my grandmother. There is a comfort to them. Kip and Jared will feel right at home here because we've done the same thing since they were born. We were a little late with the tree because of the accident, but tomorrow we're all going to make Christmas cookies and take them to Hope Retirement Home along with Mom's homemade eggnog. Now that, I have mastered."

"Even when my parents were alive we didn't have any traditions other than going to church on Christmas Eve."

"You're welcome to take part in our traditions. Miss Alice is going to help tomorrow with the cookies and go with us to deliver them."

"I wish I could, but I promised Pete I would help with some of his repairs at his house. He still has quite a bit of work to do on his place."

"Somehow I can see you doing that more than baking cookies," Kathleen said with a chuckle. "It's a lot of fun, but the real work starts after the cookies are boxed up and ready to go."

His forehead furrowed as he slowly moved forward in the line. "Taking them to the retirement home?"

"No, cleaning up the mess my boys make. Sort of like a mini hurricane blowing through the kitchen. You know flour goes everywhere and in places you don't want when you start throwing it at your brother."

"Interesting. I would never have figured that." His laughter filled the air.

Kathleen loved hearing him laugh. It invited her to join in on the merriment. She was falling for him, and she didn't know if that was a smart move. Her marriage problems were still so fresh in her mind. What if she made a mistake as she did with marrying Derek? She had more than herself to consider in this. As she reached her mom behind the first table of goodies, she shook the dilemma from her mind. She wasn't going to let worrying over it ruin her evening.

"Thanks for carrying Kip up to bed again. All this activity is wearing him out. It's hard to restrict him at this time of year." Kathleen opened the front door for Gideon.

He headed up the stairs with Jared following.

"Why does he always get to be carried up the stairs? I should have fallen asleep in the car on the way home, then you would have to carry me, too. Except I would like you to do a fireman's carry with me."

Gideon bit the inside of his cheek to keep from chuckling at the continual one-upmanship between the two brothers. At least he finally heard from *his* brother overseas. He would be returning to the United States in the spring and wanted to meet Gideon after all these years.

He had vague memories of times spent with Zach as children. Lighthearted, fun times. When he was living at some of the foster homes he'd been at, the atmosphere had been anything but lighthearted. Not all but a few—enough that he always watched his back and guarded his words.

Gideon placed Kip on the bed and covered him as he had the night they had decorated the Christmas tree. The simple action connected him to the child. He backed away, his emotions swelling in his chest, closing his throat.

"I'm going downstairs and probably fall asleep on

the couch," Jared said at the doorway. "Remember the fireman's carry if I happen to fall asleep."

Gideon strode behind the boy. "Okay, but didn't your mom say something about getting ready for bed?"

He whirled around and began walking backward toward the stairs. "I didn't hear that. I'm not tired a bit."

"Well, then I guess you won't fall asleep on the couch."

He swung around and faced forward, grasping the banister. "I can get sleepy real fast."

"Okay, I'll keep that in mind."

Downstairs, Jared ran toward the den where the sound of voices was coming from. Gideon paused in the living room and stared at the tree. True to their word, the boys had filled almost all the blank places on the tree. He could hardly see the pine beneath all the decorations.

"Hi, I thought maybe you had gone home." Kathleen came up behind him and put her hand on his arm.

The touch zapped him with more feelings of wanting to belong to a family. "I wouldn't leave without telling you good-night. Besides, I have a sneaky suspicion that Jared is going to fall asleep on the couch in the den, and I'm going to have to carry him upstairs using the fireman's carry."

"You are? So now all I have to do to get him to sleep in the future is to have you here, ready, willing and able to carry him up the stairs over your shoulder. You're hired for the job."

He tweaked her pert nose. "It's a freebie." Hooking his arm around her, he pulled her close. "I enjoyed tonight. I've gone every year to the Lights On Celebration, but this year was special."

"Because we're celebrating more than the beginning of the holiday season. We're celebrating our comeback."

"I can see that you were a cheerleader in your youth."

She laughed. "I'm gonna take that as a compliment. Someone has to cheer people on. I'm very good at standing on the sidelines and doing that."

"Not participating?"

"In this case I guess I did. I still have paint under my fingernails and probably a splinter or two still in my hands."

He grabbed one of them and turned her palm up. "Where? I'm very good at taking out splinters. Show me and I'll get a needle and alcohol."

She snatched her hand back. "I think I'll take care of it. I still have one in my hand from when I was a little girl. It would take surgery to remove it now."

"I'm a trained paramedic. I probably could do that, too."

She snuggled closer. "Don't forget our date on the fifteenth. This is your chance to tell me what you want me to cook for you."

Enjoying her close to him, he looked over her shoulder and up. "Hmm. Let me see. Lobster and T-bone sounds great. Or…" He tilted his head, pretending to be in deep thought. "Actually, surprise me."

"No lobster and steak?"

"Nope. Although I do like seafood, lobster isn't my favorite."

"I think I have the perfect recipe in mind."

"What?"

"You wanted me to surprise you so I'm not telling you."

"That day I'll be at the doctor late. Do you want to use my kitchen earlier?"

"Probably would be better than me carting all the dishes to your house."

"Are you working that day?"

"No, and I will need all afternoon to prepare my feast." She grinned. "But that is all I'm telling you about what I'm preparing."

Their easy repartee only reinforced how comfortable he was with Kathleen. Her smile encompassed her whole face, joy radiating from her. He couldn't take his gaze off her mouth. Inviting. Tempting. He had to taste it.

He slowly lowered his head. "Thank you for this evening."

Her lips parted slightly, and he swooped in to kiss them. He pulled her against him, their rapid heartbeats matching tempos, and put everything into the merging of their mouths.

From afar, someone clearing her throat intruded into his dazed mind. He didn't want to end the kiss, but Kathleen disengaged and stepped from his embrace. She shifted to the right.

"Jared is asleep on the couch. He told me when he

fell asleep I was to get Gideon. That he'd know what to do." Amusement laced Ruth's voice.

Bereft without her in his arms, Gideon nodded his head and clicked his shoes. "Duty calls."

The urge to tickle Jared was strong, but Gideon resisted it. He bent down and hoisted the child over his right shoulder. He weighed next to nothing considering some of the equipment he had to haul in a fire. Mounting the stairs, he sensed Kathleen's gaze on him. That awareness of her heightened an electric sensation that charged his nerves.

Then she was behind him, following him up the steps. What would it feel like to carry his own child to bed, to have his wife accompany him and them both put him down to sleep? The way his life was going, he'd never find out unless he was willing to make a change and risk getting hurt again.

Chapter Twelve

As Kathleen sliced up the red pepper for a salad, her hand shook. Finally, she lay it beside the cutting board and gripped the edge of the counter in Gideon's kitchen. How was she going to find the money for the medical bills for Kip? She was still paying off her husband's debt. The doctor's bill had arrived this afternoon, and it was worse than she thought. She didn't even have the energy to call the doctor's office to talk with someone about what she owed. All her mistakes from her past were crushing her, and she didn't know how to get out from under them.

She forced herself to pick up the paring knife and finish making the salad. The scent of shrimp gumbo saturated the room with its spicy seafood aroma. The repetitive motion of dicing the pepper up into small pieces didn't soothe as it usually did. That was one of the reasons she enjoyed cooking—she could forget her troubles for a while. But not this time.

Gideon would be home soon and ready to celebrate

after having his cast removed today. And that was the last thing she felt like doing. She wasn't even sure how she was going to get enthusiastic about the holidays. She had purchased a couple of gifts for her boys before Kip's accident and the car repairs. That would have to be their Christmas. Although she was already working some extra shifts at the hospital, maybe she could find another nursing job. She didn't have anything else she could sell to raise money. Most of her possessions were gone in the hurricane. The more she thought about her mounting debt the more her movements slowed until she couldn't even lift the blade.

Tears blurred her vision, and she closed her eyes, setting the knife on the counter. She didn't have any answers to her problems. She'd thought about filing for bankruptcy, but she didn't want to do that if at all possible.

The sound of the front door opening then closing underscored she wasn't alone anymore. She needed to get her composure together. This was her problem, and she didn't want to burden anyone else, even Gideon, with it. She straightened, wiped the tears from her eyes and picked up the knife to complete the salad.

"Honey, I'm home," Gideon said as he came into the kitchen. "Now does that not sound like one of those shows in the fifties like *Leave It to Beaver* or *Father Knows Best?*"

She forced a smile to her lips and turned toward him. "I think, Mr. O'Brien, you've had way too much time on your hands."

"I beg your pardon. I've been working at a dull desk job."

"Which must have given you time to daydream."

"I did find myself drifting off every once in a while, but don't tell the captain." He held up his cast-free arm and waved it. "Now that I'm back on rotation, he'd have me doing twice the work."

"Poor guy. You can't have it both ways. Either desk duty or firefighter. Which is it going to be?" She began dicing the rest of the pepper.

"No contest—firefighter." He closed the distance between them and drew in a deep breath. "Ah, that's a great smell. Shrimp gumbo. How did you know that's one of my favorite dishes?"

"A little sleuthing on my part. I called Pete, and he told me."

"And he didn't say a word to me. I didn't think Pete could keep quiet about anything."

She smiled at him. "This time he did."

"Can I help you with anything?"

"You can put the French bread into the oven at 375 degrees. Everything else is done."

"Want me to set the table?"

"I already did In the dining room."

Gideon gave a low whistle. "You are going all out."

"That's the only way to do something. I even brought two of Mom's china place settings."

"I'm feeling pampered, and all I had to do was go into a burning building and do my job."

She caught him watching her reaction to his words. "For your information I have forgiven myself weeks ago about my part in your injuries. You have convinced me I wasn't responsible."

"Good. I was ready to launch into my spiel again if I had to." He put the bread in the oven then moved toward the dining room. "I have one final touch to add to the table."

"What?"

He swung around at the doorway. "You are not allowed in here until it is time to eat."

"Okay. But that's not fair. This was my evening to do for you."

He headed out of the room. "Who said life is fair?"

Fair? No, it wasn't. Since before Derek's death, it had been one problem after another. When something went wrong, she didn't even have time to recover before another crisis occurred. The tears threatened again. She swallowed them away, but her throat burned.

"All done. I had to lend my finishing touch to the table."

She picked up the bowl of salad. "I'm done, too. I'm going to put this on the table—"

He plucked it from her hands. "Your ploy won't work. I'll take the food in."

"While you're in there, bring the bowls for the gumbo. The bread should be done in ten minutes."

"Great. I'm starved." He stopped in front of her by the stove and grasped the wooden spoon to stir the pot's contents. Bending over the heat rising from the gumbo, he inhaled and held the breath for a long moment then released it slowly. "I love that smell. I've been wondering all day what you were going to cook and was regretting telling you to surprise me. I don't like surprises normally."

"Neither do I." She threw a glance toward the dining room.

"You only have a few more minutes to wait." He inched toward her. "I can think of a couple of things we could do to pass the time until the bread is done."

His eyes gleamed as they roved over her face. He reached up and brushed her hair behind her ears, his gaze glued to her mouth. Her heart plummeted. His smoldering look spoke to her feminine side, urging her to give in to the feelings he generated in her. She couldn't, shouldn't.

When he sought her mouth and touched his to hers, she knew she needed to break it off. Her heart refused to listen to common sense that said she should get her life under control before even thinking of becoming involved with a man. She surrendered, giving him a part of herself she didn't have to give.

When they broke apart, their breathing ragged, Kathleen quickly tried to recapture that elusive part of herself—her heart. She couldn't risk it right now. She could never ask another to take on the kind of debt she had. It was *her* problem. No one else's.

He framed her face between his hands, his eyes leaving a heated trail where they roamed. "This wasn't exactly how I pictured telling you this. I wanted something a little romantic. But here goes. Kathleen Hart, I love you. I have never said that to another woman. Ever. In these past two months you've become so important to me. I hope one day you'll agree to be my wife. You don't have to say anything right now because I know you need time, but please think about it. I want to be a father to Kip and Jared. I want to be a husband to you."

Each word seared into her. *No. Don't. I can't.* She stared at him, seeing the sparkle in his eyes slowly fade, the smile transform into a look of puzzlement. Still, she couldn't say anything. It wouldn't be fair to Gideon. Her problems weren't his. She couldn't…

She backed away. "You know how I feel about marriage. I had one bad marriage and that was enough. I never want that again."

"To be married or a bad marriage?" His terse voice sliced through the air.

"Both. Not now." She whirled around and started toward the doorway into the dining room. She needed to get out of here.

He stopped her with a hand on her arm and rotated her toward him. "Stay. We can talk about this."

"No, enjoy the gumbo." The scent of burning bread permeated the kitchen. She gestured toward the oven. "You'd better take the bread out."

When he dropped her arm and turned toward the stove, she fled, hurrying past the dining room table. A gorgeous bouquet of flowers—lilies, carnations and others she didn't recognize—infused the air with their sweet fragrance. On a plate was a present in a small box. Its sight spurred her to a faster pace.

This wasn't the time to give her heart to another—not with all the complication in her life. *He'll thank me later.* But as she left his house, that thought didn't comfort her one bit.

* * *

Gideon yanked the burning bread from the oven. In his haste, one of his fingers touched the hot pan. He dropped it and jumped back. Staring at the bread on the floor, he stood rigid from the emotions bombarding him as if he were being hit over and over from all sides.

She doesn't want to have anything to do with me. She might as well tell me to get lost.

This was the reason he didn't put himself out there. Anger vied with his hurt. He wanted to be mad at Kathleen. He needed to be. Otherwise, the hurt would win, and he would be back to how it had been after his parents' deaths. He wouldn't go there again. He'd fought to get where he was today.

Lord, what do I do?

After a long day putting in overtime, all Kathleen wanted to do was put up her feet and do nothing. But tonight was the time she'd set aside to finish baking some goodies for her gifts to family and friends. It was all she could afford to do. When she entered the kitchen with her two bags of groceries, she found her mother at the table with her two sons painting the Christmas plates the goodies would be placed on. She'd wanted to help with that part, too, but when the overtime opportunity came up, her mom said she'd love to assist Jared and Kip. It would be a treat for her.

"It's about time you got home, Mom," Kip said, holding up his work of art. "What do you think? This is for Sally."

In the center of the white plate, he'd painted a green

Christmas tree and then put ornaments on it and lots of presents under it, much like the front of Miss Alice's huge card. "Beautiful. She's going to love it." Her cousin was still living with her mother at least for a few more months until her apartment building was rebuilt.

"I'm doing one for Gideon. What do you think about mine?"

All she saw was Jared's big grin as he showed her his plate with green rolling hills and a night sky with a brilliant star shining in it. "You've done a great job."

"That's the star the Wise Men followed. I remember Gideon telling me about it when we put the star on our tree." He tilted his head and furrowed his forehead. "Why haven't we seen him lately? He hasn't been down here in a week. I had to visit him to see him without his cast."

"Yeah, Mom, is he mad at us or something?"

Kathleen locked gazes with her mother. "I know he isn't mad at you two, but now that he can work as a firefighter again, he has needed to focus on that."

"I asked him to go to church with us on Christmas Eve." Jared set his plate down among the others they had painted. "He said he couldn't. It's sad he doesn't have a family to share Christmas with."

"Yes, it is," she murmured and turned away from her children before she started crying in front of them. She'd made such a mess of everything.

"We could be his family this Christmas," Kip said.

"That looks like the last two plates you need to do." Her mother glanced at the clock on the wall. "You said something about watching that Christmas movie on

TV tonight. It'll be on in five minutes. You need to wash up and get into your pajamas. It'll be late when the movie is over and time for bed."

After her boys left the room, her mom approached her. "Are you all right?"

"No. Everything is falling apart. I—" Kathleen couldn't find the words to tell her mother how much she'd missed Gideon the past week. She glimpsed him once leaving his house, and it had taken all her will-power not to run after him and beg his forgiveness.

"I haven't wanted to pry—okay, maybe I have—but talking about what happened between y'all last week might help you."

"I had just gotten the final bill from the doctor and hospital for Kip's accident that day I made dinner for him. When he told me he loved me and—"

"He loves you! Why didn't you tell me? That's great. That's—" Her enthusiasm waned. "Is that the problem? You don't love him?"

"I do love him. I didn't want to fall in love, but this whole week he's all I thought about. I miss him terribly and yet, Mom, how can I ask a man to take on my debt, especially now that thousands more have been added to it? I can't. It's not his problem. It's mine."

"Did you talk to him about it?"

"No."

"Why not? He at least deserves to know you care about him, and why you don't want to see him any-more. You aren't being fair to him."

"I believe he told me life isn't always fair."

"That's a cop-out and you know it." Her mother

sighed. "He's good with the boys. They deserve someone like him in their lives. From what you told me, their own father didn't pay much attention to them in the last few years before he died."

"Yeah, and both Jared and Kip have drunk in Gideon's attention."

"Did you think they wouldn't ask why he wasn't coming around?"

"I didn't think. I just reacted to him telling me he loved me. I got scared. I still am. What if I make a mistake like I did with Derek?"

"Gideon is a good man. He is nothing like Derek. Whether he is for you is another question and one only you can answer. Do you want Derek to control the rest of your life? He will if you let what happened between you two dictate how you live now." Her mother took her hands. "Honey, you shouldn't be having this conversation with me but with Gideon."

"Have I told you lately how much I love you?" Kathleen hugged her. "I don't know what I would have done if I hadn't come home. I was a mess after Derek died. I should have come back to Hope right away."

"I tried to get you to."

"I know. I thought I was giving Jared and Kip what they needed. Stability. When what they needed was here all along."

"Go rest. You look beat. I'm going to make some brownies and divinity for your goodie plates. Then if you want to add anything besides the lemon bars you did last night, that's fine. The kitchen will be all yours."

Kathleen dragged herself up the stairs to her room

where she was sure she would go to sleep immediately after falling into bed. But fifteen minutes later, she punched the pillow and flipped over onto her back. As she stared at the ceiling, she turned to the Lord for guidance. She needed help untangling the mess her life was in. He was the only one who could help her.

"Gideon, a lady is here to see you," Captain Fox at Station Two said as he came into the living area on Christmas Eve.

Through the open doorway, Gideon spied Kathleen standing in the bay where the fire trucks were parked. Wearing a red and green plaid dress, she looked beautiful. His heartbeat responded by kicking up a notch, and his stomach muscles cinched.

I don't want to see her. Who are you kidding? It's taken all you have to stay away from her. Not to storm down to Ruth's and demand she love you.

Gideon shoved to his feet and covered the distance to the exit, aware of his fellow firefighters looking on as he left, intense curiosity in their expressions. A woman didn't usually come to the fire station unless she was a wife of one of the firefighters on duty.

"Thanks, captain," Gideon said as he passed him.

When he emerged into the large bay, a cool breeze blew through the large open doors. Beyond Kathleen, Christmas lights shone in the darkness. He stopped a few feet from her.

Her smile transformed the tired lines of her face into a look of radiance. "I didn't realize you were working tonight. I'd gone down to your house to talk to you and see if you would go to Christmas Eve service and discovered you were working."

"I'm filling in for a guy who has a young family. He should be home tonight and tomorrow. I don't have anyone."

"Jared and Kip will be disappointed, but I can certainly understand."

"I'll be off tomorrow night. I'll come and see them then. I have some gifts for them. Is that where you're going now—to church?"

"Yeah, I'm going to meet Mom and the boys there. I told them I needed to come see you first."

"Why?"

She took a deep breath. "I had my speech all planned. That was why I had gone down to your house. But when you weren't home, it threw me off."

"You don't go with the flow much, do you?"

"I'm still learning." She turned toward a table to the side and picked up a plate with goodies covered in plastic wrap. "Merry Christmas. The boys decorated the plate, and Mom and I made the sweets."

"Thanks." He didn't know what else to say to her. He'd gotten her a heart-shaped necklace the day he'd gone to have his cast taken off. It still sat on his dresser, a constant reminder of the risk of falling in love. But he hadn't been able to bring himself to return it to the jewelry store. The couple of times he had tried he hadn't been able to do it.

Silence descended. Gideon took a step back. Kathleen looked out toward the street.

Seeing her only made him want to talk some sense

into her. Or to drag her to him and kiss her senseless until she gave in to the feelings he knew she was beginning to have toward him.

"Well…" He searched for the right thing to say. "Tell the boys and your mom Merry Christmas for me. I'll be sure to drop by tomorrow evening." He backed away some more.

"Don't leave yet." Her chest rose and fell several times. "I—I was wrong with what I said the last time we saw each other. From the beginning I've been afraid of my feelings for you. After Derek's death I'd decided I didn't want to get married again. That I would focus on Jared and Kip. Then I met you and you changed everything. I love you, Gideon. I have no doubts about that."

He clenched his hands at his sides. "Then why did you say what you did?"

"Because earlier that day I had found out the extent of money I would owe for Kip's accident. Thousands of dollars added on top of the debt my husband left me. It was too much to process. I still don't know exactly what I'm going to do, and I certainly didn't want you to be drawn into it."

"Haven't you learned by now that it's okay to ask for help? The Lord didn't intend for us to go through life alone. It's taken me years to realize that. In fact, until I met you I didn't fully realize how alone I was. After my parents died, I lost hope of finding that connection I needed to fulfill my life. You and your family gave me that hope."

"And then that night I shattered it. I'm so sorry. I

was afraid. Still am, but I had a long talk with God. I think He brought me here to Hope and to you because He wanted me to heal. I've been emotionally alone for many years, even before my husband died. I need you."

He closed the space between them. "I can help you. Together as a team we'll work it out. As a firefighter I've learned to be a team member. It hasn't always been easy because I kept those walls up. But this town, these people have helped me to break those walls down." He clasped her hands and drew her toward him. "You have. Let me be a part of your life. Fully. I'm in this relationship one hundred percent."

She wound her arms around his neck and dragged him down for a kiss. "How can I turn down an offer like that?"

He smiled and hugged her close to him. "I'm hoping you won't." He wouldn't be alone anymore. He had a family to care for and love.

Epilogue

The next evening Gideon arrived at Kathleen's mother's house with his arms full of presents. Jared and Kip were speechless as Gideon handed them their gifts. "Open them," he said as he sat next to Kathleen on the couch and took her hand.

Both boys tore into the packages, unveiling clothes and other items they had lost in the hurricane.

Glimpsing the joy on Gideon's face, Kathleen leaned toward him. "You shouldn't have. But thank you."

"They needed the clothes. I had so much fun shopping for them. And I threw in a couple of treats for them, too."

Jared held up his rock tumbler. "Yay! I have some rocks I've found that I can put in here. Can I tonight?"

Kathleen chuckled. "Somehow I figured you would say that. We'll set it up in the garage so the noise doesn't drive us crazy."

When Jared and Kip had finished, sitting among the boxes and wrapping paper, beaming, Gideon rose and drew Kathleen up next to him. "I have one more surprise for you two."

Kip looked around. "Where?"

"On the porch." Gideon started for the front door.

Jared and Kip peered at each other then went after Gideon. Kathleen took up the rear.

Out on the porch sat two boys bikes—one red and the other blue. Her sons' eyes bugged out, both Kip and Jared rooted to the cement.

"The red one is Kip's and the blue, Jared's," Gideon finally said when they still hadn't moved.

Suddenly, they surged forward, clasping the handlebars of their bikes. "Thank you. Thank you," Kip said, then Jared.

Kip swept around and hugged Gideon. "Mom, can we go for a ride?"

"Yes, but only on the sidewalk. You can ride down to the end of the block and back."

Gideon helped Jared and Kip carry their bikes to the sidewalk, the Christmas lights from the neighbors giving off enough illumination for them to see where they were going.

When they took off, Gideon moved back next to Kathleen to watch, slipping his arm around her. "I haven't forgotten you." He drew her toward the steps where the porch light glowed and handed her a wrapped box lying on the wicker chair. "This is for you."

She carefully removed the paper then the lid, and lifted a gold chain with a heart dangling from it. "This is beautiful. I love it."

"You have my heart. I wanted you to have one to wear close to yours."

"Will you put this on for me?" She turned her back to him and lifted her hair so he could.

His fingers on her neck sent a thrill through her. After fastening the necklace, he bent forward and whispered, "That isn't the only surprise for you."

She glanced over her shoulder. "You're spoiling me."

"I want to spend the rest of my life doing that very thing." He turned her around and kissed her. "The mayor heard about your medical bills and wants to help. A fund has been set up to help you pay for Kip's accident."

Words refused to materialize in her mind. She stared at Gideon for a long moment, trying to comprehend what he told her.

Gideon shifted her toward him. "Are you all right?"

Thank You, Lord, for sending Gideon to me. "I'm more than all right. After all, I'm in love with a wonderful man."

* * * * *

THE CHRISTMAS CHILDREN

Irene Brand

To our friends, Rodney and Karen Dill,
who by example have given a new meaning
to the term "adoptive parents."

For God so loved the world, that he gave his only begotten Son, that whosoever believeth in him should not perish, but have everlasting life.

—*John* 3:16

Chapter One

Darkness had fallen when Carissa Whitmore drove into Yuletide, New York, and parked her SUV in front of a fast-food restaurant. At first, she couldn't understand why she felt so let down, until she recalled her reason for being there. She'd come to this lakeside village to find the kind of holiday spirit she'd enjoyed as a child, but she couldn't see any indication of Christmas.

Carissa had anticipated a village ablaze with Christmas lights, nativity scenes and decorated trees, but except for the streetlights sparkling on the gentle snowfall as it filtered among the evergreen trees, the town was dark and uninviting. Stifling her disappointment, she entered the restaurant, sat at the counter to order a sandwich and a cup of tea. When she finished the meal, Carissa asked the waitress for directions to the police station.

The woman answered Carissa's question, then asked, "Are you the one who's moving into Naomi Townsend's house for the winter?"

Carissa smothered a laugh, but her blue eyes sparkled with mirth. She'd lived in a metropolitan area since leaving Minnesota twenty-five years ago. Carissa had forgotten how little privacy a person had in a small town.

"Yes, I am," she said. "I'm supposed to pick up the key from the chief of police."

The woman peered over the counter and nodded approvingly when she saw that Carissa wore boots. "I see you know how to dress for winter. It's only two blocks to the police station, but the streets are kinda slippery. It'll be safer if you leave your car parked here and walk, 'specially since you're from down South and maybe don't know how to drive on snow."

Carissa laughingly admitted that she had no experience with treacherous roads. When she lived in Minnesota, she couldn't afford a car.

She zipped up her heavy coat and stepped out into the chill air. The business section of Yuletide was located on the southern tip of Lake Mohawk—a small lake that measured four miles from north to south. Many vacation and permanent residences dotted the lakefront and extended into the wooded highlands.

Although Yuletide lacked Christmas ornamentation, it was a picturesque alpine village of small shops and businesses. Carissa looked forward to exploring the stores at her leisure, but she didn't dawdle tonight; the wind from the lake was penetrating her heavy parka. She gave herself a mental pat on the back for being wise enough to shop at a mall in Pennsylvania on her way north. Her Florida clothing wouldn't have been warm enough for Adirondack weather.

Warmth from a wood-burning stove welcomed Carissa when she entered the police station. The chief of police, a short sturdy man, sat behind a massive oak desk that dwarfed him.

"Hiya!" the chief greeted her. "I'm Justin Townsend. Mary, at the restaurant, called and said you'd arrived. We've been expecting you, but figured the snow had delayed you."

Carissa unzipped the front of her parka and shrugged out of the hood, revealing a head of short, curly blond hair.

"The highways were clear until a few miles south of Saratoga Springs. After that, I had to maneuver my way out of a dozen or more snowdrifts. I'd have stopped, but I didn't see any motels after the snow got so heavy."

Chief Townsend stood and reached across the desk to shake hands. "Welcome to Yuletide."

He took a ring of keys out of a desk drawer and handed them to Carissa. "Naomi's my sister-in-law. Sorry you missed her, but she left for Florida three days ago. She'd intended to show you around before she had to leave."

"I was delayed at the last minute, and Naomi already had prepaid airline reservations, so I insisted that she go ahead. I called her on my cell phone this morning. She's already in Tampa enjoying the view of Tampa Bay from my eighth-floor condo. When I called, she was sitting on the balcony drinking a cup of coffee."

A grin spread across the chief's broad face. "Well,

you won't be drinking coffee on *her* balcony in the morning."

Justin gave Carissa directions to his sister-in-law's home. "If you want to wait a while, I can drive out with you. My deputy will be back in a half hour."

"Oh, you don't need to do that, unless the house is hard to find."

"It's along the main road, but it's getting dark. I thought you might be a little skittish about going into a strange house and all."

Carissa's even teeth gleamed in a wide smile. "I've lived alone for more than twenty years, so I'm not afraid of an empty house."

"No need to be," he assured her. "Yuletide is noted for its low crime rate." He beamed expansively. "I keep it that way. Remember, Naomi's house is the first two-story log house on your left, a mile north of town. There's a security light in the yard. We have someone in the station 'round the clock, so call if you need help finding the place. Drive carefully."

Before Carissa reached the sidewalk, Chief Townsend stuck his head out the door. "Naomi turned the temperature down. The house might be a little cool, but it'll warm up in a hurry when you raise the thermostat."

Carissa waved her hand to indicate she'd heard him and hustled to her vehicle.

The drive along a narrow road, bordered by snow-covered evergreen trees, reminded Carissa of her childhood in Minnesota. And a wide smile spread across her face as she pulled up to the chalet she was to occupy for the next few months. The storybook setting was exactly what she'd been expecting.

Carissa had never met Naomi Townsend, but Betty Potter, a saleswoman for Cara's Fashions—Carissa's designing business—had called upon Naomi often. One weekend when Betty had been stranded in New York, Naomi had invited Betty to stay with her in this lakeside home. It was Betty who'd brought Naomi and Carissa together, when she'd learned that both of them wanted to spend the winter away from home.

The dusk-to-dawn pole light illuminated the two-story chalet with a soft glow. A porch, with waist-high banisters, hugged the house protectively, and a set of snow-covered steps led to the front door. Drifts blanketed the roof, and the evergreens in the yard bowed low under their accumulation of snow.

A sliver of moon hovered over the Townsend house, and Carissa remembered a portion of one of Whittier's poems: "The moon above the eastern wood shone at its full; the hill-range stood transfigured in the silver flood, its blown snows flashing cold and keen."

When she'd unwillingly memorized those words in an elementary school in Minnesota, Carissa hadn't suspected that she would ever find her way out of her dismal circumstances. But by sheer determination she had, and now stood in a setting that the poet could have been describing.

A cold wind discouraged Carissa from unpacking the car. She took the small bag containing her overnight essentials, walked up the steps and fitted the key in the lock. Expecting the house to be cold, Carissa was pleasantly surprised when a draft of warm air greeted her entrance. She could even smell food! Had she come to the wrong house? But the key had worked, so this had to be the Townsend home.

Carissa respected Betty's judgment, but still, she'd had some reservations about agreeing to occupy a home she hadn't seen. Her hesitation had been unfounded. The house could be a fitting subject for a magazine article.

She stood in the great room facing a fireplace encased in native stone. The room's furnishings were a combination of antique tables and chests with modern cozy chairs and upholstered couches. The vaulted ceiling was supported by rectangular logs, and a grandfather clock beside the stairway chimed the hour of nine o'clock as Carissa admired the setting. A teddy bear on the fireplace ledge gave the room a homey atmosphere.

Walking toward the kitchen, Carissa stopped suddenly. The television was on, although the sound was muted. Naomi had been gone for three days, and Carissa had understood that no one had been in the house since then. She looked at the thermostat, which was set at seventy degrees. Justin had distinctly said that Naomi had lowered the temperature. Had someone been in the house since then? Was someone there now? What other explanation could there be?

Suddenly, Carissa's lodging didn't seem so enticing. Should she telephone the police chief and ask him to check out the house? But if she'd misunderstood him about the thermostat, the man would think she was foolish. And she knew several people who never turned off their televisions. She reasoned that it had been a harrying day, and she was worn down, or she wouldn't be so skittish. Carissa's body ached for a hot bath and a comfortable bed, and she got ready to settle for the night.

She locked the front door and checked the windows, finding everything secure until she reached the sliding door that accessed a deck on the rear of the house. That lock had been jimmied. She turned on an outside light. The snow on the deck and steps was undisturbed, so apparently no one had entered the house through that door, but Carissa was uneasy knowing that someone *could* come in. Maybe people in Yuletide weren't as particular about locking their doors as she'd learned to be in a city.

Still, she knew she would rest easier if she had some kind of protection against unwanted guests. Barely over five feet tall, and weighing a little less than a hundred pounds, Carissa knew her appearance wouldn't intimidate a burglar. She didn't see a gun in the house, and she didn't know anything about firearms, anyway.

After years of experience in the business world, Carissa had learned to be resourceful. She brought several pans from the kitchen and stacked them in front of the door, moved two heavy chairs to provide a barrier, and put a set of fireplace implements in front of the chairs. Spying a decorative set of sleigh bells on the wall, she hung those across the entrance. It would be impossible for anyone to enter the room without waking her. But for added security, she took a poker from the hearth and carried it upstairs to use as a weapon if she should need it.

The master suite on the second floor had been prepared for Carissa—a large, comfortable bedroom with a connecting bathroom. A glass door, covered with heavy draperies, led to a balcony, and Carissa parted the curtains and peered through the door's frosty glass. Several inches of snow covered the balcony. Justin was right—she wouldn't be drinking her morning coffee outside.

Naomi had left a note on the pillow, and the words "Welcome to my home" gave Carissa the feeling of a warm, gracious hug.

The room was cool and Carissa turned the switch on the electric blanket. While the bed warmed, she bathed. A few minutes later, bundled into a warm, ankle-length nightgown, Carissa laid the poker nearby and, sighing deeply, she stretched out in the warmth of the king-size bed. A Bible lay on the bedside table and Carissa reached for it. It had been a long time since she'd looked inside a Bible, but if she was going to be successful in her search for Christmas, she knew she'd have to start with God's word. She turned to Matthew's account of Jesus's birth and read a familiar passage aloud.

"'Now when Jesus was born in Bethlehem of Judæa in the days of Herod the king, behold, there came wise men from the east to Jerusalem, saying, "Where is He that is born King of the Jews? For we have seen His star in the East and are come to worship Him."'"

Carissa remembered enough from her childhood

teachings to know that a person found Jesus through the eyes of faith. How strong was her faith? She believed that God had been her lodestar as she'd built a successful business. And she'd tried to repay Him by contributing a great deal of money to charitable organizations. To find the Christ Child, however, she'd have to go further than that. A Scripture verse she hadn't thought of for years flashed into her mind: *"You will seek me and find me when you seek me with all your heart."*

Carissa had been hesitant about opening her heart to anyone, but she knew it was the only route to the peace found in the Savior who'd been born in Bethlehem years ago. She longed to experience the close fellowship she'd once known with God—the only thing that had sustained her through a difficult childhood. Would she find it in Yuletide?

The warm bed brought comfort to her tired body, and she thought she'd fall asleep immediately, but an hour later, she was still awake. She didn't consider herself an imaginative woman, but intermittent with the wind gusts that blew tree branches against the house, she thought she heard whisperings and muffled footsteps. Finally, she went to sleep—only to awaken suddenly.

Terror as strong as a bolt of electricity flooded her body as she struggled to a sitting position. She glanced at the illuminated dial of the clock on the bedside table. Three o'clock in the morning! What had awakened her?

Her pulse fluttered when she heard a muffled exclamation downstairs, a clatter of pans and the ringing of sleigh bells. Someone was in the house, and she knew it wasn't Santa Claus.

An intruder had stumbled over the barrier she'd placed in front of the glass door. Without waiting to put on a robe, Carissa jumped out of bed and grabbed the poker. Heart in her mouth and hands shaking, she was halfway down the stairs when the pale glow of the security light revealed a tall figure disentangling himself from her self-made booby trap. He groaned softly, and Carissa assumed he was injured.

She had left her cell phone in the car. If she went upstairs to use the phone on the bedside table, the man might follow her, and she'd be trapped. The man was between her and the kitchen phone. Her car keys were in the pocket of her coat, which she'd hung in the entryway closet. Realizing she was on her own, Carissa slipped down another few steps, just as the intruder stopped in front of her and looked upward. She swung the poker and hit him on the forehead. Carissa screamed as the man folded up like an accordion and fell backward on the floor. She'd only meant to stun him.

Jumping over his body, she sprinted to the kitchen and grabbed the wall phone. She dialed 911, and recognized Justin Townsend's voice when he answered.

"This is Carissa Whitmore at Naomi's home. A man just broke in. I'm afraid… I've killed him."

Dead silence greeted her remark for a few seconds, then Justin shouted, "Don't touch a thing! I'll be there in a few minutes."

Carrying the poker with her, Carissa rushed to her

bedroom and tied a long robe over her nightgown. The intruder was stirring by the time she returned downstairs, and she breathed easier knowing he wasn't dead. Poker in hand, she waited by the door and kept a wary eye on the trespasser until a police cruiser screeched to a halt in front of the house.

Carissa opened the door, and Justin pushed by her into the living room.

He knelt beside the fallen man and checked his pulse before he took a quick glance around the room. When his gaze encountered the furniture in front of the glass door, he looked up at Carissa.

"What's happened here?"

"I sensed that someone had been in the house when I got here. I couldn't lock that door, so I piled things around it before I went upstairs to bed. This man came in, stumbled over my booby trap and awakened me. I hit him with a poker. Is he going to die?"

His eyes twinkling, the police officer said, "Nope. It'd take more than a knock on his hard head to kill this man. Don't you know who he is?"

"How could I?"

"This is Paul Spencer, Naomi's brother."

Carissa's breath rushed from her mouth, and she dropped like a deflated balloon into the closest chair she could find.

Chapter Two

Still staring at the stranger spread-eagled on the floor, Carissa wrung her tiny hands and struggled to comprehend what Justin had said.

"I thought Naomi lived alone! Why would she exchange houses with me if her brother lives here?"

"Paul doesn't live with Naomi. He works for a construction company that bids on jobs all over the world. He hasn't been home for two years, and when he is here, he lives in the garage apartment behind the house. Naomi probably didn't know he was coming home."

Carissa stared at the tall, amazingly good-looking man, lying flat on his back. His dark skin had a weathered look, and his short brown hair, thinning a bit at the temples, had streaks of gray showing around his ears. A large blue knot had risen on his forehead.

"Oh, I'm so sorry!" Carissa said. "How can I face the man when he comes to?" Eager to justify her actions, she added, "But what would you have done if you'd thought he was a burglar?"

"Same thing you did, lady. Only I'd probably have shot him," he added with a grin, patting the holster at his right hip.

Chief Townsend called for an ambulance and said, "I'll keep him from moving until the medics get here. Don't look so scared. You had no way of knowing who he was."

When the prostrate man opened his eyes and started to sit up, Carissa dodged out of his range of vision. Townsend held him on the floor.

"Stay there, Paul. I don't want you to move until the ambulance gets here."

"What happened?" Paul said, a glassy expression in his dark eyes.

"I'll explain later. You'll be all right."

Paul closed his eyes again, and Carissa whispered, "I'll go upstairs and change. I'm going with you to the hospital."

"There's no hospital closer than Saratoga Springs, but we've got a clinic here in town. It's small, but it's a good one. The doctor there will be able to tell if he needs to go to the hospital."

The ambulance crew was working with Paul when Carissa finished dressing, and she waited until they pushed the stretcher toward the door. In her own car, she followed the ambulance into town until it stopped at a small building adjacent to the police station.

The waiting room had several people in it, and Carissa and Chief Townsend weren't able to sit side by side, which was a relief to her. She didn't feel like talking. Townsend seemed to know everyone in the room, and he told them in detail what had happened to Paul. Carissa tried to block out their amused chatter at her expense.

What if she had seriously injured the man? She knew better than to strike anyone on the forehead. Her only excuse was that she was half dazed after being awakened from a deep sleep. Carissa picked up a magazine and turned the pages slowly. She had no idea what she was seeing, for her thoughts were on the strange chain of events that had brought her to Yuletide.

For twenty years Carissa had worked relentlessly building Cara's Fashions—a line of casual clothing for tall women—into a prosperous business. She'd had no intention of selling, until the building where her corporate offices were located had to be razed for a road project. While she was searching for a new location, she was approached about selling her business.

She enjoyed her work, but the purchase price was high enough that Carissa seriously considered the sale. Considering led to selling, and within a few weeks, she was carefree for the first time in years.

When she was moving out of the office building, she uncovered an antique trunk that had been sent to her after her grandmother's death fifteen years earlier. When she'd received the trunk, Carissa had put it in storage and forgotten about it, because she didn't like to be reminded of her past. But when she saw the trunk again, curious about its contents, she opened the trunk and found keepsakes from the past—textbooks, school papers and items she'd collected in Sunday school. She'd dropped those in the trash can, but she'd looked long at a large, white, wooden key decorated with golden glitter.

She remembered when, at six years of age, she'd carried that key in a Christmas pageant. She'd worn a long white dress, and appearing on stage, she had addressed the audience: "I have the key to Christmas, and I'm looking for a lock it will fit."

A first-century false-fronted village had been constructed on the stage with homes, a stable, an inn and several other businesses. She walked from door to door trying the key without luck, but when she found a lock that the key opened, a nativity scene was revealed. The Christ Child in the manger was Christmas personified, and Carissa had stood to one side while other church members presented the story of Jesus's birth.

To close the program, Carissa had turned to the audience, saying, "I've found Jesus, the reason we have Christmas. Won't you come to the manger and find Him, too?"

Carissa had known a close relationship with Jesus as a child, and the observance of His birth had been a special time. Her grandmother couldn't afford to buy many gifts, and the church program had been the focal point of their Christmas. As the years passed, however, Christmas had gradually become commercialized for Carissa, a time when huge sales boosted her income, for Cara's Fashions were popular throughout the United States and overseas. Carissa hadn't been selfish with her income. In addition to contributing to many charities and churches, she'd provided freely for her grandmother until her death. Carissa had given generously of everything—except herself.

Her musings ended when the doctor entered the waiting room and asked for Chief Townsend. Carissa caught her breath, and cold sweat spread over her body. On trembling legs she moved down the hallway and peeped into a small room where Paul Spencer, eyes closed, lay on a hospital bed.

"He's all right," the doctor said, "and I don't see any sign of concussion, but he'll have a headache for a while. Exhaustion, more than anything else, caused him to faint." He turned to Carissa, saying with a grin, "You've got a pretty hefty swing, lady. You ever play baseball?"

Her face flushed, but Carissa tried to answer lightly. "Several years ago, I played on a women's softball team." She turned to Justin. "I'm so embarrassed about this that I've half a notion to leave without unpacking my car."

"Oh, Paul's a good sport and he won't blame you. He should have told someone he was coming."

"He could be released," the doctor said, "but he shouldn't go to sleep for a few hours. Paul hasn't slept since he left Europe, so somebody will have to keep him from dozing off. Since Naomi isn't home, he can stay in the clinic the rest of the night."

"He can come back to the chalet," Carissa said. "I'm responsible for his injury, so the least I can do is watch over him for a few hours."

"I'll go in and explain the situation. He might not want to trust himself to you," Justin said and guffawed.

The doctor joined in the laughter, but Carissa failed to see any humor in the situation.

A few minutes later, she had to force herself to meet Paul Spencer's brown eyes when he walked into the hallway.

"Carissa Whitmore meet Paul Spencer," Chief Townsend said, humor still evident in his voice. "Although it seems you've met before."

"I'm so sorry, Mr. Spencer."

He shook his head and winced. "My fault! I should have let my sister know I was coming home. Our construction job had to shut down for a few weeks and I decided to come back to the States for Christmas. I tried to call Naomi when I landed at Kennedy. When she didn't answer, I came on home. The keys to my apartment are in her house, and I intended to knock on the door to get her attention. But when I discovered the door wasn't locked, I thought I could slip in without disturbing her and sleep on the couch until morning."

"I'll drive you back to her house now," Carissa said. "The doctor thinks you need monitoring for a few hours. Since I knocked you out, I'll feel better if I keep an eye on you."

Paul agreed, and the chief of police accompanied them to the parking lot. An uncomfortable silence prevailed in the SUV as they drove through the business section of town. Carissa wasn't used to driving on snow-covered roads, so she drove as slowly and as carefully as she could. Her silent passenger gave her the fidgets.

"I'm so embarrassed I could scream," she said finally.

"I'm not embarrassed, but I am bewildered," Paul said, "and it isn't all because of the crack on my head. I've got some questions. What prompted Naomi to leave her home and business and take off for Florida, and how do you come into the picture? When I talked to my sister six weeks ago, she didn't mention anything about leaving. Justin may have explained it to me, but my head was woozy, and I don't remember what he said."

"We're almost to the house, and I'll explain when we get there, if that's okay. I'm not used to hazardous roads so I need to concentrate on driving."

"I understand that. Take your time. I haven't driven on snowy highways for years. I drove cautiously from Kennedy, and that's the reason I was so late getting into Yuletide."

When they entered the house, Carissa surveyed the disheveled living area with distaste. She'd replace the furniture and kitchen utensils later.

"Do you feel like a sandwich and maybe a cup of tea?" she offered.

"That might be a good idea. It's been a long time since I've had any food, well, except for the pretzels and soda they served on the plane."

"I'll see what I can find. I've only been here a few hours, and I haven't found my way around the kitchen yet."

Paul followed her into the kitchen and leaned against a massive wooden post supporting the upstairs balcony that overlooked the living area. The kitchen was as inviting as the great room. Light oak cabinets blended with the pine-paneled ceiling. A food-preparation island filled the center of the kitchen. A round table was arranged in a window nook and four cushioned armchairs were placed around it. Several large, curtained windows blended in with the cabinets, to make the room light and airy in warm weather.

Carissa and Naomi had agreed that they'd put enough food in their refrigerators to last for a few days, but she saw now that the shelves were practically empty. That seemed strange, for in their business association, Carissa had found Naomi to be a woman of her word. There was a carton of orange juice and a gallon of milk in the refrigerator, both of which had been opened.

"We can have juice or milk. I don't see any sandwich fixin's, but what about a sweet roll? There are two left in the package. I can warm them in the microwave."

"I'll take coffee with the roll," Paul said, yawning and lounging wearily in one of the chairs at the table. "I haven't been to bed for about thirty hours. I may have to take a cold shower, too."

"It's cold enough outside to wake you up. Maybe you can take a run around the house."

"Not unless I have to," Paul said, shivering slightly. "It'll take a while for me to get used to Adirondack weather again."

Carissa heated water for coffee before she sat beside him. She said, "You already know my name, but I'll fill in some more facts. My home is in Tampa, where

I've run a fashion design business for several years. I've never met your sister, but Townsend Textile Mill has manufactured many of my designs. Naomi and I have been in touch by phone and email since she took over running the mill."

"That was when her husband died."

Carissa nodded. "I sold my business last month, and, being at loose ends, I decided I wanted to spend Christmas in the north. I was born in Minnesota, and I kept remembering the Christmases we had when I was a kid. By coincidence, Naomi's doctor suggested that she needed a vacation. He thought relaxation for a while in a warmer climate would ease the pain of her arthritis. A mutual friend arranged for us to exchange houses."

"I'm happy that Naomi's taking some time off," Paul said. "The pain has gotten steadily worse, and the stress of taking over management of the textile mill seemed to aggravate it."

"That's what she said. We decided on short notice to make this exchange, and she probably didn't have time to let you know."

"We don't stay in contact very well. Right now, my company's working on a project in an isolated part of Eastern Europe, and I call her when I get to a city. My cell phone doesn't work at our present location."

Paul's eyes were glazed from lack of sleep, and when his head drooped, Carissa knew she had to keep him talking. "What kind of work do you do?"

"I've been with the same construction company for eighteen years. I worked for them part-time in the

States while I finished college, but since then I've been working overseas. Right now, we're building an electric power plant in the Czech Republic."

"How often do you come home?"

"This is the fourth or fifth time I've been home since I left Yuletide about twenty years ago. I had an unpleasant experience here, and coming home reminds me of it, so I don't visit very often."

He stifled a yawn. Carissa stirred a heaping tablespoon of coffee crystals into a mug of boiled water and handed it to him. He took several sips of the coffee before he continued.

"Last week, we had some equipment failure that will take a month to fix, so the boss told most of us to take a vacation. I usually spend my free time sightseeing in Europe and western Asia, but since it was Christmas, I had a hankering to be with family. Naomi is the only family I have. I'll have to go to Florida to see her, I reckon—I'll be returning to Europe sometime between Christmas and the new year."

"I have a two-bedroom condo, so there's plenty of room for you. I'm sure she'll be happy to see you."

"And I want to see her," Paul agreed. "I had looked forward to spending my vacation in snow country, but I've never been to Florida, so this sounds like a great opportunity."

"There's a good view of Tampa Bay from my balcony, and the beach isn't far away."

"You've convinced me," he said, laughing. "But I'll rest up a few days before I make any plans."

* * *

It was daylight by the time they finished eating, and Carissa exclaimed in delight as she viewed the frozen lake from the kitchen window.

"I was disappointed last night when I arrived in Yuletide," she said, "because it didn't have the Christmas atmosphere I had expected, but this area looks like the winters I used to know. There are lots of lakes in Minnesota, although we don't have mountains."

While Paul showered and shaved, Carissa moved the furniture back into place and put the pots and pans she'd scattered on the floor in the dishwasher. She surveyed the room to be sure it looked as it had when she'd arrived. Something seemed to be missing, but she didn't know what until she realized that the stuffed bear she'd seen on the fireplace ledge wasn't there. She knew she hadn't moved it.

Paul returned at that time looking refreshed and more handsome than ever, in spite of his black eye and the bruise on his forehead.

"Did you move a teddy bear off the fireplace ledge?" Carissa asked.

"No," he said, adding with a mischievous smile, "I stopped playing with toys a long time ago."

"Surely at forty-five, I'm not having a 'senior' moment—as some of my friends say. But I know when I arrived last night there was a stuffed bear lying on the hearth. It isn't there now."

"Maybe Justin or the medics moved it out of the way when they came for me."

"Maybe. But I had the strangest feeling that someone had been in the house before I arrived. That's why I barricaded the door last night. The house was warm, although Justin told me that Naomi had lowered the thermostat before she left."

"Maybe Naomi was having a senior moment, too, and forgot to lower the temperature." He looked out the back door. "I'm going over to check my apartment and put my rental truck in the garage."

Still brooding over possible intruders, Carissa walked to the wide glass door and stood beside Paul. Behind the house was a three-car garage with an apartment on the floor above it.

"We inherited this property from our parents," Paul explained. "When Naomi and her husband decided to build the chalet, I built the garage and apartment. I'm never in the States more than two months at a time, but when I'm here, I want my own place to stay in."

"It's a nice place."

"Good enough for what I need," he agreed. "Want to go with me and check it out?"

"Sure. I'm still your overseer for a few hours."

She grinned pertly at him, and Paul thought how fetching she looked. Carissa had intense blue eyes fringed by dark lashes, and a spray of freckles across her nose, which only added to the beauty of her delicate oval face. Carissa seemed young and untouched. Paul found it hard to believe that she was forty-five.

"I'll put on my boots and coat," Carissa said, wondering at the speculative gleam in her companion's eyes.

His apartment consisted of a large living room and

kitchen combination with a spacious bathroom and bedroom in the rear. The absence of nonessential decorations proclaimed the apartment a man's. Carissa wondered at his age, judging that he was several years younger than she was. He'd said Naomi was his only family—but had trouble with a woman been the unpleasant experience that had caused him to leave Yuletide?

The apartment was chilly, and Carissa insisted that Paul go back to the house with her. "It'll be several hours before the apartment gets comfortable. By that time, you'll be ready to take a long nap."

"Thanks, I'll do that. But I wanted to point out the intercom system between my apartment and the house." He pointed to a speaker on the living room wall. "Just flip the switch and call if you need me. The one in the house is on the wall between the kitchen and the living room."

He yawned, and Carissa said, "Let's take a walk before we go back to the house. If you sit down, you're going to sleep."

"A good idea, but I'll need some warmer clothes, and I hardly remember what I have. I haven't been home during the winter for a long time." Paul shoved clothing back and forth in the bedroom closet until he found a heavy coat with a hood that still fit him. He changed his light boots for insulated ones.

Sunshine glistened on the newly fallen snow as Paul and Carissa crossed the road and took the path around the lake. White-throated sparrows and Acadian chickadees darted into the trees, dislodging tufts of snow that settled on Paul's and Carissa's shoulders. They observed the ungainly flight of a pileated woodpecker, its red crest conspicuous in the sunlight. Small huts dotted the surface of the frozen lake, now covered with several inches of fresh snow.

"There's a lot of ice fishing on this lake," Paul commented. "The huts are rented to fishermen for protection from the wind while they wait for a bite."

"There's ice fishing on the lakes in Minnesota, too."

"I wonder if the lake is frozen enough for skating," he said. "I learned to skate on Lake Mohawk. We used to have skating parties almost every night. I've kept up with skating as much as possible. Many Christmas holidays I've spent time in Germany, Austria or Switzerland so I could skate." He stepped out on the surface of the lake. "Seems pretty solid. Do you skate?"

"Not since I was a child. Skating isn't a Florida pastime."

Their footsteps crunched rhythmically on the frozen snow as they walked. "Why did you leave Minnesota and move to Florida? Did your family transfer?" he asked.

A somber expression quickly erased Carissa's happy mood, but she answered readily enough. "I moved there by myself, soon after I graduated from high school. I never returned to Minnesota."

Believing he'd touched on a sensitive subject, Paul didn't question her further.

Carissa's animation returned moments later when she said, "This is the first time I've seen snow for years. It's glorious." She picked up a handful and ate it. "Grandma used to make ice cream out of snow. I'll make some if I can remember how."

"Most of my visits back home have been in the summer," he said, "and I've missed New York's winters while I've been away. There were fabulous Christmas celebrations in Yuletide when we were children—lights all over the business section and most of the houses were decorated. Prizes were given for the most original ideas. We sometimes built snow palaces on the frozen lake and had them floodlighted. We had programs at the church—just a wonderful time."

"Why did they stop? I came to Yuletide thinking I'd find Christmas the way it was when I was a child. I was really disappointed when I drove in last night and didn't see any sign of Christmas."

Paul yawned. "Carissa, surely I've stayed awake long enough. I'll tell you about the tragedy that took Christmas out of Yuletide, but not until after I sleep."

Carissa was a bit surprised that they'd slipped so easily to a first-name basis, but that pleased her. Mischievously, she picked up a handful of snow and, standing on tiptoes, she rubbed it in his face.

"That oughta keep you awake 'til we get back to the house."

"Hey!" he spluttered, wiping the snow from his face with his mittened hand. "I'm an invalid and you're supposed to be kind to me." He scooped up some snow and threw it at Carissa, but she sidestepped the attack and started toward the house on a run. Paul's long-legged stride soon caught up with her.

"I'll get even with you," he warned, a gleam in his

brown eyes that belied his words. "I expected to be welcomed home as an honored guest, and what happens? I'm assaulted the minute I step into the house, and then I get my face washed with snow."

Laughing, Carissa said, "I'll make it up to you. While you take a nap, I'll fix a meal for you."

"Sounds good to me, just as long as I find a bed before I fall asleep on my feet."

While Paul slept in the downstairs bedroom adjacent to the great room, as silently as she could, Carissa unloaded the SUV and carried her luggage upstairs. Periodically, she'd crack open the bedroom door, and each time, Paul's even breathing assured her that he was resting comfortably.

She would have to wake Paul before too long because the doctor wanted to look him over again. She organized her belongings in the master bedroom, then sat on a padded window seat looking over the frozen landscape. Her thoughts were on Paul Spencer.

He seemed like a friendly, easygoing guy, possessing a spontaneous cheerfulness that answered a need in Carissa's heart. She'd never considered herself a joyful person, but when Paul's mouth spread into a toothy smile that lightened the darkness of his face, Carissa felt lighthearted, and laughter bubbled from her lips.

Having a man in the house was a strange experience for Carissa. She'd never known who her father was, and her grandmother had been widowed before Carissa was born. She'd lived alone for more than twenty years, and it seemed odd to have a man sleeping in her house. She had grown accustomed to solitude, but already she knew she'd miss Paul a little when he moved into his apartment.

Carissa had come to Yuletide to discover the faith she'd known as a child, and she was determined to achieve that goal. It had taken a long time, but Carissa finally believed that she could do whatever she set out to do.

Yet she'd never reacted to anyone as she was reacting to Paul Spencer. Her attraction to him confused her.

She found his nearness disturbing and at the same time exciting.

Chapter Three

Carissa retrieved the Christmas pageant key from her luggage and carried it downstairs. She placed it on the coffee table. Confronted by Paul's presence, she needed a constant reminder of why she was in Yuletide.

Paul was still sleeping at one o'clock, so Carissa tapped on the bedroom door. He didn't respond, so she knocked more loudly.

"Uh-uh," he said sleepily. "What is it?"

"You have to see the doctor at three o'clock. It's time to get up."

Silence greeted her. Had he gone back to sleep? She knocked once more.

"I'm sorry," Paul said. "It's taken me a few minutes to realize where I am. You're the lady who's taken over sis's home, huh?"

"Yes, the one who attacked you with a poker last night."

"Do you have the poker now?"

She imagined his white teeth showing in a slight

smile. With laughter in her voice, she said, "Not yet, but I may have to get it if you don't hurry."

He yawned noisily, and she heard his feet land on the floor.

"Be out in a minute."

Carissa was standing at the back door appreciating the landscape, when the bedroom door opened behind her.

She turned, stifled a gasp and experienced a giddy sensation as if her heart had flipped over. Paul had the broad-shouldered body of an athlete, but his waist and hips were narrow. Wearing a T-shirt and jeans, he leaned against the door, looking as vulnerable as a child. His eyes were still heavy with sleep and his hair was tousled. He yawned again.

Had she been wrong when she'd made up her mind that she could live a happy, fulfilled life without a husband? Was she old enough now that the pitfalls she'd avoided in her youth would no longer tempt her? Was it possible to disprove the opinions of her childhood neighbors, who'd often said "Like mother, like daughter"?

Deep in her own thoughts and conflicting emotions, Carissa started when Paul said, "It won't take me long to get ready. I'll bring in some fresh clothes from the car."

She winced when she noticed that the bruise had spread until both eyes and part of his cheek were black.

Intercepting her glance, he said, "I could pass for a raccoon this morning, don't you think?"

Blood rushed to her cheeks, and she covered her

face with her hands. "Don't remind me. Does your head hurt?"

He lifted his hand to his forehead. "No, but it's sure sore to the touch. I don't dare turn my head quickly."

Dropping her hands, Carissa said, "I'll get your luggage."

He started to shake his head, thought better of it and said, "Thanks, but I need a jolt of Adirondack air to help me wake up."

"I made some lunch so we can eat before we go. There isn't much food in the refrigerator, but I'll stop at a grocery store after we've been to the clinic."

"I'll need to buy a few groceries, too, though I'll probably eat out most of the time. When I'm home for such a short time, I don't want to store up any food."

Carissa was tempted to suggest that they could share their meals, but she hesitated. At her age, this was no time to become involved with a man. After all, she didn't know anything about Paul Spencer. She wouldn't become chummy with this stranger.

Why, then, did her heart insist that Paul wasn't a stranger?

Carissa sat in the waiting room, and when Paul came from the doctor's office with a smile on his face, she felt a great wave of relief.

"There's no damage except a sore head for a few days. I can live with that," he said.

"I don't know that I can," Carissa said. "I'll probably have nightmares for years about you collapsing at my feet. I thought I'd killed you."

"I'm glad you didn't," he said. He laid his hand on her shoulder.

Carissa flinched and moved away, and his hand dropped limply to his side. Paul stared at her, slightly embarrassed, a confused expression on his face. He must be wondering why she would be offended at such an innocent gesture.

Carissa knew that Paul only meant to be friendly, but she wasn't used to casual touching. She'd denied any natural tendencies toward overtures of friendship for so long that she had a complex about being touched. Several years into her career, she'd finally conquered her phobia enough to shake hands with her customers, but she apparently hadn't overcome all of her hang-ups.

Being friendly and outgoing had contributed to her mother's undoing. She could do nothing about looking like her mother, but long ago Carissa had determined that she wouldn't emulate her mother's personality and lifestyle. Her mother's vivacious personality had gotten her involved with the wrong people and sent her down the path to prostitution and, ultimately, premature death.

Embarrassed that she'd allowed a phobia from the past to make her reject Paul's overture of friendship, Carissa lifted a flushed face to him. Her blue eyes mirrored her anxiety. Her voice was strained when she said, "I'm glad, too, that I didn't injure you," and she added in her thoughts, *for several reasons.*

Paul wondered at the anxiety revealed in Carissa's eyes. She was a successful businesswoman…but had he detected a flaw underneath the facade that she presented to the world? At this moment, she seemed like a bewildered little girl unable to understand what had happened to her. For several years, Paul had made it a point to tend to his own business and keep aloof from the problems of others. Now, for some inexplicable reason, he longed to remove that confused, lonely expression from her face. Before the next few weeks passed, he would no doubt learn if it was in his power to do so.

As Paul moved his belongings into the apartment, he kept thinking of Carissa. When Jennifer had jilted him, he'd made up his mind he was through with women. He'd deliberately chosen a job that would keep him out of the United States. He hadn't been tempted to seek the companionship of women in the countries where he'd worked, and, most of the time, he was content with his bachelorhood.

Occasionally, Paul wondered if he was missing anything by not having a family. If he didn't have any children, who would carry on the Spencer name and family traditions? He often questioned what would become of the money he'd accumulated, if anything happened to him—for his sister didn't have any children, either. And what could Naomi do with the fortune she'd inherited from her husband? It was only in the past year, since his fortieth birthday, that Paul had become concerned about this issue.

Carissa was an attractive woman, and he smiled when he thought of her embarrassment over hitting him on the head. But, personally, he thought it took a lot of courage to attack a man with no better weapon than a poker. Paul admired courage in anyone.

She was a little woman—her head didn't even reach his shoulders—but at times she displayed a dignity that belied her short stature. And Paul had detected a lot of warmth and vitality waiting for release beneath that dignity.

He sensed that Carissa didn't think she was beautiful, but beauty was in the eye of the beholder. After the way Jennifer, who was tall and shapely with black hair and vivid green eyes, had treated him, Paul had decided that he'd never choose another companion based on outward appearance.

From what he'd seen of Carissa, he believed her beauty was more than skin deep.

Paul saw his sister so rarely that he was disappointed to learn that Naomi had gone to Florida. He'd called from Kennedy Airport to have his home phone connected, so he asked Carissa for the telephone number of her condo so he could call his sister. He tried three times before he finally found her at home. She couldn't believe he was actually in New York.

"Why didn't you tell me you were coming home?" Naomi cried in dismay. "I would have stayed in New York. But you can come here," she added. "The weather is wonderful. I go to the beach every day for several hours, and I'm feeling better already. I've even decreased my pain medicine."

"I'm glad to hear that, sis. I'll come down for a few

days before I go back to my job." The logical thing for him to do was to go to Tampa immediately, but as strange as it might seem to him, he wanted to see more of Carissa.

"I'd come home," Naomi continued, "but I can't because I've loaned the house to Carissa for two months. Have you met her?"

"Well, yes, we had an…unusual meeting."

He explained how they'd met, and Naomi laughed merrily before she said, "I can't imagine what happened to the door. I'm sure it was locked when I left home. Will you have it fixed?"

"Yes, I intend to."

"How do you like Carissa?"

"She's okay," Paul said nonchalantly. Naomi's ultimate goal was to see her brother married and settled down in the United States. He didn't want his sister to read anything into his meeting with Carissa. "She was embarrassed at first about hitting me, but we laugh about it now."

"Carissa is a very successful businesswoman. She sold her company for a bundle a few months ago. I've been told that the sale netted over a million dollars. And you should see this luxurious apartment!"

Paul thought he'd accumulated quite a lot of money, but he certainly wasn't in Carissa's league. His attraction to Carissa had reached its first barrier. He wouldn't fix his interest on a woman who was worth more financially than he was. But in spite of his reservations, after he'd finished his dinner, Paul kept searching for an excuse to see Carissa again that evening.

* * *

As she often did at home, Carissa prepared a taco salad, sat in front of the television and watched the evening news while she ate. Before she'd sold her company, her days had been so busy with business matters that she didn't have much of a social life. It was usually a relief to escape into her apartment at night and let the walls close around her. Her only relaxation was at the health club in the basement of the condo complex. She'd made some good friends there, and she missed them tonight.

She'd gotten a sack of Red Delicious apples at the grocery store, and while she munched on one for dessert, she reflected on her day with Paul. This time yesterday she'd never heard of the man, but they'd gotten acquainted in a hurry. Had the time come for her to seek the male companionship she'd previously avoided? Now that she'd reached the mellow years, the hang-ups she'd had about dating shouldn't be a problem. It was rather astonishing that she was even thinking about the subject, and most surprising was that she hadn't had such thoughts until she met Paul Spencer.

"Hey, neighbor!"

The loud voice startled Carissa so much that she dropped the apple core on the floor. It took a moment for her to realize that Paul was calling on the intercom.

"Hey, neighbor!" The call came again before she remembered where the speaker was.

Smiling, she picked up the apple core, hurried into the kitchen and answered Paul.

"Hey, yourself."

"I wanted to see if this thing still works. What are you doing?"

"Finishing dinner."

"I promised to tell you why Yuletide is no longer a Christmas town. If you have time, I'll come over and fill you in."

"Great! I'd like some company."

Humming a Christmas song that she'd just heard on the television, Carissa rinsed the dishes she'd used for supper and put them in the dishwasher. She prepared a bowl of grapes, cheese cubes and crackers and placed the food on a table between two large lounge chairs in the living room. She poured a jar of fruit punch over ice and was placing it on the table when Paul knocked on the back door. She motioned him inside.

"Brr!" he said, taking off his coat and laying it on the back of the couch. "The temperature is dropping quickly. If it wasn't already, the lake should be frozen enough that I can go ice fishing tomorrow. If I make a nice catch, I'll invite you to have dinner with me in my apartment."

"Can you cook?" Carissa asked as she motioned him to one of the chairs. It seemed rather odd to be acting as hostess to Paul in his sister's house.

"I'm a fair cook," he said. "I've prepared dinners many times for some of my co-workers. But I'm not such a good fisherman, though, so don't whet your appetite for a fish fry until you see the fish."

"Help yourself to the snacks," Carissa invited. "I'll take you up on the invitation. I'm *not* a good cook— I just make what satisfies my appetite, and that's not always what others like to eat. I never cook a meal for anyone. If I have guests, I take them to a restaurant for dinner."

"Since I kept you up most of last night, I hesitated to barge in on you—you'd probably like to go to bed early. I'm sleepy, too, but I want to adjust to Eastern Standard Time, so I'm forcing myself to stay up."

"Good idea. I haven't done much overseas travel, but it usually takes a week for me to get over jet lag."

Paul poured a glass of fruit juice and sipped it as he talked. "As I told you earlier, when I was a kid, Yuletide was just like a fairyland during the Christmas season. But a tragedy one Christmas Eve changed all of that."

He paused, stretched out his long legs and continued. "That night, a woman and her baby came to town asking for shelter. She went to several businesses and private homes, as well as the police station, but everybody was too busy to help. The people didn't mean to be callous, but they just expected the next person to take care of her. No one did, and on Christmas morning the woman and child were found dead, huddled in the entrance to Bethel Church."

"Oh, how terrible!" Carissa said feelingly, and memories of her own neglected childhood surfaced.

"The woman had fled from an abusive husband, and she died from complications of an unattended childbirth. The temperature went to zero that night and the baby died from exposure."

What a tragedy! Carissa could understand the reason the citizens of Yuletide hesitated to celebrate Christmas.

"The strange part of it was that the church was presenting a program that night based on an old legend of how Jesus had appeared disguised in a town one Christmas Eve. Disguised as a child, a poor woman and a beggar, He went from person to person asking for help, but everyone was busy preparing to celebrate the coming of the Christ Child, and they turned these people away."

"I'm familiar with the story. The townspeople eventually learned that if they'd helped those who came to them, they would have received Jesus, too. So the citizens of Yuletide felt that in refusing to help the mother and child, it was as if they'd refused, like those people or the biblical innkeeper, to shelter the baby Jesus?"

Paul nodded and lifted a hand to rub his forehead. Although he hid his discomfort well, obviously he was in pain.

"No one could generate any enthusiasm for a big celebration after that. Although I consider it superstition, the general feeling seems to be that when God has forgiven the people of Yuletide for neglecting those two people, He'll give them an opportunity to redeem themselves."

"Wouldn't it be wonderful if this is the year?" Carissa said. "I came to Yuletide looking for the Christmas spirit I had as a child."

"What made you start looking at this time?"

"I sold my clothing design business a few months ago, and when I was cleaning out the office and storage room, I found a trunk that my grandmother had left to me. My uncle had shipped it to me after her death.

There wasn't anything valuable in it—mostly memorabilia that I'd kept since my school years. I trashed most of the things, but I kept this—"

She picked up the white key, and Paul thought Carissa had forgotten his presence as her mind took her quickly down memory lane.

"When I was about six, I participated in a program at our church, and I carried this Key to Christmas. I went from place to place trying to fit the key into a lock, and when I finally found a door the key would open, a nativity scene was revealed. When I came across this key a month ago, I realized how far I'd strayed from the teachings I'd learned as a child. I knew then that I had to find a wintery place to relive the Christmases of my childhood. I didn't want to return to Minnesota because it doesn't hold pleasant memories for me. Besides, all of my close relatives have died. It seemed like a coincidence that Naomi wanted to change locations at the same time I did."

"As far as that's concerned, I need to be reminded of what Christmas really means, too. Carissa, I hope you *can* revive the meaning of Christmas that you once knew. Maybe we can find it together."

Their eyes met and held for a minute before Carissa looked away, too confused to even answer. She swirled the liquid in her glass, thinking that she was acting like a child.

"I guess it's time for me to go," Paul said. "I'm getting sleepy now. And you must be tired, too, unless you slept while I was napping earlier."

She shook her head. "No, I didn't sleep. I unloaded the car and settled in. Thanks for coming over tonight."

She held out her hand to him, and, unsuccessfully stifling his amazement, he tenderly clasped her hand in his.

Without meeting his gaze, she said, "Your gesture in the doctor's office took me by surprise, or I wouldn't have reacted so foolishly."

"It was just a friendly gesture," he assured her.

"I know. A foolish quirk of mine caused my reaction. I'll tell you about it someday. And I hope we can become friends." With a warm grin, she added, "It's always a good idea to make friends with your next-door neighbor."

Carissa fell asleep easily, not even worrying about the unlocked back door; she felt protected with Paul nearby. But she woke up suddenly, about the same time she'd awakened when Paul had entered the house the night before.

She'd heard something. Carissa sat up in bed to listen. The sound seemed to come from the kitchen, and she eased out of bed, wishing she'd kept the poker upstairs. Vowing that she would secure the back door before another night, Carissa ran quickly and silently downstairs.

When she reached the last step, she said, "Who's there?"

She heard a gasp and a scurry of feet.

Too frightened to be careful, Carissa snapped on the lights and rushed into the kitchen, just in time to see the pantry door close. She pushed a table in front of that door.

Standing beside the intercom, she shouted, "Paul! Paul! I need help."

Although it seemed like hours, it probably wasn't more than a minute before she heard Paul's muffled tone. Poor man! She thought, somewhat humorously, that she'd ruined another night's rest for him.

"What's wrong?"

"Somebody is in the house. Come help me."

"I'll come right away. Be careful!"

She took a knife from a cabinet drawer for protection if the intruder should break out of the pantry.

Paul rushed in the door, dressed only in pajamas and slippers, rumpled hair hanging over his agitated brown eyes.

"In the pantry," Carissa stammered.

Without asking questions, Paul motioned. "Get behind me."

He pushed the table away and swung open the door, his body hunched forward, ready to attack if necessary.

"Come out!" Paul commanded.

Nothing could be heard for moments except Paul's heavy breathing. Then there was a scuffling of feet, and Carissa stared, slack-jawed, disbelief in her eyes. Beyond words, she lowered the knife.

A teenage boy sauntered out of the pantry, followed by a little girl who held one of the red apples that Carissa had stored in the pantry. Another girl, probably eight or ten years old, peered around them, holding in her arms the teddy bear that Carissa had seen beside the fireplace the night she'd arrived.

The knife slipped from Carissa's hand and clattered to the floor. She pulled out a chair from the table and slowly lowered herself into it to support her shaking legs.

"Any more where you came from?" Paul asked, peering into the pantry.

The boy shook his head. The smallest girl handed the apple to Paul; the other child started crying.

Carissa's body trembled and a wave of nausea seized her. She dropped her head into her hands. She'd come to Yuletide looking for solitude so that she could experience a renewal of mind and spirit. She hadn't had a minute of peace since she arrived. Within twenty-four hours, four people had invaded her house.

What had given her the foolish idea to look for Christmas in Yuletide?

Chapter Four

The children bore a marked resemblance to each other, so they were obviously siblings. Of slight stature and build, the children had light brown hair and dark brown eyes. The oldest girl wore glasses, and the boy had a blue cap on his head. The smallest child sidled close to the teenage boy, and he put his arm around her.

Speechless, Carissa stared at the three children.

Paul recovered his composure more quickly than she did, and he asked, "What are you kids doing here?"

The smallest child looked at Paul fearlessly, but the boy dropped his head.

"Tell me," Paul insisted. "Who are you and what are you doing here?"

Carissa noticed that the children were shaking, and she doubted it was all from fear.

The older girl's sobs sounded as loud as thunder, and they reached a soft spot in Carissa's heart. "Just a minute, Paul," she said.

The children seemed malnourished, and the sorrow

in their eyes was unmistakable. Their clothes were worn out, and not very clean. She moved to the sobbing girl and knelt beside her.

"Are you hungry?"

Without looking up, the girl nodded. Paul and Carissa exchanged looks of compassion. Suddenly, Carissa realized why there had been so little food in the refrigerator when she arrived. These kids had broken into the house and had been living off the food Naomi had left. Carissa's arrival had probably kept them from getting any food for the past two days.

She knew that the sensible thing to do was to call the police, but Carissa suddenly remembered her own impoverished childhood. She couldn't turn these children away until she learned what circumstances had brought them here.

"Then you sit at the table, and we'll fix something for you to eat. Paul, if you'll warm milk for hot chocolate, I'll make sandwiches."

The children scuttled toward the table.

"That's my chair, Lauren," the smallest child said, and preempted the chair the older girl had started to take.

Paul and Carissa exchanged amused glances. As he opened the refrigerator door, Paul said in an undertone, "Apparently, they've eaten here before."

"Seems like it," Carissa agreed. She lifted a package of lunch meat, mayonnaise and a loaf of bread from one of the shelves. "What are we going to do with them?" she whispered.

Paul shrugged his broad shoulders. "Feed 'em."

While the milk heated, Paul set out three mugs. Carissa made several sandwiches, cut them into quarters, and arranged them on a plate that she set before the children.

"Go ahead and eat," she said. "The hot chocolate will be ready in a minute."

She looked for a package of cookies she'd bought earlier in the day. If the children hadn't eaten much, she didn't want them to founder, so she put six cookies on a tray and took the package back to the pantry.

Paul noticed the moisture that glistened in Carissa's eyes while she watched the hungry children gobble their food. The children were still shaking, and Paul, thinking it might be from cold as well as hunger, said, "I'll raise the temperature on the furnace."

Carissa turned to put the sandwich fixings back in the refrigerator. As she worked with her back toward the children, she prayed silently. *God, here's a problem I don't know to handle. Who are these children? What should I do with them?*

Remembering the legend she and Paul had discussed a few hours earlier, she continued talking to God. *Is this situation like the one that confronted the people of Yuletide several years ago? Has your Son come tonight personified in these children? Should I treat them the same way I'd treat Jesus if He came to my house?*

Recalling her early biblical training, Carissa thought of the verse "I was hungry and you gave me something to eat...whatever you did for one of the least of these... you did for me."

Was this a spiritual test? She'd come to Yuletide

to find Christmas. Would she relive the birth of Jesus through these children?

Aware that Paul was motioning her toward the living room, Carissa went to him, and he said quietly, "What do you want to do?"

"There may be a search going on for these kids. We should call the police, but…" Carissa hesitated. "I think I'd rather hear their story first."

"That's my gut feeling, too. They've apparently been living in this house for several days. Another hour won't hurt anything."

Paul had started the coffeemaker earlier, and when he and Carissa went back into the kitchen, he replenished the chocolate in the children's cups and poured a cup of coffee for Carissa and himself. Paul pulled out the other chair for Carissa at the table, and brought another chair from the living room. He sat where he could face the children.

Watching Paul warily, the boy nibbled on a cookie.

"All right," Paul said sternly. "Let's have it. Who are you? What are you doing here? And why shouldn't we turn you over to the police?"

The smallest girl started to speak, and the boy put his hand over her mouth.

"I'll do the talking," he said.

"My name's Alex. These are my sisters, Lauren and Julie. Lauren's eight, Julie's six."

"And your age?" Carissa asked.

"Fourteen."

"That's all right for a start," Paul said. "What's your last name?"

Alex shook his head.

"Does that mean you don't have a last name or you won't tell me?"

"I *can't* tell you."

"Where's your home?"

The boy shook his head again, a stubborn set to his features.

Paul laid his hand on Alex's shoulder. "It's obvious you kids are in trouble. You'd better tell me what's going on. If possible, I'll help you, but if you've run away from home, your parents must be notified."

"We ain't got no parents," Julie said.

"No home, either," her sister said, and started crying again.

Turning on his sisters, Alex said angrily, "I told you I'd do the talking."

"You're doing fine, girls. Go ahead and talk," Carissa said.

"Our mommy died," Julie said, and she slipped out of her chair and crawled up on Paul's lap.

With a helpless look at Carissa, he put his arm around the girl when she cuddled against him.

"You've got a half hour, Alex, before I call the police," Paul said.

"I ain't tellin' you our name or where we lived. Nobody wants to find us, anyway."

He looked belligerently at Paul, who stared at him until Alex dropped his head. After a slight hesitation, the boy continued. "Our mother has been real sick for two years. Something was wrong with her heart. We took care of her the best we could, and the neighbors helped, too. But she died, anyway, about two months ago."

"Where's your father?" Carissa asked.

Alex shook his head.

"Is he living?" she persisted.

"We don't know. He left when Julie was just a baby. We ain't seen him since. I don't think he's dead, though. Every so often, we'd get some money that we figgered he'd sent. No word from him since Mom got sick, so he might be dead, for all we know."

Paul's arm tightened around Julie, and he looked at Carissa, whose face was white and drawn. Lauren was still crying, her head on the table. Carissa moved closer and put her hand on the girl's trembling shoulder. She looked as if she was ready to start crying, too.

The misfortune of these children had reminded Carissa of how bereft she had been when her own mother died. If her grandmother hadn't taken her in, where would she be today?

"Surely you have some other relatives who will take care of you until your father can be found," she said around the knot in her throat.

"Just aunts and uncles. None of them wanted to take three kids, so they planned that we'd all go to separate homes in different states," Alex said. "We'd never have been together again. Mom wouldn't have wanted that. Nobody could agree on who was gonna take us, so we stayed in our home until the rent was due. The preacher and his wife kinda looked after us."

Lauren lifted her head. "We didn't want to be parted. So we run away."

Julie had relaxed in his arms, and Paul realized that she'd gone to sleep. "We'd better have the whole story before we decide what to do with you," he said. "Alex, you can't go on like this."

"We've been traveling from place to place on buses for two weeks, sleeping in bus stations, but when we got to Yuletide, we didn't have much money left. I was in the grocery store in Yuletide and heard your sister say she was leaving for Florida for two months. I found out where she lived, and thought we could stay here for a little while. I didn't know anyone was going to be living here."

"Obviously you've been eating food from the kitchen, but where have you been staying?" Carissa asked. "Last night I was sure there was someone in the house, but where have you been in the daytime?"

"In the furnace room. We took some blankets from the bedroom and fixed our beds. It was warm down there, and nobody could see the lights at night. We stayed on this floor during the daytime."

"I can't understand why you thought you could get away with this," Paul said. "Where'd you get the money to ride on buses?"

"Our neighbors collected some money for us to use until we could find a home."

"This is incredible!" Carissa said. "I'd think there would be a nationwide hunt for you."

"Maybe nobody knows we're gone," Alex said, a crafty gleam in his brown eyes.

"What does that mean?" Paul said severely.

"Alex wrote notes to our aunts and uncles so each

would think we were with another one. He left a note
for the preacher that we'd gone to visit with our uncle
in—" Lauren broke off the sentence when Alex shook
his head at her.

"Alex, what kind of kid are you, anyway? You lied
to your family, you jimmied the lock and came into
my sister's house, and you've been stealing food from
her kitchen. I know you're young, but can't you comprehend how much trouble that's going to cause you?"

Alex straightened in his chair, an indignant expression
in his brown eyes. He pulled a piece of paper from his
pocket. "I didn't steal nuthin'. I kept track of all the food
we took," he said, adding, "so I can pay it back someday."

He handed the paper to Paul, whose throat constricted when he read the daily entries: "three glasses
of milk, three sweet rolls, three sandwiches."

Paul passed the paper to Carissa.

"I was only trying to look after my sisters. What
would you have done if it had been you?" Alex asked
Paul directly.

"I don't know," Paul admitted, looking toward Carissa.

"Shall we all go back to bed and decide what to do
in the morning?" Paul asked. "Aren't there twin beds
upstairs?"

"Yes."

"Then let's put the girls in that room." He paused
thoughtfully. "My brother-in-law had a game room
in the basement. I'll check that out to see if Alex can
sleep there. But first I'll carry Julie upstairs. She's already asleep."

Cradling the child in his arms, Paul headed toward the stairs. "I'll be back in a minute," he said to Carissa.

When Paul came downstairs, he said, "Alex, let's get you fixed up for the night."

Taking Lauren's hand, Carissa climbed the stairs. Julie was lying on the bed, so Carissa didn't bother with nightclothes, if the children even had any. She removed the girls' shoes and covered them with a warm blanket in the twin beds that were ready. Impulsively, Carissa leaned over and kissed both girls on the forehead before she went downstairs.

Carissa paced the floor and waited for Paul. The few hours she'd spent in the house had been so hectic that Carissa didn't even know that there was a basement. When Paul returned, he entered the room from a door to the left of the fireplace that she'd assumed led to a closet.

"Well, what did you do with him?"

"I found just the place for him," Paul said. "After my brother-in-law died, Naomi closed up his game room, saying she couldn't go to the room alone. I knew where the key was, so I put Alex there. In addition to a pool table, there's a sleeper sofa. Alex tumbled into bed as soon as I spread out some sheets. I think he was asleep before I left the room. It smells a little musty, but it's warm. Now what do we need to do?"

They eyed each other for a few moments until Carissa said, "Pinch me, so I'll know if I'm dreaming. Is this really happening?"

Paul moved closer and pinched her gently on the arm, and she didn't mind his touch at all.

"Unfortunately, you're awake. And we have a problem on our hands."

"You're telling me! Three problems, actually. Should we telephone the chief of police now?"

"Probably we should, because we could be legally liable for not reporting the kids." Paul glanced at the mantel clock. "But it's four o'clock in the morning. I don't think it will hurt to wait 'til daylight. Justin probably couldn't do anything tonight."

"I feel so sorry for them. I hate to turn them over to the police—but what else can we do?"

"Let's decide later." Uncertainty crept into his expression. "Even if they're only children, we don't know what danger they pose, so I don't want to leave you alone. It wouldn't surprise me if Alex tries to sneak out of the house tonight and take the girls with him. That's the reason I separated them. Will it be all right if I sleep in Naomi's room tonight? I'll leave the door open so I can hear Alex if he tries to leave. Poor kid. He's probably been taking care of his sisters for months."

"Please do stay here. I doubt I'll sleep, anyway, but I know I won't if I'm here alone with our self-invited guests."

Carissa's feet seemed as heavy as lead as she went to her room. So much had happened in the two nights she'd spent in Yuletide that her former life as a businesswoman in Florida might never have happened. When she'd taken the road to Yuletide, she'd felt like a woman on a mission—a pilgrim taking a nostalgic journey into the past. But she couldn't reconcile her reason for coming north with all the things that had happened. Thirty-six hours ago she had never heard of Paul Spencer or these children, yet in a short time they'd affected her life so much that she wondered to what extent they would have an impact on her future.

Carissa hadn't expected to sleep, and she didn't. Her thoughts were filled with things that she'd successfully pushed from her consciousness years ago. In her mind's eye, she was back in Minnesota, the weather similar to what she'd experienced today. She sat in a bleak upstairs bedroom, wrapped in a blanket, hovering over her mother's dying body. Only six years old at the time, she didn't know that her mother was a prostitute dying from a drug overdose. She only knew that she was losing the person she loved most in the world. She'd felt forsaken, unwanted, unloved.

Carissa knew her mother was dead when her grandmother came into the room and pulled the blanket over her daughter's emaciated, rigid features. Carissa could almost hear her own whimpering as Grandmother Whitmore gathered her into her loving arms.

"Come, child," Grandmother had said patiently. "There's nothing we can do for her anymore. It's all in the past. Let's see what we can do with your future."

Where would she have been today if it hadn't been for her grandmother's love and tenderness during the next twelve years?

Apparently, there wasn't a grandmother to look after her present household guests. Who would see to their future?

Chapter Five

Carissa hadn't realized she'd gone to sleep until she was wakened by a small hand tapping on her shoulder.

"Hey! I gotta go to the bathroom."

Startled, Carissa's eyes flew open. Momentarily, she couldn't comprehend where she was, or why this child was in her Florida condo.

Shaking her head to clear it and smothering a yawn, she finally said, "Good morning, Julie. The bathroom is over there. Do you need any help?"

"No. 'Course not."

Just as well, Carissa thought as she stretched and glanced at the clock. Her only experience with children had been several years ago when she'd looked after a friend's son and daughter while the parents attended an out-of-town funeral. She hadn't learned enough in those two days to develop any maternal instincts, even if she had any.

It was seven o'clock, according to Naomi's clock radio. She supposed she'd have to get up, but she didn't face the day with any enthusiasm. She wondered how Paul had spent the night.

"You got enough water to flush?" Julie called from the bathroom.

"Yes," Carissa answered quickly. She had just swung her feet over the side of the bed, when, carrying the teddy bear, Lauren walked into the bedroom.

"Hurry up, Julie. It's my turn," Lauren whined.

"Just washing my hands. Okay?" Julie answered her sister.

"How are you this morning, Lauren?" Carissa asked.

"Not very good. I had bad dreams."

Could Lauren's dreams be any worse than the reality of their lives? A sick mother, and a father who'd deserted them. And not enough water to flush! Considering the terrible life these children had experienced, Carissa decided her childhood could have been much worse.

She or Paul would have to notify the police. But what would happen to the kids if they were put in state custody?

"Is it all right if I slip into the bathroom first, Lauren?" Carissa asked. "Then I can go and prepare breakfast."

The child nodded, a resigned expression on her face. Seemingly timid, Lauren had probably been in second place all of her life.

Deciding a shower would have to wait, Carissa hurriedly washed her face and hands. She slipped into a warm robe, wrapped it securely around her body and put on some fleece-lined slippers.

"It's your turn now, Lauren. Thanks for waiting."

"You sure look pretty," Lauren said. "Our mom used to be pretty, too."

Carissa patted Lauren's shoulder without speaking. She hardly knew what to say to these children.

Julie was in the adjoining bedroom making her bed, and Carissa said, "Come down when you're ready. I'll see about some breakfast."

"Okay," Julie said cheerfully, as if she didn't have a care in the world.

Paul was sprawled on the recliner, still in the dark-blue pajamas he'd been wearing last night when he'd come to her rescue. Not wanting to disturb him, she tiptoed toward the kitchen.

"Good morning," he said, shifting to a sitting position.

"Oh, I didn't know you were awake," Carissa said. "Sorry to disturb you. I thought you were sleeping in the bedroom."

He pushed his hands through his disheveled brown hair and shook his head groggily. "I decided that I couldn't hear what was going on if I was in the bedroom. I also took the precaution of piling some things in front of the door, in case our visitors tried to escape. I've known that trick to work," he said, with a quirk of his heavy eyebrows.

That brought a blush to her face.

His glance quickly surveyed her appearance. The blue fleece robe deepened the tint of her eyes. The belt, tied snugly around her middle, emphasized a slim waist that flowed into shapely hips. For the first time, Paul realized what a dainty, beautiful woman Carissa was. His scrutiny must have embarrassed Carissa, because her blush deepened to scarlet.

"My bedroom and bath have been taken over by two kids," Carissa said. "I didn't have enough privacy to get out of my nightclothes. You'll have to excuse my appearance."

"If I looked that good in a robe, I'd never put on pants and shirts," he said.

Carissa hadn't thought her face could get any redder, but she was sure it had.

Paul followed her into the kitchen and prepared the coffeepot. "If you're okay with it, as soon as we've eaten, I'm going to contact Justin. He may already know about our fugitives. The AMBER alert is active in most states now. Justin has a family of his own, and he'll be sympathetic to the kids' situation, but he'll also know the best move to make."

"I feel sorry for them, but we could be accused of kidnapping if we don't notify the authorities right away."

"My opinion, too. I'll go to my apartment, shower and dress while you finish breakfast. I'll call for Alex on my way out. I'm worried about this—we need to get it resolved."

Paul opened the door leading to the basement and called, "Alex, time to get up. Breakfast will be ready soon."

Three grim-faced children huddled together on the sofa as they awaited the arrival of Yuletide's police chief. Paul had taken care of the breakfast dishes while Carissa showered and dressed in winter-white sweats.

The sound of a squad car whizzing up the road made Carissa wonder if Justin Townsend ever observed the speed limit. When the knock came at the door, Paul opened it for the police officer. On the phone earlier, Paul simply told Justin they had a problem and asked him to come to the house as soon as possible.

"Hiya!" Justin said jovially as he entered the room. "So you're the one standing on your feet now, Paul. Don't tell me you've knocked Miss Whitmore down."

Paul motioned toward the couch, and Justin's eyes narrowed speculatively when he saw the children.

"Carissa and I are all right," Paul said. "But we do have company. Sit down."

Taking a sharp breath, Justin dropped heavily into the nearest chair. With an incredulous glance at the kids and then at Paul, the chief demanded, "What's going on?"

Briefly, Paul explained the events of the previous night and what he knew about the children. He ended by asking, "Have you had any communication about three runaways?"

"Nary a thing," Justin said. "And we get updates every day." He turned to the children. "Where's your home?" he demanded.

The girls were obviously frightened, and Alex must have been, too, for a vein throbbed noticeably in his forehead and panic was mirrored in his brown eyes. But his voice was steady when he said, "We don't have a home."

"All right," Justin continued. "Let's get at it another way. Where did you live before you didn't have a home?"

A stubborn set to his jaw, Alex shook his head.

Paul and Justin exchanged glances. With a shrug of his broad shoulders, Paul gestured in a sweeping manner with his right arm.

"That's the reaction we've had from them."

"What if I tell you I'm going to put you in jail?" Justin said severely, and Carissa gasped.

"That's okay," Alex said belligerently. "We'd get somethin' to eat, we'd be together and we'd be warm. That's all we want."

"Mommy asked Alex to look after us," Julie said, moving close to her brother. "And he's been tryin' to."

Justin looked as baffled as Carissa and Paul had felt when they'd discovered the kids in the house.

"The children were going to be separated into the homes of different relatives after their mother's death," Carissa explained. "That's the reason they ran away."

"They're too young to make decisions like that," Justin protested.

"I know that," Paul said. "And so do you. But we've gathered that the kids have been pretty much on their own and taking care of their sick mother for over a year. They still think they can manage alone."

Justin lifted himself out of the chair. "Well, I'll make a few discreet inquiries and see what I can learn." He scratched his head. "But what am I going to do with them now?" he added.

The kids seemed to cringe, and their eyes surveyed the three adults as they waited for judgment to be passed on them. Carissa closed her eyes against the entreaty she saw in their grief-pinched faces, and again her own miserable childhood passed through her mind.

"They can stay here with me until you do some investigating," Carissa said.

"That doesn't seem right," Justin protested. "You're on vacation. I can probably find a place for them in town."

Carissa looked for a moment at the children, and her glance briefly grazed Paul's face in passing.

"I thought I came to Yuletide for a vacation, but maybe God had some other reason in mind. I've not been His most obedient follower, but for the past twenty years, I've never doubted that God was masterminding my life. If He hadn't been, with my limitations, I wouldn't have made it." She glanced again at the children. "I thought I'd retired and could take it easy the rest of my life. This may be a test to show me that I'm not ready for retirement."

Paul's expression held a mixture of admiration and concern. "It shouldn't be more than a few days," he said.

"I'm not sure I should agree to this," Justin said. "Naomi won't like having you move someone else into her house."

"I hadn't thought of that," Carissa said. "Our agreement didn't provide for this situation. But as Paul mentioned, it won't be more than a few days."

The children had listened in silence as the adults discussed their fate. Now Julie took matters into her own hands by running to Paul and grabbing him around the knees.

"I want to stay here with you, Uncle Paul," she said, and compassionately, Paul lifted her and held her in his arms. He was momentarily speechless—he'd never been called "Uncle Paul."

Though Justin was visibly touched by the plight of the children, nevertheless, he looked at Alex and said sternly, "Now, young man, I want some straight answers out of you. Are you in any trouble with the law? Have you broken into any other houses?"

Alex stood as if he were a prisoner before the bench. "No, sir. We wouldn't have come into *this* house, except our money was all gone. I didn't know what else to do. We wouldn't have run away, but I'd heard our neighbors talking. No one wanted us, and if we'd gone on welfare, we might have been sent anywhere. We'd lost everything else—we didn't want to lose each other."

Justin cleared his throat huskily, pulled out a big red handkerchief and blew his nose.

Lauren was crying piteously, her glasses steamed up by her tears. Carissa, almost in tears herself, moved to the couch and gathered the girl into her arms.

Still holding Julie, Paul said to Justin, "I'll give Carissa a hand. I'm going to be home for a few weeks. I'll clear it with Naomi."

Justin ambled toward the door. "It's good of you two to take on this responsibility." And to Alex, who was still standing ramrod straight, he said, "Relax, kid. I'll do the best I can for you."

When the door closed behind Justin, Lauren peered

up at Carissa with reddened eyes. "Does that mean we can stay with you?"

"For the time being, at least."

"Do you have any little girls of your own?"

"No, and I don't know anything about little girls. You'll have to help me."

"We will," Julie said, still in the shelter of Paul's arms. "What're we going to call you?"

Carissa pondered the question. Paul was apparently going to be called "uncle." She really didn't want to become an aunt to the children, so she said, "Miss Carissa should be all right."

Julie tried to twist her tongue around those words but she couldn't handle Carissa.

"What about Miss Cara?" Paul asked.

"Miss Cara," Julie said, proud of getting it right the first time. "We'll call you Miss Cara."

In her close contact with Lauren, Carissa had detected a distinct body odor. The children probably hadn't bathed for weeks. "The first thing is for you to have a bath and put on clean clothes."

"We didn't bring many clothes, and they're all dirty," Alex said.

Carissa sighed. After having no one but herself to look after for years, Carissa wondered if she could possibly take on the responsibility of three children.

Paul noticed that Carissa's body was as taut as a bowstring, and a pensive expression darkened her blue eyes. She licked her lips nervously. Paul set Julie on the floor and knelt by the couch where Carissa was sitting.

Taking her hand, he said, "It'll work out all right.

The washer and dryer are in the basement, so Alex and I will sort their clothes and do the laundry while you take care of the girls' baths. We'll get along."

"I feel completely inadequate, but I'll do the best I can." She stood and reached out a hand to the girls. "Come on, Julie and Lauren."

Since there was a shower stall as well as a tub in Carissa's private bathroom, the girls bathed at the same time. The clothes they removed were odorous, and Carissa said, "I'll find a blanket for you to put on until Paul and Alex have clean clothes ready. You can sit and watch TV until then."

While in the other room searching for blankets, Carissa noticed that Lauren hadn't made her bed. She stopped to spread the blankets and stopped short. There was a wet spot in the middle. She had a bed wetter on her hands!

Appalled, Carissa pulled the offending covers from the bed, and breathed a sigh of relief when she saw a protective plastic cover over the mattress. At least the whole bed wasn't ruined. But what was she going to do?

Was she violating her agreement with Naomi to let the children stay, even for a few days? She would be responsible for any damage—but that was hardly the point. What was the ethical thing to do? How would she feel if Naomi took three vagrant children into her Florida condo?

When their baths were finished, she gave a blanket to each of the girls and turned on the television hanging on the wall facing Naomi's bed. Julie's tight ringlets only needed to be brushed, but Carissa struggled to comb Lauren's long hair and braid it.

"You stay here until your clothes have dried," Carissa said. "I'll take these clothes to be washed." Carissa had a keen sense of smell, and she held her breath as she picked up the girls' clothes and the soiled sheets and took them to the basement.

Paul had found a checkers set and, while they waited for the clothes to dry, he and Alex were sitting at a small table in the game room shoving the red and black disks across a board. Carissa passed them and peered into the furnace room, admiring the ingenuity of the children in providing for themselves. They'd apparently found two cots, which the girls had occupied, and Alex's bed had been laid on some cushions that Naomi probably used on the porch furniture during the summer. They would have been comfortable enough, but how they expected to spend the winter here, Carissa couldn't comprehend.

"Where are my sisters?" Alex asked.

"Wrapped in blankets, lying on my bed, watching television. A life of ease," she said, with a grimace in Paul's direction.

The washer was still on but a buzzer indicated that the clothes in the dryer were ready. When Paul started to get up from the checkers game, Carissa said, "I'll fold the clothes. Go ahead and play."

Paul had sorted the clothing by color, so there were three small loads to wash. The poor quality of the worn clothing further attested to the poverty the children had experienced. When the washer finished, Carissa emptied its contents into the dryer and put the remaining clothes and sheets in the washer.

"After Lauren and Julie have dressed, let's go outside and play in the snow," she said. "I didn't come to New York to spend my time inside."

"Sounds like a good idea," Paul said. "We'll be upstairs as soon as the clothes are washed and dry."

The children's shoes and clothes weren't warm enough for them to stay outside long, but they took a brisk walk along the lakeshore. They even ventured out to one of the fishermen's huts and waited expectantly, but the man didn't catch anything while they watched.

The five of them engaged in a snowball fight, and even though the females outnumbered the males, Alex and Paul were formidable opponents. When Paul tossed a snowball that exploded in Carissa's face, she shouted, "I give up," and hurried inside the house.

Thinking he might have hurt her, Paul said, "Go ahead and play. I'll see if Carissa is okay."

Carissa was wiping the snow from her face when Paul entered the kitchen. Her glowing eyes indicated that she was all right, but Paul said solicitously, "I didn't intend such a direct hit. Are you hurt?"

"Nothing except my pride," she said with a laugh.

"Fortunately this snow is light. It doesn't pack well."

Carissa looked out the window toward where the children were trying to make a snowman. "They seemed almost happy while we were playing. Paul, I feel so sorry for them, but I'm ill-prepared to deal with three orphan children."

"You're doing great," he said reassuringly. "I have a

strange feeling about this situation, as if God is giving us an opportunity to help. If He's orchestrating what we're doing, we can't fail."

Chapter Six

Paul spent the rest of the morning repairing the lock on the rear door. Then, early that afternoon, help arrived in the guise of Belva Townsend, Justin's wife. Belva was stocky of build, and her features were pleasant but not pretty. She had a brusque manner, but five minutes in her presence and Carissa's burden about the children lifted considerably. She didn't know what to do, Belva obviously did.

After Paul introduced Belva and Carissa, Belva said, "I came to have a look at these kids and see what they need."

"Just about everything," Paul told her. "They have one pair of well-worn shoes each. And their other clothing is sparse."

"I'll take them shopping this afternoon," Carissa said.

"I doubt you'll have to buy anything," Belva said. She lined the children up and observed them closely, talking about them as if they weren't present. "My boys have outgrown clothes that I think Alex can wear. And no doubt I can get many things for the girls from my neighbors. We also have a clothing bank at the church. I'll be back this evening with some things. Don't buy anything yet."

"Say, Belva," Paul said, "we've been wondering if any Christmas celebrations are planned. Both Carissa and I would like to experience an old-time Christmas again."

Belva helped herself to one of the cheese cubes left over from lunch. "Yuletide has never revived the large celebrations like we used to have. A few people decorate their homes and lawns, but old-timers, who still remember the past, can't get enthused about celebrating."

"Seems to me it's time to forget the past," Paul said.

"You may be right," Belva agreed. "But don't talk to me—take up your grievances with the town council."

With a cheery wave of her arm, Belva trotted down the porch steps and was gone. Her visit hadn't lasted fifteen minutes.

"Sorta feel like I've been in a blitzkrieg," Carissa said with a laugh. However, Belva's matter-of-fact approach to the situation had done a lot to calm her spirits.

"Belva can be a bit abrupt," Paul agreed. "But she has a heart of gold."

True to her word, several hours later, Belva returned with fleece-lined parkas, sweatpants and shirts for the children. She brought some books and a doll for Julie. As they looked at the books and modeled their new clothes, the children seemed happy, though occasionally, a bleak expression appeared in Alex's and Lauren's eyes.

Feeling that the children were content in their new surroundings, Paul didn't think it was necessary to guard them, so that night he went to bed in his sister's room.

Long after the household was quiet, bundled in her heaviest garments, Carissa crept down the stairs. She ventured out on the deck that Paul had swept clear of snow, and sat on a bench.

A bright moon hung over the evergreen trees, and a soft breeze wafted from the lake. The night was cold and still. In such a peaceful setting, Carissa should have been as calm as the atmosphere, but her thoughts were rioting.

She had wanted to remember the Christmases of old, but she hadn't expected to be plunged into a roller-coaster return of thoughts of her unhappy childhood. The past few days had awakened recollections of her past that she had tried in vain to forget.

In a large city, her forlorn childhood wouldn't have caused a ripple, but in a town of five hundred people, no one had any secrets. Except for the members of her grandmother's church, people in town had shunned her. Because her mother had an unsavory reputation, the townspeople had labeled Carissa with the same immoral qualities, expecting her to follow in her mother's footsteps. No decent boy had ever asked her for a date, and only a few girls befriended her—children who were also ostracized for one reason or another. Carissa hadn't been an outgoing child, and she'd made no overtures of friendship to others. She'd feared rejection then, and she still did.

She would have liked to marry and have children, but when she didn't even know who her father was, what kind of heritage would she have passed to her offspring? Any of her mother's partners could have fathered her.

She'd loved her mother devotedly, but after her death, Carissa had learned about her lifestyle and had come to resent her. She blamed her mother for bringing her into the world under such a cloud, and she didn't want children who would someday resent her for passing on a sordid ancestry to them.

She was past child-bearing age now, however, so what harm would there be in finding happiness with a husband? Carissa was a little surprised at herself.

Once she'd made up her mind years ago to remain single, she'd never thought about marriage, so why this sudden remorse that she'd remained single? Could it be the children who'd suddenly come into her life? Or was it Paul who'd triggered her desire for wedded bliss?

She feared that was the reason. During her youth, she'd missed a father figure in her life. The only close male relative who'd influenced her at all was an uncle. He was kind to her, but he had a houseful of his own kids and didn't have enough time to take Carissa under his wing.

But in those youthful days before she'd decided never to marry, she'd envisioned the kind of man she wanted to marry. Carissa had become an introvert through necessity, so she'd wanted a husband who was a friendly person, one who'd smile often, one with a strong, physical body that belied the tenderness that he exhibited so readily. And she'd wanted a man who would love her without reservation, one who would be able to understand her fears, one whose presence would calm her spirits and stir her emotions. Only a few hours in Paul's presence and she knew he exemplified all the characteristics of her dream man.

She hadn't heard a sound, but suddenly she sensed that she was no longer alone, and knew Paul had joined her. How was it possible to become so quickly attuned to this man that she could actually perceive his presence without seeing or hearing him?

"You couldn't sleep, either?" she asked.

Paul moved forward to stand near Carissa. He'd been watching her for several minutes. He hadn't made a sound, so he wondered how she could have known he was there.

"No. I'm still having a problem with jet lag."

He wasn't being exactly truthful, because actually, he'd been thinking about Carissa when he'd heard her come downstairs. After Jennifer Pruett had jilted him twenty years ago, Paul had successfully stifled any interest in women. It wasn't really difficult, for Jennifer had hurt him so badly that he didn't want another woman in his life. Since that time, he'd seldom given any woman a second thought. So what attracted him to Carissa?

Perhaps it was because, in spite of her outward appearance of success, he sensed that Carissa experienced much inner turmoil. Behind her facade of self-assurance, he sensed a little girl's wistfulness in her remote, and sometimes mysterious, smile. He'd been alone for years because he wanted it that way. Carissa was obviously alone, too, but he suspected that her natural tendency was to want people.

She was a small, slender woman with a delicate, fragile body. He could easily span her waist with his hands. But remembering the way she'd flinched when he'd touched her on the shoulder, Paul knew it would be a long time, if ever, before he could put his hands around her waist. And why should he want to?

"I don't even have that excuse," Carissa commented, turning to face him as he closed the door.

Paul had been so immersed in his thoughts that, for a moment, he couldn't remember what they were talking about.

"Oh, no jet lag? What's the problem, then?"

"I can't get the kids out of my mind. I want to do right by them, but I'm reluctant to take on this responsibility."

"Don't you like kids?"

Carissa laughed shortly. Not like kids when she'd recently signed a $200,000 check to help fund a shelter for abandoned children?

"That's hardly the point. I have a soft spot in my heart for children, especially orphaned ones like our three guests, but I'm uncomfortable about bringing them into Naomi's house. Besides, it seems to be the ethical thing to turn them over to the authorities."

"Well, Justin is working on that. And I'll call Naomi today and clear it with her."

Paul wore a parka over his pajamas, and his feet were in slippers. He shivered and pulled the parka closer to his body.

"You'll freeze out here with so few clothes on. I'm ready to go in, anyway. Sorry I disturbed your rest. I just had to deal with some of my frustrations," she said.

"Do you think you'll sleep now?"

"I should be able to," she said, but Paul was aware of the concern in her eyes. He opened the door and stood aside to let Carissa into the room.

Paul figured she'd take her worries to bed with her. But there was a limit to what he could do, so he returned to the bedroom and closed the door, as Carissa headed toward the stairs.

Carissa and Paul were lingering over their coffee when Justin and Belva came the next morning. The children were still sleeping, so Carissa invited the couple to join them for coffee. Paul got cups while Carissa poured the hot beverage.

Justin said, "I can't turn up a thing on those kids. It's inconceivable in this day of mass communication that three kids can disappear without somebody looking for them."

"You could put their pictures on the Internet and you'd soon find out who they are and where they came from," Paul said.

"I know, and I'll probably do that, but we have complications." He darted a look at his wife, and Carissa had the feeling that Justin was a mite henpecked.

"As you know, Paul," Justin continued, "Yuletide is

a small town and news travels fast. By now, everyone in town knows about these three kids. I've had a half dozen phone calls or so asking me not to relocate the children until after Christmas."

"Yuletide's citizens are deluding themselves into believing that these children have been sent to us to give us an opportunity to redeem ourselves," said Belva.

"Maybe it isn't a delusion," Paul said.

Half annoyed that she couldn't follow the gist of their conversation, Carissa remembered what Paul had told her two nights ago. "Oh, now I understand. They're tying the present situation to the Christmas Eve tragedy of the past."

"That's right," Justin said. "People are begging me not to do anything until after Christmas. The mayor wants the town to adopt them as our special guests for the next few weeks. Even the pastor of Bethel Church stopped by the office last night, suggesting that the children might give us a second chance to show our generosity and faith."

"But can't you get into a lot of trouble by not trying to find out whose children they are?" Paul asked.

Justin slanted an uneasy look toward his wife, who took a sip of coffee, seemingly oblivious to his gaze.

"But I might get into a lot more trouble if I don't do what the Yuletide citizens want me to do. Besides, I *am* trying to find out who the kids are."

When Belva didn't comment, Justin asked, "What do the two of you think about it? You're more involved than anyone else."

Paul's eyes registered concern when he looked at

Carissa. He hadn't anticipated spending his vacation in this manner, but he was willing to help out. And what about his visit with Naomi? He wouldn't go to Florida and leave Carissa with the responsibility.

"You'd expect us to be the children's guardians until after Christmas?" he asked Justin.

"Others in town would be willing to give them a home," Belva said, "but I'm not sure anyone can take all three of them."

"Then they'd be separated!" Carissa said. "That's what they were trying to avoid when they ran away."

She moved from the table to stand in front of the window. Hoarfrost decorated the windowpane in lacy, geometric patterns. Ice fishermen already huddled over holes in the lake. As she watched, one man pulled a foot-long fish from the frigid water.

Carissa saw the scenery, but her thoughts were far removed from the beauty of the winter morning. For years she'd been a heavy contributor to children's charities—but was God now giving her the opportunity to donate hands-on help to children whose needs exceeded hers as a child?

She'd been anticipating two months of inactivity, and deep down in her heart, Carissa didn't want to take on this responsibility. She hadn't been in Yuletide a week, and if she assumed the care of these children until after Christmas, over half of her time there would be gone. And what about her quest for Christmas? She couldn't continue that as long as she was playing mother.

Or was God giving her the opportunity to find Christmas through the three children?

"Do unto others as you would have them do unto you." The Scripture verse she'd learned as a child flashed into her mind.

Why couldn't she put memories of her childhood behind her? She'd buried her past while she built up Cara Fashions, so why did her past intrude upon her thoughts now? Obviously, she hadn't dealt with the youthful heartaches she'd experienced, or she would be able to forget them.

"If Paul can get Naomi's okay, I'll look after the kids," she said, her heart speaking instead of her head. She wasn't sure what she was getting into.

"Good!" Belva said, a full smile lighting her irregular features. "I've already talked with the teachers, and the children will be welcome to come to school." She stood up. "Come, love," she said to her husband. "We have lots of things to do. Thanks for the coffee."

"I still think it's too big a risk for all of us to take," Paul said, as Justin pushed back from the table. "We don't know that these kids are even telling us the truth. They may have a family looking for them."

"You don't really believe that, do you?" Justin asked.

"No," Paul said slowly, and he looked at Carissa's tense features. "But I know Carissa is reluctant, and she'll be bearing the brunt of this because they'll be living in her house. She has a lot at stake."

With her accumulated wealth, Carissa realized that she'd be ripe for plucking if anyone wanted to sue her. But she remembered what her grandmother had said the day she started to Florida: "It's a big change for you, my dear, but you'll never be happy living in this town. Always remember God's promise, 'The Lord is my helper; I will not be afraid. What can man do to me?'"

"If I thought of myself, I couldn't do this," she said. "For some reason, God sent these children to this house when I was here to receive them. If I told you I wasn't afraid, I'd be lying. I don't know anything about cooking for children or buying their clothes."

"Listen, my dear," Belva said. "I've raised five kids. If you need any help, I'm as close as the telephone. And don't you worry about clothing. The church's clothing bank has good items. You bring the children in at two o'clock this afternoon, and we'll outfit them in whatever else they need."

When the door closed behind the Townsends, Paul laughed softly. "Belva has always liked to be in charge of things," he said, "but she will be a source of wisdom to us."

"Well, we're committed. What do we do now?"

"Let's get the kids out of bed and tell them about the town's plans for them."

Carissa said, "I dread checking Lauren's bed—she's apparently a bed wetter. I hoped the first night's incident was caused by stress, but if the bed-wetting persists, I'll have to talk to Belva about it. I won't ruin Naomi's furniture."

"Which reminds me—I have to talk to Naomi. I'll go to the apartment and call her."

"Please be candid with me. If she doesn't want the

children in the house, I'll take them to a motel and keep them."

"I know my sister, and she'll understand the situation. But we'd better resolve the matter of where I'm going to live. If you're uncomfortable about staying alone with the children, I'll continue to sleep in Naomi's room."

With her gaze downcast, Carissa wondered which situation would make her more uncomfortable. She was uneasy about being in the house alone with the kids. They didn't seem to be dangerous, but the media often carried reports of children who were violent.

But was it wise to share a house with Paul, when his every movement demonstrated his masculine attractiveness? She had sensed something exceptional about him from the very beginning, as if the qualities she'd always admired in men were all wrapped up in one bundle, Paul Spencer. Physically and emotionally, she was aware of his every move—his ready sense of humor, the lurking smile in his eyes, his warmheartedness, and the one lock of hair that consistently fell over his forehead. It wasn't worry over the children that had kept her awake last night, but Paul's presence in the house.

She tried to force her swirling emotions into order. For years she'd denied herself the companionship of any man. And suddenly the thought that had been nagging for entrance into her mind surged forward. She was five years older than Paul—too much of an age difference to become more to him than a friend. She'd never approved of women who married men younger than themselves. She'd have to be careful she didn't reveal any of her thoughts to Paul, which would be embarrassing to both of them.

Annoyed that she was again thinking of marriage, she turned to Paul, hoping that her face didn't reveal the tumult of her thoughts.

"If you don't mind, I'd prefer it if you'd stay in the house with us. But you have to go to see Naomi, so don't let my hang-ups prevent you from going to Florida. If you stay here a few days, I'll be more accustomed to the kids by then."

"I would like to see Naomi, but I won't leave you with all this responsibility. I committed to watching out for the children as much as you did. I'll find time to visit my sister."

Paul shifted his eyes from her intense expression, afraid to contemplate why he craved Carissa's company. He could plead the necessity of helping with the children, but was that the real reason he intended to spend Christmas in Yuletide?

Chapter Seven

Overjoyed that they were going to stay with Paul and Carissa, Lauren and Julie enthusiastically jumped into Carissa's SUV to go into town. Paul noticed that Alex was uneasy, and he glanced often from side to side. When they reached the church—a stone structure built from native materials and topped by a tall steeple—Paul drew Alex to one side.

"Alex, we aren't trying to trap you. Unless something else turns up, you can stay with Carissa and me until after Christmas."

Alex shuffled his feet in the light dusting of snow that had fallen the night before.

"So be honest with me. Is there somebody looking for you?"

"I don't think so. I can't tell you anything else, because I want to keep my sisters together like Mom said. She was an adopted kid, and she didn't have any idea whether she had any sisters or brothers. My aunts and uncles are all on my father's side. If they took us, they'd just do it so they could get state money for giving us a home. I promised Mom I'd look out for the girls."

Paul privately thought that his mother had laid a heavy burden on the back of a fourteen-year-old. He put his arm around Alex's shoulders. "We'll help you keep your promise. Come on inside, and we'll find some more clothes."

Belva met them in the church basement and introduced the church's pastor, Philip Erskine. The pastor was a young man who'd come to Yuletide three years ago.

"If you'll allow Belva to take care of the children's needs, I'd like to talk to you in my office," Philip said to Carissa and Paul.

Knowing the children's insecurity, Carissa said, "Is that okay with you, kids? Belva will show you around the clothing room."

"Where you gonna be?" Lauren said fearfully.

Pastor Erskine pointed to a door directly across the hall from the room that held the clothing. "That's my office. You can come in with us when you're finished. We'll leave the door open."

"Remember, Belva," Carissa said. "I'll purchase anything they need, but you'll have to tell me what to buy."

Belva nodded. "We'll see what's available here in their sizes."

Inviting them to sit, Pastor Erskine said, "This is my second Christmas in Yuletide. It's inconceivable to me that these people won't celebrate the birth of Jesus in their homes or the church. I don't believe that God has withdrawn His blessing from their town because of what happened twenty-five years ago, but I can't convince my congregation."

With a smile, he continued. "If the local citizens feel that they've been given a chance to help the children and atone for that previous oversight, I believe I should take advantage of it. I'm not above exploiting that superstition to accomplish what I want."

"Which is to have the town celebrate Christmas?" Paul said with a laugh.

"Right! Chief Townsend told me this morning that the two of you wanted to revive an old-time Christmas in Yuletide. Will you help me?"

Carissa and Paul exchanged glances. A faint light sparkled in the depths of Carissa's blue eyes, and Paul knew she was willing to do what the pastor asked.

"Suits me," Paul said, "but we don't have much time."

"So we must start right away," the pastor said. "I'll call a meeting of some of the town's influential people tonight at seven. Will you come?"

"I wouldn't like to leave the children alone—they might run away," Carissa said.

"Tonight is our monthly youth rally with activities for all ages. Your children could profit by attending the meeting."

Surprised at herself because she'd made all her decisions since she'd been on her own, Carissa looked to Paul for an answer.

"I'm willing," he said. "For one thing, it will give the kids some diversion. Carissa and I aren't exactly gifted in entertaining children." He glanced in Carissa's direction. "All right?"

"Yes. We'll be here tonight."

Twelve people attended the meeting, and due to an intense spirit of cooperation, plans were formulated quickly.

"We've got our work cut out for us if we plan on getting all of these things done in the next two weeks," Paul said as they were driving home. "The decorations should be up now, so people from out of town can come to see them."

"If we extend the time until after the first of the year, tourists will have the opportunity to stop by," Carissa added. "Especially if the mayor gets coverage in big-city newspapers."

The committee had decided that within the next week, the stores would be decorated, and a large spruce tree, in a vacant lot near City Hall, would be covered with colored lights. The pastor had referred to a catalog featuring lighted commercial displays, wishing they could erect an exhibition along the lakefront.

When he bemoaned the fact that even a modest display would cost five thousand dollars, Carissa had said, "I'll pay for the display. Go ahead and order what you need."

All heads had turned in her direction, and she wished she'd waited until later to tell the pastor. Normally, she made her charitable contributions more discreetly.

"That's good of you, Miss Whitmore." Pastor Erskine had surveyed the group seated in his small office. "But is there time to get these things and have them erected?"

The pastor's secretary had said, "I looked through that catalog, and the company sends representatives to erect the displays and put them into operation."

Embarrassed when, at the close of the meeting, several of the people thanked her warmly for contributing the money for the light display, Carissa had wished again that she hadn't made her donation public. Paul had made no comment one way or another.

On the way home, as Carissa expertly handled her vehicle on the slippery roads, Paul realized that he had apparently been the only one who wasn't pleased about Carissa's generous offer. He should have complimented her, too, but he was wary of people, and especially women, who had a lot of money. Although Jennifer had insisted she loved him, she'd jilted him because he was poor. When she'd had the opportunity to marry a rich man, Jennifer had chosen money over her love for Paul.

Carissa had noticed that Paul seemed to be the only one at the meeting not overjoyed that the town would have a light display. And even as they talked in the car, she wondered why he didn't mention her offer.

"You kids have a good time?" he asked the children, as Carissa parked, and the kids tumbled out of the SUV.

Julie grabbed Paul's hand and held up a Christmas ornament she'd made. "Look, Uncle Paul. The teacher told us to put this on our tree."

"Are we gonna have a Christmas tree?" Lauren asked. "We couldn't have one last year."

Carissa looked to Paul for that decision, too, and he answered easily enough, although she sensed his preoccupation.

"Of course we'll have a tree. We can cut one on the hill behind the house."

"What did your group do?" Carissa asked Alex as they entered the house.

"Played games. My team got the Ping-Pong trophy for the most wins. We played Bingo, too. I won three candy bars. Here, girls," he said, handing a bar to each of his sisters.

"Maybe we'd better save ours until tomorrow," Lauren said, when Julie started opening the package.

Carissa couldn't determine whether Lauren was concerned because they shouldn't eat chocolate at bedtime, or whether she'd developed the habit of hoarding because of the scarcity of food in their home. Wondering how many times these children had gone to bed hungry, Carissa said, "Why don't you eat half of the candy now and keep the rest until tomorrow?"

"We had 'freshments at the church," Julie admitted. "And Mommy didn't want us to eat before bedtime."

"Then, by all means, save the candy until tomorrow."

The fragrance of coffee awakened Carissa the next morning. She'd slept well in spite of her concern over Paul's attitude last night. When she tried to pinpoint when he'd changed, she traced it to the time she'd volunteered to pay for the light display. Did he think she was flaunting her money? After being so poor through her childhood and feeling inferior to most of the other children in her school, Carissa had made an effort not to offend anyone with her prosperity.

She peered into the other bedroom. Lauren and Julie were still sleeping, so Carissa closed the door between the rooms. She showered and dressed in jeans and a turtleneck sweater before going downstairs.

Paul was busy in the kitchen. He'd prepared a pitcher of frozen orange juice. Sausage patties were laid out ready for the microwave, and he was mixing something in a bowl.

"You're energetic this morning," Carissa said when she entered the kitchen. "Are you making a cake?"

He grinned at her in his usual way, saying, "This is pancake batter. I decided we should have something besides sweet rolls this morning. Do you like pancakes?"

"Very much, but I get mine from the freezer section in the grocery store, then pop them in the microwave. I haven't had homemade pancakes since I lived with my grandmother. It isn't much fun to cook for one person."

"I'm no fancy cook, but I like to putter around the kitchen."

"Good!" Carissa said, a teasing quality in her voice. "Then, you can be the cook for this joint venture we've taken on."

"Suits me! You can take care of any homework that has to be supervised, as well as discipline the kids."

"I'll pass on that, too," Carissa said. "I believe parents should work as a team in disciplining their children. I grew up in an all-female household, and I always felt I'd missed a lot by not having some male influence."

"What happened to your father?" Paul asked.

"Well, about that…" Carissa started. At the strain in her voice, Paul looked at her questioningly. Before she could finish, Alex walked into the kitchen.

"Hey!" he said. "I smell food."

"And good food, too," Carissa said, obviously relieved that Alex had interrupted them. "I'll see if Julie and Lauren are out of bed."

"What can I do to help?" Alex asked Paul as Carissa turned toward the steps.

She was tormented by confusing emotions. Why did she find it so difficult to talk about her teen years?

She hadn't wanted any of her business associates to know of her past, and she'd never told anyone about her sordid family background. When she left Minnesota at eighteen, Carissa had believed that her unsavory past would follow her, but miraculously, it hadn't. Therefore, for over twenty years, she'd been spared talking about that period of her life. If Alex hadn't walked in, would she have told Paul?

Carissa supervised the girls while they showered and changed into some of the clothes they'd gotten at the clothing bank. She couldn't imagine that two sisters could have such opposite personalities. Julie only took a few minutes to decide what clothes she wanted to wear, and dressed quickly without much supervision from Carissa.

Lauren, on the other hand, chose one shirt, but when

she put it on, she started crying. "Miss Cara, Julie's clothes are all prettier than mine."

"But, Lauren," Carissa said, "you had the opportunity to choose what things you wanted."

"Yes, but the clothes in my size weren't very pretty."

"Of course they are," Carissa said. She turned Lauren to face the mirror. "The brown in this shirt is the color of your hair, and these little yellow stripes reflect the golden flecks in your eyes. I think you made a great choice."

"Do you *really* think so?" Julie asked worriedly.

"Yes, I do. And let's leave your hair hanging over your shoulders instead of braiding it today. You have such pretty, soft hair, it's a shame to braid it."

"Julie's hair is curly."

"It's pretty, too, but not any prettier than yours. Stop comparing yourself to Julie. You're different girls, so you should be what God made *you* to be."

"Oh!" Lauren said, and reached her hand to touch Carissa's cheek.

Carissa blinked away the unaccustomed moisture in her eyes. Taking Lauren's hand, she said, "Let's go for breakfast. Paul has made pancakes with sausages this morning."

Soon after breakfast, Paul herded the three children into his pickup and took them into Yuletide to go to school. Since they'd met children their ages the night before, they didn't seem to mind going to a strange school.

"I'll help decorate the central Christmas tree while

I'm in town. I'll stay until school is out—probably at three o'clock. Hope you have a nice, quiet day."

In fact, the house seemed too quiet after they left, and Carissa marveled that a few days had changed her perspective. Without Paul and the children, the silence seemed strange as she straightened the house for the day.

The girls had spread the covers over their beds. Although it was a makeshift effort, after Carissa checked to find that Lauren's sheets were dry, she left the beds alone. She wouldn't take away from the independence they'd learned from their mother.

Carissa had finished tidying the house by midmorning, and she was restless. She walked along the lakefront for an hour, and then decided to go into Yuletide. She needed to open an account at the local bank, and she thought she might be helpful in decorating the community tree. Did she really have a yen to decorate the tree, or did she want to be where Paul was? If so, it was a new sensation for her to deliberately seek the company of a man.

She arrived at the town hall just as the eight volunteers stopped for lunch. She eyed the twenty-foot-tall spruce tree and the ladders that leaned against it. "Any place for a person who prefers her feet on the ground when she works?"

"We're taking a break now," Paul said. "Come along and eat with us, and then we'll find a job for you."

They went to the café Carissa had visited on her first night in Yuletide. It was the only place to eat in town, except for the restaurant in the lobby of the hotel, and it was crowded.

A decorated pine tree stood in one corner of the room, red candles were placed on each table and Christmas music mingled with the voices of the diners.

"We should put some outside decorations at the house," she said. "If people are driving around the lake to see the light display, the houses should be attractive, too. Where could we go to buy decorations?"

"There won't be anything in Yuletide," Paul said. "Saratoga Springs would be the closest place. We could go tomorrow and get what we need. I told the kids we'd have a Christmas tree, but since it will be a real one, we shouldn't put it up until a few days before Christmas."

"I couldn't get into the spirit of Christmas in Tampa when the temperature on December twenty-fifth is often in the seventies. I have a two-foot artificial tree that I place on the coffee table in my living room. That's the extent of my decorating. It'll be nice to have an evergreen scent in the house."

"Even the years I've been away from home I've always managed to spend Christmas where there's snow. I've spent several Christmases skiing and skating in the Alps."

They met Pastor Erskine as they left the restaurant. "The lighting company will erect the display a week from today. We can't hope for anything better than that, when our order went in so late. But the manager said that the weeks prior to Christmas are slow for them because their customers usually order months in advance. And I've come up with another idea."

"Uh-oh!" Carissa said, feeling mischievous. "That sounds like more work to me."

"I'd like to have a progressive outdoor nativity pageant. The manger scene could be set up beside the town hall, the shepherds and angels could congregate on one of the hillsides outside town, and the Wise Men could travel into Yuletide from the far side of Lake Mohawk."

"Got any camels?" Paul asked.

Pastor Erskine's face suddenly drooped. "I hadn't thought of that. But we don't have any biblical proof that the Wise Men rode camels. They'll have to walk into town."

"A pageant would be a memorable event," Carissa said. "If you need any help with costumes, let me know. I'm a fashion designer, and I make my creations on my own sewing machine before I send out the patterns to the manufacturers."

"Miss Whitmore, I believe in providence. God must have sent you to Yuletide to help us revive the spirit of Christmas. The town is coming alive again."

Silently, Carissa agreed with him, for more and more, she believed that her choice of Yuletide had not been happenstance.

Chapter Eight

The next week passed quickly. Paul and Carissa made a trip to Saratoga Springs to buy decorations. When each insisted that they'd pay for the items, they finally agreed to split the expenses.

"If this year's observance goes well," Carissa said, "Yuletide will probably throw off its fixation about not celebrating Christmas. Perhaps Naomi can use them for another season."

"I don't know," Paul said. "Naomi sounds like she's having such a good time in Florida. She may never spend another winter in the north."

"Yes, I know. I called yesterday to apologize for the way we were misusing her home, and she said that her New York home was the furthest thing from her mind now."

"I thought a change of scenery would be good for her, but I didn't dream she'd become a new person. Management of the textile mill was apparently too much for her. She says the staff can handle the work, and she isn't worrying about it. She's made new friends. One man from Wyoming has rented an apartment in the complex where you live, and they've been going to dinner together."

Paul spent the next two days draping the evergreens with strings of lights, and he put icicle lights around the eaves of the house. Carissa started decorating the great room.

Thinking that Naomi might also want to decorate, Carissa telephoned to let Naomi know where her meager supply of Christmas decorations was stored. She made three attempts before she finally caught Naomi at the condo.

"You're an elusive lady," Carissa said. "You must spend all your time at the beach."

"I go walking every morning, but there are so many other things to do. My new friend, John Brewster, and I go to a different restaurant for dinner every night."

"Is he the man from Wyoming?"

"Yes. Since he retired, he's spent the past five winters in Florida."

"I'm happy you're enjoying my place as much as I like yours. Since I'm decorating your house today, I thought you might like to put out some decorations, too. I don't have many things, but you'll find what I do have in my storage area in the basement. The key is on the key ring I left for you. If you want more things, I'll pay for them. I can always use them next year."

"Thanks, but I probably won't do any decorating. I'm out of the habit now, since we haven't done anything at Yuletide for several years."

"And, Naomi, if you want to come home for Christmas, please do so. One more person in the house won't be a problem. I'm encouraging Paul to come visit you, but he insists he feels responsible for the children, too. I don't want you to be lonely."

"I thank you, but I'll be content to stay here. I've made many friends, and we have so much in common that I feel as if they're family. John took me to the large church two blocks west of your condo. They have a Bible class especially for northern people who spend the winter months in Florida. Twenty-three people attended, and we're planning many activities for the holidays. Two of the couples live in RVs, and they've rented the clubhouse at their RV park for a big party. We'll all take food and exchange gifts. And we're planning to take a Caribbean cruise for several days, so I won't even be home on Christmas Day. I'm happier than I've been since my husband died, so don't worry about me being lonely."

How could Naomi have made friends so quickly— friends she preferred to see more than she did her own brother? But Carissa reflected that she'd also become acquainted with many new people in the past three weeks. In the frenzied rush to bring Christmas to Yuletide, they didn't seem like strangers.

Carissa had bought a wooden nativity scene for the mantel, which she surrounded with pine cones and greenery from the trees around the lake. She placed the wooden key she'd carried in the Christmas pageant when she was a child in a prominent place. Each time she looked at it, Carissa was reminded of her reason for coming to Yuletide. She had ropes of tinsel and red poinsettias to tie around the wooden supports in the great room and on the stair railings.

When Paul came home from taking the children to school on Wednesday morning, Carissa was placing electric candles in the windows. He carried a large paper bag that held several sprigs of a plant with small green leaves and clusters of white berries. With a boyish smile, he handed the plants to Carissa.

"What's that?" she asked.

"Mistletoe! I stopped at the farmer's market for a bag of oranges, and he'd just received a shipment of mistletoe. I thought you could use it for decoration."

Frowning, Carissa said, "I'm not so sure. I've heard that mistletoe berries are poisonous to people. With three kids in the house, I don't want to take any chances."

"I didn't buy this for eating. Haven't you ever heard of kissing under the mistletoe?"

She glanced at Paul questioningly. "I can't see that we'll need it for that purpose, either."

"Oh, you never can tell," he answered. "I think our visitors could benefit from a few hugs and kisses. They probably haven't had much affection since their mother became sick."

"Whatever you do with the mistletoe, be sure it's out of reach of the children. And you can take care of the affection, too. God must have left maternal instincts out of my makeup. I'm capable of clothing and sheltering our visitors, but I don't seem to have many hugs and kisses to give."

And I wonder why you don't, Paul thought. From the tense expression on Carissa's face, he felt sure it was a discussion he couldn't initiate at that time.

They chatted companionably the rest of the morning while Paul tied sprigs of mistletoe not only on the chandelier in the great room, but also on the light over the kitchen table. He inserted some of it in Carissa's mantel decorations. It did look pretty as an extra touch, Carissa thought, but she was uneasy about having the mistletoe in the house. She couldn't decide which disturbed her the most—her concern for the children, or what Paul had said about hugs and kisses.

By noon, the great room was festive, and Carissa stood in the middle to survey their efforts. "I suppose we should have waited for the children to help decorate," she said, "but I didn't think about it. I'm so used to doing things alone that I can't easily include others. We'll let them help trim the tree. Looks good, doesn't it?"

Carissa had inadvertently stopped beneath the mistletoe-decorated chandelier to admire the room's new look. Watching her, and the look on her face, Paul thought she was an exquisite woman. He moved closer, and, putting his left hand on her shoulder, he pointed up at the mistletoe.

"After all, it is a Christmas tradition," he said, and bent his head, meaning to kiss her on the forehead.

Carissa quickly lifted her face, and his lips touched hers in an electric moment. Dazed, her eyes closed, Carissa swayed toward Paul.

After a second's hesitation, when he briefly recalled

his long-standing vow to avoid women, he hugged her to him in a delight too profound for words.

His kiss was surprisingly gentle, and Carissa was surprised at her eager response to the touch of his lips. She seemed to be drifting through space, her spirits soaring, filled with an inner excitement that was foreign to her. Then suddenly she remembered! Her eyes flew open. A glint of wonder had transformed Paul's gaze.

Wrenching out of his arms, Carissa pushed Paul away from her. Caught off guard, he stumbled backward and sprawled in a crumpled heap on the couch, mashing the boxes that had held the decorations.

Running toward the stairs, Carissa said in a tearful voice, "Don't ever touch me again."

Angered, not only by his own emotional reaction to Carissa, but also by her rejection of his advances, Paul shouted angrily, "I don't intend to. I'm going to the apartment. When you decide to act like a sensible woman instead of a skittish girl who's never been kissed, I'll come back to help you."

Running into her room and slamming the door, Carissa thought that if Paul waited for that, he'd never come back. Why, after guarding her emotions for years, had she suddenly succumbed to the magnetism of Paul Spencer? Always before, she'd been so careful to keep men at an emotional distance, but for the past week, she'd been out of her element. Her usual contact with men was on a business basis and she often played the dominant role in those relationships. She'd never had a male friend, and because of his friendship, Paul had broken down her defenses.

She wanted to leave Yuletide, but she'd never run away from an obligation before. They had promised to take care of the children until after Christmas. If Paul didn't want to honor his promise, she'd manage alone, as she'd always had to do.

Paul untangled himself from the plastic bags and boxes, wondering if he'd injured himself. He'd felt a sharp pain when he'd landed on his left shoulder, and he sat up gingerly. If she'd injured him again, he wouldn't have the nerve to go to the local emergency room for treatment. He moved his arm back and forth, and found that it wasn't broken. Still angry, he went into the bedroom, picked up the clothes and personal articles he'd brought to the house and walked across the yard to his apartment.

Carissa Whitmore had been bad news for him from the first minute he'd laid eyes on her. The last thing on his mind when he'd bought the mistletoe was that he'd kiss Carissa. Up until that minute, he'd thought of her as an interesting companion, and he'd admired her courage in taking on the responsibility of the children. He'd started to be wary when he'd learned she had a lot of money. That should have warned him to keep their relationship impersonal. But they'd had so much fun together while they were shopping and decorating the house that his defenses were down.

When Carissa had pushed him away, the humiliation he'd experienced when Jennifer jilted him had flashed before his eyes. Carissa was the only woman who had interested him since that time. To have her reject his advances had touched a raw nerve that he'd thought had healed a long time ago.

But regardless of what she'd done, Paul couldn't excuse himself for the vitriolic words he'd hurled at her. He'd never talked to anyone like that in his life. Not even to Jennifer, who'd hurt him so much. And he'd had the nerve to accuse Carissa of acting like a child! Well, he'd made a fool of himself, but if Carissa wouldn't make the first overture, it was all over between them.

But if he wasn't at the house, he wouldn't be able to help with the children. Serves her right, he thought. Hadn't Carissa brought this on herself by the way she'd reacted to a simple kiss? But was it a simple kiss? As best he could remember, his innocent, youthful intimacies with Jennifer hadn't given him the electric jolt he'd felt when his lips had touched Carissa's. Happiness such as he'd never known had made his spirits soar, and at that moment, even if he'd tried, he couldn't have resisted Carissa's appeal.

Well, the fox is in with the chickens now, he thought, recalling the old expression, and he didn't know what he could do about it.

When it was time to pick up the children, he drove into town as usual. It wasn't fair to Carissa to expect her to explain to the children why he wouldn't be staying at the house. Even a few days of tender care had made a difference in them. Uneasiness still lurked in the eyes of Alex and Lauren, but Julie was as carefree as if her future was certain. He would miss being at the house with them.

Paul was pleased to see that their children—and he wondered when he'd started thinking of them in that way—had made friends. Lauren and Alex seemed to have one or two companions when they left the school building, but Julie was always surrounded by several other children. She usually talked most of the time on the way home, telling of their school experiences.

When she'd finished, she asked, "What're we gonna have for supper, Uncle Paul?"

Now was the time to tell them. "I don't know. I'm staying in my apartment now, so Carissa will be doing the cooking."

Alex, who was sitting nearest the door holding Julie on his lap, glanced quickly at Paul.

"She's no cook. Said so herself," Alex said.

"I'm sure she'll have a good meal for you, but don't expect too much. She worked hard today decorating the house."

Julie's lips drew into a pout. "You said you'd watch cartoons with me tonight."

"I know I did, and I'm sorry. Some things came up, and I need to stay in my apartment."

"Uh-huh!" Alex said, and his expression became hard and resentful.

Paul stopped in front of the house and said, "I'll see you in the morning when I take you to school."

"I'm gonna stay with you," Julie said, a determined set to her little jaw.

"Forget it, Julie," Alex said, and he lifted her out of the truck.

When Carissa opened the door to greet them, she donned a smile.

"Oh," Lauren said as she looked at the decorations. "Pretty!"

Carissa hoped the Christmas decor would take their minds off Paul's absence.

"Let me help you out of your coats," she said with forced cheerfulness. "I bought some cookies at the deli yesterday, and you can have some with milk while we wait for dinner."

"I'm not hungry," Alex said, and stomped through the great room toward his room.

Lauren and Julie threw their coats on the couch and followed Carissa into the kitchen. They answered Carissa's questions in monosyllables, and as soon as they ate the two cookies and drank the small glasses of milk she allotted them, they picked up their coats and went upstairs.

Carissa sat at the table, her chin resting in her hand. What had Paul told the children that had upset them? Or had something happened at school?

Dinner, too, was a silent affair. As soon as they finished eating, Julie and Alex went into the great room, while Lauren stayed behind to help with the dishes.

Carissa soon became aware of an argument between Alex and Julie.

"I want to watch cartoons," Julie shouted.

"And I want to watch the hockey game," Alex said. "You're spoiled, Julie."

"Am not!"

"You are, too."

Julie tried to snatch the remote from Alex's grip. Carissa was surprised at Alex's reaction, for she'd noticed that both he and Lauren gave in to Julie. She knew it was time for her to intervene, but she didn't have the first clue about how to stop a quarrel between siblings.

"Thanks, Lauren, for helping," Carissa said, and with a sinking heart, she went into the great room.

"Julie, you've been watching cartoons for a half hour," she said. "It's Alex's turn to choose a show."

A belligerent light glittered in Julie's brown eyes. "No!"

"Then, go upstairs and watch the television in my room."

"No!" she shouted. "I'm gonna go and watch television with Uncle Paul. He'll let me watch my shows."

Julie started determinedly toward the back door. Carissa moved quickly and blocked the exit.

"No!" Carissa said. "Your place is here."

Julie started screaming, and kicked Carissa's leg savagely.

Carissa couldn't believe that this child, who'd been so sweet and outgoing for the past week, had turned into a little monster before her eyes.

Julie fell to the floor, kicking and screaming. Alex continued to watch television. Lauren stood behind the couch staring at her sister.

Rubbing her injured leg, Carissa said, "Well, what do we do? I told you I don't know anything about children."

"Nothing," Alex said. "She'll wear herself out after a while and cry herself to sleep."

"Sometimes Mama gave her time-out—made her go in a room by herself until she could behave," Lauren said.

"I wouldn't try that here," Alex advised. "When she has these fits, she sometimes throws things. Didn't matter at home, 'cause we didn't have nuthin'. I don't want her to tear up this house."

Carissa certainly didn't want her to destroy any of Naomi's things, either, but she didn't know if she could stand the screaming much longer. Her nerves were already frayed from the emotional scene with Paul earlier in the day. He'd said he wouldn't come back until she needed him. She certainly needed him now—but she wouldn't call for him.

"Does she do this often?"

"Anytime she can't get her way," Lauren said.

"When our mom was so sick," Alex said, "we let her get by with a lot of stuff, so's not to worry Mom. But I'm tired of it."

Carissa limped to a chair and Lauren came to her.

"Did she hurt you bad?"

"Just a bruise, I think. I'll be all right."

Carissa made room in the chair for Lauren to sit beside her, but she held her hands over her ears. The child's piercing screams seemed to compound the pain in her head, which had been hurting for hours. She put her arm around Lauren, and the girl snuggled close to her. She knew these children needed a mother's love, but did she have any maternal love to give?

Julie's screams lessened gradually over the next

hour and finally ceased. Lauren peered around the chair at her sister.

"She's asleep," Lauren whispered.

"Now what?" Carissa asked, feeling very foolish for having to ask for advice.

"Wait a while, and then we can take her to bed," Alex said.

After another half hour, Julie was still sound asleep. Lauren awakened her, and she docilely accepted Carissa's hand and went upstairs to bed.

"Is it all right if I stay up and watch television?" Alex asked.

"Keep the volume low and don't stay up too late," Carissa said. "I've had a hard day. I have to get some rest."

Lauren helped Julie undress and slip into her nightgown. "I'd better sleep with her," Lauren said.

"Surely that isn't necessary," Carissa said. There had only been two nights that Lauren had wet the bed, but she didn't want her to have an accident in Julie's bed. If these kids stayed much longer, she'd have to refurnish Naomi's house.

"I ought to, Miss Cara," Lauren responded, compassion in her voice. "She knows she's been bad, and she needs to know that we still love her, anyway."

Words of wisdom from such a small child, Carissa thought. She reached out and hugged Lauren tightly, for she needed love, too. Carissa swallowed a sob when Lauren leaned into her embrace.

"You're a good sister," Carissa said. "I'm going to bed, too, but call me if you need anything."

Carissa couldn't believe that such a tiny girl could have caused so much pain, but Julie had kicked her on the shinbone. She rubbed the affected area with some liniment she found in the medicine cabinet. She also took a couple of ibuprofen for the pain and swelling.

But she didn't go to sleep. All day long she'd avoided any thoughts about her altercation with Paul. She didn't blame him for his harsh words. She'd had them coming. Why hadn't she been wise enough to accept his kiss under the mistletoe as a friendly gesture and let it go at that? If she hadn't been so captivated by his words and leaned toward him, he wouldn't have done anything more. Why, oh why, had she let down her defenses to become enamored of Paul? For twenty years she'd built a wall between her and the male population—a wall high enough to keep all of them at a distance. When a man made romantic overtures, she froze him with a glance. Why hadn't she done that with Paul? The answer was simple—she hadn't cared about any of her other admirers. Paul was different.

She wanted him around her, so much so that she was afraid to admit it to herself.

Chapter Nine

Carissa finally drifted into a light sleep, only to be wakened by Lauren, who was shaking her shoulder.

"Miss Cara, come quick!" she said. "Julie's sick in the bed."

Fearing the worst, Carissa rushed into the other room. Julie was sitting up, gagging, and Carissa said, "Hurry. Into the bathroom."

"Too late," Lauren said, pointing at the comforter where Julie had already spewed the contents of her stomach.

Groaning, Carissa eased into a chair beside the bed to get her breath. The room smelled like a hospital, and nausea gripped Carissa. But she forced herself to deal with the situation.

"If you still feel sick, come to the bathroom with me," she said.

Julie took Carissa's hand and walked docilely to the bathroom with Lauren trailing behind. Julie's gown was soiled.

"Could she have eaten something at school today that made her sick?" she asked Lauren.

"We had vegetable soup," Lauren said, "but she usually gets sick when she throws a temper fit."

"Please bring a clean nightgown, Lauren, while I wash her face and hands. Are you still feeling sick, Julie?"

"I don't think so."

"You'll have to sleep in Lauren's bed the rest of the night. I'll get some ginger ale from the refrigerator, and if you sip on that, it will settle your stomach."

When she went downstairs for the beverage, Alex was still watching television, and it was one o'clock in the morning.

"Julie's sick, huh?"

"Yes, and since you're still up, I'm going to take the soiled bedclothes to the basement and put them in the washer."

She cracked the upstairs window to clear the odor, tucked the girls into bed and covered them with a heavy blanket. Impulsively, she leaned down and kissed both girls' foreheads.

"Try to sleep now."

When she came up from the basement after putting the bed linens in the washer, she sat beside Alex on the couch. He muted the television volume.

"You should be in bed," she said.

"I'm too worried to sleep." When she didn't comment, he said, "You and Paul had a fight, didn't you."

"Do you think that's any of your concern?"

"Yes, it is. You both agreed to look after us, and I

was starting to think things might work out for me and my sisters. We're gonna be dumped again."

"We didn't promise you anything permanent."

"I know, but I could hope, couldn't I? I can tell that you and Paul like each other, so I thought maybe you'd get married and adopt us."

Carissa put her hand over his clenched one. "Alex, Paul and I haven't known each other any longer than we've known you. We've lived into our forties without getting married—we're not apt to take such a step now. Marriage is a serious move for anyone, and especially for two people who are set in their ways. I'm sorry that you were expecting more than you'll get, but you knew this was a temporary situation from the first."

"I know that in a few weeks, it's going to be up to me to look out for my sisters again. But I trusted you to help us."

Trying to control her temper, Carissa crossed the floor and turned off the television. "Go to bed, Alex. I've had all I can handle today."

Sulkily, he obeyed her, and Carissa went upstairs wondering if Alex would try to run away again before morning. Without even changing into nightclothes she took off her shoes and slipped under the blankets. Emotionally and physically spent, at that moment, Carissa didn't care what happened.

Paul could tell by the woebegone expressions on the children's faces that all wasn't well. He drove slowly, hoping to find out what had happened the night before.

"Nice morning," he said, motioning to the snow-topped evergreen trees glistening in the morning sun. "Looks like nature is getting ready for Christmas, too."

No answer.

"How'd you like the decorations Carissa put up yesterday?"

"Nice," Lauren said.

After another period of silence, while Paul grew tense with apprehension, Julie said, "I was bad last night."

"You were worse than bad—you were a monster!" Alex said.

Julie's lower lip trembled. "I missed you, Uncle Paul."

"And when Miss Cara stood in front of the door to keep her from coming to your apartment," Lauren said, "she threw one of her fits and kicked Miss Cara on the leg."

"That wasn't a nice thing to do," Paul said, angry at himself because he'd deserted Carissa when she needed him.

"But it got worse," Alex said. "Julie screamed and carried on until she cried herself to sleep."

"Then she got sick and threw up in the bed," Lauren said. "We changed Julie's clothes. Then Miss Cara had to wash the sheets and things."

"And if Miss Cara puts us out, it will be Julie's fault," Lauren said.

"What makes you think she'll put you out?" Paul said.

"I wouldn't blame her if she did," Alex said.

"She looked awful sad while she was fixing our breakfast this morning," Julie said.

"Did you tell her you were sorry?"

Julie shook her head.

They had arrived at the school by then, and as the children left the truck, Paul said, "Don't worry about it today. You can apologize to Miss Cara tonight."

Paul parked the truck at the café and went inside to order his breakfast. In his anger, he'd told Carissa he wasn't returning until she asked him to. If she hadn't called for him the night before, when she was having so much trouble, it was obvious she wouldn't bend. Was it up to him to make the first move?

Paul had his pride, too, and it wasn't his nature to apologize for his actions. He knew he'd never forgiven Jennifer for her treatment of him. He hadn't railed at her the way he had at Carissa, but when Jennifer had written that she was breaking their engagement, asking for his understanding, he hadn't answered. He'd left Yuletide the next day and he'd neither seen nor heard from Jennifer since.

He sipped absentmindedly on his cup of coffee and stared into space. Through his stubbornness, was he going to allow his relationship with Carissa to fail? She was the only one who'd touched his heart in twenty years—in fact, he'd decided that he was incapable of loving again. He didn't think he was in love with Carissa yet, but given time, he believed he could learn to love her.

Pastor Erskine interrupted his reverie when he stopped by the booth where Paul sat and said that he wanted to have a committee meeting in the afternoon. Paul went back to his apartment and waited, hoping that Carissa would contact him and tell him about the episode of the night before. She didn't. He didn't see any sign of life at the house. Still not knowing what move to make, he waited until eleven o'clock before going over.

His heart pounding like a jackhammer, and wondering if Carissa would even speak to him, Paul stepped softly up on the deck. He lifted his hand to knock, and halted. Carissa was lying on the couch, on her back, one arm resting over her face in a defensive gesture. He watched for a few minutes, started to walk away, but then turned and knocked on the door. Carissa swung into a sitting position, rubbed her eyes and looked toward the door.

Would she turn him away?

She favored her right leg as she walked toward the door, and Paul realized that Julie's kick had hurt her.

She unlocked the door and turned back into the room. Presented with her back, Paul didn't know how to proceed. Somehow he perceived that apologies weren't necessary or perhaps even wanted.

"I saw Pastor Erskine in the café," he said. "He wants to have a meeting of the planning committee at one o'clock."

Carissa glanced at the clock. "Then I'd better get ready." Without looking at Paul, she went upstairs.

He watched her rigid back with alarm. Her eyes had been icy and unresponsive. He wondered if he should call out his apologies to her. But he let her go without saying anything.

Carissa wondered if Paul intended for them to go

together to the meeting, or if he'd return to his apartment and drive to town on his own. At that point, it really didn't matter to her. The episodes of the previous night had left her so depressed that she didn't care about anything. Not Paul. Not the Christmas celebrations. Not the children. Nothing.

When Carissa came down an hour later, feeling a little less exhausted after a shower, shampoo and a change of clothes, Paul was waiting in the kitchen.

"I'll have lunch ready in a few minutes," he said, as if no harsh words had ever passed between them.

Without answering, she sat at the table. He placed two grilled-cheese sandwiches and a plate of apple slices on the table. He'd brewed a pot of tea.

"I thought hot tea would go well. The bank sign registered zero this morning."

"I like a cup of hot tea on a frosty morning," Carissa replied.

They talked very little during lunch.

"The meeting will probably last until time for the kids to be out of school. If you want to take your SUV, we can bring them home."

When they left the house, she handed him her keys. "Will you drive, please?"

He took the keys, wondering why she wanted him to drive. Had Julie's kick injured her badly? Should she stop by the clinic? But Carissa had been making her own decisions for a long time. She didn't need a nursemaid, and in her present frame of mind, she'd be quick to tell him so. But Carissa didn't seem to be angry at him. She conveyed an "I just don't care" attitude, which alarmed him more than if she'd vented her anger on him.

The meeting lasted for two hours, and by the end, Carissa's head hurt so much that she could hardly concentrate. The lack of sleep and tension were taking their toll.

She wrote a check to pay for the light display that was already being erected on the lakeshore and gave it to Pastor Erskine. He said it would be operating a week before Christmas, and would stay lighted through New Year's Eve.

Two other women had volunteered to help Carissa with the costumes for the progressive nativity scene. The pastor asked if she and Paul would play the roles of Mary and Joseph in the pageant, which would take place on the Sunday night before Christmas. They both agreed, but Carissa felt, rather than saw, the frequent glances Belva Townsend sent her way. As soon as the meeting adjourned, Belva drew Carissa aside and into a vacant room.

"I told you to contact me if you had any trouble," Belva said.

Eager to unburden herself to this knowledgeable woman, Carissa rubbed her head and said, "I have a headache now, but my role as surrogate mother is really wearing me down." She told Belva about Lauren's bed-wetting habits, Julie's tantrum and the subsequent results, and Alex's hopes that she would keep them permanently. She omitted any mention of her relationship to Paul, and if the woman suspected that Carissa hadn't told her everything, she was wise enough not to mention it.

"Lauren's problem is a common one among children. The cause is usually a small bladder—it hasn't grown enough yet. Encourage her to go to the bathroom often, and, if you're awake in the middle of the night, see that she goes then. Pediatricians don't all agree with me, but I think the situation can be magnified by emotional distress. And the same thing probably caused Julie's tantrum. These children's mother died only a few weeks ago. They don't have a home, and they've been wandering around the state on their own. I noticed in school this morning that all three of them were not as exuberant as they'd been. Alex probably thinks you'll put them out because of the way Julie acted."

"No matter what they do, I'll keep my promise to look after them until after Christmas," said Carissa. "I tried to tell Alex last night that they need parents who know what they're doing. I'm ill-equipped by practice or temperament to take on a family of three. I'd be miserable, and they would be, too."

"Paul promised to help," Belva reminded her.

"But he has to return to his job before the first of the year."

"It *is* a dilemma," Belva agreed. "They need love more than anything else—if we can only find someone to give it to them! I've put the situation on the prayer chain—our church family is praying for a solution. We'll have to find out who those children are and where they lived."

"Julie has taken a distinct liking to Paul. He might

be able to surprise the information out of her. But I don't suppose we should disrupt them any more until after Christmas."

After the children were strapped into their seat belts for the drive to the house, in a quiet little voice, Julie said, "I'm sorry for being so mean, Miss Cara."

Carissa nodded and felt the pain increase. "I know you are, Julie. Just forget about it. I'm sorry you were upset—perhaps I let my own problems override your needs. How did things go at school today?"

"Somebody stole some money," Lauren said, "and the pastor called us all into the auditorium and talked to us about stealing."

"Do they know who took the money?" Paul asked.

"He didn't say," Alex said.

When they arrived at the house, Julie tugged on Paul's hand and drew him inside. "I missed you last night," she said.

"It's good to be missed," he answered. "I'll make up for it by fixing what you like for supper. What do you want?"

"Spaghetti!" Julie said.

"No, pizza!" Lauren said.

Seeing Julie's pouting look, Paul knelt in front of her and helped her take off her snow boots.

"No more tantrums out of you, young lady. If you hadn't been so nasty, we'd have had spaghetti, but as it is, you'll have to wait until another time for your favorite. I guess I shouldn't have asked for suggestions, Lauren, because I don't have any pizza ingredients.

We'll have pizza tomorrow night. Alex, you choose tonight's menu."

"I'd like to have chicken and mashed potatoes like Mom used to fix."

"Didn't we buy some chicken, Carissa?"

"Yes, it's in the freezer."

"Then I'll thaw it in the microwave and pop it in the oven to bake while I make the rest of dinner, which ought to be ready by six o'clock. Girls, you take your things upstairs, then come down and help me with dinner. Alex, you can bring in some wood from the deck so we can have a fire tonight. If you have homework, we can take care of it after dinner."

When all of the children denied having assignments, Paul looked keenly at Carissa. "You'll probably find some headache medicine in Naomi's medicine cabinet. Close your door, and I'll keep the kids quiet while you take a rest."

Tears misted her eyes, and she went upstairs without answering. Paul had evidently come back to stay, and she hadn't had to ask him to.

She didn't take any medication, but she did stretch out in the large recliner chair in the bedroom. She pulled a hand-crocheted afghan over her shoulders and dozed contentedly. She glanced at her watch occasionally, and at six o'clock, she went downstairs.

The aroma of food, mixed with a smell of burning wood, filled the house. She paused on the bottom step. All the decorations seemed enhanced by the gently-burning fire, making the great room the most home-like place Carissa had ever seen.

"We were going to let you sleep a little longer before we called you," Lauren said.

"I didn't sleep, but I rested some. Dinner smells great," she said.

"All of us helped," Alex said.

"Then I suppose I'll have to take care of the dishes—since I didn't help cook."

The children were cheerful again—so different from the way they'd been the previous night. As they ate together and then sat on the floor around the fireplace to pop corn the old-fashioned way, they seemed like a family. Paul and Carissa exchanged questioning glances, but Carissa could see no further than the present. She was happy they could provide some security for the children for a few weeks, but she couldn't conceive of this being a permanent arrangement.

The warmth of the fire and the cessation of her headache made Carissa very sleepy, and after watching her yawn every few minutes, Paul said, "I don't think anyone got much sleep last night. Let's go to bed early tonight."

"Girls, head upstairs and get ready for bed. I'll be up in a minute," Carissa said. Remembering Belva's observation that the children needed love more than anything else, she went to Alex and put her arm around his waist, giving him a slight squeeze. "Thanks for helping with your sisters. I'm sure your mother would be proud of you."

He hung his head and moved out of Carissa's embrace. "I don't think she would be," he said, and went to his room.

Carissa lifted troubled eyes to Paul. She'd thought her gesture would encourage Alex, but apparently it hadn't. Whenever she thought she was learning how to treat the children, she ran into a wall.

"The teen years are difficult ones," Paul said. "You're doing okay."

She shook her head. "I don't know."

When she turned away, Paul said, "Are we going to keep pretending nothing has happened? Or are we going to talk?"

"We'll talk, but not when there are three pairs of interested ears in the house. Besides, I'm too weary to talk tonight."

Halfway up the stairs, Carissa turned to find Paul watching her. He captured her eyes with his, and his look of tenderness made her heart ache. She'd told him they would have to talk tomorrow. But how could she explain her fondness for him, while at the same time revealing the reason she'd reacted so strangely to his caresses? Would the hang-ups she'd carried from youth into maturity ruin her friendship with Paul?

"Goodnight, Carissa," he said softly. "Sleep well."

When she tried to answer, her voice faltered, but before she made a hasty retreat to her bedroom, she threw him a kiss.

Chapter Ten

After Paul left to take the children to school, Carissa cleared the kitchen table and started making sketches for the costumes needed for the nativity scenes. She had an afternoon appointment at the church with the other two women who were helping with the costumes. Belva had said there was a fabric shop in town where they could buy the necessary materials at a discount. They would need twenty-five garments, and it would involve a lot of sewing. Luckily, she had brought her favorite portable machine with her.

She hadn't gotten far with her designing when Paul returned. She heard his truck in the driveway, and she wondered if he would go to the apartment. If he didn't, the long-overdue talk must take place.

"Am I interrupting?" Paul said as he entered the kitchen, bringing the outdoor fragrance of wintertime with him.

Carissa's hands wrapped tightly around her pencil. "I'm making sketches of the costumes we need for the pageant."

"I thought we could talk now, but if you're too busy..." His voice trailed off.

"Let me finish the lines of this shepherd's robe so I won't forget what's in my mind. I'll join you in the great room in a few minutes."

Even as she finished the sketch, Carissa's heartbeat accelerated and she had trouble focusing on what she was doing. The hour of reckoning had come—the time when she knew that, for her continued happiness, she must talk about things that would be difficult to reveal.

She poured two glasses of apple juice, and handed one to Paul as she entered the great room. He sat on the couch, and she chose a chair directly opposite him. She needed to look him in the eye while they talked.

"I want to apologize for what happened," Paul said. "I can't say I'm sorry I kissed you, because I enjoyed it, but I am sorry I did it when you didn't want me to."

Carissa waved aside his apologies. "I'm not mad at you—I'm mad at myself. I accept the blame. There's no excuse for my behavior. It was only a brotherly kiss at first, but my reaction invited more."

Paul wondered at the look of humiliation in Carissa's eyes.

"Why does my touch disturb you?"

She shook her head. "This isn't easy for me to say. You accused me of acting like a girl who'd never been kissed. And that's true. I hadn't been kissed before."

Paul stared at her in disbelief. "What's the matter with the men you've met through the years?" he asked, a tinge of wonder in his voice. "You're a vivacious, charming woman."

Her heart hammered foolishly at his words, but she made an effort to speak calmly. "I made up my mind a long time ago that I wanted to avoid a close relationship with any man."

She swallowed hard, gripped the sides of the chair and closed her eyes for a moment.

Paul was aware that this revelation was hard for Carissa, and he wondered if he should tell her that she didn't have to explain. He didn't speak, however, for he sensed that Carissa needed to unburden herself of the frustration that had blighted her emotional life.

She opened her eyes. "I'm an illegitimate child," Carissa started, in a voice that was barely more than a whisper. "My mother never married, and she had lots of male companions, so I have no idea who my father is. My mother died when I was a child, before I knew what kind of person she was. After her death, it didn't take long for the kids to let me know that my mother had been a prostitute."

After a few minutes of silence, she glanced at Paul. His face revealed consternation at what she'd told him.

"Like me any less than you did?" she asked with a wry smile.

"Of course not! You aren't accountable for what your mother did."

"You'd have thought I was if you'd lived through my childhood in a small town. I had a few friends, but they were mostly older people in our church. But I looked very much like my mother, and I heard more than once

'Like mother, like daughter.' By the time I reached my teen years, everyone was expecting me to turn out just like her. I couldn't do anything about looking like her, but I made up my mind that I wouldn't be promiscuous, too. The only way I knew to avoid that was to stay away from the opposite sex. I refrained from any casual friendships with men, fearing they might develop into something more. I was determined that I'd never have children who would be ashamed of me as I am of my mother."

"I'm sorry to hear about your parentage and the difficult childhood, but…" He paused, wondering how to continue. "But why did you push me away? I had nothing to do with that."

Sadness had darkened her blue eyes while she'd unloaded the trauma of her past, and she couldn't meet his gaze now. She stood and walked to the window that looked out upon the wooded mountain behind the chalet.

"Because I *wanted* you to kiss me, and I didn't want you to stop. When I realized that I'd let my emotions overrule my principles, I was scared. Terrified of how I was feeling—strange, uncomfortable feelings I'd never experienced before."

She felt Paul's presence behind her, and she clenched her fists, praying he wouldn't touch her again. How would she react if he did?

He didn't touch her, but his voice was tender when he said, "I know it wasn't easy for you to reveal this, and I'm honored that you'd tell me. But you're not a vulnerable girl anymore. And there's nothing wrong with the emotions you experienced. You're a mature woman who won't submit to the shortcomings of your mother. Come and sit down."

Noting the weary droop of Carissa's shoulders, Paul's arms ached to embrace her. He almost believed that Carissa wanted him to take her into his arms, but he'd have to be more sure of that to try again. She turned away, and he hoped she would sit beside him on the couch, but when she didn't, he knew he must be cautious in what he did and said.

"To be honest," Paul said, "I wasn't too happy with my reactions to our kiss, either."

She lifted her head quickly, and her expressive eyes revealed a hint of sadness. Had he used the wrong words?

"Since you've been so honest with me, I think it's only fair to tell you why I've never married. During my last two years in high school, I dated a local girl, Jennifer Pruett. We were in love. We planned to be married after graduation and attend college together."

Carissa watched the play of emotions on his face. Pain and anger glittered in his dark eyes.

"The summer after our graduation, Jennifer went to visit her aunt in New York City, where she met a man she wanted more than she wanted me. An older man who could give her a lot more than I could. He was wealthy, and when she compared all he had to the four years we'd have to spend in college living from hand to mouth, she chose riches instead of me. She sent me a 'Dear John' letter, which I didn't answer. I left Yuletide and I haven't seen Jennifer since. Her mother still lives in town, but I've been fortunate enough not to encounter Jennifer during the few visits I've made here."

"Where is she now?"

"Last I heard she'd divorced her husband, but was still living in the New York City area. I'm not sure I've ever forgiven her, but the way she treated me convinced me that I was better off staying a bachelor. I didn't want to get hurt again. So when I kissed you, I wasn't happy about it. I thought I'd put those emotions out of my life. Then, when you pushed me away, I experienced the same sense of rejection that I'd had after Jennifer jilted me."

"I'm sorry I made you remember."

"Maybe it's just as well for me to remember. As long as the past festers in my heart, I'm not the kind of person God wants me to be. And the longer we work toward bringing Christmas to Yuletide, the more it makes me realize that I've not honored God by the way I've lived. My only concern has been Paul Spencer, and no one else."

"I understand what you mean," she said. "Helping with the celebration and looking after our children has caused me to look at my own spiritual needs."

"So now that we know and understand each other's hang-ups, where do we go from here? Seems to me we've been getting along pretty well the past three weeks, so if you're willing, let's forget our past problems and concentrate on finding Christmas—the way we'd both planned. I believe we'll find it by caring for the children and bringing Christmas to Yuletide."

He reached out a hand to her. After only slight hesitation, Carissa took it, and he helped her to her feet.

"Of course I'm willing. I haven't had many close friends, and I've enjoyed our few days together. And the children will be relieved, too. They detected the tension between us. Alex even asked if we'd had a fight, and said he supposed he'd have to start looking out for his family again."

"And speaking of that, I'm concerned about something else. I wonder if Alex took the money that disappeared from school. Maybe he's accumulating some money so they can run away again."

"Oh, no! I've coped with Lauren's bed-wetting problem and Julie's tantrums. I won't overlook stealing."

"You won't have to. I've already set a trap for Alex. I had an old billfold in the apartment. I put a few dollars in it and placed it on a shelf beside the washer and dryer. We'll see what happens. I suspect that Alex was stealing, even before his mother died, to help with the family's upkeep."

"Stealing was one offense I wouldn't tolerate in my company," Carissa said grimly, her blue eyes darkening. "Evidence of theft meant automatic dismissal. And to think I've taken in a child who may steal."

"We don't know that yet," Paul said. "But I wanted you to know my suspicions so you'd watch your purse."

"Yes, I will. Thanks, Paul, for listening to me. It's been too convenient through the years for me to ignore things that bothered me. But now… I have to go back to my work. The sketches have to be finished before this afternoon. I've promised to cut out the patterns, and the other two ladies will do most of the sewing."

"I'm going out on the lake now to try some fishing. That will give you some peace and quiet to work. I'll drive into town with you this afternoon and help with the rest of the street decorations."

A half hour later, Carissa watched through the window as Paul, heavily clothed, walked toward the lake. His presence did disturb her peace of mind, so it was just as well that he had left the house for a short time. Still, she couldn't tear her gaze from his long athletic stride and the proud set of his head. Carissa knew that her feelings for him were intensifying to a point of no return.

Paul returned, empty-handed, at eleven o'clock, but he'd had a good morning. The cold air had added a ruddy hue to his dark skin, and contentment gleamed in his eyes.

"It's a good day for skating," he said. "Maybe we can rent some skates and take the kids out on the ice."

Carissa had finished her sketches and had a light lunch ready, which they sat down to. The doorbell rang, however, before they finished eating.

They'd had no visitors other than Justin and Belva, so Carissa was surprised to answer and find a woman at the door.

Carissa took in the visitor's appearance quickly. Tall and willowy, with black hair and glowing green eyes, this woman would be a perfect model for Cara's Fashions. Her leather jacket was open, and, coincidentally, her sweater was one of Carissa's creations.

"Hello," the woman said. "I'm looking for Paul Spencer. I understand he's living here."

"Well, yes," Carissa said slowly as she opened the door. "Come in. Paul," she called, "you have company."

He sauntered into the great room and glanced at the visitor, and his face whitened. His eyes widened in astonishment.

The woman went toward him with outstretched hand, and when Paul ignored her hand, she leaned forward and kissed him lightly on the lips. He moved away, and she laughed.

"That's not the way you reacted the last time I kissed you," she said. "I thought some things would never change."

Turning as if she'd suddenly remembered Carissa's presence, the woman said, "Maybe I'm out of line." Nodding toward Carissa, she said, "I hadn't heard that you were married."

His astonishment soon turned to annoyance, and in a curt voice Paul said, "I'm not married. This is my friend, Carissa Whitmore." And with a meaningful glance toward Carissa, who had an unfathomable expression in her eyes, he continued, "Carissa Whitmore, meet Jennifer… Pruett. I don't remember your married name."

Jennifer smiled. "It's Colton. Jennifer Colton. It seems you've forgotten a lot of things about me, while I've never forgotten *anything* about you." She slid her fingertips across his left cheek in a provocative gesture before walking to the couch and sitting down without an invitation.

"If you'll excuse me," Carissa said, "I have some work to finish."

Uneasy, Paul wondered what Jennifer was up to now. How he wished she'd stayed out of his life!

He watched Carissa climb the steps, wanting her to stay but knowing he shouldn't ask it of her. If Jennifer wanted to talk to him, he might as well get it over with. As he waited for Jennifer to speak, he compared the present Jennifer with the one he'd loved. Had she always had that determined thrust to her jaw and that hardness in her eyes? Or had the eyes of love and youth blinded him to her true character?

"I've wanted to see you since we parted," Jennifer said, "but apparently you haven't spent much time in Yuletide."

"Only a few times to visit Naomi. Yuletide held nothing else of interest to me."

"I came to visit Mother for a few days, intending to take her home with me for Christmas. Now that I find you're here, I may just spend Christmas in Yuletide." She nodded her head toward the upstairs. "Or do your interests…lie in that direction?"

Paul was determined that Jennifer wouldn't learn how much she'd hurt him, and he forced himself to speak in a composed voice. "Carissa and I met about three weeks ago. She and Naomi have traded houses for a few months. Your mother may have told you that three runaway kids have come to Yuletide. Carissa and

I are looking after them until further arrangements can be made."

"How cozy!" Jennifer exclaimed.

When Paul remained silent, Jennifer stood and said, "Well, you won't be baby-sitting all the time. Perhaps we can have dinner some evening."

He followed her to the door. "Carissa and I are helping with the town's celebration, so we're very busy."

"Oh, well, I'll see you around somewhere," Jennifer said breezily as she strolled down the sidewalk, jaunty and self-assured.

Chapter Eleven

Carissa sat in the window seat and leaned her head on her knees. Jennifer Colton's physique was the kind Carissa had always dreamed of having. Carissa had resented the fragile features and the light coloring she'd inherited from her mother. As a child, she'd often fantasized about being a tall, slender brunette, and she'd created Cara's Fashions for that type of woman. Jennifer could easily have been one of the cover girls that appeared on her company's brochures.

The woman's arrival today had ruined the friendship that she'd started to enjoy with Paul, ruined whatever relationship might have developed between them. Anyone could tell from the predatory look in Jennifer's eyes that she intended to go after Paul again, as she'd done in her youth. And what were Paul's feelings toward her? He had said he'd loved her once. Had that love disappeared when Jennifer jilted him and married another man? Carissa doubted it, thinking that might be the reason Paul hadn't been interested in any other women.

Not for the first time, Carissa wished she'd never made this move to Yuletide. She'd been getting along very well on her own, but in just a few days, she'd become dependent on Paul's companionship for her emotional needs. It would be doubly hard when she had to go alone again.

She heard a car leave the driveway and assumed Jennifer was leaving. Carissa dreaded to find out Paul's reaction to seeing his former girlfriend. Her stomach churned with anxiety when she heard his soft tread on the steps. He tapped lightly on the half-closed door. She straightened on the window seat, grateful that in spite of her sadness, she was dry-eyed.

"Come in," she said.

Paul walked in, and Carissa's suspicion that he was pleased that Jennifer had reentered his life was immediately dispelled.

He said bitterly, "I don't know why she had to show up at this particular time. How she has the nerve to face me I can't imagine."

So his reaction to seeing her again was anger, Carissa thought. But sometimes anger covered other emotions. He could be angry and still love Jennifer.

Paul paced for a few minutes. "After I got over the blow to my self-esteem when she broke our engagement, I was able to realize that her emotions weren't as deeply involved as mine had been. She wanted a husband, and Yuletide didn't offer a large selection. I suppose I was the best one she could find here. When she visited the big city, she found men that suited her more."

He sat on the edge of the bed.

"Maybe she's back in your life for a reason," Carissa said. "When I talked to you about my anger and frustration with my mother, it relieved me of a burden I've carried for years. Maybe you haven't resolved your anger, and this will give you an opportunity to do so. Harboring such sentiments for years isn't easy. I know."

Paul knew one reason he was so angry: for the first time since his attachment to Jennifer, he'd become deeply interested in another woman. Carissa had been on his mind constantly since he'd met her, and it was pleasant to contemplate the rest of the month with her. When they had to part on the first of January, he didn't know what commitments he might want to make.

Now he had the feeling that Jennifer hoped to rekindle their romance. Surely he had enough willpower not to succumb to her charms, which had fascinated him when he was a teenager. But he remembered that Jennifer could be very persuasive and was unsure of how he'd react.

"Maybe she's had time to realize what she gave up when she let you go."

"I'm not that much of a catch," he said. "Not with all the possibilities in the Big Apple."

Knowing how she was drawn to him herself, Carissa wasn't so sure. Obviously Jennifer had everything a woman could desire. Wealth, charm, good looks—perhaps everything except the devoted love of a man. If love had eluded her, then Jennifer might look for it in Paul.

* * *

Carissa vowed to put aside thoughts of a possible reconciliation between Jennifer and Paul as she helped Yuletide prepare to resurrect the Christmas spirit.

The night that the display of lights around the lake was turned on, Paul and Carissa went with the children to the opening celebration, when the mayor threw the switch to illuminate the Christmas Fantasy show.

The five of them walked the mile-long route to view the wonderland of lights. The largest display represented a tall ice castle. Others represented the joy of the holiday season—an ice-skating family, a group of carolers standing beside a lamppost, a horse-drawn buggy, and many animated toys.

The real meaning of Christmas was commemorated in scenes depicting the birth of Christ—three Wise Men approaching on camels; angels announcing the birth of Jesus to shepherds watching a flock of sheep; and the nativity scene with Mary, Joseph and the baby in the stable surrounded by several farm animals.

Paul had prepared logs for a fire before they left, and when they returned to the house, while Carissa prepared hot chocolate, he and the children popped corn in the fireplace.

It occurred to Carissa that it seemed unnatural that the children seldom talked about their home life. Their mother had been dead only a short time. Surely they missed her. By refusing to voice their sorrow, were they pretending they were happy?

But tonight, instead of sitting with the others around

the fire, Lauren huddled in a deep chair, and Carissa pondered if this sensitive child was remembering the past.

"Don't you want to sit closer to the fire, Lauren?" Carissa asked, touching her hand. "You feel cold."

"The last time I touched Mommy, she was awful cold," Lauren whispered, and her eyes filled with tears.

Carissa moved to the chair and sat beside the child.

Tears brimming in her eyes, Lauren asked, "Is she still cold? They buried her in the ground."

Carissa lifted terrified eyes toward Paul. She didn't know how to deal with Lauren's hurt.

Julie rushed over to pat Lauren on the head, and Alex said, "I told you people don't get cold in heaven."

"Is that true, Miss Cara?" Julie asked.

Praying for guidance, Carissa tried to remember the words her grandmother had used to console her when she lost her mother.

"When your mother died, she left her earthly body behind. She has a new, spiritual body, and I'm sure she isn't cold." Carissa's mouth seemed parched, and she looked to Paul for help.

"From what you've told us," he said, "your mother had been very sick for a long time. Maybe God took her to be with Him so she wouldn't hurt anymore. Try to think of your mother being in a place where she's happy."

"She didn't have happiness here on earth," Alex said bitterly. "I miss her, but I was glad when she died because she wouldn't be sick anymore."

"That's the way to look at it, Alex," Paul said. "Why

don't you remember the good times you had with your mother—that's a good way to forget her illness."

"We've got a picture of all of us before Mama got sick, but Alex won't let us look at it," Lauren said.

Carissa turned on Alex. "Why not?"

"Because they both start crying, and I can't stand it."

"They need to cry," Paul said, "and so do you. You're only a boy, even if you've had a man's burden put on you. Where is the picture?"

"With my things."

"Go and get it. I'd like to see your mother's picture," Carissa said gently.

Reluctantly, Alex went into his room and came back with a large photo taken by a professional photographer. He handed the picture to Lauren, and Julie hung over her shoulder to look.

"See, that's me," she said, pointing to a curly-headed toddler on the lap of a sad-faced but beautiful woman sitting in the center of the photo. Lauren and Alex stood on either side of the woman. All three children had pleasant, carefree expressions on their faces, so apparently their home life hadn't been too bad before their mother became ill.

"We couldn't afford anything but the free copy," Alex said.

"It's a very nice picture, and the next time we go to Saratoga Springs, we'll take this picture and get a copy for each of you," Carissa said. "Your mother was very pretty. And I know how much you miss her—I was about Julie's age when my mother died."

"Is there a tombstone on your mother's grave?" Alex asked, his face troubled.

"Yes. Not a big one, but my grandmother marked the grave."

"There's none on Mom's, except the little metal marker the undertaker put on it."

Carissa was tempted to tell him that she'd buy a marker for the grave, but she'd have to know where the cemetery was. That might be a sly way to dig into their past, but tonight wasn't the time to be devious. The children needed to be loved.

"Let's sing some Christmas carols," she suggested. "While we sing, think about the good times you had with your mother. Instead of being bitter about the past, all of us should think about positive things," she added with a pointed look at Paul.

Smiling, he lifted his hand in a salute to show that he'd gotten her meaning and swung into the opening lyrics of "Joy to the World."

The next day when Jennifer Colton attended the committee meeting, however, Carissa was hard put to follow her own advice.

"I'm so proud of my hometown for resurrecting Christmas," Jennifer said as soon as the pastor started the meeting.

Even Carissa with her suspicions about Jennifer couldn't tell if the woman was being honest. "But there's one more thing needed to make this celebration like the ones we used to have. We need to have a skating party." Jennifer looked with glowing eyes at some of the older people in the room, whom she apparently knew.

Paul's heart plummeted, and he turned a despairing glance in Carissa's direction.

"Do you remember the great times we used to have?" Jennifer asked. "We had competitions and gave prizes for the best acts. If you're interested in trying this again, I'll organize it and take care of all the expenses."

Paul thought Jennifer must have learned about Carissa's generous contribution for the light display. As he remembered, Jennifer always wanted to outdo everyone else.

When the committee chairman put the idea to a vote, only Paul dissented. Regardless of the way Jennifer's presence had disturbed her, Carissa knew she couldn't let personal bias rule decisions that would be good for the town, so she voted in favor of the skating party.

Carissa didn't think her emotional roller coaster could plunge any lower, but it did when, with a hearty laugh, Belva asked, "You and Paul going to perform like you used to?"

"I hadn't thought of that—" Jennifer said.

Carissa believed she was lying, that this was another ploy to get her hooks in Paul.

"That would be great. What about it, Paul?" Jennifer asked.

Paul was convinced that Jennifer had planned this whole thing with the goal of forcing him back into a relationship with her. In the days of their courtship,

Paul had overlooked some of her obvious faults. Disillusioned now, he remembered character traits that hadn't been endearing. The boys had liked Jennifer, but she hadn't cultivated the friendship of girls.

"I haven't had many opportunities to skate lately," Paul said, "so I'm out of practice. Sorry."

"I figure skating is like riding a bicycle," Belva said. "Once you learn how, you never forget."

"That's true," Jennifer said excitedly. "And I've kept up with skating. It won't take long for me to teach you any techniques you've forgotten."

Paul shook his head. "And I weigh about fifty pounds more than I did when I was in high school. I'm not very graceful anymore, so it wouldn't be much of a performance."

"But you're still in good shape," Jennifer said, unashamedly admiring his solid shoulders and trim waist. She reached out and patted Paul's forearm. "It'll be fun." With glowing eyes, she turned to the pastor's secretary. "Put us down for a performance. I'll come to your office in the morning to make plans about getting others enrolled in the competition."

Paul felt like a drowning man searching for a life preserver. "I don't know that I'll participate," he said. "I'll think about it and let you know in a day or two."

"But time is running out. We'll have to move quickly," Pastor Erskine said.

"I'll think about it and let you know in a day or two," Paul repeated evenly, and he looked at Jennifer.

"If you make an announcement indicating that we'll be skating before I agree to it, you'll skate alone."

An angry look crossed Jennifer's face, but she said with a strained laugh, "All right! All right! But decide as soon as possible."

"Have you had another fight?" Alex said as they were driving home.

Paul turned furiously toward the back seat, but Carissa nudged him in the side.

"Paul and I haven't had the *first* fight, so how could we have *another* one? Just because you're living with us doesn't give you the right to involve yourself in our personal affairs. But I will tell you that Paul has been upset by something that has nothing to do with you or your sisters. So stop being nosy!"

"Yes, ma'am," he said. "Sorry."

As they drove the rest of the way in silence, Carissa considered the aunts and uncles who'd not wanted to take all three of these children. She could understand why, because all three of them had distinct personalities. She thought she could deal well enough with any one of the three, but she didn't think she could cope with all three. Natural parents became accustomed to their children's differences gradually, but to suddenly take on the responsibility of caring for three children was daunting. Short of adopting these children, what else could she do for them?

After Paul helped with the dishes, he said, "I'm going out for a walk."

"I want to go with you, Uncle Paul," Julie said, and headed for the closet to get her coat.

"Not tonight, Julie," he said. "I have some thinking to do."

Julie stamped her feet. "I want to go."

He knelt beside her. "Julie, you *are not* going with me. Sit with your family and watch television for a while and then get ready for bed."

"Please!" Her chin quivered, and Paul wasn't unaffected by her gesture. It had been balm to his heart that this little girl adored him so much, but he knew it wasn't good to give in to the child's demands. Besides, he had to be alone tonight.

"No," he said firmly. "Give me a hug and then behave yourself."

Sniffling, Julie hugged his neck, and Carissa wondered if she'd throw a tantrum as soon as Paul was out of the house.

Looking at Carissa, a resigned expression on his face, he said, "I don't know when I'll be back, so don't wait up for me. I have a key."

Julie's eyes followed Paul until he was out of sight. Still sniffling, she sat on the floor and watched the program Alex had chosen.

Carissa was sympathetic to Julie's feelings. She would have liked to accompany Paul, too. The uneasy nagging in the back of her mind refused to be silenced. Paul needed some time to decide if he still wanted Jennifer. Carissa dreaded the decision he might make during his walk.

Chapter Twelve

Paul avoided the lakefront, where he would encounter other people looking at the Christmas Fantasy lights. He took a flashlight from the glove compartment of his truck and headed up the mountain. He soon accessed a trail made by loggers several years ago, which was kept in usable condition for safety purposes during the forest-fire season.

The days he'd spent with Carissa and the children had been the most satisfying time he'd known in years. After the first dreadful months following his breakup with Jennifer, he'd been content with his nomadic life. But recently, he'd started thinking about settling down in one place, wondering if he was too old to become a family man. Many men he knew had married in their forties, and had fathered children.

So why, when his thoughts were veering in that di-rection, had Jennifer come back into his life? He had no doubt that he'd loved Jennifer at one time, but he believed it was over. When she'd shown up yesterday, he hadn't experienced any of the pleasure or excitement she had once caused. Didn't that indicate that he was indifferent to what she said or did?

After Jennifer ditched him, Paul had pushed all memories of their painful relationship into the background. But today, little by little, as he walked, Paul dredged from the depths of his memory the two years he and Jennifer had dated.

Jennifer's family had moved to Yuletide when she was sixteen. She'd been the most beautiful girl in their school, and he was flattered when she chose him. He wondered now if he'd been chosen not because she loved him, but because he was the most eligible guy in school. Yuletide was a small place, and Paul had been captain of the football team and had played on all the other sports teams. He was also the only man in town who excelled at skating. Had she loved him or had she chosen him only because he fitted her needs at the time?

In retrospect, he realized that even as a teenager, Jennifer had been manipulative. He remembered with sorrow one time when his parents had planned for all of them to attend a family reunion in Vermont. The date conflicted with the time that Jennifer's family was going to the beach. He still didn't know how it happened, but Paul ended up going to the beach with the Pruetts.

He'd felt lousy for disappointing his parents, who had gone to the reunion with Naomi and her husband. He'd promised, "The next time I'll go with you," but his father died before the next reunion.

He'd apparently been putty in Jennifer's hands, for he remembered countless other times that he'd set aside his plans because she'd wanted him to. He'd tell himself that he wouldn't do it, but the next thing he knew, Jennifer got her way.

Paul's mother hadn't liked Jennifer, and now he could understand why. His mother had told him when they announced their engagement that he was making a mistake—that Jennifer would ruin his life.

Jennifer hadn't been pleased with his plans to be an engineer. She'd wanted them to become professional skaters. He liked to skate, but he wasn't thrilled with the intense competition and the rigid life of a professional. After Jennifer broke their engagement, he'd moved to California, finished his engineering degree and started his overseas work. He'd blocked Jennifer out of his mind and life. But now she was back. He didn't want her—but was he strong enough to withstand her charm and seductive ways if he saw her every day? She'd wrapped him around her finger once…so should he avoid her now? Or was it better to skate with her and prove to her and *himself,* once and for all, that she had no hold on him?

And what would Carissa think about it? After yesterday—when he and Carissa had unburdened their past hang-ups and explanations about why they'd never married—his feelings for her had intensified, as if the future held something more for them than they realized.

He didn't want anything to jeopardize their relationship, if that was what God wanted for them. If he skated with Jennifer, he might lose an opportunity to explore a future with Carissa. On the other hand, he didn't want to go through life wondering if Jennifer had any hold on him.

Breathless, he reached a clearing on the top of the mountain, affording a view of Yuletide and the lake. He easily picked out Naomi's house. What were Carissa and the children doing now? As he watched, the lights faded on the first floor, and he knew they'd gone to bed. When the deck light came on, he realized that Carissa had left a light for him. How much would Carissa care if he and Jennifer were reconciled?

He sat on the boulder until the crisp night air chilled his body. He knew what he had to do—but was he man enough to do it? He'd lived for years in a man's world, one that had given him very little experience in dealing with inner emotions and needs of the heart. He now faced a new situation—his emotions in conflict between two women. One whom he'd once loved, and another whom he believed he *could* love, given time and opportunity.

He had already committed to being Joseph in the living nativity and Carissa would be Mary. They would be together often, planning and practicing for their roles. And if he accepted Jennifer's challenge, and he believed that was what it was, he'd be with her every day, too. Which woman would win his heart?

He considered the five-year age difference between Carissa and him. He had trouble believing that Carissa was forty-five, because she had a vulnerable, untouched air that prompted him to protect her. He believed he could help her forget her unfortunate past—but he didn't have much time. In two weeks, he had to return to work in Europe.

Discouraged, and still undecided about what to do about Jennifer, Paul strode quickly down the mountain trail. The waning moon provided some light, and the glow on the deck served as a beacon to guide him. Or was Carissa the lodestar that lighted his way?

Carissa heard the wind blowing around the house, and she shivered under her warm blanket. The illuminated clock face indicated it was past midnight. Paul had been gone for more than three hours, and she wondered if he was all right. She'd dozed a little, but for the most part she'd stayed awake, worrying that Paul would go back to Jennifer.

She indulged in several minutes of self-pity, wishing she had Jennifer's beauty. She compared her small body and insignificant features to the perfection of Jennifer's appearance. If it came to a choice between her and Jennifer, she wouldn't blame Paul if he chose Jennifer. And Jennifer was closer to Paul's age. Being five years his senior didn't make her eligible for a romantic relationship with him.

Carissa didn't like Jennifer's flamboyant personality, but she attributed that to jealousy. She disliked pettiness in anyone, and she was disgusted that she'd stoop so low, even in her thoughts.

Remembering Belva's admonition that Lauren should take frequent trips to the bathroom, Carissa went to the other bedroom and awakened the child to go. Carissa hadn't put on a robe, so she was colder than ever when she got back to her bed. She turned the blanket heat up a couple of notches, hoping she would go to sleep, but she was still awake when she heard Paul enter the house an hour later. She would have liked to talk to him…. No, Paul would have to initiate any conversation about his relationship with Jennifer.

"Brr!" Paul greeted her when she entered the kitchen the next morning. He pointed to a dual thermometer on the wall. The outside temperature hovered slightly above zero.

"No wonder I felt cold last night," Carissa said.

"The furnace is on a timer that reduces the temperature a few degrees at night. Naomi and her husband didn't like to sleep in a warm house."

"I'm worried about the children's clothing," she said, trying to talk of mundane matters to keep her mind off Paul and Jennifer. "The things they got at the church are all right, but they need heavier footwear. I'll pick them up after school and take them shopping. I noticed a department store in Yuletide that should have what they need."

"I'll share the expense with you, Carissa. Remember, this a joint venture."

"Then you might as well go along with us as we shop. I don't know anything about buying boots for kids."

Their routine was well established. Paul prepared breakfast for everyone, and she took care of the dishes while he drove the children to school. Carissa was vacuuming when Paul returned. When she finished, he put the vacuum cleaner in the broom closet, then stood by the fireplace, his arm resting on the mantel.

"Well, Jennifer really wrecked my plans for a laid-back Christmas celebration," he said. "She wasn't content to be a disruptive element in my life twenty years ago—she had to come back now."

"I assumed you took the walk to decide what to do. I've had no experience along this line, but I suppose once you love someone, the emotion is always there."

He looked at her quickly. "I'm not in love with Jennifer now, if that's what you're suggesting."

Carissa's heart exploded with a little leap of gladness. "Then why should her return to Yuletide disturb you? Obviously, it has."

"Jennifer is always determined to get what she wants."

"And you think she wants you?"

He flushed. "I know that sounds conceited, but she acts as if she does. Last night, I remembered many things about our previous relationship. She always liked a challenge. It might sound less arrogant to say that she might not want me, but she's just curious to see if she can maneuver me into another relationship."

Carissa sat on the fireplace ledge and looked up at him. "It takes two to make a relationship. If you're unwilling to take up where you left off twenty years ago, I don't see why you need to worry."

He walked to the kitchen and turned on the faucet to draw a glass of water. "I told you Jennifer usually gets what she wants."

Carissa's eyes narrowed. "Are you afraid you won't have the willpower to resist her?"

Paul's face flushed again, and he drank a full glass of water before he answered. "That sounds rather cowardly, doesn't it."

If he was that fearful about Jennifer's attempts to snare him, was he as unaffected by her presence as he said?

"What do you want to do?"

"Avoid her. But I've come to the decision that I should go ahead and skate with her. If she throws any romantic lures my way, I can prove that I'm not interested by ignoring her."

"But what if you can't ignore her overtures?"

He shook his head, for he had no answer.

Carissa lowered her head, knowing that she had a similar problem. She wasn't sure she had the willpower to keep Paul at arm's length. If he kissed her again, how would she react? Just thinking about a romantic relationship with him caused her spirits to soar. And what if that thought became a reality? Her heart danced with excitement if their hands touched casually when they were working around the house. She wasn't sure he was affected, but she believed that if a web of attraction was building between them, she was powerless to prevent it.

She moved away from him and started to finish the interior decorations. Paul came over to help, and she sat on the steps while he stood by the railing as they decorated the stairway with garlands of poinsettias and evergreen.

Paul groaned when Jennifer appeared at the back door. She peered through the glass, saw them and entered without knocking.

With a short laugh, Jennifer said, "Paul, do you spend all of your time over here? Mother said that the apartment behind the house is your home. I've called several times without an answer."

"I'm seldom in the apartment and I *am* living here. When the three children invited themselves into Naomi's house, Carissa and I assumed responsibility for them."

"How long have the two of you known one another?"

"Since the day after Thanksgiving," Carissa said.

"Mother said you'd traded houses with Naomi."

Carissa didn't answer, and Jennifer turned her attention to Paul.

"We must talk about the skating party and our participation."

Carissa started to stand, but Paul put a gentle hand on her shoulder to keep her in a sitting position. She continued to wrap the greenery around the posts.

"I'm not interested in doing the exhibition. But Carissa and I have pledged to help Yuletide revive the spirit of Christmas. And since the skating party was once part of the celebration, I'll skate with you, but don't expect me to be light on my feet. I've skated sporadically over the past twenty years, so we can't perform a difficult routine."

"Then meet me at the skating rink this afternoon

and we'll see how much you've forgotten. Two o'clock okay?"

"Let's make it one o'clock. Carissa and I are taking the children shopping when school lets out at three."

"How about having dinner together tonight to plan our strategy?"

"No. I'm committed to Carissa and the children every evening. We're trimming the tree tonight."

Shrugging, Jennifer said to Carissa, "Mother tells me that you're the owner of Cara's Fashions."

Carissa taped the last garland to the bottom step before she answered. "Not anymore. I sold the business two months ago."

"I've worn some of the clothes."

"Yes, I noticed that you had on one of Cara's sweaters yesterday."

Jennifer turned toward the door without saying whether she liked the clothes or not.

Carissa's comment about the sale of her business brought to Paul's mind his reluctance to become involved with a rich woman. But that point wasn't bothering him so much now. During his last conversation with his sister, Naomi had told him that when Carissa sold her company, she used a large portion of the income to establish a foundation for abandoned children. Not only was she not as wealthy as he'd feared, but her charity had convinced Paul that Carissa was a compassionate, caring woman.

"This must be our day for company," Carissa said, when the doorbell sounded at about noon.

A police cruiser stood in the driveway, and Paul opened the door for the chief of police.

Stomping his feet to get rid of the snow on his boots, Justin said, "Hiya! I have some news for you about the children."

"Come in. Got time to have a sandwich with us?"

"Sounds good to me. I worked all night and I'm finally heading home for some shut-eye."

Justin shrugged out of his heavy coat and laid it over the back of a chair.

"Is it good news or bad?" Carissa asked as she poured a cup of coffee for him.

"Not bad," he said, settling into a kitchen chair. "And for the good of everybody concerned, I think we'd better keep this information to the three of us until we decide what we want to do about it. If I tell one other person, including Belva, the news will be all over town by nightfall."

Paul set lunch meat, cheese and mayonnaise on the table. Carissa took a bowl of grapes and a loaf of bread from the refrigerator.

While they made their individual sandwiches, Justin said, "There was a message on the Internet last night about three missing children in Aberdeen, Vermont. The profiles sounded a lot like our Christmas children, so I telephoned the sheriff there. We had a long chat. There's no doubt we're dealing with the same kids."

A wave of disappointment spread through Carissa. Had she actually been hoping that the children couldn't be traced?

"Have they told us the truth?" Paul asked.

"Pretty much so, it seems. Their family name is Garner. Their mother was sick for several years and died about three months ago. The father hasn't been seen for several years. I gathered from the sheriff that the neighbors had been taking care of them for months."

"Is their family looking for them?"

"The sheriff said that a local preacher and one aunt had initiated the search. The kids are from a poor family. The extended family members aren't necessarily heartless, but none of them can afford to take in three children."

Carissa pushed back her plate. She'd lost her appetite. Her mouth was dry, and she swallowed with difficulty. "So, what do we do now?"

"The sheriff is going to contact the local welfare service, which has been supporting the Garners for several years. I told him of Yuletide's desire to include the children in our Christmas plans and that they are in good care. He thinks there won't be any demands to have them returned to their hometown before Christmas. They'll probably be put in foster care, though it's unlikely they'll find one family that will take all the children."

"So they'll be pushed from pillar to post?" Carissa said.

"More'n likely," Justin agreed.

"Shouldn't we tell the children what you've learned?" Carissa asked.

"That's up to you. I thought the kids should hear

it from you rather than from somebody else." Justin stood, yawning. "I'm headin' for home, folks. I'll keep you posted on what I hear. Thanks for lunch."

While Paul chatted with Justin as he put on his coat and left the house, Carissa put away the food and placed their dirty dishes and silverware in the dishwasher. She went into the great room and absently picked up items that belonged to the children: Lauren's bear from the fireplace ledge, a book on football that Alex had been reading the night before and one of Julie's mittens lying on the couch.

When Paul returned he didn't interrupt her musings, but went into his bedroom to prepare for the afternoon's ordeal with Jennifer. Carissa was staring out the glass doors when he returned. He'd changed into a pair of gray sweats, and he sat on the couch to pull on his snow boots.

"I don't know whether I feel better or worse now that we've learned more about the kids," he said.

Carissa sat beside him. "I feel worse. There just doesn't seem to be a happy ending for them, unless I adopt them."

Impulsively, he laid his hand over hers—conscious, and relieved, that she didn't rebuff his touch. "No, Carissa, that isn't the answer. Haven't you seen enough already to know it wouldn't work? Where would you live? Would you take them back to Florida with you? It's too much for you to take on Lauren's physical problems, Julie's tantrums and Alex's stealing."

She looked at him quickly.

"Yes, he took ten dollars out of that billfold I planted in the basement. I hadn't seen any need to bother you with the knowledge."

"But don't you think they'd change a lot if they had the security of a home?"

"I'm not thinking about anyone but you. You've worked hard, and now that you're financially secure enough to retire, you ought to have a life of your own."

"But a life doing what? That's one reason I started thinking about finding Christmas. I didn't have anything else to do."

"Trust me, Carissa—this isn't the answer. You can find many worthwhile things to do without becoming a mother."

"You think I'm too old to do it," she accused.

"I don't think you're too old to do anything you want to. I'm not as old as you, and I wouldn't want to take on the single parenthood of three kids. I admit I've become attached to them, and I'd help you with them if I could. But in a few weeks, I'll be thousands of miles away."

He couldn't read her expression, but he didn't think he'd convinced her. "At least promise me that you won't make a hasty decision about this. Who knows—maybe their father will show up."

She looked at the clock. "You only have ten minutes to get into town."

Carissa didn't seem a bit disturbed about his association with Jennifer, so apparently Carissa wasn't experiencing the same feelings for him that had started infiltrating his mind and heart when he was with her.

"I'll meet you at the school by three o'clock," she said as he left the house.

Carissa seldom had any time alone anymore, so she took advantage of the peaceful moment to read the Bible. For years, Carissa had devoted all of her energy to making a success of Cara's Fashions, to the neglect of her spiritual nature. But since the pressures of business had been lifted from her shoulders, she'd tried to read the Bible every day. She was pleasantly surprised to find out how much she remembered of the spiritual truths she'd learned from the Bible as a child.

When she'd received such a large payment for her business, she'd recalled the Scripture verse, "As we have opportunity, let us do good to all people." She'd pondered a long time about how she could do this, until she heard about an organization that was devoted to helping abandoned children. She'd felt that she should share some of what she'd gained, to help children who'd had the same misfortune she'd had.

Now, as she sat, Bible in hand, considering the Garner children, the story of Queen Esther came to mind. Esther, a Jewish slave girl, had become queen in the Persian Empire. Esther may have thought that she'd reached the pinnacle of success and that her life from then on would be one of ease. Yet, when her countrymen were on the verge of extinction, Esther had been told, "And who knows but that you have come to royal position for such a time as this?"

Right from the first, Carissa had thought it strange that she'd been inspired to look for the meaning of Christmas in a town she'd never seen, among people she didn't know. God's spirit was everywhere. Couldn't she have found the Christmas spirit in Florida? She didn't need to travel a thousand miles to find new meaning for her life.

Yet it seemed right for her to be in Yuletide, New York, in this house with Paul and the children. Had she, like Queen Esther, been brought to this locality for a specific purpose? During the few times she'd contemplated adopting the children, she'd always thought of doing it with Paul at her side. It seemed obvious that he had no inclination in that direction. And she could understand that he had a job to do. With Paul's cooperation she believed they could set up a happy home life for the Garner children. But where? Naomi would be returning to New York in a few weeks. They couldn't live in this house, which was too small for five people, anyway. Besides, soon after Christmas, Paul would return to Europe.

Could she handle the adoption alone? But would she *be* alone? If God had brought her to Yuletide because the Garner kids were here, wouldn't He be with her through parenthood as helper and guide? Queen Esther had had the prayer support of God's people to accomplish her goals. The local Yuletide church members had already demonstrated their willingness to help feed and clothe the children. She was sure that any church congregation anywhere would offer the same loving support.

But Paul had asked her to use caution, and she would. She'd seldom acted on impulse, but since making the hasty decision to travel to Yuletide, she'd been jumping into troubled waters with both feet. Which way should she jump now?

Chapter Thirteen

Paul also felt the need for extra strength as he drove into Yuletide. He prayed for help in keeping his guard up against Jennifer's wiles. It wasn't his nature to be rude to anyone, but during this skating performance, he must keep their relationship on a strictly impersonal level.

He knew his task wouldn't be an easy one when Jennifer showed up at the skating rink wearing tights that looked as if she'd been poured into them.

"Oh, why are you wearing sweats? You'd be more comfortable in tights," she said, tapping him playfully on the shoulder.

"I'm not wearing tights until we're ready to perform. Besides, I *am* comfortable." He tied on the rented skates. "All I intend to do today is to learn how much endurance I have. I haven't been on skates for several months. You can explain what routine you have in mind, but we can't skate as partners today."

Lifting first one leg and then the other, Paul tottered

for a few moments before his body movements adjusted to the sensitive balance necessary for skating. Only a few other skaters were on the ice, and he spent several minutes circling the rink. He leaned forward, lifting his left leg and stretching it behind him, his arms extended in a straight line from his shoulders.

As always, he thrilled to the feel of the cold air drifting past his face as he glided across the smooth surface. Confident that he hadn't lost much of his agility, Paul tried a two-foot spin. With his feet slightly more than shoulder-width apart, he put his weight over his left thigh, his left toe gripping the ice. With his right arm pressed behind him, he positioned his left arm across his body, fingertips pointed behind him. He bent both knees equally, and with his arms held taut, he snapped his arms around and to the front, stretched his knees, straightened both legs, planted both blades on the ice, initiating the spin. He was pleased that he experienced only a slight dizziness, and decided he could probably do a creditable job of skating for the exhibition.

He glided across the glistening ice several more times, then experimented with cutting figure eights on the smooth surface. He tried several rotation jumps, and while he considered his movements clumsy, at least he didn't fall.

All during the practice session, he was aware of Jennifer. How could he help it when she circled him dozens of times? Her body was as youthful and glamorous as it had been when she was a teenager. When they made eye contact, she gave him a tantalizing smile as if to remind him of other times they'd performed together.

After a half hour, Paul's heartbeat was more rapid than he would have liked, so he skated to the side and sat on a bench. Jennifer executed a graceful waltz jump directly in front of him, then joined him.

"You haven't lost much of your grace," Jennifer said admiringly.

He rubbed his legs and went through a few stretches. "Maybe, but my muscles didn't appreciate the exercise." Hoping to hasten Jennifer's departure, he said, "I'll be here tomorrow at the same time, and we can work on our act. What routine are you considering?"

"Nothing too difficult. The last time we performed together, we skated to the music of 'The Tennessee Waltz.' For old times' sake, it would be fun to do that again. What do you think?"

"That's okay." He started to remove his skates, and Jennifer hovered over him.

"Then, how about going into Saratoga Springs with me now to choose our costumes? I have to make arrangements for the spotlights that have to be set up for the presentation, too. You could help with that."

Paul didn't want to spend any time alone with Jennifer, but several people were involved in various activities around the rink, so Paul indicated the bench beside him. "Sit down, please."

She sat close to him, her thigh grazing his. The contact was distasteful to Paul, but he didn't move.

"I told you earlier that I have other commitments this evening, and I intend to keep them. Before we go any further, I want to make one thing clear to you. Jennifer, I agreed to this performance because I want to see Yuletide glow with Christmas again. But I have no interest whatsoever in a relationship with you."

Her lips curled ironically. "You flatter yourself, Paul."

"Perhaps, but how else can I interpret it? You put me on the spot in front of the celebration committee. I had little choice but to accept your challenge."

"So you haven't forgiven me for breaking our engagement?" she said, her shoulders drooping pathetically.

"I don't know whether or not I have. But that's beside the point—it's in the past and I want it to stay there."

"You're making a mountain out of a molehill. I was so pleased to see you again that I thought it would be nice to skate together. Our practice sessions will be more pleasant if we're friends."

"No, Jennifer, I don't want to be your friend. You use your friends. We're acquaintances, nothing more."

"Have you fallen in love with Carissa Whitmore?" she demanded.

"I've known Carissa less than a month—it's a little soon to be in love with her. We've committed to take care of the children until after Christmas. That will take all of my time."

"Have fun, then," Jennifer said, and resumed skating. He didn't give her a backward glance as he turned in his skates, asked that they be reserved for him until after the exhibition, and left the rink. He doubted that Jennifer would give up so easily.

* * *

After they visited a department store and bought boots for the children, Paul suggested, "Anybody interested in eating out tonight? You're probably tired of my cooking, and I know *I* am. There's a special on hamburgers and fries at the café."

"Yeah!" Alex said, giving Paul a high-five. "The coach gave us a good workout in the gym today."

Julie grabbed Paul's hand. "The pastor said they're gonna make us do something in the parade."

Paul's eyes questioned Carissa as they got into the SUV.

"The pastor mentioned it to me," she said. "They want the children to be the town's guests and ride on a special float during the Christmas parade next week."

"That sounds like quite an honor," Paul said. "You want to be sure you deserve it."

He sensed rather than saw the suspicious glance Alex gave him.

Apparently the Garner children hadn't had many opportunities to eat in restaurants, but they were delighted to be able to order exactly what they wanted. Carissa asked Lauren to drink water instead of a soda, but otherwise, each child chose his or her food. When Alex ordered both french fries and onion rings, Carissa glanced questioningly in Paul's direction. He shrugged.

Carolers were singing along the streets of Yuletide when their meal was finished, and Carissa and her temporary family listened as the music faded into the distance. Paul and the children sang as she drove them home.

Once they were back, while the children went to their rooms with their belongings, Paul stepped near Carissa. "Are we going to tell them what we learned this morning?" he asked quietly.

She nibbled uncertainly on her lower lip. "I've been worrying about it all day, but I think we should. I'm tired of just thinking of them as 'the children.' We know their last name now, and I think we should use it. We're in the clear legally, since Justin has reported their whereabouts and gotten permission for them to stay here through the holidays."

Lauren brought a book downstairs with her and sat beside Carissa on the couch. Alex turned on the sports channel and was soon engrossed in a hockey game. Julie nestled down beside Paul, and he started reading a story to her.

"I read a book like this in my other school," Lauren said as she leafed through the pages.

Paul and Carissa exchanged glances, and taking a deep breath, he said smoothly, "Did you attend a big school in Aberdeen, Vermont?"

Julie apparently didn't notice the import of his question, but Carissa felt Lauren tense beside her. A dark, angry expression spread across Alex's face, and he stared at Paul. Obviously very disturbed, he turned off the television, his interest in sports interrupted.

"So you've been snooping around behind our backs?" he snarled.

Lauren started sobbing, and Carissa enveloped her in a tight hug. Paul's body stiffened, and he opened his mouth, no doubt intending a sharp retort, but Carissa shook her head.

"We did not snoop around," she said. "Chief Townsend received a bulletin yesterday that three children, with the last name of Garner, are missing from Aberdeen, Vermont. The children's first names were the same as yours, so he knew it was you."

"What'd he do about it, besides blabbing to you?"

"He did what he had to do," Paul said, trying to stifle the harsh words he wanted to say. "He contacted the authorities in your town and told them where you were."

"And I suppose they're sending someone to pick us up," Alex said bitterly.

"No. Justin told them we were taking care of you, and guaranteed your safety, which has been approved by the authorities in your area. There won't be any changes until after the first of the year."

"And then what?" Alex demanded.

"I don't know," Paul said, "but I wouldn't advise you to keep stealing money so you can run away again."

A hangdog expression replaced the anger on Alex's face, and he turned away.

"If the people of Yuletide have honored you by giving you a special place in the parade," Paul continued, "the least you can do is stop stealing from them."

Lauren's sobbing ceased, and she lifted a moist face. "Alex! You promised Mommy you wouldn't steal no more!"

"You'd have gone hungry more than once if I hadn't," her brother retorted without remorse.

"Stealing is never justified," Paul said sternly. "And I speak for Carissa, as well as myself—if you want any further help from us, you'll stop taking things that don't belong to you. I understand that you want to accumulate some cash to take care of your sisters when you're not with us anymore. But if you get caught stealing, you'll be in so much trouble that you won't be able to help anyone, not even yourself."

A look of despair spread over Alex's face, and Carissa wanted to comfort him, but she knew Paul's method was needed now.

"You must return the money you took from the school to the pastor tomorrow. And I want the money you took from my wallet."

Alex reached into his rear pocket and took out a worn wallet. He passed over two five-dollar bills and a twenty. Paul felt like a heel for taking the money, but the boy *had* to stop stealing.

"The twenty is what I took from the school. Will you give it to the pastor?"

"No. If you're man enough to look after your sisters and mother, you're man enough to own up to what you've done."

Alex took the twenty and replaced it in his wallet.

"Now I know it isn't easy to be without money, and the three of you have been doing lots of work around here by bringing in wood and helping in the kitchen. I intend to give you an allowance for each week." He reached into his own wallet, replaced one of the fives, and took out some dollar bills. He handed the five back to Alex.

"Since you've done more work than your sisters, I'll give you five dollars a week. The girls will get two dollars each."

Alex turned the money over and over in his hand, and Carissa thought he was on the verge of tears.

"I'm sorry," he whispered, "but Mom told me to look after the girls. I'm not old enough to get a job, and I didn't know how else to do it."

Paul couldn't imagine why his mother had placed such a burden on Alex, but he supposed the poor woman was frantic, knowing she was dying and leaving her family without any help.

"If you're caught stealing, then who'll look after your sisters?" Paul asked.

Alex dropped his head into his hands, and Paul went to him and pulled him into his arms. Alex buried his face in Paul's shirt, his shoulders shaking with sobs. Julie slipped out of the chair and ran to grab Paul around the legs. He dropped his left hand to her head, while still holding Alex in the circle of his right arm.

Hardly conscious that she was speaking, Carissa said, "Stop all of this! I'm going to adopt you."

Three tear-striped faces lifted and stared at her.

"Carissa!" Paul said. "You shouldn't promise that."

Alex ignored his comment. "All three of us?"

"Yes. Legally, I don't know that I can adopt you, but I'll at least apply to be your guardian. It will take a long time, but perhaps I can be your foster parent until we see what we can do."

"Uncle Paul, too?" Julie asked.

Paul cast an angry look toward Carissa, as if to say,

Now see what you've done! "Julie, I have to go back to my job after Christmas," he said.

Already Carissa was regretting her rash promise, but she couldn't stand the grief and fear these kids were obviously feeling. If she could do something to help them, for her own peace of mind, she had to do it. She was sorry that Paul was angry with her. Did he think she was trying to manipulate him into staying in Yuletide?

It would be so much easier if they could have joint custody of the children. She recognized how expertly he'd handled Alex tonight. She might be able to meet the girls' needs, but would she fail with Alex? She didn't know much about child psychology, but she believed Alex needed a father figure in his life. Paul had proven that he could provide that. Perhaps she shouldn't have promised. What if she made a worse mess of their lives than they'd had before?

She wasn't up to a confrontation with Paul tonight, so she said, "Girls, it's time for showers. I'll read a Christmas story to you before you go to sleep."

With a meaningful glance, Paul said, "Come down after the girls are in bed."

Carissa didn't respond. Paul was angry at her, and she was scared of what her impetuosity would lead to. If she waited until tomorrow, he might be over his anger.

She was halfway up the stairs, with the girls running ahead of her, when Paul spoke again.

"Carissa?"

She turned, unable to meet his gaze.

"All right. After the girls are in bed and I hear their prayers, I'll come."

"You gonna talk her out of adopting us?" Alex demanded.

"Carissa makes her own decision, but I think she's promised something she can't do. With your father missing, it could be years before anyone could adopt you."

"But somebody will have to look after us until then. I can't think of anyone else who's willing to take us. Not even you."

Paul could understand why Alex had a belligerent attitude, so he tried to explain. "I'm a bachelor and probably wouldn't be allowed to adopt kids even if I wanted to. When I go back to my work, I'll be living in a shack about the size of the kitchen. The job is in an isolated area, without phones or television. A few men take their wives, but I honestly think the living conditions are too rough for women and children."

Alex's expression, which had been so joyous when Carissa said she'd adopt them, was woebegone again. Paul gave him a quick hug. "Don't start worrying about it. Carissa is a determined woman, and if she's made up her mind to adopt you, nothing anyone says will stop her. So take a shower and go to bed—tomorrow may be a new start for you."

Paul's anger had cooled considerably by the time Carissa came downstairs. She paused uncertainly on the bottom step.

"Our talk can wait if you're tired," he said.

"Not physically tired—but emotionally I'm drained.

If you want to bawl me out because you'd advised me against adopting the children, I'll save you the trouble. I admit that I shouldn't have spoken up as I did, but the children's grief got to me. I should have had a lawyer look into their situation before I promised them. I didn't build Cara's Fashions by giving in to my emotions, and I shouldn't have acted impulsively. But I did, so I'll live with it."

He took her hand and led her to the couch. He turned off the overhead light, leaving only a small lamp to illuminate the room. When she didn't rebuff him, he pulled her gently down beside him, relieved that his temper was under control. Had he been angry because Carissa had spoken, or because she had alerted him to his own responsibility?

"My concern is for you. This is too much for you to handle alone. Your agreement with Naomi is for two months. Where will you take them after that? You'll have to establish a residence somewhere."

"I have a house in Florida."

"But when the state of Vermont has custody of our children, you might have to live there."

"Don't ask me such questions. I have no idea what I've gotten myself into, and I can't even think about it. I've lived alone for years and I don't know what I'll do with three extra people in my home. Since I've been in Yuletide, I haven't had more than an hour to myself at any given time. That's frustrating. No wonder I'm making foolish mistakes."

Paul remembered that Carissa had been reluctant to assume supervision of the children, and he'd more or less pushed her into it. "It isn't a mistake to have compassion for others, Carissa. It's a trait more of us should have." He moved closer and, wondering if he dared, drew Carissa into the shelter of his arms.

"It didn't seem as if I was the one who spoke," Carissa said softly into the fabric of his shirt. "It was almost as if God was speaking through me. I've read in the Scriptures that sometimes God puts words in our mouth. Deep down, I don't *want* to do this, but it seems to be the right thing to do."

He patted her back comfortingly. "I'll do what I can to help you as long as I'm here. I'll ask Justin to contact that sheriff again and learn everything he can about the children's father. In the meantime, we'll show them we love them and give them a Christmas to remember. You'll make a wonderful mother."

Pleased by his praise, Carissa stared up at him in astonishment, and the expression in his eyes made her heart beat very fast.

Her thick, curling lashes dropped in confusion. Paul touched her chin and lifted it upward. The pale gleam from the lamp lit her face with a dancing glow, and her eyes were very bright. A half smile hovered about her lips. Even as he bent closer, Paul struggled for control. He wanted to kiss her, but what if he upset her again? Emotional gravity seemed to pull them together, and when their lips touched in a gentle kiss, Carissa didn't pull away. Slowly her arms slipped around his neck, and she eased comfortably into his embrace. His heart thudded when he realized that emotions he'd thought he killed long ago were still alive and well.

The touch of Paul's lips brought an irresistible sensation to Carissa's heart, and she was happy at her own eager response to his gentle touch. Lying trustingly in his arms, she experienced no guilt. Once, she'd thought that to enjoy kissing and touching was immoral, but these few moments in Paul's arms had brought a new awareness that *real* love between a man and woman was more than sensual, it was also a meeting of mind and soul. After having known Paul for such a short time, could she possibly be in love with him? As incredible as it seemed, Carissa believed that was the case.

"Oh, Paul!" she murmured. Carissa eased out of his arms, not knowing that her eyes were glowing with an intensity that Paul found hard to resist. A rosy hue stained her cheeks.

As he watched the play of emotions on her face, Paul knew that his kiss had unlocked her heart. Carissa's lips parted in a smile as intimate as a kiss, and she studied his face feature by feature, her eyes dancing with excitement.

Paul was humbled to witness her metamorphosis from an emotionless woman to this vibrant, lovable person with a heart full of affection. Once he'd witnessed the emergence of a golden-winged butterfly from its cocoon. He knew now the same awe and unworthiness he'd experienced then.

"Thank you," she whispered.

"For what?" he murmured, his lips hovering in the soft curve of her throat.

"For making me feel alive. For letting me experience the kind of closeness I've often envied among other couples. For causing me to lose my misguided notion about the results of affection between a man and a woman."

"That kiss taught me several things, too."

Afraid to ask what he meant, unwillingly, Carissa stirred from his embrace and stood. "Why'd you ask me to come downstairs?"

He grinned sheepishly. "I've forgotten. But it was a good idea, whatever the reason. We'll talk about what happened in the morning. Good night, Carissa."

She sensed his eyes following her as she mounted the steps. Carissa felt as if she were dancing on clouds, and so intense was her perception of the wonderful thing that had happened to her that later she hardly remembered preparing for bed.

The next thing she knew, her pleasant dreams of Paul were interrupted.

"I tell you they were kissing."

Lauren's muffled words pierced Carissa's semiconscious state, and her eyes popped open.

The girls were tiptoeing their way to the bathroom.

"How'd you know?" Julie answered.

They entered the bathroom, but Carissa heard the rest of the conversation through the partially closed door.

"I got up to come to the bathroom last night. The lights were still on downstairs. I peeked over the rail. They were on the couch huggin' and kissin'. It's the truth—cross my heart."

"Then that means we might get a daddy as well as a mommy," Julie said.

The relief and delight in the child's voice stunned Carissa. It took so little to bring hope to the children. And she feared it was a false hope. Regardless of their mutual affection, Paul had made it clear that he would return to work. There had been no mention of love—and she wouldn't marry someone who didn't love her. And now that they were so physically aware of each other, they couldn't continue in their present situation.

Chapter Fourteen

At the breakfast table, Lauren and Julie looked from
Paul to Carissa and giggled intermittently.

"What's the matter with you girls?" Alex demanded
crossly. He seldom awakened in a cheerful mood, and
this morning was no exception.

Carissa thought the poor child had little to be cheer
ful about. For all of his grown-up airs, he *was* only a
boy. And it had been a humiliating experience for him
to be confronted with his thefts last night.

Paul's eyes sought Carissa's, and she shook her head.
She'd have to tell him part of what she'd overheard,
she supposed, though she didn't intend to tell him all
that Julie had said.

In the few minutes that she had alone with Paul before he took the children to school, Carissa said, "Lauren saw us on the couch last night. She put two and two
together and came up with five."

"I wasn't doing a lot of thinking at that time, but

even if I had been, I'd have thought we had some privacy."

"I'm beginning to wonder if there *is* any privacy with three children in the house."

"I suppose not! We had to learn the hard way."

Feeling motherly, Carissa checked to be sure that Julie and Lauren were buttoned up securely against the cold weather. Paul stopped beside her as she stood at the door, and his eyes caressed her.

"Oh, well! Since they know anyway…" He stooped and brushed a gentle kiss on her soft cheek.

Tears misted Carissa's eyes as they drove away.

God, she prayed, *thank you for giving me this opportunity to* feel. *I didn't think I had any maternal instincts, but I believe I could love these children as my own. And though I'd successfully suppressed all romantic emotions, thanks for allowing me to meet Paul and be awakened emotionally by his caresses. Is it love I feel for him? Am I deluding myself to think that he shares my feelings?*

As the relationship between Paul and Carissa deepened, Yuletide moved full-speed ahead with its resurrection of the Christmas spirit. For three hours each night, a steady stream of cars passed the house, as people from as far away as New York City came to view the Christmas Fantasy.

The costumes for the progressive nativity were finished and the cast had practiced several times.

The skating show was scheduled for two nights before Christmas on the lake near Yuletide.

Paul didn't comment on his practice sessions, and Carissa was jealous of the time he spent with Jennifer. If he would only mention Jennifer, she wouldn't be so miserable about it. Carissa feared that he had succumbed to Jennifer's charming magnetism again, and he didn't know how to explain it to her.

She needn't have worried.

Now that Paul suspected he was falling in love with Carissa, he wasn't disturbed by Jennifer's ploys. She was a beautiful woman and he enjoyed skating with her again, but Jennifer was cold. Now that he'd uncovered Carissa's softness and compassion, he only had to draw forth her image as a shield between him and Jennifer.

Since the children would be the honored guests in the parade, Carissa and Paul took them into Saratoga Springs to outfit them for the event. Neither one of them had any idea about the clothes children liked, so they permitted the children to choose their own, reminding them that the clothes would be part of their Christmas presents. Obviously, the kids were expecting nothing; their delight in the new garments made it apparent that they'd have been pleased with nothing more. Paul and Carissa had already shopped for the children's other gifts. Remembering her own meager Christmases, and wanting to compensate for the Garners' poverty, Carissa would have liked to lavish gifts on them. She refrained, though, knowing that too much at one time wouldn't be good for their character.

When they were passing through the adult section of a big-mall store, Lauren paused beside a display of women's dresses. She lifted a maroon evening dress from the rack.

"Look, Alex," she said. "Wouldn't Mama have looked pretty in this?"

Alex ducked his head. "Don't talk like that," he said. "We've got to forget her."

Unaware that she was blocking the walkway, Carissa stopped and took Alex's hand. "Oh, no, Alex," she said. "Never forget your mother."

"If I think about her, I'll be crying all the time. I see the pretty clothes you wear and it makes me realize how little she had. I don't ever remember her having a new dress until the preacher's wife bought one for her to be buried in. She couldn't see it then."

He broke away from Carissa and ran to catch up with Paul, who was walking in front of them, holding Julie's hand. Paul hadn't witnessed the incident that had brought such misery to Carissa's heart.

Carissa's mother hadn't had many new clothes, either. She took the dress from Lauren's hand and hung it back on the rack.

"I miss Mama," Lauren said, tears forming in her eyes.

Carissa didn't try to stop Lauren's crying because she believed it was best for the child to weep away her sorrow. Besides, tears were welling in her own eyes. She took the child's hand and hurried to join Paul. She shook her head at the question in his eyes.

When Julie saw that Carissa and Lauren were in tears, she started wailing, and Alex turned away to hide his own sobs.

"What in the world happened?" Paul asked, bewildered, but he stooped to lift Julie with his left arm.

Carissa, blinded by tears, held to his right arm.

"Let's sit down on this bench," he said, moving out of the flow of mall traffic to a secluded area. Still holding Julie, he put his other arm around Carissa, who held Lauren's hand. Alex knelt in front of Paul, trying to quiet Julie, who didn't even know why the others were crying.

Carissa took a tissue from her pocket and blew her nose. "I'm sorry," she said between sniffs. "But Lauren saw a dress that her mother would have liked. Alex couldn't remember his mother ever having a new dress until the preacher's wife bought one for her burial. That reminded me that my mother didn't have nice things, either. I don't usually lose control, but I'm more vulnerable to my emotions now than I used to be." Forcing a smile, she said, "I'll be all right."

Paul felt like a drowning man grasping for a straw. He closed his eyes, praying silently for wisdom—he didn't know how to handle this situation.

God, I'm in over my head, going down for the last time. I need help.

"Looks as if you've got your hands full, sir. Anything I can do to help?"

Paul's eyes popped open, and he knew his face must mirror his astonishment. He glanced up at the tall, angular man standing before them.

"I hope so. The children's mother died a few weeks ago, and something in the store reminded them of her. What should I do?"

"Let them cry. Bottling up grief can be harmful. Tears can wash away a lot of misery. Are you their father?"

Paul shook his head, almost on the point of tears himself. "No, they don't know where their father is. My friend and I are looking after them for a few weeks."

The man glanced at the packages piled haphazardly around the bench. "Then I'd say you're doing all you can do. They need to know somebody cares for them." He shook hands with Paul and Carissa, gave each of the children a five-dollar bill and disappeared into the crowd of shoppers.

"He's a nice man," Julie said, a smile replacing her tears.

Paul prayed. *Thank you, God.*

The man hadn't done anything spectacular—nothing that Paul couldn't have done. But Paul needed some sign that what he and Carissa were doing was right, and God had sent His messenger to tell him.

"Is there anything else we need to buy?" he said to Carissa.

She shook her head, and handed Lauren and Julie tissues to wipe their faces.

"Let's have some food and then head for home," he said, thankful that they'd passed another hurdle in soothing the children's sorrow.

Carissa noted that Paul seemed to tolerate the practices with Jennifer, although each day, either by innuendo or by her sinuous movements, she tried to tempt him. She dropped by the house almost every day.

Paul asked Carissa to stay with him any time Jennifer came, and sometimes he wondered if he was afraid to be alone with her. But as long as he kept Jennifer's past actions in mind, and focused on his growing interest in Carissa, Paul felt confident that Jennifer was his past, not his future.

Paul put the letter in his pocket and walked out of the post office with foreboding. The message had come from his employer that the work project would resume the first of January, and that he was booked on an overseas flight from Kennedy International Airport, December twenty-seventh. Normally, Paul would have been delighted with the news because he enjoyed his job; he was usually ready to return to work long before the appointed time. But he'd been so busy with Yuletide's celebration, and being with Carissa and the kids, that the days had flown by.

With so little time left, he should go to see his sister, but he didn't want to leave his unofficially adopted family. And when he didn't want to be separated from them for a few days, how would he feel when he boarded the plane, knowing that it would be months before he'd be back in the United States?

Faced with this anxiety, he wasn't sleeping well. He paced around his bedroom in the dark, wondering what he should do. He believed he was in love with Carissa, and judging from his youthful feelings for Jennifer, he knew that his present emotions ran much deeper. His love for Jennifer had been more physical than true affection and admiration. Now he wasn't content unless he was with Carissa. Since their first kiss, he'd kissed her occasionally, and he knew she looked forward to his caresses. She often kissed him with her eyes, if their gazes met when the children were with them.

What would life be like if he married Carissa and became a father to the Garner kids? He'd been on his own for a long time. Could he so drastically change his habits without feeling trapped?

During one of his nocturnal musings, Paul looked out the window, amazed to see a man standing in the shadow of a spruce tree, watching the house. The next morning he checked the area and found many tracks, as if someone had watched the house more than once.

The person, whom he assumed to be a man, returned the following two nights. Paul became concerned enough to talk to Carissa about it. He'd learned that with three kids in the house, there were no secrets, so he didn't approach Carissa until he returned from taking the children to school.

"For the past three nights, someone has been watching the house," he said, "and I don't know how long before that."

At her gasp and startled look, he said, "I didn't want to disturb you about it, but you are a rich woman—do you think it might have something to do with you?"

"Oh, I'm not *that* rich," she protested. "If I lived twenty years in Florida without anyone having designs on my money, I'm surely safe in Yuletide. Could there be some connection with the children?"

"I've wondered about that," he admitted unwillingly. He didn't want to believe that the children were in danger. "I'll be out tonight practicing, and I didn't want to leave you alone without warning you."

"Should we tell Justin?"

"I can't decide. If the guy comes back tonight, I'm going to confront him."

"Oh, you shouldn't do that. Let Justin handle it."

"With all the visitors coming to town, Justin and his deputy have their hands full now, but I'll tell him what's going on, and that we'll notify him immediately if we need him. When I come back this evening, I'll put my car in the garage as usual, but instead of coming to the house, I'll stay outside and be on the lookout for our visitor."

"I don't like it," Carissa said worriedly. "But I'll wait up until I hear you drive in. I'll flip the light on in your bedroom, and after about fifteen minutes I'll turn it off. Perhaps the guy will think you've gone to bed."

"The times I've seen him, he watches from underneath that grove of spruce trees across the road. After you turn off the light, watch from my bedroom window. Or you can see just as much from the window in your bedroom. If I get into trouble, I'll signal you with my flashlight and you can call Justin."

If Paul was attacked, he might not be able to give a signal, but Carissa didn't point out what must be as obvious to Paul as it was to her. Carissa still wasn't willing to put a name to her feelings for Paul, but she realized that she'd be devastated if anything happened to him.

But while Paul and Carissa were on guard, no one spied on the house that night.

* * *

After school was dismissed for the holidays, the children were at the house all the time. It was difficult for Paul and Carissa to discuss the situation or for Paul to get much rest. On December twenty-second, the day of the skating exhibition, Carissa took the children shopping to give Paul an opportunity to sleep.

"I'd like to go with you and the children," he said, "but that skating routine is rigorous and I've been staying up late to watch, because I told Justin I would. I have to catch up today."

"You might get more sleep in your apartment."

Carissa wondered if her concern was for Paul's rest, or if she just didn't want Jennifer to come to the house when Paul was alone. He didn't seem to have any affection for Jennifer; in fact, Carissa thought he simply tolerated her, but she was still dubious about Jennifer's motives.

"Good idea. And I'll leave my cell phone over here."

Broad-beamed spotlights highlighted the area of ice where the skating party would take place. Carissa had rented skates for the children and herself so they could participate in the general skating after the program. She'd never been graceful on the ice, although she'd done some ice skating in Minnesota as a child; she didn't think she'd forgotten how. Carrying the skates, the four of them found seats on the bleachers that had been erected along the shore of the lake.

Twenty acts, single and pairs, were entered in the competition. Three stern-faced judges had seats close to the ice. Paul and Jennifer's routine would be the grand finale of the program.

Booths were set up, with eager-faced youths selling hot cider and cocoa. The smell of popping corn permeated the crisp evening air, along with the scent from pine trees. Carissa sat on the bleachers, and sipped a cup of hot chocolate and watched "her" children mingle with the friends they'd met at school. She was pleased that they'd adjusted so easily to a new life.

What would happen if they were forced to leave Yuletide and were sent to separate foster homes, or even forced to live with their father? If the man watching the house was their father, or even another relative, he would take precedence over her attempts at adoption. She should have talked to a lawyer, but in the pre-Christmas rush, she hadn't had time. If she waited until after Christmas, it might be too late.

Carissa enjoyed the amateur performances of the youthful skaters, but during Paul and Jennifer's routine, she was miserable. Jennifer was dressed in crimson tights, a short white cape over her shoulders. Paul's tights were light green, his cape bright red.

Their program lasted about ten minutes, every moment of which was agony for Carissa. When the music started, they performed separately, cutting figure eights in the ice, executing side-by-side solo jumps and spins. They skated in unison, close to each other. Once Jennifer got a lift from Paul that made her jump higher, longer and more spectacularly. She landed gracefully, gliding backward on one foot. They did a spin by connecting their legs and whirling together.

The crowd cheered lustily when Paul tossed Jennifer into the air, watched her turn around and caught her. These feats executed, they skated to the center of the rink.

The volume of the music decreased as Paul took Jennifer in his arms, and they danced in perfect rhythm to the waltz music, dipping and swaying as gracefully on ice as if they were on a ballroom floor. Although the movements were rapid, sometimes they were so close it seemed as if only one body danced. The music stopped, and hand in hand Paul and Jennifer skated to the center to take their bows.

Well, she'd lost him! Carissa decided. No man would be stupid enough to want her when someone as clever, fascinating and beautiful as Jennifer Colton had set her cap for him. If Paul was in a position of comparing her and Jennifer, Carissa conceded that she wasn't even in the running. And if she lost Paul, as well as the children, her future looked bleak.

"Penny for your thoughts," Paul said. She'd been so engrossed in her worries that she hadn't heard him approach.

"It was a magnificent performance," she congratulated him. "Both of you skated perfectly as far as I could tell."

"Thanks. We didn't make many mistakes. It's easier than when we were competing. I was relaxed tonight." He took her hand. "Come on. It's time for you to skate."

"I'm waiting until the ice is full of people. Then, if I do a lousy job it won't be so noticeable."

She handed Paul the empty cup, which he took to the garbage can while she put on the skates.

When he returned he said, "I'll hold your hands until you get the feel of skating again."

How she wished he could hold her hands the rest of her life!

Carissa was wobbling from one foot to the other when Jennifer, wrapped in a white wool coat and looking unbelievably beautiful, stopped beside them.

"Oh, you're going to skate?" she asked Carissa.

Although annoyed that Jennifer had seen her awkward movements, Carissa forced herself to say sincerely, "Your performance was excellent. Congratulations."

"It was the most exhilarating experience I've had for years! I'm sorry now that I didn't continue my dreams and become a professional skater instead of getting married. But we don't always make wise decisions when we're young, do we, Paul?"

She fixed him with a predatory glance that worried Carissa.

"I made some good decisions in my youth, and I don't regret any of them. Let's go, Carissa."

"I'll see you shortly, Paul." Jennifer leveled a glance at Carissa. "I've invited all the participants to my house for a party, so I have to hurry and be sure the caterers have everything under control."

Since the children didn't have school tomorrow, Carissa had planned to have snacks when they got home and let them stay up later than usual. She'd counted on Paul being there, too, but she didn't betray that fact by her expression.

Paul held her hands to be sure she was balanced on the ice before he skated away to check on the children. It was so crowded on the ice, Carissa couldn't have fallen if she'd wanted to, but she didn't enjoy the experience. Her legs soon became tired from the unaccustomed exertion, so she went back to the bleachers, changed into her boots and huddled in her comfortable coat to wait for the children.

Brilliant lights focused on the gaily garmented skaters—the scene reminding Carissa of a Currier-Ives painting. As she waited, she contemplated the past month. She'd come to Yuletide to find Christmas. How well had she succeeded in her quest? What had she really accomplished?

She'd found Paul Spencer—a man she admired very much. She'd taken three orphaned children into her home. She'd also found new purpose in life—at least temporarily—to replace the many years she'd devoted to Cara's Fashions.

But so much was still uncertain. She was afraid to adopt the children, even though she wanted to take them. Could she do it alone? With Paul helping, the task wasn't so difficult. Why couldn't she stop imagining how it would be if they were really a family—if she and Paul married and adopted the children?

Her fantasies about Paul had to stop. He'd opposed her adopting the children, and he'd made no bones about the fact that he was returning to Europe after Christmas. Although he'd been affectionate, and she believed he was attracted to her, he hadn't given the slightest indication that he intended to make a lifetime commitment. And then there was Jennifer!

It had been agony for her to watch them skate together tonight. And she was honest enough to admit that her reaction was jealousy. Although Paul seemed indifferent to Jennifer's charm, how could he not have been affected by her nearness during the hours they'd spent perfecting that skating routine?

But even without Jennifer, was marriage an option? For one thing, she'd have to be sure that she loved Paul for himself, not as a way for her to adopt the children. Never until now had Carissa realized how she'd suppressed her maternal longings. When she'd decided not to marry, that had meant no children, so she'd subconsciously put aside any thoughts of motherhood. Now she was amazed to realize that she'd always wanted to be a mother.

If she did adopt the children, Carissa knew that she could rely on God to help her. If God put His approval on the adoption—and she believed that He would—she would manage.

"Why such a gloomy face?" Paul asked, halting in front of her with the children beside him. "I didn't know you weren't skating, or we'd have come sooner. Are you cold?"

"I'm very comfortable sitting here—much more than being out on the ice. I remembered the knack of skating but my joints and muscles didn't. Thinking about that long walk we'll have tomorrow night on the road to Yuletide's Bethlehem, I decided I'd better rest."

Their happy faces were answer enough, but she asked, "Did you kids enjoy yourselves?"

"I falled down and hurt my knees, but it was fun," Julie said, clinging tightly to Paul's hand.

Paul walked with them to her SUV, and after he checked to be sure the kids were buckled in, he looked in the window at Carissa, whispering, "I'll help take down the bleachers and other equipment now. Be sure and keep the door locked until I get home."

"I'll watch, and I'll be careful," she said. She wanted to caution him too, for she considered Jennifer a predator of the worst kind. If Paul went to her house, he'd be lucky to get home at all tonight. But Paul might not appreciate her advice. Instead of speaking, she stood on tiptoes and put her arms around his neck. Daringly, she planted kisses on his neck, face and lips.

As she jumped in the SUV and started the engine, she heard Paul gasp. Feeling heady, Carissa thought, "Let Jennifer deal with that!"

Chapter Fifteen

Thrilled by Carissa's kisses and the promises of the future they offered, Paul wished he could skip the party Jennifer had planned, but, not wanting to be a spoilsport, he'd agreed to put in a brief appearance. It took longer to dismantle the bleachers and the light equipment than he'd expected, and it was well after midnight before he was free. When he turned into the street where Jennifer's mother lived, he stopped abruptly. Not a single car was parked in front of the house. Could the party have broken up so soon? The porch light was on, indicating that the welcome mat was out.

Suspicion began to dawn in Paul's mind. Had Jennifer invited anyone other than him to the "party"? Suddenly, he was sure she hadn't. Anger burned in his heart that she would try to trap him.

As he looked back on the past, he remembered that she'd invited him to a party the night he'd asked her to marry him. It turned out that he was the only guest then, too, and her parents weren't at home. Twenty years ago, he'd been gullible, but not now. Jennifer wouldn't deceive him again. He made a U-turn in the street, hoping she'd see him leaving. He was far more intrigued by what waited for him at his sister's house.

Carissa was watching from Paul's bedroom window when he drove in. She went to the rear door and opened it for him.

"I didn't know if you had a key," she said.

"Any trouble?" he asked.

She wanted to ask him the same thing, but she said, "I haven't seen anyone loitering about. Maybe the person was just looking at the Christmas lights. Our decorations have turned the house into a beautiful sight."

"I hope that's it." He shivered. "It is cold tonight. And it's going to be cold tomorrow night for that pageant. We'd better wear thermal underwear."

"I bought some for myself and the children last week."

"And I have some in the apartment."

She was annoyed at him. How could he stand there talking about underwear when she wanted to know how he felt about Jennifer?

Carissa drew the draperies over the sliding doors.

"I'm sorry to keep you waiting. I didn't go to the party, but it took longer to dismantle the bleachers and spotlights than we'd expected."

His words brought joy to Carissa's heart. Paul obviously hadn't fallen for Jennifer's charms.

On the other hand, he didn't have any plans for Carissa in his life, either. If she'd foolishly dreamed of a life with Paul, it was her own problem. He hadn't promised her anything.

The two-mile walk seemed long to Carissa, but as she and Paul walked slowly, she was conscious of the many people who stood along the road watching them. Paul played the part of the solicitous mate quite well. At times, he simply held her hand; other times, he circled her shoulder with his arm. He carried a walking stick, and swung it occasionally at an imaginary animal that menaced them.

They passed the knoll where the shepherds watched over the small flock of sheep. After a short interval they, too, would hear the angels' song and come to the manger. The three kings wouldn't leave their starting point until an hour after Mary and Joseph had departed. Slowly, they would wend their way on camouflaged horses toward the imaginary Bethlehem.

The sidewalks of Yuletide were crowded with onlookers, and the silence was almost unbelievable as Carissa and Paul walked slowly through the streets of the beautifully decorated town. Carissa saw their three children in the care of Belva Townsend, who'd volunteered to watch them during the pageant.

A huge electric star hung over the vacant lot beside the town hall where the false-fronted inn was located. But Carissa looked heavenward and nudged Paul to call his attention to the glittering star, millions of light years away, that hovered in the sky above Yuletide. It seemed to her that the star's radiance was a sign of approval of what they were doing tonight. Yuletide had indeed reclaimed Christmas. But had she?

Carissa and Paul were taken by the innkeeper to the stable, and after a short interval, Carissa appeared with the live baby in her arms. It was the first time she'd ever held one. The soft, cuddly infant felt strange, just as it must have felt for Mary when cradling her firstborn. Holding the baby gave Carissa an insight into what she'd missed by not bearing children. Perhaps she'd been wrong in her decision, but if she'd had a family of her own, she probably wouldn't be in a position to help the Garners. If God did indeed control the destiny of His creations, perhaps He'd kept her maternal longings bottled until this particular time for a reason.

As she sat beside Paul and waited for the remaining participants to find their places around the manger, Carissa thought of Zechariah and Elizabeth, the parents of John the Baptist. Elizabeth had been barren until long past the time for childbearing.

Although Zechariah and Elizabeth were righteous and kept God's commands blamelessly, they'd had no children. In Jewish culture barrenness was usually considered a curse for sin—a sign of God's disfavor. This childlessness must have been a lifelong disappointment. No doubt, they had prayed daily for a son and couldn't understand why God's answer was no.

But God intervened in their lives. Elizabeth had a son, John, who was destined to be the prophet who would prepare people for the coming of the Messiah. Their prayer was answered; their disgrace was wiped away in God's time. To be the parents of a prophet was a privilege greater than if they'd had a houseful of children.

Carissa was caught up in the pageantry. The way Paul squeezed her hand, when the shepherds appeared and bowed before the manger where she'd laid the child, she was sure he was experiencing the same emotions. A hidden choir sang "O Come Let Us Adore Him" during the adoration of the shepherds.

After the departure of the shepherds, the Wise Men came, their arrival heralded by the lyrics of "We Three Kings."

At the stroke of midnight, the crowds that had converged around the stable in the final moments of the pageant began to disperse. The mother came to reclaim her baby, and even though the manger was empty, Carissa had an uncontrollable urge to kneel beside that crude wooden structure. Yuletide had found the meaning of Christmas and so had she. Tears stung her eyelids when Paul knelt beside her and hugged her close to him.

Although she'd often doubted that she was where God wanted her to be spiritually, she knew now that she'd never forgotten what she'd learned that Christmas many years ago in Minnesota. Without Jesus in one's life, there was no meaning in Christmas. God had sent His Son to earth not to stay as a baby to be worshiped, but to die for the sins of humankind. Without the death and resurrection of Jesus, Christmas would never be commemorated, for there would be nothing to celebrate. The baby in the manger would have been forgotten long ago without Christ's death on the cross.

Had God been working in her life all along to prepare her to become the mother of the Garner children? It was difficult for Carissa to consider that God would single her out for this role. But she considered that as one of God's children, she had been chosen to carry out His purpose. She perceived the eternal truth that God wanted to give her every desire that was in line with His will for her life. Like Zechariah and Elizabeth, she only had to wait for the right time.

Once and for all, Carissa committed her life to God's Son. "Whatever Your will for my life, God, I accept it," she murmured aloud. "Please provide daily guidance on the path I should take."

Paul must have heard her words, for his grip tightened around her waist.

"God," he prayed quietly, "I, too, want to draw closer to you, make you an integral part of my life. You've given me the answer to many things these past few weeks, but I'm still uncertain of other decisions I need to make. My heart guides me onto a certain path that I don't think I can take. Don't I trust You enough for the future? Why can't I leave my life in Your hands? Please remove the veil of my uncertainty and show me Your way."

He knew what he wanted to do—but was it practical to do so? How could he quit his job and take on a family of four without the means to support them? No doubt Carissa had all the money they'd ever need, but he wanted to do his share. Paul had peace in his heart about his spiritual security, but the immediate future was still uncertain as he assisted Carissa to her feet.

"Come, my dear," he said. "It's been a long night. Let's go home."

At that moment, he wanted nothing more than to have the four walls of the house surround him, Carissa and the children.

Caught up in the excitement of the pageant, Paul had forgotten about the man who'd been watching the house. But long after Carissa and the children were asleep, he was awake, trying to make difficult decisions. Walking around his room in the dark, he chanced to look out the window. The security light's faint rays revealed a man standing again in the spruce trees.

"Enough is enough," Paul muttered. In the darkness, he struggled into his outdoor clothes, and without telling Carissa, he slipped out the back door. He had to approach the man from behind, and that meant crossing the road at some point. Using his flashlight sparingly, he walked a half mile north of the house, keeping under cover of the evergreen trees. When he was out of sight of the house, he crossed the road to the lake path. Walking quietly, he maneuvered toward the grove of spruce trees.

The man was leaning against a tree. As Paul neared, he jerked up his head and started running. With one big leap, Paul caught the man by the arm.

"No, buddy," he said. "You don't get away that easily. Why have you been watching our home?"

Paul became aware that the arm he held was scrawny

and that the man was trembling. Compassionately, he said, "Come on into the garage. It's warmer in there, and we can talk."

The man didn't answer, nor did he resist Paul's iron grip, but Paul held tightly to his arm while they crossed the road and entered the garage. There were no garage windows facing the house, so he wouldn't disturb Carissa. He turned on the light because he wanted a look at his captive. Once inside, Paul released the man, who crumpled to the floor.

Frightened, Paul felt for a pulse, which he found readily enough. The man was a rack of bones—whether from illness or malnutrition, he couldn't tell. After scrutinizing the unconscious man's face, Paul picked him up and carried him upstairs. The stranger was unshaven, but his clothes were clean enough, so Paul laid him on the couch. He raised the thermostat, and heat had already filled the room by the time he'd brewed some coffee. The man was stirring when Paul returned to the couch, and he shielded his eyes from the light.

Paul heard static on the intercom from the house. Carissa must have seen the lights.

"Paul," her frightened voice called.

"I'm all right," he answered. "I can't talk to you now, but please believe me, I'm in no danger. Go back to bed. We'll talk in the morning."

Sounding unconvinced, she said, "All right."

Since Paul had been taking his meals with Carissa and the children, there wasn't much to eat in his apartment. He found a half loaf of bread in the refrigerator, so he took two slices, toasted and buttered them. He carried the food to the table beside the sofa.

The man was sitting now, his head in his hands.

"Here, drink the coffee and eat some bread."

Without meeting Paul's gaze, the man lifted the coffee mug to his lips with shaking hands. He ate the bread hungrily. Pitying the man, Paul sat opposite him and watched. He supposed he was foolish to bring the man into the apartment. It was no wonder Carissa was worried. For all he knew, the man might have a gun. At least Carissa and the children wouldn't be at risk in the main house.

When the man finished, still not looking at Paul, he said, "Thank you."

"Well, let's have it," Paul said. "Who are you? Why are you here?"

"Keith Garner. I'm looking for my kids."

"It's a little late for you to be worrying about that, isn't it, Mr. Garner?" He wasn't surprised at the revelation, for Alex bore a marked resemblance to the man.

Keith Garner's haggard face flushed.

"How did you find out where they were?"

"A cousin of mine is the custodian in the sheriff's office in Aberdeen. I went back to town, not knowing my wife had died. I was beside myself when I learned the kids had run away. How did they get this far, and why did you and your wife take them in?"

"The lady isn't my wife." And at Keith Garner's stunned expression, he quickly explained why Carissa was living in the house. Paul briefly told him how they'd discovered the children in Naomi's house, and gave a brief rundown of how and why they'd run away. "What kind of a man are you that you'd desert your family and leave your children to cope with their dying mother?"

"I'm the kind of man who is more harm than good to them," he said bitterly. He pulled up his shirtsleeves and revealed the evidence of multiple needle marks in his arms. "It started out with alcohol and mild drugs when I was a teenager, then I started using the hard stuff. I'd steal my wife's money to buy drugs, and I finally left, knowing she and the kids would be better off without me."

Paul was angry at the man, but he detected remorse in his eyes. He could heap a lot of recriminations on Keith Garner for his neglect, but he suspected he couldn't say anything the man hadn't already said to himself.

"I've been in and out of a lot of rehab places, and they'd dry me out for a while. Then, I'd find a job and send some money to my family. I'd send it to my cousin and he'd take it to them as if he was providing it. I hoped they'd think I was dead, and I wish I was. The kids would be better off."

"Julie doesn't even remember you, but Lauren and Alex think you're still alive. You must talk to them."

Keith Garner half rose from the couch. "No! I can't face them looking the way I do."

"If you won't assume your responsibility as a father, at least make some arrangements to give them up for adoption. They're terrified that they'll be separated if Social Services get involved. Miss Whitmore has volunteered to adopt them. She's financially able to give them a home."

"Are you and the lady going to marry?"

"I'm only in New York for a leave of absence from my job in eastern Europe. I'm leaving the country in less than a week. Carissa will do it on her own."

"I'd feel lower than a snake to give my kids away, but I'm afraid to take them. My record is so bad, I can't get a decent job. People don't trust me, and I don't even trust myself."

"Mr. Garner, you have to see the children and tell them why you abandoned them."

"They're too young to understand."

"Believe me, Alex and Lauren have grown up mighty fast in the past five years. You can't walk out on them again without giving them some closure and making provisions for their future. Look me in the eye and tell me, man to man, if I can trust you to stay here in the apartment and see those kids tomorrow. It's the best Christmas gift you can give them. They're feeling very alone in the world."

Keith Garner reached out his hand to Paul, and Paul clasped it firmly. "I'll do what you ask. I'll be grateful for a warm place to sleep."

"Where have you been staying?"

"In the fishing huts on the lake at night and in the woods during the day. I've been here four or five days."

Taking in the man's lightweight clothing, Paul didn't know how he'd survived the cold weather. And judging from the pallor of his skin and the lackluster look in his eyes, Paul figured that Keith Garner was seriously ill.

He knew he was taking a chance, but what else could he do? Perhaps he should guard the man all night, but first, he needed to tell Carissa what had happened.

"I have a disposable razor in the bathroom that you're welcome to use. I'll also lay out some towels and other things for you to use as you shower."

When he returned to the living room, Paul carried two heavy blankets. "I'll leave the heat where it is, so you should be comfortable."

"Thank you, Mr. Spencer. In spite of what you think, I do love my kids. I won't desert them this time."

Paul didn't lock the apartment. If Keith Garner had a mind to, he could get out. But in his condition, he wouldn't get far before the authorities picked him up.

Right now, he was more worried about Carissa than he was about the kids or their father. She didn't know what she was getting into taking on the responsibility of caring for three children, but she would be disappointed if Keith Garner took them with him. Paul hated to disturb her, but he doubted she was asleep, anyway, and he had to talk to her before morning.

Inside the house he took off his boots and went quietly upstairs. He could hear Julie and Lauren breathing softly as he tiptoed across their room. In the faint glow of the bathroom's night-light, Paul saw Carissa sitting upright in the bed, her hand to her throat.

He went close to the bed and whispered, "Come downstairs—we need to talk."

When she joined him a few minutes later, he said, "Let's go in my bedroom and close the door."

There he motioned Carissa to a chair and sat on the

side of the bed. "The kids' father is over in the apartment."

Carissa gasped. "What!"

He put his hand softly on her lips in a bid for silence. "He's the one who's been watching the house. I saw him tonight and waylaid him. He's skin and bones, so it wasn't any trouble to confront him."

"Where's he been for five years? And how did he find out where the kids are?"

Paul told her briefly what Keith Garner had said.

"What have you done with him?"

He explained how he'd found Keith Garner and brought him to the apartment, and left him there for the night.

"Is that wise?"

"Probably not, but I couldn't turn him out into the cold. He's been sleeping in the fishing huts on the lake."

Carissa shivered and pulled her robe tighter.

"I don't want him to get away again. He's willing to let you adopt the children."

"Oh!" Carissa said, not knowing whether to laugh or cry.

"I still think it's too much responsibility for you, Carissa. Naomi will be back in a month. Where will you take them to live?"

"I don't know. I'm scared stiff, but I told them I'd adopt them if I could. I won't back out now."

Paul leaned toward her, and she lifted her face to his. "They couldn't find a more wonderful mother," he said, "but I don't want you to do it."

It flashed into his mind that without the children,

he could take Carissa with him on the job site. It was crude living compared to what she was used to, but he figured she would be able to cope with the rigorous life. He thought of the sightseeing they could do in Europe—almost like a two-year honeymoon. But would he still feel the same if they hadn't been involved with the children, who had seemed to give them a sense of closeness they might not have had otherwise?

"What kind of man is he?" she asked, interrupting his thoughts.

"He seems to have some pride, and he probably could have been a useful citizen if he wasn't addicted to drugs."

"Just like my mother. That's what started her downhill slide."

He didn't want her to start thinking about her mother. "I shouldn't have bothered you tonight, but I thought you should know before the kids did."

"I wasn't asleep, anyway. I heard you go out, and I was worrying about you. When I saw the lights on in your apartment, I was really scared."

"It's nice to have someone worrying about me," he said softly, taking her hands. She was so close and so desirable, but Paul set bounds on his emotions. He was in no position to offer Carissa anything except this moment. So he lifted one of her hands and placed a kiss in the palm.

As she left the room, Carissa felt a deep sense of disappointment. Paul would soon go out of her life, and she couldn't do anything about it.

Chapter Sixteen

They'd opened one gift each on Christmas Eve, but the thought of packages under the tree catapulted the kids from their beds as soon as it became daylight. Carissa hadn't had more than an hour of sleep, so she reluctantly left her warm bed to follow the girls downstairs to where Paul and Alex waited.

Paul and Carissa had agreed that they shouldn't go overboard in buying gifts, but each child had one large gift of clothing, and smaller gifts of books or games. They'd bought a piece of jewelry for each of the girls and a pair of skates for Alex.

Carissa's gift to Paul was a digital camera, and her box from him contained a diamond bracelet. Carissa's heart was touched by the gift, but her eyes promised Paul that she'd thank him properly when they were alone. His answering smile indicated that he understood.

"Let's pick up the paper and ribbons, then get dressed so we can have breakfast," Carissa said.

"Want us to take our presents upstairs?" Lauren asked.

Carissa shook her head. "No, let's leave them under the tree for now."

After the kids scampered to their bedroom, Paul said, "I'll check on our visitor. Shall I bring him over?"

"Might as well get it over with. If he's still here."

"Do we have anything the children could give him as a gift?" Paul asked.

"I bought a tin container of butter cookies that hasn't been opened. Would that do?"

"I should think so. Undoubtedly, the man hasn't had enough to eat."

"Should we invite him to eat breakfast with us?"

"Let's play it by ear—see how the children react to him."

Keith Garner was sitting on the couch watching television when Paul entered the apartment. He'd shaved, and trimmed and washed his hair. He'd tried to make himself presentable, and it helped that his clothes were wrinkled but not dirty.

"I helped myself to another slice of bread—hope you don't mind."

"Not at all."

"Have you told the children I'm here?"

"No—it will be a surprise."

"Maybe not a very pleasant one."

"I don't know. They've opened their Christmas gifts, and they're dressing now. In the meantime, let's talk. If you do let Carissa adopt the children, their future is secure. But what about you? You can't be more than in your late thirties. I hate to see a man throw his life away. If Carissa adopts the children, I can at least do something for you. I'll pay for a rehabilitation program for you at a good facility."

"It's too late for that."

Suspecting strongly that Keith Garner didn't expect to live long, Paul still insisted, "It's worth a try."

"I'll think about it."

Paul went into the bedroom and brought out a heavy coat that he'd worn when he was several pounds lighter.

"Try this coat on. It will be warmer than the one you have. I'm not in this country much in the winter, so it's practically new."

After spending a night in the warmth of the apartment, Garner appeared less haggard. Perhaps the children's first look at their father wouldn't be too shattering, but Paul figured that five years had made quite a change in Keith Garner's appearance.

When Paul and Keith stepped up on the deck, the children were sitting on the floor around the Christmas tree, examining their gifts. Carissa was working in the kitchen, and she looked up quickly when Paul opened the door.

Hiding Keith Garner behind him, Paul said, "Kids, you have another gift, too."

He stepped aside to let their father enter the room first. Carissa came from the kitchen as Alex jumped to his feet, his face flooded with a mixture of emotions that she couldn't figure out. He was such a bewildering boy. What if he rejected his father!

"Papa," Lauren cried, and she ran to him. "Mama died," she said, sobbing and clinging to the man, whose own cheeks were stained with tears. He patted her back.

"I know, Lauren."

Julie stared at her father as she sidled over to Paul and leaned against him. The questioning, lost look she turned on him threatened his composure.

"It's your father, Julie. Go speak to him."

While she hesitated, Alex, who'd been standing like a statue, turned an angry look on his father. "Where have you been?" Alex said defiantly. "Mom wanted so much to see you before she died. I hate you."

"I don't blame you, son. I hate myself."

"Let's sit down," Paul said. "Your father has a few things to tell you. Mr. Garner, this is Carissa Whitmore. She's been looking after the children for about a month."

"For which I thank you, ma'am."

When they sat down, Carissa coveted Julie's position in the safe harbor of Paul's arms. She felt alone and vulnerable. Lauren sat in the chair beside her father. Alex stood in front of the fireplace, his back to the rest of them. A tense silence surrounded them.

Awkwardly, Keith Garner cleared his throat, and his hands moved restlessly on the arms of the chair he occupied.

"I've been a drug abuser since I was a young man, and I was too weak to break the habit. Anytime we had trouble of any kind, I'd forget my worries by taking drugs. It finally got me."

The two daughters obviously didn't comprehend

what their father meant. But the bleak look on Alex's face as he glared at his father indicated that he knew all too well what kind of life his father had led.

"Don't you see, son? You were better off without me. When I was at home, I'd use all of our money to feed my habit. You were better off without me," he repeated, his eyes begging for understanding.

"If you really cared, you could have kicked the habit," Alex said.

"Alex," Paul said, "you don't know what you're talking about. You've never walked in your father's shoes. Try to be more understanding."

"I've tried, Alex, I really have. I've been in and out of a dozen rehab centers, and I'd go straight for a while."

"And that's when you sent us money?"

Keith Garner nodded. "But the addiction was too strong for me. With my record, it got harder and harder for me to find a good-paying job, and I didn't have much money to send your way."

He started coughing and gasping. Paul put Julie aside and went to Keith. The children stared in horror as their father struggled for a breath, and Carissa wondered if they'd have been better off not to have seen him.

"Shall we have some breakfast? Maybe some hot coffee will help you," Paul said.

Carissa bolted out of her chair, glad to have something to do. "You'll eat with us, please, Mr. Garner?" she said.

He was weak from the coughing spell, but he said, "Thank you. Something hot to drink would be fine."

Paul pulled chairs around the table for the six of them and got everyone seated while Carissa put frozen waffles in the toaster. She poured orange juice, and filled Mr. Garner's mug with coffee, which he sipped gratefully.

Lauren eyed her father nervously all through the meal. He ate very little, but he asked for another serving of coffee. Paul didn't think anyone enjoyed the meal, for Keith Garner was uneasy, the children's insecurity had surfaced, and Carissa was edgy. When he invited the Garner family to return to the great room, he, too, was doubtful about the outcome of the reunion between this man and his children.

Carissa had been fretting about their Christmas dinner before the appearance of Mr. Garner, and she hardly knew what she was doing. Leaving Mr. Garner alone with his children for a while, Paul put a ham roast in the oven. Carissa prepared a packet of dressing, knowing that her grandmother would have been horrified that she hadn't prepared it from scratch. She'd bought a cranberry salad, pumpkin pies and yeast rolls at the deli—all no-no's to her grandmother, who'd probably never heard of a deli. But Carissa was grateful for the advanced technology today, for her emotions were so mixed that preparing food was the furthest thing from her mind.

Would Keith Garner agree to let her adopt the children? What would happen to them if he decided to take his children with him? In less than a month, Carissa's life had become so involved with the three kids and Paul that she couldn't contemplate the future without them.

Perhaps sensing her confusion, Paul pulled her into a close hug.

"Everything is ready," he said. "I've peeled the potatoes, and they'll cook slowly while we wait for the ham to bake. We might as well get this over."

Carissa took the tin of cookies with her into the great room, where the children were showing Keith Garner their Christmas gifts. Lauren and Julie were chatting easily with their father. Alex had thawed to the point that he was sitting on the floor beside his father's chair, and Keith had his hand on Alex's shoulder.

"Lauren, would you like to give your father a gift?" Carissa asked, handing the box of cookies to Lauren.

Julie jumped up. "I want to give it to him," she said.

"Why don't both of you hold it?" Carissa said.

Keith's head bowed over the gift. "Thank you," he mumbled, and a sob rose from his throat.

He lifted his head and looked from Paul to Carissa.

"And I thank both of you for what you've done for my children. It gave me nightmares to think that they might have fallen into the wrong hands. If there is a God, I pray that He'll bless you for what you've done."

"There *is* a God, Mr. Garner," Paul said. "I've always believed that, but my belief was renewed last night when I again met the Son of God, Jesus, in a life-changing experience. He's already blessed us by giving us the opportunity to care for your children. Now the question is—where do we go from here? I'm sure the three adults in this room want the same thing—what is best for Alex, Lauren and Julie."

"I understand, Miss Whitmore, that you want to adopt my children," Keith said.

"I told them I would adopt them, but that was before we knew you were still alive."

"I love my children," he said sincerely, "but they'd have a worse life with me than they had when their mother was ill."

"We'd take care of you, Dad," Alex said, standing at his father's side.

"I know you would, Alex, but I can't ask it of you. I don't know Miss Whitmore's position, but it's obvious she can give you the things I can't. A comfortable home, food on the table, nice clothes, a college education, maybe even love…." His voice trailed off, and he looked at Carissa expectantly.

"Yes," she said simply. "I love the children already. I've worked most of my life establishing a good business and I've never married. I didn't know my life lacked anything until this month. Being with your children has brought a completeness to my life that I've never known before. To be honest with you, I don't know what kind of a mother I'll be, but in many ways, I can empathize with the children. My mother died when I was a girl, I never knew my father and my grandmother raised me. I know what it's like to be alone."

"Kids, you need to be involved in this decision," Paul said. "What do you want to do?"

"I want to stay with Miss Cara, but I want Papa, too," Lauren said.

"That's what I want," Julie shouted. "And Uncle Paul, too."

Paul knelt beside her, his face white. "Julie, I've explained that I have a job. I still want to be a part of your life, but I have to work."

Alex looked at Carissa. "Can't we just go ahead and live with you without you adopting us?"

Taken aback by this turn of events, Carissa hesitated.

Before she could answer, Mr. Garner said, "No, it won't work, Alex. Miss Whitmore has to have full authority if she takes you. I don't want to be in a position to undermine her decisions." He turned to Paul. "How soon can we sign the necessary papers?"

"I know nothing about adoption procedures, but there's a lawyer in Yuletide who handles my sister's affairs. He'll be able to advise you. I'll try to get an appointment for tomorrow. I've heard that adoptions usually take a long time, but since both you and Carissa are agreeable to this, there shouldn't be any hitches."

Paul invited Keith Garner to stay in his apartment until they could find more information, so Keith went to retrieve his backpack from one of the fishing huts on the lake, and Alex went with him. Paul wondered if Alex wanted to keep his eye on his father, fearful that he'd disappear again. When they brought the pack to the house, Paul judged that it didn't weigh more than ten pounds. Was this all Garner had to show for a lifetime? No wonder he wanted something better for his children.

Keith asked Carissa if he could wash some clothes, and he and Alex spent time alone in the basement taking care of that chore.

Carissa hoped they were able to do some bonding as father and son. Alex needed to forgive his father.

After Paul arranged an appointment with a lawyer for the morning, he telephoned Belva Townsend, asking if she'd come to the house and stay with the children while they were with the lawyer. At the office the lawyer explained the adoption rules, and Keith Garner signed the necessary papers to initiate the proceedings. Carissa gave the lawyer permission to check her financial standing.

Knowing that Belva would take care of the children, after they left the lawyer's office the three of them went to the café for lunch.

"I hope Alex won't give you any trouble, miss," Keith said as they waited for their food to be served. "I don't want him to take after me."

Secretly, Carissa had been hoping the same thing. She believed she could cope with the girls' problems, but she knew nothing about boys. Despite the fact that he'd abandoned his family, during the few hours she'd spent with Mr. Garner, Carissa had formed a better opinion of his character. Still, he'd admitted in front of his family that he'd started using drugs and alcohol when he was a teenager. Bitter as Alex was about his family life, would he follow his father's example? The possibility sent shivers of fear up and down her spine.

"I'm going to give Alex a good talking-to," Keith said.

"But what about you, Mr. Garner?" Paul said. "Even if you are no longer legally responsible for them, you're still their father, and they'll want the best for you. It's obvious you are ill. For the children's sake, if not for your own, why don't you see a doctor? I'll pay for the initial tests, and if you need further treatment, I'm sure you'll be eligible for financial help."

After some hesitation, Keith said, "I've tried to keep going because of my kids, but now that they'll be taken care of, I don't really have much to live for. But if you think it will help them for me to stick around a little longer, I'll do it. Besides, I'll need to stay close by, so I can sign the adoption papers when they're ready."

"Good!" Paul said. "I have a flight out of Kennedy tomorrow night, so I'm leaving early in the morning. If you'll go with me, I'll drop you off at a hospital in Saratoga Springs and make the necessary financial arrangements for you to be admitted."

"I appreciate it. You know, I've never had much use for religious people because I've never been able to tell the difference between people who profess to be Christians and the ones who don't. But I've been wrong. I've looked in the wrong places to find Jesus in people. The preacher and his wife in Aberdeen looked after my kids, and the church members paid for my wife's funeral. I'm a stranger to you, but you're willing to pay my hospital expenses. And Miss Whitmore is adopting my kids, although she's scared to death to do it."

Carissa gasped and felt her face flushing. Was it that obvious?

A slight grin appeared on Keith Garner's face. "I shouldn't have mentioned it, but it's normal for you to be afraid to take on a job like this. Are you sure you want to do it?"

"It's too late to back out now, and I *do* want to take your children. I only hesitate because I'm not sure I'll be the kind of guardian they need."

"When I was a child, my mother took me to Sunday school, and I remember the preacher saying that 'Jesus went about doing good.' I'm seein' that in the two of you."

"Oh, no!" Carissa said. "I'm not worthy to be compared to my Savior."

Paul covered Carissa's hand with his. "Remember the story we talked about a few weeks ago? The people who'd heard that Christ was coming to visit them missed their opportunity by turning away several needy people because they were waiting for Christ. You came to Yuletide seeking Christmas, and you've found Him by opening your heart to others. When we sacrifice to help others in need, we're doing what Jesus would do. Don't you see, Carissa? You've found Christmas through the Garner children."

Tears filled in Carissa's eyes and eventually found their way down her cheeks. "Yes, I suppose I have. With God's help, I'll do the best I can for your children, Mr. Garner."

"I've never doubted that for a minute, or I wouldn't have agreed to this adoption."

Painfully aware that this time tomorrow night they'd be separated, after dinner Paul and Carissa left the children alone with their father and took a walk along the lake on a path not illuminated by the Fantasy lights.

"I suppose I'm feeling motherly already," Carissa said. "I'm uneasy about leaving the children with him. What if he decides to steal them from us?"

"That worries me, too, but he is their father. I thought we should give them some time together. I believe that he wants the best for them."

"Do you think he has a communicable disease?"

"No. I don't believe he would be around his children if that were true," Paul replied. "But I wouldn't be surprised if Keith Garner knows he has a terminal disease, and that he's trying to provide for the children while he's still alive. Let's forget them for a few minutes. I had to have you to myself for a little while tonight. I can't believe that tomorrow night I'll be gone."

Soft snow covered their shoulders as he leaned against a towering evergreen and pulled Carissa into the circle of his arms. "I love you, Carissa. It must have been love at first sight. I don't know what was in that poker you used to whack me on the head, but it was as powerful as Cupid's arrow."

She laughed softly. "I love you, too. It's such a strange feeling for me because I've loved so few people. Only my mother and grandmother, now you and the children. It's rather scary to be overwhelmed with love for another person."

He cupped his hand around her face and held it gently. "I can't bear the thought of leaving you tomorrow."

"Then stay here."

"Don't tempt me. I want to marry you and adopt the

kids with you, but I won't live on your money. If I had another job comparable to what I have now, I wouldn't hesitate a minute. But overseas work is profitable and I can retire after twenty years of service. I can't throw all that away."

"How long before you retire?"

"Two years."

"How much do you love me?" she asked.

"Enough to want to marry you."

"Then delay your flight until we can get married and you can take the kids and me with you."

"I've considered that, but I don't think we could take the children out of the country with the adoption pending." A thoughtful expression crossed his face, and his brown eyes gleamed with eagerness. "And don't think I'll marry you and leave you behind!"

"Then, we'll come to you as soon as their adoption is complete. We can get married when I arrive."

Paul thought of his reservations about the living conditions on the work projects. But the pleasure of having Carissa and the children with him overturned his concerns. "You'd be willing to do that?"

"I'll do it in a heartbeat, Paul. Besides the fact that I don't want to be separated from you, I need you. It hasn't been too difficult with you here, but I'm terrified to face all the children's problems alone. And I know there will be problems."

"It's an option, certainly, and something that will make my leave-taking a little easier. Several of the engineers on our job take their families with them, so it isn't impossible. I'll look into it."

He picked Carissa up and swung her around and around.

"Stop it, Paul. I'm getting dizzy!"

"It's just that I haven't been able to see any possibility of marrying you, and now there's a light at the end of the tunnel."

Paul's brown eyes held great tenderness. Reveling in the feel of his arms so close about her, Carissa said brokenly, "I'm going to miss you."

Paul whispered his love for her even as he claimed her lips. At length, he rested his head against her soft hair.

"The time will pass quickly, love. We'll find a way to be together. I promise you."

Paul's pickup was parked in front of the house, and the children were outside saying a final goodbye to their father as he stepped into the truck.

Paul stood in the foyer of the house, and Carissa was weeping in his arms. His eyes roved over the room where they'd been so happy.

"My dear," he said, "God will provide some way for us to be together. We've committed our lives to Him—we mustn't underestimate His power."

"That's the only comfort I have—knowing that God will help me with the children until you come home again."

Carissa stirred in his arms and broke their embrace.

"I feel like a heel, leaving without seeing my sister, but there wasn't enough time to coordinate my schedule with hers," Paul said.

"I'm sure she'll understand."

"I tried to call Naomi again this morning," Paul said. "I thought she would have returned from that cruise. I'll try to reach her after I'm checked in at the airport."

"If she calls after you leave, I'll tell her to expect your call."

"Well, I can't delay any longer."

He led Carissa to the door, his arm tight around her. She lifted her lips and he kissed her hard. She sobbed when the phone rang.

"Please answer it," she said. "I can't talk to anyone right now."

Unwilling to lose a minute with her, Paul drew Carissa beside him toward the ringing phone. He peered at the caller ID.

"It's your phone listing," he said. "It must be Naomi!"

He lifted the receiver and pushed the audio button so Carissa could hear.

"Hey, sis," he said. "You almost missed me. I'm ready to step out the door."

"I called as soon as I could. Our group traveled back from Tampa to Miami by bus. On our return trip last night, the bus had engine trouble and we didn't get home until fifteen minutes ago."

"A belated Merry Christmas, sis."

He held the phone toward Carissa.

"And Merry Christmas from me, too," she said. "Did you enjoy the cruise?"

"Oh, it was wonderful!" Naomi said, and Carissa thought she seemed very bubbly for a woman who'd spent the night on a bus.

"Paul, I've never been so happy. I'm going to get married."

Paul almost dropped the receiver. "What!"

"Don't you approve?" Naomi said, disappointment in her voice.

"It's not up to me to approve or disapprove. I'm surprised, that's all!"

"I'm surprised myself. I never intended to marry again."

In an excited voice, Naomi said that she was going to marry John Brewster, the man from Wyoming who'd been so friendly to her. "We didn't know we were in love until we were on the cruise. It was so romantic. Aren't you happy for me?" she added.

"Of course," Paul said. "But isn't it a quick decision? You've only known this man a month."

Carissa playfully nudged Paul in the ribs. He looked quickly at her, and she stretched to brush his lips with hers.

"Love often comes on swift wings," Naomi said, and Paul chuckled merrily.

"I agree with that," Paul said, and as Carissa's fingers caressed his face, he pressed a kiss on her hand.

"What about the children?" Naomi asked.

"They're still here—"

Before he could explain further, Naomi said, "Paul, I'm glad I caught you before you left. I have a proposition for you. Can I persuade you to take over management of the mill for me? I'll give you twenty-five percent of the stock, and you set your own salary."

"What!" Paul's voice was incredulous.

"You know I've never been happy managing the textile mill—it's been a burden to me. John lives in Wyoming six months of the year. I want to move there with him, and in the winter come back to Tampa. But that mill is my only income, and I need someone I can trust to manage it."

If Paul ever had needed confirmation that God was in control of his life, he had it now. He made up his mind quickly—or perhaps God had already made it up for him. As part owner of the mill, he'd have financial security, so he'd have no hesitation about leaving his engineering job.

"I'll do it, if you'll sell me additional stock so that I'll own forty percent of the company. And," he added, smiling, "if you'll agree on Carissa working with me as a consultant. She has more business experience than I do."

"But she's retired—she doesn't have to work."

Paul's eyes darted toward Carissa. She nodded agreement. She could certainly combine her parenting responsibilities by working part-time at the mill. Especially if Paul was by her side.

"You aren't the only one who's fallen in love. Carissa and I are going to be married, too."

"Oh, that's wonderful news!" Naomi said. "You've missed so much happiness living alone."

"Well, I won't be living alone much longer," he said with a laugh. He would wait until later to pass on the news about their ready-made family.

Naomi yawned audibly. "I'm too sleepy now to talk about the nitty-gritty details. I just wanted to get your agreement before you left the country—Carissa, are you still there?" she asked.

"Yes."

"I'd love to stay in your condo the rest of the winter. John won't leave for Wyoming until the last of March. Are you interested in continuing our arrangement for a few more months?"

"Yes, that would work for me, too."

Paul replaced the receiver and enveloped Carissa in a hug that threatened to crack her ribs. The touch of his lips was like a promise.

When he finally lifted his head, Carissa felt protected, loved and desired. Wrapped in the security of his love, she was speechless, but she still had enough breath to whisper, "Let's go tell the children."

Epilogue

Four years later

Paul and Carissa sat hand in hand, as Alex took his place among the graduating seniors. When he walked on the platform to receive his high school diploma, Paul whispered, "Whew!" and wiped imaginary sweat from his forehead. His clownish gesture hid the pride he felt for his adopted son.

Alex had already been accepted on a sports scholarship at a state university. To have gotten the willful Alex this far was evidence that they'd done a pretty good job of parenting. Who'd have thought that the undernourished, tense, gangly boy they'd taken in would develop into this tall, handsome youth who walked with catlike grace.

Julie sat with her hand resting on Paul's arm, for the years had not lessened the bond that had been forged at their first meeting. At ten, she was a happy-go-lucky girl with lots of friends, although her grades left much to be desired.

Lauren sat at Carissa's left. A quiet, tenderhearted girl, Lauren was a superior student, and now that she was happy and secure, her fragile beauty won the affection of her peers, as well as many adults.

Although mothering the children had often tried Carissa's nerves, she'd never spent more rewarding years. After Paul had agreed to take over management of the mill, he'd returned to his job in the Czech Republic for two months to give his employer time to find a replacement. The short separation, which had seemed like years to Paul and Carissa, had provided enough time for them to realize that their hasty decision was the right one. They were married as soon as he returned to the States.

By that time, Naomi's lawyers had drawn up the necessary papers for Paul to take over the management of Townsend Textile Mill. They'd established their permanent residence in Saratoga Springs, but they'd traded Carissa's Florida condo to Naomi in return for the house on Lake Mohawk. They spent the summer months, as well as the Christmas holidays, at the lake house. Participation in Yuletide's Christmas festivities was a highlight of their family.

By the time Paul had come back from overseas, Jennifer Colton had apparently given up forging a new relationship with him; she'd sold the family home in Yuletide and taken her mother to New York. She hadn't returned.

Mr. Garner died a few months after the adoption proceedings had been completed. The children had made weekly visits to him in the hospice, and these visits had solidified their relationship. Having those months with their father had reconciled them to his illness. And he'd also been instrumental in steering Alex on the right path. Paul and Carissa had arranged a funeral for the children's father, and his body had been taken to Vermont for burial. A granite marker was erected to mark the graves of both parents.

The ceremony now over, Alex headed in their direction. Paul greeted him with an affectionate grip on the shoulder, and Carissa hugged him and stood on tiptoes to kiss his cheek.

"We're proud of you, son," Paul said.

Alex ducked his head in embarrassment. After clearing his throat a couple of times, he thrust his diploma into Carissa's hand.

"I don't say thanks very often, but all during the program, I kept thinking of where I might have been if you guys hadn't taken me in. You earned the diploma, not me. Thanks."

Paul and Carissa exchanged a look of satisfaction and surprise. More than once, they'd wondered if their children had any comprehension of the sacrifices they'd made for them. But they'd been repaid over and over for anything they'd given up.

Carissa had come to Yuletide to find Christmas, but she'd found so much more—an affectionate husband, a loving family and a closer relationship with her Lord.

* * * * *

SPECIAL EXCERPT FROM

❧

LOVE INSPIRED
INSPIRATIONAL ROMANCE

An Amish man gets more than he bargained for
when he moves next door to a large spirited family
during the holiday season.

Read on for a sneak preview of
The Amish Christmas Secret
by Vannetta Chapman.

"Get back!"

Definitely a female voice, from the other side of the barn. He walked around the barn. If someone had asked him to guess what he might find there, he wouldn't in a hundred years have guessed correctly.

A young Amish woman—Plain dress, apron, *kapp*—was holding a feed bucket in one hand and a rake in the other, attempting to fend off a rooster. At the moment, the bird was trying to peck the woman's feet.

"What did you do to him?" Daniel asked.

Her eyes widened. The rooster made a swipe at her left foot. The woman once again thrust the feed bucket toward the rooster. "Don't just stand there. This beast won't let me pass."

Daniel knew better than to laugh. He'd been raised with four sisters and a strong-willed mother. So he snatched the rooster up from behind, pinning its wings down with his right arm.

"Where do you want him?"

"His name is Carl, and I want him in the oven if you must know the truth." She dropped the feed bucket and swiped at the golden-blond hair that was spilling out of her *kapp*. "Over there. In the pen."

Daniel dropped the rooster inside and turned to face the woman. She was probably five and a half feet tall, and looked to be around twenty years old. Blue eyes the color of forget-me-nots assessed him.

She was also beautiful in the way of Plain women, without adornment. The sight of her reminded him of yet another reason why he'd left Pennsylvania. Why couldn't his neighbors have been an old couple in their nineties?

"You must be the new neighbor. I'm Becca Schwartz—not Rebecca, just Becca, because my *mamm* decided to do things alphabetically. We thought you might introduce yourself, but I guess you've been busy. Mamm would want me to invite you to dinner, but I warn you, I have seven younger siblings, so it's usually a somewhat chaotic affair."

Becca not Rebecca stepped closer.

"Didn't catch your name."

"Daniel…Daniel Glick."

"We didn't even know the place had sold until last week. Most people are leery of farms where the fields are covered with rocks and the house is falling down. I see you haven't done anything to remedy either of those situations."

"I only moved in yesterday."

"Had time to get a horse, though. Get it from Old Tim?"

Before he could answer, a dinner bell rang. "Sounds like dinner's ready. Care to meet the folks?"

"Another time. I have some…um…unpacking to do."

Becca shrugged her shoulders. "Guess I'll be seeing you, then."

"Yeah, I guess."

He'd hoped for peace and solitude.

Instead, he had half a barn, a cantankerous rooster and a pretty neighbor who was a little nosy.

He'd come to Indiana to forget women and to lose himself in making something good from something that was broken.

He'd moved to Indiana because he wanted to be left alone.

Don't miss
The Amish Christmas Secret *by Vannetta Chapman,*
available October 2020 wherever
Love Inspired *books and ebooks are sold.*

LoveInspired.com

*Before he testifies in an important case, businessman
Michael "Mikey" Fiore hides out in Jacobsville, Texas,
and crosses paths with softly beautiful Bernadette, who
seems burdened with her own secrets. Their bond grows
into passion...until shocking truths surface.*

Read on for a sneak peek at
Texas Proud,
the latest book in
#1 New York Times *bestselling author Diana Palmer's*
Long, Tall Texans series!

Mikey's fingers contracted. "Suppose I told you that the
hotel I own is actually a casino," he said slowly, "and it's
in Las Vegas?"

Bernie's eyes widened. "You own a casino in Las
Vegas?" she exclaimed. "Wow!"

He laughed, surprised at her easy acceptance. "I run it
legit, too," he added. "No fixes, no hidden switches, no
cheating. Drives the feds nuts, because they can't find
anything to pin on me there."

"The feds?" she asked.

He drew in a breath. "I told you, I'm a bad man." He
felt guilty about it, dirty. His fingers caressed hers as they

neared Graylings, the huge mansion where his cousin lived with the heir to the Grayling racehorse stables.

Her fingers curled trustingly around his. "And I told you that the past doesn't matter," she said stubbornly. Her heart was running wild. "Not at all. I don't care how bad you've been."

His own heart stopped and then ran away. His teeth clenched. "I don't even think you're real, Bernie," he whispered. "I think I dreamed you."

She flushed and smiled. "Thanks."

He glanced in the rearview mirror. "What I'd give for just five minutes alone with you right now," he said tautly. "Fat chance," he added as he noticed the sedan tailing casually behind them.

She felt all aglow inside. She wanted that, too. Maybe they could find a quiet place to be alone, even for just a few minutes. She wanted to kiss him until her mouth hurt.

Don't miss
Texas Proud *by Diana Palmer,*
available October 2020 wherever
Harlequin Special Edition books and ebooks are sold.

Harlequin.com